TWILIGHT

Also by Elizabeth Atkins Bowman
from Tom Doherty Associates

White Chocolate
Dark Secret

Also by Billy Dee Williams
from Tom Doherty Associates

PSI/Net (with Rob MacGregor)

BILLY DEE WILLIAMS

and

ELIZABETH ATKINS BOWMAN

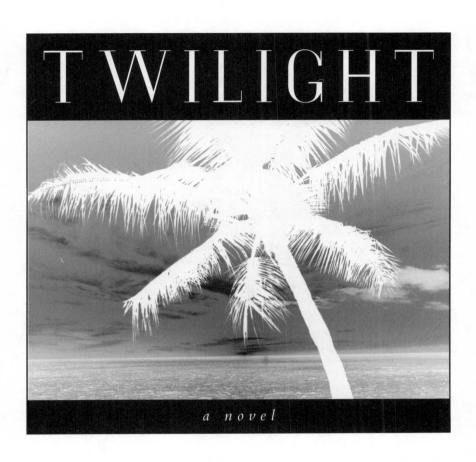

TWILIGHT

a novel

A TOM DOHERTY ASSOCIATES BOOK
NEW YORK

TWILIGHT

This book is printed on acid-free paper.

Book design by Jennifer Ann Daddio

A Forge Book
Published by Tom Doherty Associates, LLC
175 Fifth Avenue
New York, NY 10010

www.tor.com

Forge® is a registered trademark of Tom Doherty Associates, LLC.

Library of Congress Cataloging-in-Publication Data

Williams, Billy Dee.
Twilight / Billy Dee Williams and Elizabeth Atkins Bowman.—
1st ed.
p. cm.
ISBN 0-312-87909-1 (acid-free paper)
1. Hollywood (Los Angeles, Calif.)—Fiction. 2. Motion picture
actors and actresses—Fiction. 3. Custody of children—Fiction. 4.
Women judges—Fiction. I. Bowman, Elizabeth Atkins. II. Title.

PS3573.I4475 T87 2002
813'.54—dc21
2002016474

First Edition: July 2002

Printed in the United States of America

0 9 8 7 6 5 4 3 2 1

For my children,
Hanako Ann Williams Riley
and
Corey Dee Williams
—BILLY DEE WILLIAMS

May the soft blossoms of gratitude sweeten the lives of those who care,
Enabling me to live this dream through the gifts they share.
First and foremost, eternal thankfulness to God up in the sky,
Along with my father's protective spirit, beaming down, nearby.
Then my mother's dedication and sacrifice to show how wishes come true,
Her words of wisdom are cast in gold; her helpful acts speak volumes of virtue.
A husband who understands the goal, the hours, the fantasy of creation,
"Darling, can I get you some tea? It's three a.m., isn't your brain aching?"
A cherubic smile and big, happy eyes saying, "Mommy, can I write, too?"
Yes, anything you like, because the message in this book is for you.
A sister who knows just what to say in a mellow, calming tone,
Far more brave and graceful in the face of fear than anyone I've ever know.
A network of family and friends whose love and support are always there,
Whether it's to celebrate or cheer me on or just say they care.
An editor whose expertise and enthusiasm are icing on the cake,
An agent whose vision predicted what a cool project this would make.
A romantic hero and intelligent man who charmed me from page one,
Creating a lush drama with progressive themes until the work was done.
The mentors and advisors sitting at the table around a lavender wish,
Believing that the magic is as real as Sonny and Simone's first forbidden kiss.

—ELIZABETH ATKINS BOWMAN

Thank You: Thomas Atkins, Marylin Atkins, Victor Bowman and family, Catherine Atkins, Kevin and Sonja Horton, Natalia Aponte, Susan Crawford, Jeff Wardford, and Billy Dee Williams

. . . day must join with night to bring forth the dawn and twilight

which are more beautiful than they.

—VICTOR HUGO

TWILIGHT

1

Simone Thompson cringed deeper into the plush lounge chair as the yacht splashed and hummed toward the emerald dot coming into focus on the shimmering horizon. Her stomach cramped as the jagged tops of palm trees grew larger, arching like giant green sawblades toward the seamless infinity of sea and sky.

With damp fingertips, Simone clutched the legal document propped against her white linen pantlegs. But the double-spaced black text blurred under the hypnotic shimmer of heat and light on the turquoise water and white sand beach ahead.

"There's—" she whispered into the hot, salty wind, toward the two nearly nude women glistening with coconut oil in chaises at her sides. "There's Sanctuary Island."

"You say it like we're about to dock at Alcatraz," Paulette teased from behind the rustling gray curtain formed by her open *Los Angeles Times.* Her gold wrist bangles clinked as she turned a page. "For heaven's sake, Simone, it's a *tropical* island. A five-star resort. A movie mogul's wedding. In the most exotic place in the world—"

"I'm not safe anywhere," Simone said toward her own face on page one of the *Los Angeles Times.* The black and white picture, in which she wore glasses and her hair pulled back, joined four other faces under the headline: HOLLYWOOD-HATING STALKER TARGETS JUDGE, ACTORS.

"Or so they tell me," Simone said, "that LAPD detective who came to my chambers yesterday says Narcissus could be filing the hate letters from anywhere. Including Brazil. So I would appreciate a little comfort and concern from my friends—"

"This guy is crazy," Paulette said. Her outstretched legs were leaching suntan oil onto a stack of celebrity gossip tabloids under her knee. Her long red fingernails gripped the newspaper, and a wild, feathery twist of brunette tendrils billowed atop her head.

"I don't know if it's a man, like that Greek god who fell in love with his own reflection," Simone said. "All I know is, I want him, her, it, caught—"

"It's so hot," Paulette said, extending her right arm toward the small table between their chairs. She grasped her *caipirinha*—sugar cane liquor with lime slices crushed in sugar and ice—which sat next to her silver camera and Simone's tiny white ceramic cup of Brazilian espresso.

"That *cachaça* smells so strong," Simone said, as Paulette raised her drink behind the newspaper. "Makes my stomach ache."

"I'll give them credit, this is *some* national cocktail," Paulette said. "Sure takes my mind off the bills waiting for me back home. You have no idea how good it feels to get away from the mail, the phone, and my constant cash crisis—"

"If you'd stop indulging your champagne taste with a beer budget, you wouldn't need to run away," Simone said, turning rightward toward three security guards, standing before the gleaming black windows in dark suits, sunglasses and coiled earpieces. "Just like I can't escape the fact or the fear that someone wants to kill me."

Paulette rattled the paper, making her bracelets clink. "You're better off here than back home," Paulette said. "Listen to what he wrote: 'Judge

Simone Thompson's black cloak is but a costume for her save-the-children masquerade. Now the wrongs of her past will reap revenge—' "

Simone reached for her *cafezinho*. It was so strong, despite all the sugar, that one sip made her shoulders twitch. "I already read it. Along with the hate letters faxed every day last week to the courthouse." Simone set the cup down, then dug her bare heels into the cushion. She pressed down the top of her straw hat to stop it from rising with the wind.

"To tell the truth," Simone said, poising a yellow highlighter pen over the legal brief, "I can't wait to get back to work, to the cool, controlled comfort of my courtroom. I said I would *never* come back here." She inhaled the salty sea air and read her work: *four children now in the custody of maternal grandparents, until stability of mother and father is re-evaluated—*

French-manicured fingernails and a seven-carat canary diamond fluttered over the page.

"Girl, it's time to cure your workaholic ways," Marie said softly from the lounge chair on the right.

"You're the one who changed your wedding date three times." Simone tensed as she turned toward her friend. The black rectangular lenses of Marie's tortoiseshell sunglasses obscured part of her pug nose and almost half of her narrow face. Marie's skin—as rich in color and as smooth in texture as maple syrup—glowed as if the sun were shining within her. "Marie, I'm coming halfway around the world to a place I hate, for your movie set marriage. In the middle of two important trials *and* bizarre death threats. So—"

"Simone, honey, we're worried about you," Marie said, finger-combing her short, 1920s-style flapper coif that shined copper; her opalescent coral maillot formed a svelte Y from her freckled shoulders to her waxed bikini line and bare legs. Her fingernails made a delicate *tap* as she stroked the three strands of her pearl choker.

"My new life with Norris has made me realize, all work and no play was making Marie a very boring girl. Now Paulette and I want you to have what we have—love, sex, big smiles—"

Marie's full lips, shimmering with the same pink-orange hue as her bathing suit, broke into a smile around the tiny gap between her two front teeth. C-shaped laugh lines framed her mouth with thin folds of skin that showed no trace of the acne that had splotched her face back during college.

"Good for you, Marie," Simone said, yanking her work toward her chest. "Now if you'll just blow away the blushing bride cloud that's obviously taking over your brain, you'll remember there's something I have to do before—"

Marie shook her head, pulling the brief. "No. Right here, right now, Paulette and I are staging an intervention—"

Simone snatched the thick document back, slicing her index finger on the top page. "Ow! I'm not one of your patients, Dr. Cartwright. And I'm not laughing. At all."

"Exactly," Paulette said, crumpling the newspaper onto her lap. Her bright brown eyes twinkled from her round, sun-pinkened face. The hot, heavy breeze danced brunette tresses over her full cheeks, her thin, highly arched eyebrows, her triple-gold-hooped ears. And the word PAULETTE glistened in gold script on a chain between her round breasts, which were suspended by a red bikini top.

"It's our goal," Paulette said playfully as her braces glimmered. "Before Marie and Norris say, 'I do,' you'll be saying to some gorgeous stud, 'do me!' "

"You need balance, Simone," Marie said. "Not just work-work-work. How 'bout work-play-fun—"

"M-A-N." Paulette walked her fingernails up Simone's arm. "Forget about finding your daddy, for once, and indulge in the delights of the flesh—"

"We've spent half our lives supporting your"—Marie squeezed her hand— "*quest* to put your love life on hold until you find your father. But now—"

"Four months until I'm thirty-five," Simone said. "If I have to go to Washington and use a wrench to pry answers from my mother, I will. I have to know who I am before—"

"Start living and loving now." Paulette shared a mischievous smile with Marie. "As your best friends, we are hereby enrolling you in Abstinence Anonymous—"

"I'm telling you, I resent this," Simone snapped. "Paulette, when you got pregnant, I supported your decision to get married and finish school later. And Marie, when you started your own practice, I was there for you. Now how about you reciprocate. I have too many questions to answer before I indulge in your fun and games—"

"Questions that may never get answers," Marie said.

"But with your very own twelve-steps-to-love program—" Paulette raised her drink. She puckered sheer-glossed lips around the red straw, then winked as she sucked it down.

"We'll help you savor the sensuous delights of life—" Paulette lay back, and tilted her face toward the sky. "Below the equator, in this to-die-for heat." She sighed as two hard peaks formed under her bikini top. She writhed in her red thong. "Follow my lead. Before we hit land, I'm going to have a sun-gasm."

The sudden scent of sweet tropical flowers and fiery cooking spices made Simone's stomach cramp, and the overwhelming spiritual power of Bahia, here on the Atlantic coast in the northeastern part of Brazil, raised the tiny hairs on her body. She glanced forward.

Flowers—white, blue, yellow, pink—exploded in great sprays with green ferns from two big baskets, bobbing in tiny wooden boats on the water about twenty feet ahead. Simone closed her eyes, trying to block out a sad barrage of unfulfilled childhood wishes. . .

"Look," Marie said, flattening her hand like a visor over her eyes. "Flowers for the goddess of the sea. Simone, help me remember, what's her name—"

"Iemanjá," Simone said softly, opening her eyes. "As much as I hated all the trips to Rio as a kid, I loved Copacabana Beach on New Year's Eve. Brian and I felt like we were standing with angels. All the Brazilian women in flowing white lace, launching huge baskets of flowers and candles into the water—"

"But it's February." Paulette snatched up her silver camera and dashed to the rail, her oiled curves glistening. The camera clicked. "Why in the world would someone put lipstick, perfume and mirrors in a basket—"

"They think Iemanjá is vain," Simone said. "She's like the female Poseidon. If your offering comes back to shore, you're out of luck. If the sea accepts it, your wish is supposed to come true." Simone's throat burned as the baskets spun in the yacht's splash. "My baskets never came back. I really thought my father would just show up. Or my mother would magically start being nice." She cringed further into the cushion. "Can't you feel it?"

"You're giving me goosebumps," Paulette said, lowering the camera. She spun around, bright brown eyes wide. "Is it like voodoo?"

"It's more religious," Simone said. "This part of Brazil, it's where the Portuguese first brought slaves. You can see by the people—" A young man with green eyes, a bronze complexion and pin-straight black hair approached with fresh white towels. Bright blue sky framed his white polo shirt and shorts, which hugged a buff chest and muscular legs. "Every-body," Simone whispered, "is a blend of Indian, African, European—"

Marie raised Simone's right hand, then pushed her sunglasses to the tip of her nose to inspect Simone's fingers. "Then your mystery mix, Miss Buttercream, fits right in—"

Paulette faced the sun. "This Caucasian mutt is going home with a killer tan—"

"Daddy Thompson's gonna show up one day," Marie said playfully, "and we'll have to add some chocolate to girlfriend's ingredients list."

Simone bristled. "I hate not knowing."

"Look," Marie said. "The marina. Sanctuary is so spectacular."

To the left, tall coconut palms and coves of lush greenery fringed a long white beach. At the water's edge, a nutmeg-toned woman in a pink thong and a high ponytail was frantically shaking her hips, facing dozens of nearly nude people doing the same. To her right, three men pounded huge drums strapped to their chests, while another man played the trombone. Their biceps and pecs and abs glistened; their complexions ranged from hazelnut shell to beige-white.

"God, those samba drums sound so sinister," Simone said, hugging herself as the primitive pounding vibrated through her chest, "beating up every bad memory of what happened here—"

"I wish we could stay for Carnival," Paulette sighed. "The biggest party in the world is ten days away, and we have to go back home—"

"We were supposed to honeymoon in Rio," Marie said, "but the trial." She shrugged. "Norris says we'll have our own last hurrah to fun before, after and during Lent."

"You're bad," Paulette cooed. "Look, the bungalows. Oh man, three days alone, no husband, no kids, no bills. In the picture of paradise."

Thatch-roofed cottages of richly stained wood peeked through the foliage. Pink, purple and yellow flowers cascaded from oceanfront porches and spiral staircases leading to second-story balconies.

"The pool!" Paulette pointed toward water streaming over boulders into the cobalt tank, where dozens of kids and adults splashed about.

"That's the house where they're filming, right now," Marie said, pointing up to a yellow mansion with a terra cotta roof. It sat on the cliff over the marina, straight ahead. A small white footbridge with a silver SANCTUARY arch extended from the dock over jagged rocks to the crowded public beach. "Norris is supposed to meet us when they wrap—"

"May I tempt you ladies?" The waiter offered bite-sized mounds of spicy red shrimp on golden circles of fried manioc flour.

Simone held her breath, but the Brazilian cooking aromas of palm oil, cilantro and malagueta peppers were already wafting down into the deep-est, darkest spot in her psyche, stirring up long-buried horrors—

"No!" she exclaimed.

The waiter paled.

"I mean, *nao, obrigada*," Simone said softly. "No, thank you."

Paulette returned to her chaise lounge. "I'll take some, please." Her bangles jangled as she took a bite and sucked crumbs from her fingers. "So spicy! I am loving this! Marie, have some. If you get any skinnier, you're going to blow away—"

"That's not something *you* have to worry about. Neither does Miss Marathon Queen," Marie said, tapping Simone's leg. "*Senhor*, our friend would like a drink. One of these"—she raised a slushy red concoction in a martini glass with yellow star fruit— "guava, ice and rum."

"*Sim, senhora.*" The man strode around the curved black front win-dows, down the outdoor walkway, past the bodyguards.

A purple speedboat shot by next to them. Two buff, hairy-chested men with mirrored sunglasses and hearty grins waved up.

"They're too close," Marie shouted over the roaring engine.

The yacht's horn blasted. The security guards stared down, thick hands poised over black handguns in clear view.

"What the hell?" Paulette cried. "You think they're Narcissus on a renegade boat?"

Simone's heart hammered. "I will not live in fear."

With a great spray and roar of engines, the men zoomed toward a cir-cular clump of white sand and a palm tree or two, one of dozens of tiny islands dotting the bay.

"How macho was that?" Paulette said with an annoyed tone.

"Boys will be boys," Marie said. "But with Narcissus lurking in the shadows, I'm not in the mood. Where's my drink?"

"This'll keep me alert." Simone raised her *cafezinho*.

"It'll give you a buzz, too," Marie said, "but you need to relax—"

"The first and last time I drank that stuff," Simone said, "I was seven-teen, at Carnival with Brian. This gang of teenaged boys walked down from the ghetto, dozens of them, they came after us—"

"I got it!" Marie sipped her drink while staring up at the house on the cliff. "The cure for Simone's workaholic, abstinent ways."

"Who?" Paulette squealed, holding up her camera. "Say it now!"

"Sweet," Marie said seductively, stroking Simone's arm, "Sonny Whittaker!"

Click!

"Brilliant, Dr. Cartwright." Paulette lowered her camera. "I captured it the moment you put it into the universe." Paulette's braces glistened as she smiled. The newspaper crinkled under her leg as she glanced toward the water. "Now, where are those baskets? We'll make a wish to that goddess, too—"

Simone grasped the crumpled pages, icy goosebumps prickling her skin. There, next to her picture: Norris Haynes, Jenn Ryder, Cheyenne Moore and Sonny Whittaker.

"Tell me you're *not* serious." Simone tapped the paper. "Sonny Whittaker is on the hit list, too—"

"All the more reason to get together," Paulette said. "Sounds like one of his movies. Man and woman, pursued by a lunatic, find love at a tropical resort—"

"Which happens to be called Sanctuary," Marie said.

"I love it!" Paulette raised the camera. "I'll document every heart-throbbing second—"

"You're both being insensitive," Simone said.

"This is a good diversion," Marie said. "I lost my dad to a stalker; I'm sure as hell not going to lose my future husband to one, too. And Paulette can stop wondering if the repo man is coming after her Benz, or if the boys are being barred from school because their tuition is late."

"Late doesn't begin to describe it," Paulette said, sipping her drink.

"Norris is hiring more security for our wedding than the Oscars and Golden Globes put together," Marie said, glancing toward the three guards standing about a dozen feet away, scanning the water.

"Both of you," Simone said. "I do not want a man, especially not a movie star whose divorce trial will bring media mayhem to my court-house Monday—"

"It's not your case," Paulette said, "so who cares?"

"Not everyone shares your loose interpretation of ethics," Simone said. "Selling houses to young athletes after Ted's agency signs them—"

"So?" Paulette said.

"You saw those reports during the mafia trial." Simone stiffened at the memory of that week-long "Double Jeopardy" series on *Entertainment Exclusive.* "Who is Simone Thompson?" had flashed like a headline across the bottom of the screen, over video footage of her jogging around the UCLA campus near her home, and even grocery shopping!

"Is this attractive woman," reporter Roxanne Jones had asked over video of Simone playing volleyball with the kids on the sprawling ocean-front grounds of The Tree House Orphanage, "as goody-two-shoes as our secret cameras are finding? Or is Simone Thompson leading a double life, just like her married-to-the-mafia colleagues? Is she, too, putting your right to a fair trial in jeopardy?"

"I'm still enraged," Simone said through tight lips, "that Roxanne Jones cast me in such a suspicious light. As if she were trying to give the Judicial Tenure Commission ideas on who to disbar next."

"I'm sure Roxanne set out to prove you could only get into your position by sleeping with someone," Paulette said. "The governor. The chief judge—"

"She's been calling my chambers all week. About Narcissus. But she will not be getting a return call from me."

"She might ask you in person," Marie said. "Norris gave her an exclusive to the wedding."

"Tell me you're kidding," Simone said.

"Relax, girl," Marie said. "She'll be so busy trying to scope out celebrities, she won't even notice you. We're worlds away from all that courthouse stuff."

"Well," Simone said, "I'm staying worlds away from Sonny Whittaker. If he ends up in my courtroom, and I've so much as blushed at him, it just wouldn't feel right."

"Come on, listen to my new idea for a career change," Paulette said.

"What get-rich-quick scheme do you and Ted have in the works this time?" Marie said. "What ever happened to your plan to become a makeup artist, or start a limo company—"

Paulette raised her camera. "Photography is my first passion. I need more excitement, something more glamorous."

"*What* are you going to photograph?" Simone asked.

"I'm thirty-four years old, still trying to get my fifteen minutes of fame," Paulette said, raising her drink over Simone. "Let's toast. Jesus, if I could be single for a day and meet Sonny Whittaker. I think this old, over-worked supermom would just faint—"

Marie clinked Paulette's glass; water droplets plunked on the smooth white legal brief on Simone's lap. She coughed on the fruity liquor fumes.

"Be careful." Simone raised the brief toward her chest. "Your timing is all wrong—"

"Oh, girl, the timing couldn't be better," Marie said. "I guarantee,

Sonny Whittaker will turn you out so tough, you won't know your own name."

"I do not want to meet him," Simone said. "Even though it's true that in the few happy memories I have of that witch who birthed me, a Sonny Whittaker movie is always playing."

For hours, Simone would secretly watch the big television in the media room inside the Andersons' mansion back in Washington, DC, while her mother and Bianca curled up under a cashmere blanket on the couch, nibbling brie and sipping champagne from crystal flutes that cost more than what the Andersons paid her mother in a week. Crouching behind the sofa, Simone would fantasize about escaping her opulent prison by stepping through the giant screen, becoming Sonny Whittaker's leading lady in some far-off romantic adventure.

"My mother and Bianca used to say," Simone said, "that when they died, they wanted Sonny Whittaker to whisper those lines he told his dying lover in *Destiny*."

Marie imitated him: " 'If I awake tomorrow without you, the color in my world will fade to gray. The scent of roses will turn sour. And the sweetest strawberry will—' "

Paulette finished: " '—make my lips, these lips made for kissing you, burn with bitterness.' His voice is like an orgasm to your ears."

Simone smiled. "When my mother left me alone for hours on end, I would imagine him coming to the carriage house, taking me away to a happier place . . ."

"Tell him that," Marie said. "He'll melt."

"I'm married, I'm married," Paulette said, holding up her left hand and making her diamond wedding band glimmer in the sunshine.

"I've definitely got Norris whipped, dipped and addicted to these hips," Marie said with a sultry tone, using her open palms to air-trace her trim hourglass shape. "Now it's your turn, your honor—"

Simone stiffened.

"He's got this intense magnetism," Marie said, "intelligent and smoldering. He'll talk about Jung and world politics, then stare down to your very core and set you on fire—"

Simone pulled her hat down and ran her hands over her sunbaked arms and shoulders exposed by her white tank top. Her mother's voice cackled through her thoughts: *Your own father doesn't even want you. So don't ever believe a man will want daddy's little discard, either.*

A deep horn sounded. The sharp white bow of another yacht shot by, dangerously close. A slight, silver-haired man stood on the top deck with topless, long-haired brunettes on each arm. He raised his dark sunglasses, then blew a kiss. Judge Johnston's lecherous stare made Simone's mouth taste sour.

"Yet another reason," Simone said, pulling the document toward her chest, "for me to stay curled up in my bungalow with this."

"Norris adores Judge Johnston," Marie said. "He's just a harmless old fart who's damn lucky he's not in prison with the other judges-for-hire."

"I'm bearing the brunt of it," Simone said. "A triple docket, and Charlie breathing down my neck every minute about following the rules—"

"Why?" Paulette asked. "You wouldn't even oversee your dentist's divorce!"

"Johnston is on a mission to burn me at the stake, for testifying in the Katie Moore case."

"That was so long ago," Marie said. "But it still feels raw."

"Every little thing I do," Simone said. "Like the posters for the 5K race at the orphanage. He went ballistic when I put one on the bulletin board in the lounge, saying my position would intimidate employees into donating—"

"Speaking of ballistic," Paulette said, snatching up a copy of *Famous*. "Marie, the rumor is—"

"Tell me why you pay money for those lies." Simone glared at the celebrity gossip tabloid. "They're invasive, offensive—"

"It's my brain candy after a hard day of selling houses," Paulette said, tapping the actress's face on the cover. "I can't believe it. Cheyenne Moore says Norris is using an interracial marriage as a PR stunt, to hype the movie."

Marie stroked her choker. "That woman is stone cold crazy."

"Huh," Paulette sighed, "I'd be crazy, too, if Sonny Whittaker dumped me."

"She's a witch with a beautiful face," Simone said. Shining silver masts and bright flags fluttered over yachts in the marina. There was the flag of Italy. France. Jamaica.

"Seriously," Marie said. "Cheyenne is out to destroy Norris and Sonny. She sent a nasty letter to the house, saying Norris should cast her in *The Colony*—"

"But she's had no good roles since *Come Back, My Love*," Paulette said. "Sonny Whittaker became a superstar. She didn't. Now she's bitter—"

"I was only ten," Simone said, "but his face and voice from that movie are imprinted on my mind—"

"I'm surprised Cheyenne hasn't dropped a bomb on *The Colony*," Marie said.

"What do you call her book!" Paulette said. "She's airing all the sheets she stained with Sonny Whittaker, and your husband-to-be, or so she claims—"

"She'll be hearing from the lawyers," Marie said. "I wouldn't be surprised if she's Narcissus. Maybe she still hates you, Simone, for all that happened during her divorce—"

"Not after all this time," Simone said, tapping the brief. "I'll tell you what, though. No other child will end up like Katie Moore while I'm on the bench. God, I wonder where she—"

"Your drink, ma'am." The waiter stepped close with red slush in a glass.

"No, thank you," Simone said.

"Enjoy," Marie said. "Just one. To take the edge off before we land."

"Nice advice from a therapist." Simone reached for her *cafezinho*.

The yacht's horn sounded; Simone startled, almost spilling her coffee.

"You're a nervous wreck." Paulette took the drink from the waiter. "Thank you. Here, Simone."

Simone shoved the thick stack of legal papers toward the end of the chaise; her bare feet hit the white carpet.

Paulette thrust the drink at Simone as she stood.

An icy splash on her stomach—

"Ugh!" Red slush and brown coffee soaked Simone's tank top, her pants, the white carpet, and her work. She jumped as the slush seeped into her panties.

Paulette and Marie dabbed napkins and towels on Simone and the puddle forming on her legal brief. Simone grabbed it, shook it off. "Where's the luggage?"

"Sorry, girlfriend," Marie said. "The cargo hold is locked until we hit land."

Chilled, Simone glared at her friends. "Marie, Paulette, end your little intervention scheme, now. Or I'll be on the next plane home."

2

Sonny Whittaker squinted toward the ocean, where sleek yachts, battered fishing boats and colorful windsurfers sliced white wakes across the vast aquamarine shimmer. Blade-like bamboo leaves and blood-red hibiscus blooms swayed in the salty breeze, forming a lush frame around the blufftop balcony. He gripped the glass railing and sucked in the steamy air, keeping his back to all the scrutinizing eyes, cameras and voices on the set.

The director's raspy shout of *"Cut!"* still pounded in Sonny's mind as violently as waves crashed against the jagged black rocks below. The wind hissed in the jade canopy of palm and poinciana leaves, as if the ancient spirits here in the soul of Brazil were whispering warnings too sinister for words.

"Nothing, and no one, will stop my legacy," Sonny whispered. He would soar as gracefully as those two orange birds on the rocks—a sharp wave curled over them, but they fluttered up through the spray. Sonny turned as they flew over the garden patio toward the yellow mansion. They nestled in the purple bougainvillea adorning the black wrought iron balcony, just above the man in the director's chair.

"Norris," Sonny said, his New York accent stretching out the "no" and emphasizing the "r." With a mask of cool, Sonny strode toward his creator and destroyer, who was sitting between two black cameras, shrouded by thick foliage and fuchsia hibiscus. As Sonny's brown leather sandal made one final slap on the pale pink tile, he let out his famous chuckle. Deep, slow, in control.

"Norris," Sonny said firmly. "We need to do one more take. Now."

"I said 'cut,' Whittaker, not 'come here,'" Norris snapped with a deep rasp.

A shard of sunshine illuminated Norris's beige PRISM FILMS baseball cap, making his green-tinted aviator glasses cast an eerie hue over his brassy lashes and large, honey-colored eyes. The glasses rested on a straight nose that reminded Sonny of a statue he'd seen in Pompeii of the Greco-Roman god Apollo. The skin on Norris' nose, broad forehead, square chin and high cheekbones was so tan and smooth, his face looked airbrushed. The white patches of hair sprouting at his temples were the only hint that he was pushing sixty.

"Maybe you didn't hear me," Sonny said deeply. "Let's do this scene one more time."

"It's a wrap, Whittaker." Norris's light brown wavy hair danced over his muscle-pumped shoulders and the sleeveless beige vest embroidered with the word PRISM. He raised the silver watch on his thick right wrist. "I'm meeting with resort security in a half hour, and Marie—"

"Look around, Norris," Sonny said over the chatter of dozens of cast and crew members, bodyguards and that flash-from-his-playboy-past TV reporter by the huge brick barbecue.

Norris closed his eyes and pinched the tip of his nose. He pursed his figure-eight-shaped mouth, which reminded Sonny of a pink ribbon tied in a bow.

"Norris 'Midas Touch' Haynes," Sonny mocked. "Every film he touches turns as golden as Oscar. Including *The Colony*. So Norris, look around this fantasy film set and tell me, what do you see?"

"I see red." Norris's white suede loafers thumped the stone. With a waft of his usual smoky-incense scent, he stood eye-to-eye with Sonny. "I see a man who's going to writhe on the courtroom floor Monday when my daughter cuts his heart out—"

"Never," Sonny said through burning lips. "You know she used me just to spite you. And she doesn't give a damn about putting our little girls on the battle line—"

"You should've thought about that before you let Cheyenne slander me in her book of lies." Norris grasped the silver cell phone clipped to the belt on his safari shorts. "Sweet Sonny Whittaker, diggin' your own grave—"

"No, you are," Sonny said. "You need me, and this film, to save your ass—"

"Time out, Whittaker. It looks like you're the one who's trying to throw the fight." Norris raised his voice to a shout. "Because you keep fucking up!"

Sonny raised his chin. "You know, Norris," Sonny said so deeply his throat burned, "you should get a grip on your anger. It's not healthy."

"Fuck you, Whittaker." The hot breeze whooshed through a feathery clump of giant bamboo behind him, exposing a stone statue of Iansa, the Brazilian goddess of love and death. The sick-sweet scent of flowers and moist earth and sea salt stole Sonny's breath.

"No, you're trying to burn me, by shouting 'cut' when I'm giving a flawless, eloquent performance over there!" Sonny turned to point at the long rattan table where he'd been sitting just minutes ago. "Now, I want one final take. It would be ridiculous to start cold, after two weeks away—"

"If the accountants keep cracking the whip," Norris said, "we'll take a raincheck altogether—"

"I will be back here in two weeks to finish this movie. The world is waiting."

"Christ."

"And nobody is going to stop me," Sonny said. "Not you, not Erica, not the lawyers and judges, and especially not whoever wants to kill us all. Even these threats, they reek of another Norris Haynes publicity ploy. Your wedding, your new wife, it's all about PR for you."

Norris's forehead crinkled slightly; sadness roiled in his eyes.

Sonny lowered his voice: "A truce, Norris. Now. For our film. And our family."

Norris pinched his nose, closed his eyes, and shook his head. "The clock is ticking. Marie will be here any minute—"

"One more take. Jenn and the girls, they're hating this armed guard situation."

"It was misguided to cast them," Norris said. "They should be back in LA with Erica—"

"Never." Sonny was sure his glare would draw blood from Norris's cheek. "If I lose my heartbeat, you lose three actors. The twins. And their dead father. Then you have nothing. Because without this project, Prism gets boycotted, and you—"

Norris snatched off his green glasses. "Whittaker!"

Sonny's lower lip trembled as he stared into the soft brown eyes that had once glowed with pride as they took home Oscars for *Come Back, My Love*. Norris had had that same look the first time the twins had uttered the word "Grandpa."

"The girls stay with me, and they stay in the film," Sonny said. "I wrote *The Colony* for them. For the world that they're going to inherit—"

"Cut the crap," Norris said. "You give yourself too much credit. One film won't change the world."

"Tell that to the NAACP."

Norris' eyes sharpened. "I won't be bullied by you, by them—"

"The Colony," Sonny said, "is your only ticket to getting the civil rights group off your back. Otherwise, you can put your dad's white hood back on—"

"Motherfucker," Norris hissed. "I *made* the international phenomenon of Sweet Sonny Whittaker. Not because you're black. Because I saw the fire in your eyes—"

"You were running from your dad's demons then, too," Sonny said, his painter's eye recording the yellow swords of sunshine slicing the translucent jungle mist like out-of-control floodlights at a movie premiere.

"I created you," Norris said raspily, "and I can break you down—"

"God created me," Sonny said. "Sometimes you let your one and only film role, as *Jesus of Nazareth*, go to your head. You're just a man, Norris. Now, call security and tell them you're held up on the set."

Norris glanced at his watch again. "Christ, if the stalker is here, this place could be a bloodbath once half of Hollywood arrives for the wedding—"

"I canceled the interview," Sonny said.

"Uncancel it." Norris's gaze danced over Sonny's shoulder, where the *Entertainment Exclusive* reporter was still posing in her tight red dress. All morning, her cameraman had captured every cuss word, every angry look.

"I will not indulge Roxanne Jones with a moment of my time," Sonny said. His memory offered up a split-second slide of Roxanne's chocolate-brown breasts bubbling in a Jacuzzi overlooking the sparkling night lights of LA, as she slipped between Sonny and Norris. "My days of being tricked by temptresses are long over."

"We need the publicity," Norris said.

"You need a cold shower," Sonny said. "You're so dazzled by Roxanne's body, you can't see her vindictive scowl. She talked to Cheyenne—"

"Do it," Norris said. "I promised her an exclusive on the wedding, too."

"No. She's Erica's friend. I will not be cast as a heartless womanizer—"

Norris's hot hand came down on Sonny's shoulder. "We'll add some time to the clock for one more take, if you work some Sweet Sonny Whittaker magic, and we wrap this scene once and for all. *If* you do the interview with Roxanne this afternoon. Game?"

Sonny's fingertips dug into the hot, damp flesh of his palms. Flames of anger threatened to burst through his flesh and melt his silky olive tunic to his arms, his chest, his legs. Why were so many forces suddenly crashing into his life, threatening to sear all that he cherished?

"Norris, nothing will stop me from leaving my Hollywood legacy behind," Sonny said. "Not Cheyenne or your daughter or your lusty liaison with that media vulture over there. I have a half century of film and television under my belt—"

"And about fifteen extra pounds you need to lose," Norris said.

"Fuck you, Norris," Sonny said. "My trainer almost killed me this morning, running on the beach. I'm getting back to work. All of me." Sonny spun on a heel, his lines poised on the tip of his tongue.

"Everyone in your places." Norris clapped behind him. "Let's do this one more time. Where are the twins?"

"I'll get them." Sonny stepped toward the white shuttered archway leading into the house, where the girls had gone for a bathroom break with the nanny. Looking into their happy amber eyes would infuse him with even more determination to bring this final film of his life to fruition.

"No, Norris!" Jenn Ryder shouted. "I refuse to fry in this sun anymore."

Sonny spun around. His female costar stood over Norris, shielding her face with a flat hand at her arched eyebrows. Her hazel eyes blazed, her thin face glowed pink, and the blunt ends of her platinum hair flipped over her thin shoulder.

"What's the problem?" Sonny turned toward them.

"I'm getting so many wrinkles," Jenn yelled, "I'll never get another role—"

"Stop whining and take your seat," Norris snapped. An assistant handed him a tall bottle of water; his adam's apple rose up and down as he chugged it.

"Norris," Jenn said, bending slightly, making her snug olive dress hug the tiny Us of her behind. "The heat, the bodyguards, the two-week break in production—these are cruel and unusual working conditions—"

"So I'll replace all of you," Norris said flatly. "Now get to work."

"Jenn," Sonny said. "There's a TV crew watching our every move."

Jenn cocked her neck as she glared up at him. He never should have listened to Norris's pitch about how Jenn Ryder's name, face and Play-boy-bunny past guaranteed a box office blockbuster. The role of Xavier's wife demanded someone more mature, someone with a more nurturing warmth.

"We hand-picked you for this role," Sonny said softly. "But my God, had I known your prima donna ways . . ."

"Excuse me, oh great god of the silver screen," Jenn snarled, narrowing her eyes up at Sonny. "I'm just not used to getting death threats on the job!" She hurried to the table, where she asked the two native actresses in white romanesque dresses to cool her with the palm fronds that they used to fan Sonny's character.

"Christ," Norris hissed. "What next?"

"*Entertainment Exclusive* is the only TV crew allowed on the exotic set of budget blowout thriller *The Colony*—"

In front of the huge brick barbecue near the house, Roxanne Jones stood with her back to the set, her black hair bouncing in a swoop as her red dress squeezed in a V-shape down to two grapefruit-sized mounds, shapely brown calves and red heels.

"We've got the latest on a terrifying stalker scandal," she gushed into a microphone, toward a black camera emblazoned with "EE" in yellow letters, "and behind-the-scenes fireworks between Norris Haynes and Sonny Whittaker."

Sonny's veins burned as he glared back at Norris.

"Roxanne!" Norris shouted. "All due respect, we got work to do."

The curled-up tips of her hair bounced on her shoulders as she spun around. Her flawless makeup made her look like a brown porcelain doll, from the unnaturally perfect black arches of the eyebrows, to the heavily lined dark eyes, the powdered button nose, the thin lips, the white-as-snow teeth.

"There are no fireworks," Sonny said, propelled toward her by a blast of anger, "and do not refer to this film as a budget blowout."

"I speak the truth," she said, stroking the microphone. "I hope you'll do the same when we get together later. Just like Cheyenne and Erica did."

She leaned around Sonny. "Norris, sweetheart, I'm sorry," she said with a sudden Southern drawl. "I thought you were finished for the day." She turned her back on them, telling her cameraman, "Definitely get this last take, in case Sonny Whittaker screws up again and Norris cusses another blue streak."

Sonny's male parts contracted upward. He curled his fingertips into his palms. He hated this feeling of being trapped, of having to follow someone else's—especially Norris's—rules. But he wanted to do this last take, and expressing himself to Roxanne would only delay that. Even though she embodied all that was wrong with his life right now.

His blood boiled. Beautiful women were stepping out of his past one by one to lob missiles of lies and jealousy and hatred at him. Threatening to incinerate all that he cherished, all that he was working so hard to rebuild after Norris had tried to obliterate his career.

But Sonny Whittaker would win, and live to experience his grand-mother's vision:

"You see that, Sonny," Grandmama said, the cowrie shells securing her silver braids clinking together as she pointed to the Caribbean sunset, where magenta streaks and fiery red fingers were clawing the day down into the ocean. "Someday she'll shoot into your life like a flame. And you'll know she's the other half of your soul, because her eyes will make you shiver . . ."

Goosebumps prickled Sonny's damp skin.

"Uncle Sonny," a deep voice called.

"Jared," Sonny said as his nephew approached. My God, the closer he got to thirty, the more Jared favored Andrew at the time of his death. Just as tall at six-foot-six, with the same smooth brown skin, from his bald head to his close-cut goatee, and the same muscular build.

"Where are the girls?" Sonny asked. His insides hummed with the sense of honor that came from the responsibility of helping his nephews navigate careful and confident routes through adulthood. Hiring them as bodyguards was a good way to jumpstart their private security business.

Jared came out of the house, then stopped. He stared down with dark, gentle eyes.

"They're coming," Jared said, resting his big hands on the black belt that held his gun. Sweat stained the top of his white tank top, in the valley formed by his pumped-up pecs. He glanced around, then pulled a black phone from its clip on the front pocket of his army green shorts. His giant finger pushed one button, then he held the phone over the tiny gold hoop in his ear. "Josh, it's clear."

"Uncle Sonny," Jared said, slipping the phone back on his pocket, "Asia and India, they were kinda upset. Kindred, too—"

A spark of paternal machismo propelled Sonny toward the house.

"Daddy!" Asia and India cried in unison. Black ringlet curls sprung over the shoulders of their silky olive pantsets as they sprinted toward him. Their brown leather sandals pattered on the tiles. Tears glistened in their wide-set, amber eyes, clumping the black fringe of lashes and streaking their plump, crème-caramel-hued faces.

"Angel Eyes." Sonny's heart hammered as he bent down and held out his arms. His every cell went numb and exploded with pain all at once. Sweat prickled his skin, plastering his costume to his back.

"Double jump, Daddy!" The girls leaped up. Sonny's arms were like safety nets as he scooped them up toward his chest. Asia and India laced their fingers on opposite sides of his neck, hanging on as they pressed damp cheeks into his jaw.

Sonny's arm muscles burned as he rose. "You know daddy doesn't do well when you cry."

The nanny stepped behind them, sniffling as she rested her large hands on their backs.

"My God, Kindred, you, too? Why the tears?"

Kindred stood almost eye-to-eye with Sonny's six feet three inches. Soft wisps of dark hair framed her round, dewy face, as smooth and unblemished as the inside of an almond. Redness ringed her slightly up-slanted, honey-colored eyes; dark smudges of makeup accentuated the worried emotions that were causing tears to well between her black lashes. The sun cast an opalescent sheen on the black pearl earrings that he had given her and the girls to celebrate the deal with Prism, when the film company had agreed to produce and pull out all the stops for *The Colony*.

"Come here," Sonny said softly, tilting his head to invite her into the hug. As Kindred stepped close, a droplet rolled down her cheek, past her scoop of a nose—a triangle so small that she could hide it by pinching it between her thumb and forefinger. The tear dripped onto the round neck of her T-shirt, which was the same shade of ballerina pink as the patent leather mules and tennis shorts that were showcasing her basketball-star legs.

"The fear, it's making us all a little bonkers today," Kindred said with her usual lullaby smoothness and softness. But the two sharp peaks of her upper lip pursed into her half-circle lower lip; her mouth whitened under the carnation-hued gloss. "We saw a TV report—"

Kindred's long ponytail lashed her back and sent up a waft of pear-scented shampoo as she turned toward the house. "It upset us," she said, raising her hands to her face. Her short, pink fingernails glistened over her dark, Greta Garbo-arched eyebrows. She shook her head, then lowered her hands to stroke the girls' backs. "It's just getting to us."

"I told her to relax," Josh said, coming out of the house behind Kindred. He was a carbon-copy of Jared, without the goatee and a year younger. His eyes focused on Kindred's backside, his hand on his gun. "Me and Jared, we're double the protection."

"We'll be home in a couple days," Sonny said. "We'll all be fine. Just don't cry." Even as screaming newborns, his daughters' tears had sliced his heart, inspiring him to hold one writhing doll in each arm, pacing on the terrace of their Moroccan-style home overlooking Los Angeles. The sun would set, the stars would twinkle, and he would sing, hum and make faces until they giggled or fell asleep.

"Looks like," Sonny now said playfully, craning over their heads, "I'm gonna have to go searching for some worry bugs. For all three of you!"

The twins cringed toward him, exclaiming, "No!"

"It's okay, little princess girls." Kindred smiled, showing large, curved teeth as the sun shimmered on the inch-long scar on her jaw. "Josh and Jared are good guys. Your cousins. To protect us from the bad guys. Your daddy won't let anything happen to us—"

"Daddy, I want to go home," Asia whined. "Who is Nar—"

"He's not gonna get us," India said, rubbing the pink tip of her triangle of a nose. She extended her arm with the silver astronaut cuff that Sonny had bought her at Cape Canaveral. Her fascination with space travel had been sparked as an infant, when a shuttle launch on television had evoked a gummy grin and a mesmerized sparkle in her eyes. "I'll shoot my laser—"

Sonny glared at Kindred. "What did you tell them?"

"We passed a television," Kindred said, "inside. That woman"—she nodded toward Roxanne by the barbecue—"was doing a report about the wedding, how the girls are going to sing for Norris and Marie. But then she talked about the movie." Kindred ran her hands up and down the goosebumps raising fine brown hairs on her bare arms. "The scary stuff that's going on—"

"I'll have every TV removed from here," Sonny said. "And down in the bungalow."

"I'm sorry, Mr. Whittaker." Kindred stroked the twins' heads. "It happened so quickly—"

The girls' slender arms pressed harder into Sonny's jugular veins. Their warm, velvet cheeks touched his. He kissed their foreheads.

"Oh, I need a double hug," he said. "Thank you, Angel Eyes of Dawn."

Sonny watched Jared and Josh scanning the dozens of people around the set, the lush bushes, the balcony. No one was going to harm one hair on these girls' heads. They could survive anything, even their terrifying birth:

"They are not blind," the doctor said in the small lounge outside the OR. "They appear to be very healthy, despite their low birth weight—"

Sonny turned toward the window, his eyes welling with gratitude—and rage at Erica for starving and poisoning their babies in utero. As he wiped his eyes, the first golden rays of daylight broke over the mountains around LA.

"My flesh and blood," he whispered a few minutes later, as a nurse offered a white-wrapped bundle in each arm. Their light caramel skin symbolized what he had thought was colorblind love. And when they opened their puffy, pink eyelids, four amber eyes harkened the dawn of a better world—

"No, I'm the dusk!" India's bow-shaped lips now broke into a smile. "Because that's when the space shuttle is gonna launch. Tonight. Daddy, remember, you said I could watch it—"

Sonny chuckled. "Of course—"

"I want Mom," Asia said, her chin quivering, tiny nostrils flaring. "When is she coming?"

"Right after we shoot this scene one more time," Sonny said. He pressed a fingertip to the gold chain at Asia's neck. "I don't remember Xavier's daughter in a diamond—"

"Daddy," Asia said, "this is how we interpret our characters."

Sonny laughed. "When I was seven, I wasn't *interpreting* anything. Now, how 'bout we try this scene once more. Then a picnic on the beach—"

Asia crossed her arms, her tiny elbow jabbing Sonny's stomach. "I don't wanna eat," she said with downturned lips. "I wanna see Mom. And I don't wanna be in this scary place—"

"Or be around guys with guns," India said. "They're not my cousins—"

"Yes," Sonny said, "Jared and Josh are my brother's children. You never met Uncle Andrew—" Because he died on his fifty-fifth birthday. Just like Popa.

"I'm not gonna eat," Asia said, "till we go to Montserrat with Grandmama—"

"Oh, she'll fatten you up good," Sonny said softly. His heart warmed at the idea of taking the girls to her sprawling home on the lush volcanic mountainside, far from the violent and decadent land of lollipop women like their mother and his costar Jenn Ryder, whose stick-slim bodies made their heads look extra large. "We'll call Grandmama tonight—"

"I don't want to get fat," Asia cried, withdrawing into Sonny's shoulder. "I want to stay this size, but taller."

Kindred poked a finger into Asia's tummy. "You have to grow as big and strong as me."

"Our Amazon warrior." Sonny smiled at Kindred. "She looks like a sister, loves you like a mother, and beat out twenty other nannies for the job. Now she, and your cousins"—Sonny cast a warning glare at Josh and Jared, then back at Kindred—"are going to watch your every blink and breath, without distractions, so you'll be safe and strong."

Tiny arms squeezed Sonny's neck. He coughed.

"Angel Eyes, listen to me," he said softly, inhaling their coconut-scented hair. "I promise you, nothing bad will happen. To you, or me. Now," he nodded toward the lion-tiger hybrid which was rolling between two chairs at the long rattan table. "The cub. You get to play with him again in this scene."

Their eyes sparkled, but their cheeks paled just as quickly.

"That lady"—a disgusted tone passed over India's trembling bottom lip as she glared at Roxanne Jones—"was talking about you and mom, in a court ring."

Sonny pressed his cheek to hers. "Court*room*."

India's eyebrows, as delicate as if he'd used his smallest paintbrush to draw black silk threads, came together. "She acts like she knows us. Make her stop."

"Daddy," Asia cried, "this isn't fun anymore."

The two terror-pinched faces made Sonny's chest squeeze. Had he been wrong to bring the girls here? On every other of their quarterly trips to Brazil, staying at this resort owned by his good friend Rico Miranda, the twins had loved the people, the exotic fruits and animals, the beaches.

"Angel Eyes," he said, "I wrote this film for our future. I want you to be proud of me, and live in a better world. Do you understand that?"

The twins nodded.

"Remember what we're learning about the Buddha? How sometimes we have to go through things that are hard?" Their eyes widened. "This little bit of time that's 'not fun' will make going to the premiere of *The Colony*, and living on Montserrat with Grandmama, all the more happy."

Even though right now it felt he would have to jump through increasingly small hoops of fire to reach the serenity of Nirvana.

Sonny kissed their foreheads, then set the girls down.

"India, wait!" he said, finger-combing her corkscrew curls to expose a squiggly part. He pinched gently against her scalp, making a *pluck!* sound.

"I got it!" He held the imaginary insect before her face. "The worry bug!"

Her silver astronaut cuff glimmered as she doubled over, laughing.

"Wait, Asia," he said, repeating the act on her head, "You have a giant one, right here! There, go away, worry bugs!"

Asia's eyes sparkled. "You're the silliest daddy!"

"Come on, girls," Kindred said, tapping their backs. "Métisse wants to play." With one girl on each side, Kindred took their hands. The bodyguards walked alongside them past the archway to the house.

A muscular, swarthy man dashed out in front of them.

"Uncle Rico!" the girls cried, looking to his hands. But he carried none of the sugar cane cubes on sticks that he'd been giving them since they'd grown teeth. The twins and Kindred froze, three sets of wide, amber eyes mirroring the terror roiling in Rico's gaze.

"My God," Sonny whispered, his heart hammering. He placed a hand on the sweat-soaked white cotton of his friend's shoulder.

"Christ, what now!" Norris exclaimed behind him.

"Sonny, my friend, I am sorry," Rico said with a Portuguese accent. He raised a Popeye-thick forearm protruding from a rolled-up sleeve, running a hand over his bronze-hued, bald head. He pressed a palm on the W-shaped wrinkles formed by his raised, black unibrow.

"This was just faxed," Rico said, holding out a large white envelope. He looked as distressed as he had that day back in the seventies, when a female guest at Sanctuary had slipped off the jagged rocks by the beach and drowned. Rico would never interrupt a shoot unless something terrible—

Grandmama. Alone in the house, hundreds of miles away in Montserrat, except for Grandpopa's buried remains under the almond tree overlooking Sunset Cove.

"What is it, man?" Sonny asked.

Rico's eyes darkened. "Sonny, my friend, the FBI, the CIA, the local police, they are on alert. I am expecting the American Embassy and the ambassador—"

"Daffodils," Sonny said, pinching the edge of the paper, which had a floral design around the black type. He knew every ridge and shade of that flower; he used to sketch and paint it during his two-year scholarship at the National Academy of Fine Arts and Design in New York. "From the Narcissus plant family—"

"The ID on the fax was blocked," Rico said. "The sender could be here, or thousands of miles away—"

Two black and olive blurs drew Sonny's focus; the twins ran toward him.

"Is Mom okay?" Asia cried.

"What's wrong, Daddy?" India demanded.

Kindred's large hands cupped their shoulders. "C'mon girls, let daddy—"

"Just a moment, Angel Eyes," Sonny said softly. Their tangible fear torched through him, superimposing their faces on the paper as he read:

Sonny Whittaker
You are what every man can never be, what every woman desires,
With your face, your voice, starring in a cast of Hollywood liars.
You're a symbol of fantasy and romance that can never be real,
Named the world's sexiest man, with your multi-million dollar film deal.
Too caught up in your own lust and greed to notice our pain,
You just keep making us feel inadequate, unattractive, insane.
But now it's time to repent for all the hope and hearts you've crushed,
So no other man or woman will ever crave your touch or your trust.
Should I be forced to write my message using your family's blood as ink,
At least, the shock will make the world stop worshiping you, and think.
I may strike on this set or your palace on the hill,
Just know for sure, Aries man, that more than tears will spill.
Sonny Whittaker, you and your perfect little dolls will suffer now,
Because with my very last breath, I'll be your angel of death, this I vow.
Narcissus

The paper rustled; Rico grasped Sonny's quaking wrist.

"My God," Sonny groaned. "Why?"

His veins felt like steampipes, rattling and hissing as blood coursed past his ears. Every heartbeat exploded again and again, sending molten surges of rage from the top of his zigzag black waves, combed back into a curlicue ponytail, down to his toes. Sonny crumpled the poem and shoved it into his pants pocket.

Norris yelled behind him, "All due respect Mr. Miranda, we got a movie to shoot here. Sonny, let's play ball!"

Sonny clasped the girls' little hands, casting a long, silent pledge into their faces that he would always protect them with his life. As Kindred led them away, Sonny turned to his friend.

"Triple security, Rico," Sonny said. "I want our bungalows checked. And . . ." He leaned toward Rico's large ear. With a quick nod toward Norris, Sonny whispered, "Keep an eye on my wife, and him."

3

Blue waves crashed on sharp black rocks, drowning out the clicking sound of typing on the gray laptop computer. Screeching gulls obscured the laughter. It was time to write another poem, to scare the shit out of the next person on the list. Then do something to show that this was serious business. Show business of another sort: to make them stop brainwashing the world.

"These rocks are killin' me."

The *Los Angeles Times* crinkled under the laptop. Had to get more comfortable, by scooting toward a smoother spot overlooking the beach. Why couldn't Americans be like these Brazilian women? All around, on the palm-fringed sand, the native vacationers showcased voluptuous hips and rounded stomachs—even those with the proud markings of motherhood—in *fio dental*. As in, thong bikinis so tiny, the Brazilians called them "dental floss."

But no, that x-ray bitch Jenn Ryder and her pimp Norris Haynes were up there, creating yet another movie celebrating an ideal that would make more girls starve themselves to death, and more guys search in vain to find such an impossible clone. An ideal who would make men get hard-ons, then spit at their fat-and-getting-fatter wives. An ideal whose shampoo-commercial hair, dermatologist-perfect skin, and artificially white teeth would make women spend money and time and anxiety trying to be like her.

"Who's next?" That row of pictures on the front page of the newspaper offered so many choices: Norris Haynes, Jenn Ryder, Sonny Whittaker, Simone Thompson.

"Hmmm. How 'bout—" Dark letters popped onto the screen: *Dear Simone Thompson: You may be wondering why I hate you. Or what you have to do with the Hollywood machine that I'm going to smash—*

"No." The delete button made the screen go blank. Maybe this next note would have more impact after Jenn Ryder's quick-change artist act. From sex symbol to hideous freak, all in a day's work.

"Cheyenne Moore, maybe." Didn't that maniacal manipulator know she was a washed-up whore with no chance and no right to be happy? After what she'd done to so many people—

A palm-sized green lizard scurried over the rocks onto the keyboard. Its tiny fingers pressed onto the keyboard, typing: *awefsdaweasdx.*

A swat, a balled fist, a smashed lizard, its scaly head flat. Beige goo—brains?—squirted onto the rocks. Its stubby legs convulsed. A quick dash down the rock, to rinse the slime in the foamy waves, then back to the keyboard.

"Now, what about Sonny Whittaker?" He was up there right now, looking so handsome and worried about his children and his movie. Didn't he know how many hearts he'd broken? Did he have any idea how much women loved him?

"He will. Yeah, once those little girls are dead, he'll start to understand."

4

Simone Thompson's insides jittered as she charged through the sleek black double doors leading into the plush cabin of the yacht. She hurried past gray suede couches and a long white marble bar.

"Tell me you have something clean and dry," she told Marie as they descended the polished teak stairwell into the master suite. "And not some thousand-dollar, thigh-high, low-cut Frederick's of Hollywood ensemble that you and Paulette probably have on hand as part of this scheme."

A mischievous smile lifted Marie's cheeks in her reflection in the wall of mirrors leading to the black-tiled bathroom.

"Seriously," Simone said, "something appropriate that fits me." She squinted in the bright sunshine pouring through windows on the ceiling, illuminating the white sheared mink bedspread and walls tiled with iridescent seashell. "This is obscene. Norris could feed half the children of Brazil with what this costs. Your jewelry could feed the other half."

Marie pulled Simone's straw hat off, grasped her sunbaked shoulders. "Stop carrying the weight of the world—"

Simone gasped at her reflection in the mirror. "An hour in the sun down here, and I already look like someone else!"

"I love it," Marie said, pulling her own bathing suit strap over her shoulder to inspect her tan line. "But of course, anything that feels and looks this good, *has* to be bad for us—"

"My mother would spit bullets," Simone said. A deep golden glow enhanced the buttery hue of the soft, slender bell shape of her nose, her full but sculpted cheeks, and the delicately defined line of her jaw. Her wide-set, silver-blue eyes seemed brighter against the suntan. But her jaw was tight; a tiny wrinkle formed between her naturally thick eyebrows.

"I can still hear my mother screaming about how dark I would get in the sun down here," Simone said. "She forced me to come. Three, four times a year, with the ambassador's family. But after a day on the beach with the Anderson kids, man, she'd just go off." Her pillowy lips pursed slightly. "Marie, you said—"

"Here, let your hair down," Marie said, unsnapping the plain silver barrette holding her ponytail. Simone's hair expanded into a cloud of wild sandy waves tumbling over her shoulders.

"She'd assault my head with a blow-dryer," Simone stroked her hair. "Until every curl, every wave, was pin-straight."

"That stain," Marie said, glancing at Simone's stomach, "is like a Rorschach: your mother's abuse is a big ugly blot on your life."

"Thank you, Doctor."

"You need to let go of all the shit that happened to you here," Marie said, aiming a black remote at the mirrors, which retracted into the wall to reveal a closet. "I confess, having the wedding here was not just Norris's idea. I want you to deal with your demons—"

"Men's suits?" Simone snapped, peeling off her wet clothes, then her beige cotton bra and panties. Her almond-hued nipples stiffened in the cool air.

"Damn, Simone," Marie said, glancing toward Simone's Brazilian bikini wax. "For someone who hates Brazil and doesn't want a man—"

"I do it for myself," Simone said. "Tell me, what demons?"

"Blaming yourself for Roland Anderson's death."

"Marie, I haven't brought that up in years."

"No, but we'll be in the very place where it happened," Marie said, "in a matter of minutes. I saw you wince when Paulette pointed to the pool."

"It wasn't my fault," Simone said, crossing her arms. But the images kept shooting up like burning embers . . .

"Thank you, Little Simone," Roland Anderson said, reaching for the plate of cookies that Simone offered. The silver hairs on the back of his thick knuckles caught the sunshine as he picked one, then sat back on the chaise lounge. "You're the most polite five-year-old I know."

"Marco!" Rosa shouted as she jumped into the pool. She was a blur of black hair, dark tan skin and a green tank suit with the number 6—the birthday they would celebrate that night after Bianca, Mr. Anderson and Simone's mother returned from a reception in Salvador.

Simone set the cookies on the umbrella table. She gulped down some more coconut milk right out of the shell, then set it next to the cookies. And she splashed into the water.

"Polo!" Simone and Brian yelled in unison.

Then, in a flash . . . their grandfather's barrel chest keeled over; he thudded on the cement patio. Half-chewed cookie oozed from his glistening blue lips.

In the chaos, as the nanny screamed for an ambulance and someone else said "heart attack" and someone else said "asthma attack," Rosa spotted the cookies. She smelled one.

"Cashews!" Rosa screamed at Simone. "You fed him nuts!"

Simone shook her head. "Marie, I've told you, they never let the grandfather be in the same room with nuts. He'd start coughing and—well, they didn't like that he was amending his will. I'm the scapegoat."

"You obviously haven't gotten over it," Marie said, reaching into the closet, "I can see it in your eyes. That, and Narcissus. If you need to talk—"

"I don't," Simone snapped. "Now, please give me some clothes."

Marie held up three dresses. "Pick one."

"Be real," Simone chided. "I prefer to wear a whole dress."

"Try this," Marie said, shaking a shimmery beige sheath.

Simone pinched the tag, scowling at the number four. "Please. Do these size-eight hips look like they'd fit into that tube sock?"

Marie held up the white one. "This one's a six. A roomy six."

Simone spread two triangles of gathered white chiffon that formed the halter top. "Where's the rest?"

Marie laughed. "You'll be gorgeous! Just put it on—"

"Absolutely not." Simone took the dress, making it flutter against her body. In the mirror, the skirt swayed like a white cloud over her toned legs. "This is so not me. Tell me you and Paulette aren't trying to stage your own *My Fair Lady*. Call it *My Freaky Lady,* starring me as Eliza Move-Somethin'. No telling what'll happen when we hit land."

Marie laughed as she opened a drawer built into the closet. "You're worried about Judge Johnston and Narcissus? Well, nobody will even recognize you—"

"And if they do, they'll think the tropical heat has all but melted away my judicial restraint."

"Everyone who lays eyes on you will thank me," Marie said, pulling a white bikini from the drawer. "Sonny Whittaker, Hollywood's who's who, Norris—"

"Never met a photo op he didn't like," Simone said.

Marie froze. She tossed the bikini toward Simone and whispered, "Simone, honestly, as my friend: do you believe the rumor?"

Simone drew her brows together, handing the skimpy bikini back. "I need underwear and a bra—"

"That's all I have." Marie shrugged. "Simone, what does your heart say about me and Norris? Do you think he loves me for me? Not my skin or my profession—"

"You know my rule on the bench: consider the source," Simone said as she dashed into the gleaming black bathroom. In the shower, hot water rained down on her sticky skin. "Even when someone is under oath, you have to trust your gut feeling, whether they're telling the truth."

"Cheyenne is a liar," Marie said. "Even if she and Norris do have a past."

"Norris loves you, so trust that," Simone said, pulling a plush white towel from the warming rack. From a long silver bowl, she took one of a dozen fresh aloe vera stalks, squeezed out the clear gel, and massaged it into her sunbaked skin.

"It's just, the way we met," Marie said. "Sometimes I wish I didn't have so much insight into Norris's mind."

"He fell in love with your super-sleuth mind," Simone said, eyeing the bikini on the bed. "I'm still in awe of you, Marie. You were just a girl, but your description and persistence—"

"Don't forget the modern miracle of DNA testing," Marie said.

"Of course," Simone said. "But you helped the detectives catch your parents' killer. Norris was so impressed, he made a movie about it! What more proof do you need?"

"I hear you," Marie said. "Simone, are you just gonna stand there naked?"

"I am going to run to my cabin," Simone said as she slipped on the bikini.

"You're going to bungalow eighteen, and Paulette is in nineteen," Marie said, tying the bikini top and the halter top of the dress. She fluffed Simone's hair over her shoulders. "Shoes." Marie rose from the bed, dashed to the closet and retrieved mules with clear acrylic wedge-heels and a silvery strap.

"Absolutely not," Simone said. "First the Marilyn Monroe dress. Now Cinderella slippers? I can't wear those. If I trip and hurt my ankle, I can't run. And if I can't run, I'll lose my mind."

"Yes!" Paulette shrieked as she dashed into the room. "I am loving this! Simone, you are drop-dead gorgeous." She laughed. "Sorry, bad choice of words. So put the shoes on—"

"Simone, girl," Marie said. "Don't you dare wear those espadrilles up on the deck with this dress."

Paulette laughed as she stepped into the bathroom. "Oooh, check out this bathroom. Marie, you are livin' in the lap of luxury. So glad I'm your friend—"

"What's mine is yours, girl," Marie said. "Now you, Simone, the shoes—"

The yacht's horn blared. Simone slipped on the shoes. "They don't feel as painful as they look."

"You look as painful as you feel. Ever since you broke up with Clark—"

"Ugh," Simone said, turning toward the door. "With all his dot-com fortune, he wouldn't give a dime to the orphanage. I only asked him once—"

"Oh, I meant to tell you," Marie said, "I got Norris to write a huge check to that charity you told me about. They're building shelters for street children in Rio and Salvador."

"Wonderful." Simone's stomach cramped. Sister Margaret's sad eyes filled her mind, along with the image of one hundred children marching along the sprawling lawn, pulling suitcases and wiping tears. "God, bring me a small fortune to keep The Tree House open—"

"The answer is right under your nose," Marie said. "Norris is on the cover of *Veja* right now for his donation to that program that stops farmers from destroying the Amazon. He would be happy to help my friend's pet project."

"No," Simone said. "With his daughter's trial coming up, it wouldn't look or feel right. It'd look like he was buying influence—"

"It's not your case," Marie shrugged. "Besides, who would know Norris's donation had any connection to you?"

"I would know," Simone dug her toes into the carpet. "And it wouldn't feel right."

"You're too uptight."

"Not according to Appeals Court Justice Caroline Drew," Simone said. "Last week, at the state judicial conference, she moderated a panel on ethics. Afterwards she pulled me aside and said, 'Judge Thompson, you set the standard when it comes to the personal and professional conduct that is expected of a judge.'"

"Half my clients waste their lives trying to live up to expectations," Marie said. "Parents, spouses, kids, neighbors—"

"Judge Drew said, 'in light of what's happened at your courthouse, that's quite a feat. We need guiding lights like you, to balance the damage done by a few bad apples.'"

"I'm proof," Marie said, "you can have both—"

"Your superior attitude is so aggravating," Simone said. "I know you're excited and worried. But where's the humility I know and love? Especially with all these rumors that Norris has less-than-noble reasons for choosing *you* to walk down the aisle—"

Marie fingered her pearl choker. "Hearing that from Paulette's gossip-filled head is one thing, but from you it contradicts your advice to trust my heart. I want an apology."

"So do I," Simone said. "You're in love, so I don't question your motivations for marrying Norris. So respect my need to find my father—"

"I can't keep quiet while you waste away—"

"Then don't expect me to ignore the rumors that you're just one more pretty spoke in Norris's golden PR wheel."

Marie peeled off her bathing suit and grabbed a robe from the closet. "You know, Simone, it seems like yesterday. You, me, Paulette, in our dorm room, looking out over Westwood. You said, 'My father is out there somewhere. A judge. I'm going to become one, too, so other kids won't grow up like I did. And I'll find him if it kills me.'"

Simone lowered her lids over stinging tears. She could still smell the cherry vanilla candles on their dorm room dresser. And see the Georgia O'Keeffe posters on the walls over Marie's desk where she'd chomp red licorice sticks while reading huge stacks of psychology books.

"We were teenagers," Marie said, squeezing Simone's hands. "But your mom hasn't given you anything but grief since you came to California. Not one clue about your dad. And I can't stand by and watch you waste—"

"I'm not wasting anything!" Simone said through tight lips. "I have my career—"

"Simone, honey," Marie said, her voice cracking and her eyes glistening. "You're all I have in this world, besides Norris. But awards and accolades can't hold you when you're afraid, or kiss you until your very bones catch fire—"

"I don't need you or Paulette to worry about my bed or my bones." Simone grasped the wispy skirt. "I'll have a bellman bring you this dress as soon as I get to my bungalow. I feel absolutely ridiculous."

Anger pumped her legs as she dashed out of the room, up the steps.

Her heart pounded as waves of questions flooded her mind. What if it *were* time to stop trying to find her father, to let go of her lifelong dream, and start looking for a mate? But could a man truly love her, unanswered questions and all? Could she be happy without ever knowing the second half of her genetic equation? Of where she got these unusual eyes, this yellowish skin tone, and—she flexed her calves—these runner's legs?

She stopped at the white marble bar to retrieve her purse. In the mirror, her eyes flashed like silvery neon question marks.

"Quitters never win, and winners never quit," she said aloud, quoting her track coach whose scholarship offer had been Simone's only ticket to UCLA. "I will find my father." She pulled her cell phone from her purse, dialed the Anderson's home in Washington.

"Bianca Anderson's office, may I help you?"

"Yes," Simone snapped. The overly polished secretarial tone in her mother's voice stiffened Simone's every muscle. "If you don't tell me the truth right now, I'll come there—"

"Simone, I'm very busy. I'm on the other lines with the caterer and the band for Bianca's party tomorrow—"

"I don't care. I'm your daughter. And I want answers."

"Simone, where are you? We have an awful connection—"

"The line is perfectly clear to me," Simone said. "I'm on All Saints

Bay, for a wedding. But all I can think about is the wretched way you've treated—"

"The static—" her mother said over ringing phones. "Try me back later, Simone."

The silence on the line made Simone feel as if she were underwater, hearing only her pounding heartbeat and air bubbling from her tight chest. Damn her mother for always putting the Andersons first. Always. Never giving straight answers or affection or even praise for Simone's straight A's and track trophies.

The yacht's horn blared. Bungalows, shrouded by lush tropical trees and flowers, appeared in the oblong tinted windows above the gray suede couch.

Simone's heart raced. The acrylic sandals pinched her toes. She shifted, catching her reflection in the mirror over the bar. All her life, her mother wouldn't tell her who she was. Now her friends were literally trying to make her into someone else.

No! Simone speed-dialed the chief judge's chambers at the Santa Monica County Building.

"Charlie, anything new on Narcissus?"

"Not unless he's poisoning our food," Charlie said. "Half the staff is sick to their stomach. The health department is trying to figure out if the cafeteria is the culprit."

"You sure it's in-house?" she said. "Remember last year, that coleslaw we ate at the bench meeting, from the fish and chips joint on the Third Street Promenade—"

"Don't remind me," Charlie said. "You're still coming back Monday?"

"That's the plan," Simone said.

"Good. Because you, me and Judge Johnston might be the only judges still standing. By the way, another note was faxed to your chambers. Sort of a poem, signed by Narcissus."

"Then he doesn't know I'm here," Simone said.

"Simone, this person comes across as very intelligent," Charlie said. "A skewed view of the world, but as passionate in his hatred for Holly-wood and the legal system as the Unabomber was about technology. And we saw what *he* did before he was stopped."

The yacht slowed; the horn blared again. Dread pumped through her like ice water. If only she could stay on this boat.

"Simone, just be careful," Charlie said.

5

Sonny Whittaker's every cell flamed with fear and determination as he took his seat at the head of the long rattan table. The twins sat an arm's reach to his right, facing the spread of earthenware pots that filled the air with the fiery-sweet scents of Bahian cuisine. At the other end of the table, Jenn faced him. Three actors sat on Sonny's left, their backs to the native beauties fanning the table with palm fronds; the woman playing his mother-in-law was between Jenn and the twins.

"Quiet on the set!" Norris said. "Speed?"

"Speed," the sound man answered.

"Scene five, take fifteen," the assistant director said. The black and white striped slate with red electronic digits closed.

"And, action!" Norris commanded.

Sonny cast his character's unfocused gaze upward, into the yellow-green haze of jungle mist and leaves. An adrenaline surge activated the actor's autopilot that Sonny had tuned and tweaked since his stage debut at age five on Broadway. And now, despite that wicked poem crinkling in the right front pocket of his pants and the worries searing his senses, he would not let Norris shout "Cut!" until the last syllable of this scene had passed perfectly over his burning lips.

"As leader of The Colony, blindness is required for me," Sonny said with the deep, practiced tone of authority. "It enables me to see with profound clarity that we are cultivating a utopia here on this island, for all the world to emulate."

"Never, Senhor Xavier," said the actor playing one of the World Council investigators. His face was a shiny, ebony oval against the lush wall of bamboo and fuchsia blooms. "If you do not cease the deliberate mixing of races and cultures and religions here, we will wage war against this abomination of nature!"

"Even if that means bloodshed," said the actor playing the second investigator. Silver bristles of a beard and crew cut framed his pinkish, round face. "Here, and anywhere else on the planet that your people have preached this desecration of humanity."

Sonny stiffened. That hot wind coiling around his neck dusted the salty taste of danger on his tongue. The rustling leaves seemed to whisper the words of Narcissus that he had read in this morning's *Los Angeles Times: I will punish Sweet Sonny Whittaker for his crimes of passion, by stealing the babies spawned by his international escapades of lust and greed—*

No! He remembered the excitement of writing this script, of basing the idea on Valley of the Dawn, a real community near Brasília. When he had visited the dusty village years ago with Rico, they were greeted by women in silver-sequined robes and men in Renaissance outfits. Residents explained that they communicated with black, Indian and extra-terrestrial spirits in their brashly colored temple. And despite the bizarreness of the community founded by a former trucker named Aunt Neiva, the Brazilian media was always consulting with people there about eclipses and the millennium. And just as folks flocked there for healing, Sonny decided that residents of his colony should travel outward to heal others.

"Gentlemen." Sonny stifled a cough as the fiery-sweet food scents burned his throat. "Your threats—"

He cast a split-second glance at the twins; their unblinking stares warned, *Don't mess up, Daddy.*

"Your threats cannot stop us," Sonny said deeply, as the girls' faces blurred, "because we are creating a twilight race of people, and our children are ushering in the dawn of a new day."

Sweat plastered Sonny's silky olive tunic to his back; his fingertips tingled with the need to grasp a paintbrush at the easel back at his bungalow. Yes, he would release all this worry onto a canvas, right after this shoot.

First, he would paint a black metal rake, glowing red as it dragged hot coals marked WORRY and FEAR and LONGING from the dark shadows of his mind. Then, leaving in their wake the white-hot clarity and concentration to execute this final and profound role of his life, he would paint a golden Oscar, and an NAACP Image Award, maybe even a Nobel Peace Prize, rising from the ashes of this angst.

"In fact," Sonny said, raising a hand toward Jenn as she sauntered from the other end of the table, "my wife—"

His wife. Erica Haynes Whittaker, who would be arriving here any moment, teetering on sky-high stilettos, defying gravity with her enhanced chest, but keeping her balance on the arm of her latest European boy-toy. The pools of ice that were her blue eyes chilled Sonny's mind—

"—my wife," Sonny said with a proud tone, lacing an arm around Jenn Ryder's waist, onto the padded curve of her belly, "is again with child."

Jenn gazed toward the gray-haired woman at the table.

"Mom, Dad, I changed my name to Aurora." Jenn's hip pressed into Sonny's thigh, rousing the hot, stiff ache of abstinence.

"That's Portuguese for 'dawn,'" she said, "because that's how I see myself now, as a mother. Xavier and I believe our children blend the brilliance of the brightest day with the black elegance of night. We—" Her soft fingertips on his cheek were his cue to speak.

Asia and India were pointing up at the waxy green leaves and tangled branches of a banyan tree. There, a monkey with a striped tail and fan-shaped ears was devouring a mango. They giggled softly as droplets fell on the pots of fiery malagueta sauce, pepper fish steamed in banana leaf, and *quindim* coconut pudding cakes.

He had to keep that happy sparkle in their eyes. In real life—

"Our children," he said, "grow up without seeing race. They carry that message of colorblind love out into the world. They are the salvation—"

"This is damnation, Senhor Xavier!" shouted the World Council investigator. "And I dare say, The Colony harkens the downfall of mankind."

Sonny tilted his chin higher. "Sir, our founders chose Brazil because for five centuries, blood from Europe, Africa and native Indians has blended into what they call *Mistura Fina*. An exquisite mixture."

The villain slammed his glass on the table. "The charter submitted to the World Council spoke of a nurturing community for the blind, shielded from the dangers of the outside world. This," he said, glaring at India and Asia, "was never the intention—"

"This twilight race," Sonny said, "is the future. Skin from alabaster to ebony. Hair in every shade from gold to onyx, as soft as cornsilk or coarse as sheep's wool—"

"Senhor, I can plainly see—"

"That's the point," Xavier said. "The very differences that arouse such hatred and malice within your heart, are what we are blind to. Instead, we feel. We love with our hearts and minds, not our eyes and skin. And—"

The *plunk* of an earthenware pot on the table and the cocoa-butter scent wafting from the cook as she leaned between Xavier and the villain cued Xavier to turn slightly rightward.

"Thank you, Anna," Xavier said, inhaling the aromas of garlic, cilantro and palm oil. He faced his foes as the cook ladled a steaming portion into his bowl. He spooned up a mouthful, then dabbed his lips with a satin-soft, caramel-colored napkin.

"Indulge, please," he said. "*Moqueca* is an impossibly delicious mix. Softshell crabs, coriander, tomatoes, coconut and our native *dende* oil. Anna, our tastebuds thank you."

"My pleasure, Senhor Xavier," said the actress with slanted blue eyes, blond dreadlocks and deep olive skin.

"A freakish race of mutts is what you are," said the silver-haired actress. She grasped Jenn's hand. "We want you out of this genetic science experiment."

The older actress's lip trembled. "Honey, when you were born blind, we brought you here because, well, the doctors never told us this was going on!"

"What do you mean, this, Mom?"

The ebony man glared at Asia and India. "What do you call your-selves? These girls, the cook, the petri dish you're making of your wife's womb! Even that animal there. I can't tell if it's a tiger or a lion!"

"Her name is Métisse," Jenn said. "Half lion, half tiger. Technically, a liger."

"She saved me from a green python," India said, making a swatting motion. "It was coming at me but Métisse just hit it on the head."

"Then," Asia said with a playful wrinkle of her nose, "Métisse bit the snake in half!"

"Disgusting," the silver-haired actress said under her breath.

Xavier said with a serious tone: "Sir, madame, have you ever stopped to listen to yourselves? We are helping the world see a better way—"

"What I *see*, Senhor Xavier, and *feel*, is that I'm on the Island of Dr. Moreau—"

Xavier patted Jenn's behind. They both stood.

"Sir," Xavier said, "I want to thank you."

"Thank me?"

"Yes, for reminding us that our twilight race must persevere with even more passion—"

"The World Council will stop you!" The man rose to his feet, making his chair scrape the patio. He threw his napkin toward the table. "And if bloodshed is required—"

Xavier was supposed to keep his unseeing gaze on the villain. But something made him peek from the corner of his eye at that napkin. It fluttered like a wounded dove, free-falling into the pot of pepper sauce. Blood-red liquid seeped through the fabric that was the same color as his daughters' skin. And Narcissus's words torched his mind: *Should I be forced to write my message using your family's blood as ink—*

"No," Xavier shouted. "You cannot stop us."

Sonny focused on the twins. Roxanne Jones and her TV camera. Norris, who was financing his daughter's wicked ploy to steal his babies. The bodyguards.

Sure, he had had threats and crazy letters and even women staking out his hotel rooms, all but shoving nipples and panties into his mouth when he showed up. Sometimes the dramas required a call to the police, a restraining order, even extra security at the house for a couple weeks. But things always blew over. And never had anyone threatened his children.

"We will fight!" Sonny shouted. "I pledge—"

The lines waiting to stream out of his mind, over his tongue, onto film, vanished. As if all the distractions around the set were pushing a giant ERASE button in his mind.

Sonny breathed deeply. India widened her eyes as if to say, *Daddy, concentrate!*

The relentless drum beat of a samba band rumbled up from the beach.

Xavier put his hand on his heart. "Sir, I will fight to the death—"

"You may have to," the World Council investigator said.

"Then we will be martyrs," Sonny said. "We will photograph the slaughter of our beautiful children—"

Those words caught in Sonny's throat. A hot bolt of panic shot through him, making his heart skip a beat. No! No one would hurt Asia and India—

He coughed. Grasped his throat. Doubled over, hacking.

"Cut!" Norris shouted. "Cut! Cut! Cut!"

A red cloud billowed inside Sonny's head, setting fire to his senses, making him tremble. Rage was burning away all he'd learned from the Actor's Studio and the Stanislavsky Method at The Group Theater, and dozens of films. This paralysis was a sacrilege to his childhood pledge to shield his children from the fatigue and fear he saw in his own mother's eyes, her fingertips bloodied after long hours as a seamstress in Harlem while Popa worked three jobs, six days a week, to send Sonny and Andrew to school with full stomachs and fresh clothes.

"We're through, Whittaker!" Norris shouted.

Sonny shot up so quickly the chair tumbled over behind him. He placed a hand on the girls' outer shoulders, bent down between them and said, "I'll see you at the bungalow. Stay with Kindred and the bodyguards. No matter what."

He kissed the tops of their heads just as Kindred approached.

"Your mom will be here soon," she said softly. "Maybe we can all go for a boat ride later, and watch the ocean swallow the sun."

The girls's eyes widened up at Sonny. "Can we, Daddy?"

"Whatever will make you smile, Angel Eyes." Sonny strode toward the bodyguards, who stood at the archway into the house.

"Guard them with your lives," Sonny said.

Josh grasped the gun strapped to his waist. "Consider me a human shield."

"Whittaker," Norris yelled, his shoes slapping the stone. "You better think long and hard—"

Sonny could feel Roxanne Jones staring, her cameraman aiming at him, and Norris in the background. He dashed toward the wooden staircase leading to the beach, the resort, the marina.

He had to be alone for a few moments, to extinguish the fury threatening to sear his very soul. With every step downward, the hypnotic rhythms of samba music became louder. Far below on the beach, men and women formed a fleshy snake of dancing and drumming as they practiced for Carnival. Sonny ached to escape into the abandon of their erotic expression.

Near the dancers, a cluster of women sunbathing on the sand waved to him. One of the women flipped a shiny black mane and rolled onto her back, offering up to the sun nipples as sweet and succulent as the swirls of steaming cinnamon rolls.

"Obrigado," he sighed playfully, saying thank you in Portuguese as his sandals scraped the sandy, flower-lined sidewalk leading to the marina.

A fiery surge slackened Sonny's neck, shoulders, and fingers, arousing a tingly warmth far lower. His every cell craved the oblivion of lust, the opiate of a woman's hot hiding places. There, he could climb into a sensual sanctuary, far away from the dread, the rage, the anxiety that was so viciously clawing his entire being. But a deep, regretful ache seeped through his gut, as if he'd indulged in an extra fingerlick of frosting after eating the whole cake.

No more women. Unless she could pass Grandmama's prophesied shiver test.

Sonny ran; his leg muscles burned. Lush vegetation shrouding the pebbled stone path formed a green tunnel, dotted with sweet-smelling purple and orange flowers. The docks and gleaming white yachts were a blinding-bright mirage at the end.

"My God." Sonny ran faster, sucking down air, his legs pumping with white-hot rage. He had to get away, escape to the serenity of his boat. Watch the water, the sun, perhaps meditate. With every step, waxy leaves shaped like giant hands sliced against his shoulders, his elbows, his ankles. He tripped on a rope-like vine.

And during that split-second when his body lurched forward, a painting came to mind: the lush green leaves of life closing in, trying to trap him, to stop him from fulfilling his life's work as a father, an actor, a painter, a citizen of the world with so many gifts to share. Sonny ran faster, until the hot sun, screaming seagulls and lapping water overcame his senses.

"You should not be alone, Senhor Whittaker," said a police officer who stood with another man in uniform at the marina entrance. One officer grasped the silver pole supporting the SANCTUARY archway. He nodded toward the shadowy path. "Especially there."

"I'll be on my boat," he said, sandals pounding the white wooden planks of the dock. Sonny dashed past schooners, where fishermen were assessing their catches. He ran by more pairs of police officers, who were scanning gold-chain-draped older men with deep tans sitting like kings atop gleaming yachts where women sunbathed and children zoomed off on jetskis.

"Dharma's Dream." Sonny announced the black script letters painted on the back of his fifty-foot red cigarette boat. It rocked in the very last slip closest to the open water. All around, the hot, humid air rang with samba music, splashing water, buzzing motors and sun-revelers' snippets of Spanish, Portuguese and English. He jumped over the red, black and white stripes on the leather seat across the back.

Sonny unlocked the thick gray Plexiglas doors leading down to the cabin, to the left of the steering wheel and raised white leather bucket seats. Once inside, he pulled his sweat-drenched tunic over his shoulders.

His hands were still trembling as he removed his sand-filled sandals. The note crinkled in the pocket of the drawstring pants of Xavier's costume. Sonny put on loose-fitting beige silk shorts and slipped the poem into the right front pocket of the shorts. He had to relax. Because he would explode, or implode, with angst if he kept this up. The thought of anyone wanting to hurt his beautiful babies—

Sonny shot up the steps, over the narrow side ledge, to the red leather cushion on the long, A-shaped front of the boat. A huge basket of flowers floated in the blue-green water about a dozen feet away.

"No, not mine, but go back to sea anyway," he said. Just last week, on February second, he had taken Asia and India across All Saints Bay, into the city of Salvador, for the festival of the Queen of the Sea.

"Angel Eyes," Sonny said, the salty water frothing around his ankles on the yellow sand of Itapoa beach, "let's make our wishes and let them set sail."

Sonny put his basket of flowers into the water as the girls launched their two-foot-long boats of soap, lipstick and barrettes into the waves.

"Yay!" the girls cheered as the little vessels headed toward the sunset, which Grandmama was watching further north in the Caribbean, to tell him just what it might portend on this evening. He would have to ask her during their Sunday teleconference.

He and the twins held hands and closed their eyes. In unison they recited their bedtime prayer: "Please keep us happy and healthy, safe and strong. Please keep us with our Daddy, and make our movie the best ever!"

As the girls clapped, Sonny whispered toward the shimmering pastel heavens,

"And please bring me that woman who will make my very soul shiver."

Now, Sonny stared at the turquoise horizon. "Yes, a woman as mystical and powerful as Iemanjá. Beautiful and brilliant. I've seen enough she-devils." He laughed toward the sky as he lay back on the leather cushion, making the poem crinkle in his pocket. "Now we deserve nothing short of a goddess."

Sonny closed his eyes, savoring the hot sunshine on his face, his bare chest, his legs, his palms. Through his nose, he breathed slowly and deeply.

"Fome," he whispered. That mantra signaled his muscles to slacken, his heartbeat to slow, his blood to cool. He had chosen the word with the help of his Buddhist spiritual guide back in Los Angeles.

"Fome." It was Portuguese for hunger, but was often used in context with sexual desire. Other times he would say *comendo*, a word for eating that was also used to describe intercourse. The words often brought to mind Gabriela, the lusty heroine who seduced men with sex and food in *Clove and Cinnamon*, a novel by one of Brazil's foremost authors, Jorge Amado.

Sonny smiled, remembering the madame on New York's Upper West Side, who had taken Sonny into her home for a whole year. Wearing lace and satin outfits of every color, Lovelee would feed him an international smorgasbord by week's end—Indian, Vietnamese, Nigerian, Italian, Brazilian, Mandarin—all while teaching him about Eastern religion. And rescuing him from the emotional abyss that had sucked him into a zombie-like void after his parents died some thirty years ago.

"Fome," Sonny whispered into the steamy breeze.

The deep horn of a yacht vibrated the air. Hot shards of worries shot back through his mind as Norris's sleek white yacht approached with its round black windows, a helicopter on top gleaming in the sun. A boat Sonny had enjoyed many times.

"Sonny!" Marie blew a kiss with her left hand from the second-level deck where she stood with two other women.

"Better wave with your other hand," he called back. Then again, Norris could get just as much publicity out of her losing that boulder of a diamond as he'd gotten out of giving it to her on live TV.

Marie smiled, lifting her left hand to her trademark pearl choker, then finger-combing her hair that shined as brightly as a new penny. How could a sister so successful and intelligent be blind to Norris's ulterior motive? It seemed everyone but prim, professional and just-black-enough Marie knew the wedding was another Norris Haynes PR stunt. Like last year, when he checked himself into the hospital for a mysterious stomach ailment. The media went wild just in time for the release of *Death Ranger*, a box office blockbuster about a renegade doctor. This time, Norris was getting married to tame his image, just in time for Oscar.

The starboard side of their boat hummed closer, now about ten yards away. Sonny squinted in the bright sunshine reflecting off the azure water. Marie turned to her companions.

"My God," Sonny groaned. "That's her."

She was tall. Clear, buttery skin. Was she a fair-skinned Brazilian mulatta, an interpreter? A friend of Marie's from the States? Her loose, sandy-colored hair blew back toward the horizon like yellow flames shooting behind a meteor. Not his usual preference—Sonny typically found himself drawn to more petite women with dark eyes framed by lush brunette or black hair.

But this woman's unconventional beauty was mesmerizing. If only he could see her eyes behind those oval, black sunglasses. They rested on a nose shaped like a little golden bell, pinched into a point.

Her full lips puckered slightly in the wind. They were the same shade of deep, dewy pink as the long-stemmed roses Popa used to bring home to Momma every Friday, after his shift at the flower shop. The same flowers Sonny placed on their side-by-side eternal resting places whenever he visited New York, and kept in his home as reminders of their hopes and dreams for him. And their lifetime of love.

My God, I could latch onto those lips and never let go . . .

The wind carved her white dress around an hourglass of bosom, waist and hips. The halter top cradled full breasts and a triangle of ripe, creamy cleavage.

"Welcome to Sanctuary," he said deeply, staring at her.

She faced him, her eyes still hidden behind the sunglasses.

But he could feel her soul. It was whispering to him across the water so intensely, with such yearning, his head spun. The magnetic power between them made Sonny envision fingers of red fire shooting down from the sun, whirling in a yin-yang circle with sharp waves churning up from the ocean, glowing with diamond dots glistening on the water. But if they tried to touch through this awesome karmic connection, would one of them get burned, or drown?

His blood was pumping so fiercely, with such heat, that it provoked a faint ringing in his ears. And it only got louder as her bare shoulders faced him squarely. Her delicate jaw rose slightly. She wrapped long fingers around the silver pole atop the rail. And she seemed to step forward.

"Yes, come to me," Sonny whispered. His shoulders twitched. Goose-bumps rippled from his face to his nipples and abdomen, thighs and toes.

He had a sudden vision of himself at the bottom of the sea, helplessly holding up outstretched arms, and she, like a golden mermaid, swimming from a boat called *Destiny*, splashing down to rescue him from the dreary depths.

"Come all the way to me," he whispered.

His skin felt electric, like when he walked through the billowing orange sheers between his paint studio at home, onto the terrace to watch the sun set over Los Angeles. On particularly dry nights, static electricity made little popping-crackling sounds, and he could actually see blue-gold sparks as the fabric brushed his skin. That was how this woman—this goddess delivered by Iemanjá at his request—was making him feel right now. Electrified.

Was that a smile raising the corners of her beautiful mouth? The boat was drawing closer. The primitive rhythm of samba drums echoed his pounding heart; the lusty screams of dancers on the beach expressed all he wanted to say.

The woman's lips, parting slowly, triggered a sharp gasp from deep inside him. It escaped into the salty wind and screams of gulls.

She raised a delicate hand, a supple arm. The color of her skin brought to mind the name of one of his paints, *butterscotch cream*. The orange and white tube was sitting on his easel back home.

A thousand images and ideas for paintings flashed like an out-of-control slide show in his head. A glass bottle shaped like a woman's body, scrolled with ELIXIR, topped with a porcelain knob painted like her face. Or the two of them holding hands, running through the treacherous jungle of life as a volcano spewed fire in the background, and they sprinted toward a glowing yellow ball around a house with a white picket fence. Or himself, bloody and beaten, crawling up a jagged, muddy mountain, where a lavender halo glowed around her and Asia and India, the three of them in angel wings—

"Sonny!" A man's voice called from the dock.

But Sonny could not look away from the woman. No, his brain clicked and snapped like the camera he often used to take pictures of people and places, for future reference at his easel. Because now, in case he never again saw this lovely vision of all that a woman should be, he had to make a detailed mindprint. The texture of her hair, the oval shape of her face. He would immortalize this vision tonight, after the girls practiced their song at the rehearsal dinner, after they were safe and sleeping . . .

He would make love to this woman's image with the most sensuous sketching, the most tender brushstrokes. And if he could see her up close, to meet her, to know her name, to hear her voice—

"Sonny!" Yes, that was Myles. Hard footsteps echoed on the dock. But he could not turn around. The woman, she was removing her black sunglasses.

"C'mon," Myles shouted with his New York accent, "somebody's tryin' to cast the *Sonny Whittaker Horror Show*, and you're down on the boat alone! Bad deal, man."

Heart exploding, palms slick, Sonny tried to look back at his best childhood friend and lawyer. "Are the girls—"

"They're fine," Myles said, jumping into the boat. "But Sonny, I'm hustling to get ready for this trial, and I need your help. So stop with the dreamy gaze and let's go."

The woman's eyes were like two full moons shining toward him. Like his metallic paint called *moonbeam gray*. Milky blue in the center, ringed by an almost silver glow.

My God . . .

His very core turned white hot.

A sudden shiver made his breath catch in his throat. His every muscle seemed to stiffen and slacken at once. And he felt as though his entire length, from his tingling toes to the hair on his head, was bursting into flame under her gaze.

6

The hair on the back of Jenn Ryder's neck prickled as she struggled to turn the brass key in the door of her bungalow. A sour scent wafted from the lush vegetation shrouding the stained-wood, two-story structure. She glanced back and up at Norris and the two bodyguards behind him, hating the bright sunshine in her eyes and on her face. "What, am I such a ditz, we came to the wrong—"

"Number eight," Norris said. The number was carved on the cinnamon-brown wood to the right of the door. Closed shutters obscured the windows on each side of the entrance.

"The first day here, the idiot from the office did give me the wrong key," Jenn said, turning so hard the key ached against the pads of her fingers. "Ugh! No chance of a psycho getting into my bungalow when *I* can't even get in!"

"Hurry up, Jenn," Norris said. "You got ten minutes on the clock. Marie won't take kindly to it if I'm not at the marina to greet her. So whatever you wanted to talk about, let's play ball."

"Dammit, Norris, I'm sick of being scared," she said.

Jenn's key turned; she pushed open the door. The ocean, framed by double glass doors at the back of the bungalow, calmed her. And she loved the earthy design of the knotty wood paneling, vaulted ceilings and bamboo ceiling fans, the cushy couches and chairs in the open living room and kitchen.

Except for all the footsteps as the bodyguards looked around.

"You guys," Jenn said. "In a few minutes I'm just going to wash my face and change clothes. So leave me alone, will you?"

"Christ," Norris said. "Just relax! Sonny's right next door—"

"I can't wait to go home to my high fence and video cameras and regular security team—"

Jenn dashed up the open, stained-wood staircase to the bedroom loft. "Could Sonny have designed a hotter costume?" she called down to Norris, as he chugged bottled water and plopped into the fan-shaped wicker chair by the fireplace.

She just wanted Norris to agree to some changes on the set. Her pulse pounded as she stood at the end of her fluffy white bed and pulled off her dress.

"If you gotta go through your whole face routine," Norris barked, "we'll talk later."

"Wait," she said, unhooking her bra. She loved the sensation of letting her heavy, damp breasts breathe. She cupped them, letting cool air from the ceiling fan hit the sweat where they rested on her ribs. "I can't believe my picture is in there," she said, peering down at him through the stained, polished tree-branch collage that formed the balcony railing. He was flipping through the latest edition of *Veja* magazine. "That's like Brazil's *Newsweek*."

"Why not, you're in every other magazine in the world," Norris said. "They're making as big a deal out of *The Colony* as they did when we shot *Come Back, My Love* on the Amazon twenty-five years ago." Norris laughed. "You weren't even born."

"I'm not as young as you'd like to think," Jenn said, pulling on a white cotton tank top she had laid out on the bamboo bench at the foot of the bed. "I'm old enough to appreciate what you and Sonny are doing with *The Colony*. And it's an honor to be part—"

"Save it for your Oscar speech," Norris said, flipping pages.

Jenn sat on the bed, raising her long, waxed legs up toward a pair of white shorts. She smiled at the bold-faced SIZE 2 on the label. "They even say, in that article, this film has the power to transform the way we relate to each other."

"Yeah, yeah," Norris said.

"Great picture of you on the cover," Jenn said, securing her hair into a ponytail with trembling hands. "Flattering article, except the guy who says you love green plants and money more than people—"

"Just call me Poison Ivy from *Batman*."

"And I love how they're giving Sonny the credit he deserves for trying to do a film with so much substance." Jenn jumped to her feet, pulling up the shorts, the tight elastic flattening her stomach even more. "Especially considering the danger—"

"I'm not worried about it," Norris said. "Usually turns out to be some harmless teenager with too much time on his hands, just playin' around on his computer."

"I hope that's all it is," Jenn said, her bare feet thumping down the steps.

She pressed her fingertips to her cheek. "I can't wait another second to wash these ten layers of sunscreen off." She dashed to the kitchen island, where a white washcloth, face towel and small bottle of anti-wrinkle cream awaited her daily post-filming wash routine.

"Norris, you know, it took me fourteen years to make it in Hollywood. Now I'm thirty-three. My face is my livelihood."

"And what a lovely face it is," he said, pinching his sunburned nose.

"Thank you." She held a washcloth in the warm stream of water. Her shoulders trembled; the words she'd been thinking for the past month of filming shot from her mouth: "But if I have to fry in the sun, take after take, you can take my SAG card right now. I'm wrinkling up like a prune. And I don't want my next role to be as a teenager's mother!"

"Jenn, this is Brazil. It's hot. Don't be so vain. Besides, you got a good four, five years before the crows start making footprints around your eyes."

She buried her face in the warm, wet washcloth. She made gentle circles, the way her dermatologist had showed her, so as not to stretch or pull, which could cause wrinkles. Or worsen the ones she already had.

"Norris, I want to shoot the rest of the scenes indoors, or at night—"

"Are you nuts?" He shot to his feet. "That would fuck everything up. Without the outdoor scenery here, we might as well be on a sound stage in LA."

Jenn cupped water, splashing her face. "Norris, I believe so much in this movie—"

"Then do what you have to do to play the part," Norris said. "You want extra security, I can understand. Your face should be the least of your worries."

Jenn patted her cheeks with the towel. "I guess these editorials from Narcissus have gotten me thinking. The tragedy is, I agree with him."

Norris put his hands on his belt. "You *have* been in the sun too long."

"It's true, Norris. When I read that editorial this morning, along with my eggwhite omelet and grapefruit, after my workout, I thought, I couldn't agree more."

"Jenn, you *choose* to be an actress. You choose to work in an industry that demands you look your best—"

"Exactly. Yet I'm caught in a Catch 22 because the working conditions are frying my skin, and the food here is so heavy, from that disgusting palm oil."

Norris glanced at his silver watch. "I tell you what, Jenn. My future wife, the brilliant psychologist, will be here in just a few minutes. How 'bout you express these anxieties to her? You're sounding like her patients with that body dysmorphic syndrome. So I'm sure she'd be delighted to—"

"No—"

"Jenn, you're at the top of your game right now. Enjoy it while it lasts—"

"Yeah, because when I'm fifty-five like Sonny, the roles will be few and far between. Is that what you're saying?"

"I think the timing for this break will be good for you," he said, stepping toward the door. "So you can come to your senses."

"It's just not fair. I shudder to think about even turning thirty-five."

"Jenn, if you want to go back to waiting tables, along with the thousands of beautiful young women in LA, all trying to get exactly where you are right now—better yet, why don't you go back to that shithole trailer park in Vegas with your booze-guzzlin' pops—"

"I didn't say I was quitting," she said. "I just want to do something before the sun makes faultlines in my face."

"I'll be making faultlines in the cast if you don't stop whining," he said, opening the door. "You've been a pain in the ass from day one. Having that feng shui guy come in here to arrange your furniture. The personal masseuse. Now this. A couple more weeks on the set here won't make or break you."

Norris stepped outside; the sun illuminated the top of his wavy hair. He put on his PRISM baseball cap.

"You can't honor my one simple request?"

He slammed the door.

"What a jerk! Oh, shoot—" She still needed to put on her anti-wrinkle cream. She returned to the kitchen island sink, ignoring the bodyguards sitting at the table. She grabbed the jumbo bottle and took it into the back bathroom, off the bedroom suite overlooking the beach.

"Come out!" she shouted at the upside down bottle.

Pffftttzzz.

"There." She wanted to smooth it on an inch thick, to make up for all her time in the sun today. Her reflection in the mirror revealed a face that felt tight and dry enough to crack. Worry glowed from her cosmetic-free eyes. Her pointed nose was sun-pinkened.

"It's gonna peel," she sighed. The word "damage" blared in her mind. Maybe she did have body dysmorphic disorder. Maybe she was internalizing the pressure to look young to the point that she was seeing wrinkles where they did not exist.

She had no concept, no perspective. Just like it seemed normal and rational to skip meals or feel lightheaded or not eat for days before she had to walk the red carpet in a slinky gown for an awards ceremony.

She frantically squirted out the yellow cream. She used her fingertips to massage it around her eyes, her mouth, her forehead.

"This doesn't feel right," she said, looking at the meringue-like swirls of cream covering her whole face. The slight burning sensation was more like the one chemical peel she'd had just before the Oscars last year, when she won for best actress.

She snatched up the bottle; it looked the same as it always did. She smelled the top. Nothing strange. Her face was getting hotter by the second. And now the palms of her hands, the lengths of her fingers, under her nails . . .

Her eyes became huge. Narcissus. Could someone have gotten in here and tampered with her lotion? Suddenly, something yellow on the bathroom wall, behind her, caught her eye. A daffodil.

She spun around. A silver nail pierced the green stem of the fresh flower, holding it and a sheet of white paper to the wall. She ripped it down, speed-reading the black type:

> *Jenn Ryder*
> *The movies and magazines say you're the fairest of them all,*
> *Skinny and happy and rich and tall.*
> *But I want you and Hollywood and the world to see,*
> *How much you're hated by ordinary people like me.*
> *You make us feel ugly, fat and so depressed,*
> *Measuring our worth by white teeth, pretty hair and big breasts.*
> *Who gave you and all of them the power to decide,*
> *To let looks and things on the outside make us hurt so much inside?*
> *Mirror, mirror on the wall, watch it crack and fall to Hell,*
> *No more fame and fortune for girls like you, as I sound Jenn Ryder's*
> *death knell.*
>
> *Narcissus*

"Oh my God!" Her lips, her face, her hands, burned horribly. And that smell—

Melting skin.

Her arm shook as she reached for the faucet handle.

She had to wash this off her face! What was it?

"Help me!" She frantically glanced around. The bodyguards and Sonny next door would never hear her. Her excruciating fingers quaked just above the faucet.

Somehow, despite the pain shooting up from her palms, she grasped the knobs. Turning. The water hissed.

A strange tearing sensation . . . *skin.*

She raised her hands, flipping them over.

She screamed. Inch-long sheets of skin hung, dripping blood—

"No!"

She had to get this off her face. She clawed her cheeks to scrape it off—but her hands felt like burning mitts wiping up clumps of flesh.

Water! She tried to cup her hands under the faucet. She splashed water up onto her face. Over and over.

Yes, she could get it all off. The cool water dripped down her jaw, to her neck, down her arms. The water in the sink was pink. Red. Dotted with pieces of—

No! Her head spun. Eyes burned.

My eyes. I'll go blind! No, I can do this. I can rinse it all off . . .

7

Simone Thompson quivered as the yacht splashed through the shimmering turquoise water toward Sonny Whittaker in the marina. His thigh muscles rippled with every step he took toward the front of his boat, closer to her. And his smoky-brown eyes provoked tingles deep below her belly button. As if his gaze were luring her soul to flow toward him like molten gold and pour into a cast of embracing lovers, hewn by this surreal sensation.

"No, Marie, don't let me near that man," Simone said, her bare arm pressing her friend's shoulder as they stood at the starboard side of the foredeck.

"I told you," Marie said playfully. She turned toward Paulette, on the other side of Simone. "Intervention of the most magnetic kind."

"Looks like she'll only need one meeting at Abstinence Anonymous," Paulette cooed. "That man is beyond sexy—"

"No," Simone said. "I'm not ready. Not now. Not here." She did not want to let her face broadcast this sudden rapture, because it would give Marie and Paulette fuel for their love connection quest.

"But I feel," Simone sighed, "he's talking to me, touching me, with his eyes."

"Who's that with him?" Paulette asked. The ruffled neckline and bell bottoms of her mint green jumpsuit fluttered, while the tapered waist and snug pants hugged her curves. Her feathery brown hair cascaded from under a wide-brimmed straw hat and whisped over her bare, plump shoulders.

"Probably an assistant," Marie said. The second man was a mere blur of white fisherman's hat, mirrored sunglasses, plain white T-shirt and khaki pants. He turned his back, stepping onto the dock with a bottle of water. "But I've never seen Sonny with an entourage. Or even a cell phone, for that matter. He's humble as pie."

Sonny stared straight at Simone.

"Whew," Paulette said, fanning herself with her hand. "Let me get my camera."

"Paulette," Marie said sternly, "go easy. I know you're excited to meet celebrities, but—"

"Don't tell me how to act," Paulette said, stepping toward her straw bag on the chaise lounge. "I've sold houses to more than a few stars."

"Then act like it," Marie snapped. "Norris is having *People* and *In Style* here. Period." Marie fingered her pearls. "Help me, girlfriends," she said, smiling as she turned toward Sonny. "The first time I met him, I couldn't make a sentence to save my life."

"Talking isn't what I had in mind." Paulette gathered Simone's hair into a ponytail, then let it fall. "Let me live out my seventeen-year itch through you, Simone."

"What is he *doing* to me?" Simone sighed. The sudden tickle of her nipples against the bathing suit top softened her voice to a sultry depth: "My goodness, I feel like I've known him forever. Like he's making love to me with his eyes—"

"But a man with that much magnetism," Paulette cooed, "needs the sampler plate as opposed to a single entree. Even if it's filet mignon. And from what I've read—"

"Sonny!" Marie called. "Where's Norris?"

"He's coming to meet his blushing bride," Sonny answered, smiling. His deep voice lulled Simone's senses along with the gentle splash and chirping birds. He stood at the front V of the red boat, which had no rails, rising and falling with the rocking vessel against a backdrop of palm trees, white sand beach, blue water and sky.

"Never thought anyone would call me that at thirty-eight," Marie sighed. "But look how he's looking at you, Simone."

"I shouldn't have come here." Simone's mouth moistened with the urge to taste the luscious bronze hue of his sculpted cheekbones, his clean-shaven angular jaw, and a nose that reminded her of an Indian chief. His full lips . . . they suddenly parted, revealing a flash of straight white teeth, as if he were releasing a breath he'd been holding since he first saw her. His eyelids lowered under lush black crescents of lashes, then raised over a smoldering gaze.

She wanted to close her eyes and savor this mellow, intoxicating sensation, as if she were floating and soaking inside the voluptuous curve of a crystal snifter of warm brandy. Yet, she could not break the sparkling channel of energy between their eyes.

"Am I really blushing?" Marie asked.

"No, *he'd* blush," Simone whispered, "if he heard what I was thinking right now."

"I am loving this!" Paulette exclaimed.

"Face it," Marie said, "you're just a lusty, repressed Lolita who's feeling the Brazilian heat. To hell with all the rules you have to follow back home. Toss off that black robe and samba, baby!" Marie raised her hands, snapping her fingers, shaking her hip against Simone's, then Paulette's.

"Hey, I wouldn't care if I were Chief Justice of the Supreme Court," Paulette said playfully. "All the judicial restraint in the world wouldn't stop me from getting some of that." She waved at Sonny, who waved back. "Just one kiss!" Paulette's nipples made their presence known like two marbles under the green fabric of her jumpsuit.

"I'm keeping my chastity belt on." Simone's stomach cramped as she inhaled the salty-sweet, nose-burning heat. They were close enough to swim to the shore of this land where so many times Simone had sat as a child and teenager, mesmerized by the waves rolling in, crashing, foaming, rolling out—never providing answers to all her questions. About why she had no father. About why the Andersons blamed her for their patriarch's death. About why her mother chose to keep working for people who hated her daughter.

"I could stare at him all day," Simone whispered as Sonny Whittaker's gaze trailed over her nose, her mouth, her hair. The words "We Are One" streamed through her mind, as if he were typing a stock ticker on her brain.

Simone sucked a sharp breath through parted lips. Her pounding heart sent blood wailing past her ears like sirens. She imagined pressing her breasts into his broad chest, letting him wrap his arms around her.

Even her first and only real love had not roused an attraction this strong. "Super sexy Simone, make me cry and moan, I'll never love another, just Simone forever," teenaged Brian would whisper during heart-pounding orgasms, on all those days when he would sneak up to the carriage house to see her. So his father the ambassador would not catch him saying "I love you, Simone" or whispering that Brazilian term of honey-sweetheart endearment, *Fofa,* to the hired help's daughter.

Their romance had become even more clandestine after Brian's sister, Rosa, had screamed: "I hate you for stealing my brother!" Rosa had thrown the Monopoly game into the murky water in the boat house, where Simone and Brian often stole away to play Scrabble or kiss.

But even after that, Brian's eyes expressed only tenderness. Always, whether strolling through the Smithsonian, sharing coffee at some tiny café in Georgetown, phoning from Oxford University in England, or whispering to her in her dreams after fever burned his life away during a safari in Botswana.

Now, Simone bristled at the memory of his memorial service, when Rosa had stood beside her architect husband and hissed that some day she would punish Simone for taking Brian's attention away for so many years.

"I'm getting worried about Norris." Marie's brows drew together as she scanned the dock and the empty slip where the yacht was approaching.

"He's probably still tied up on the set," Simone said. "What are you worried about?"

"If you think Norris is having a private bachelor party with some star-let," Paulette tapped her fingernails on the metal rail, "forget about it. I see how he looks at you, Marie. Just like that." She pointed to Sonny, whose eyes were sparkling at Simone.

"Look at yourself, Judge," Marie said. "Father or no father, how many times in your life do you think you'll come across a man who stares at you like *that*?"

Paulette chimed in, "That man wouldn't care if your daddy were Godzilla."

"If fame and fortune impressed me," Simone said, "we'd be having a double wedding: you and Norris, me and dot-com what's-his-name."

"You and Clark made a better couple than you want to admit," Paulette said.

"He was fun, and his cooking—that pesto!—was incomparable," Marie said. "But again, your phantom father chased Clark away. It's maddening to me—"

"Both of you, get off my case. I don't feel—"

"You feel *what* as we ogle Sonny Whittaker?" Marie studied the dock again, as the yacht turned. "Norris better have a good expla—"

"Nostalgia," Simone said flatly. She looked down at her butter-hued hands as the fingertips of her right hand stroked the knuckles of her left hand. "The good old-fashioned, Hollywood heartthrob kind. Just like every other woman in the world who's seen Sonny Whittaker in person for the first time."

An incoming yacht sounded a deafening horn.

"Look," Paulette said. "The women here are so open." On the upper deck, a tall brunette in a black thong arcing over deeply tanned curves rose from a chaise lounge. Her bare breasts poked through a tousled mane as she shouted in Portuguese to a petite, topless redhead waving from a docked boat.

Simone stiffened. "The tall one is a Bianca look-alike. Every direction, there's a reminder of something bad—"

"I'm going in to get my phone," Marie said as she dashed away.

Simone tried to look back toward Sonny. But the yacht pulled into the slip next to the boat they'd seen earlier, carrying her colleague. And blocking Sonny's boat.

"Hello, Simone," a man called over groaning gears.

Simone's heart pounded as she looked up.

"What a lovely surprise," Judge Johnston said, as the two women rubbed his arms. "Let's share a cocktail."

"If the dirty old man stereotype fits," Paulette whispered as Marie returned with the cell phone, "wear it. What a creep."

"Marie, you are radiant," he said, raising a drink.

"Hello, Judge," Marie said, smiling over electronic beeps as she dialed. "Norris will be thrilled you could make it down."

"Norris wishes Judge Johnston were doing the divorce," Marie said.

"Erica would get the kids, hands down. Jake always favors the mother—"

"And I have to clean up the mess when the kids should've been placed with the father," Simone said. "But that's why I'm a judge, to protect kids."

"Like it or not, he and Norris's dad go way back," Marie said, stepping toward the little ramp to the dock. "Come on."

"Just be glad," Paulette said, "you won't have all that drama in your courtroom."

"Thank goodness," Simone said. But if the other judges had food poisoning, would they recover by Monday? "Judge Evans is fair, and won't get distracted by the celebrity chaos."

Through her dark sunglasses, Simone watched Sonny walk on the dock toward land, with the man in the white fisherman's hat. Sonny was shaking his head, his lips a silent, slow-motion wonder unto themselves, as he spoke to him. Flashes of his bare, bronzed shoulders appeared between the silver poles and bikini-clad women and luxury boats. She watched his beautiful black wavy hair as he headed toward the resort.

The pool . . . Roland Anderson keeling over . . . Rosa screaming, "You killed him!"

A hot-cold wave of nausea cast a clammy sweat over Simone from her neck to her feet.

"I can't do this," she said, clutching her stomach as the yacht's engines quieted.

"Don't ruin my wedding," Marie snapped, "by obsessing about ghosts of your past."

"I think," Paulette said, smiling, "she just saw a ghost of her future."

"No," Marie said. "Now that I think about it, it's a bad idea. As you can see, our friend here doesn't just have emotional baggage. She's got cargo."

Simone glared at Marie as anger and resentment flooded her senses. The superior glow in her friend's eyes, the know-it-all cock of her chin, roused a string of expletives that threatened to steam from Simone's taut lips.

"Marie," she said, "I moved across the country to get away from my mother's insults. Now I'm going home to get away from yours."

Simone turned to the men in green polo shirts who were toting luggage over a ramp to the dock.

"Faz favor," Simone called. It was customary here to hiss or snap fingers or clap to get someone's attention. One of the men looked up at her.

"*Faz favor,* bring the black suitcase back up here." She turned to Marie and said, "So I can change into more respectable clothes. Will you please ask the captain to take me back to Salvador?"

Marie grasped Simone's hand. "Come on, honey. Stay. I'm sorry. I'm just on edge about everything—"

Simone looked down, away from her friends. She focused on blue ropes and a silver ladder on the white-washed wood of the dock.

"We promise," Paulette said. "Not another word about men or work or anything. We'll let you stay in your bungalow and work."

"Besides," Marie said, "the captain can't leave. Norris is taking us out for a sunset sail after the rehearsal dinner. We can't risk—"

"I'll take a schooner or a ferry," Simone said, scanning the bustle of sailboats, speedboats and yachts all around. Somehow, she would get a ride back to the mainland. Then, she would not have to face the prospect of meeting Sonny Whittaker face-to-face.

"That's Sonny's wife," Paulette said over the deep drone of a speed-boat.

The banana-yellow vessel with a flame design down the sides approached from the open water. At the wheel stood a man with a dark crew cut and big shoulders. Dark sunglasses, a flow of white-blond hair and three tiny black squares adorned the deeply tanned face and curves of a woman holding his arm.

"Erica," Marie scowled. "I thought *I* brought a lot of luggage. She must have a half-dozen Louis Vuittons—"

Simone could not pull her gaze away as the boat pulled into a slip on the other side of the dock. If *that* was Sonny Whittaker's type—

"Does she eat?" Paulette exclaimed. "I read she has hair extensions."

Erica pushed up blue-tinted sunglasses to hold back her platinum hair, which squiggled down her thin shoulders, over her tiny bikini top, and at the sides of her ribs like a yellow cape. Heavy eye makeup matched the blue-and-black leopard-print fabric of her bikini. She turned; a single black strap made a double arch over her bare, suntanned behind. She took a step up, with the help of men on the dock. Then, in impossibly high heels, she straightened, fastening sheer black fabric around her hips.

"How modest of her," Marie said as the boat's driver hopped out to take Erica's arm. "I think when she got her boobs done, they used her brain as an implant, and put a saline bubble in her head. It's full of boys, clothes, parties. You'd never know she's pushing thirty-six."

"How'd she get *twins* out of those hips?" Paulette asked.

"Sonny Whittaker's super sperm, I guess," Marie said with a shrug. "He's a wonderful father, too. But Erica is about as fit for motherhood as a fifteen-year-old."

"*Senhoras,*" one of the men on the dock called. "This way."

"She hates that I'm marrying her dad," Marie said as her heel tapped the metal ramp. "She's pretty distracted with the divorce, though. And she'll probably get her way, because Norris hired the best divorce lawyer—"

"Brett 'Half' Robinson," Simone said, grasping the rail. "I cringe every time he steps into my courtroom. You know the California law saying someone suing for divorce is entitled to fifty percent of their spouse's worth?"

"What wife doesn't?" Paulette said playfully.

"Especially those of us who just signed on the dotted prenuptial line," Marie said.

"Well, Brett Robinson probably recites that law verbatim before he goes to bed at night," Simone said. "And as far as his razor tongue, I know firsthand. I was only nineteen, but I bleed inside every time I remember facing him during the Katie Moore trial."

"Brett was on *EE* the other night," Paulette said, "getting some award for being a pioneer for African American lawyers. You have to look twice to notice that he's black. His complexion, it's bright, like he was dipped in gold with some bronze mixed in. I just kept staring at him—"

"It's the contrast of his unusual skin tone and his bright blue eyes," Marie said.

"You should see the contempt in those eyes when he looks up at me," Simone said, envisioning the golden disc of his clean-shaved face and his combed-back, blond-brown waves that he wore in a neat row of curls over his starched shirtcollars. "Brett Robinson still hasn't gotten over little college student me, taking the stand for Katie. There was pioneering alright, putting him in the loser's corner for the first time."

"Well not anymore," Marie said. "Brett met with Erica at the house the other day. He told me, after he wins the Whittaker case, he won't do a divorce unless you show him a million in cash, first."

"He needs it," Paulette said, "to keep his personal tailor at Hermès on Rodeo Drive. *EE* interviewed him. No wonder the man is so impeccable!"

"I'm telling you, that's all he cares about." Simone's voice rose with anger: "I just hope Sonny Whittaker's little girls don't get caught in the crossfire like Katie."

"Our judge has a grudge," Marie said, glancing at Paulette. "It's not even your case and you're making a fist about it—"

"You have no idea how many times I've threatened to throw him in jail for contempt," Simone said as they stepped onto the white wooden slats of the dock.

"Simone, maybe if you got laid, you'd work off some of that aggression." Marie laughed coolly.

Simone stomped forward, stopping inches from Marie's face. "Maybe if you weren't being such a bitch, I'd feel happy for you and want to stay here. But you're so caught up with these crazy people, I don't want to be around."

"You guys, this is a happy occasion," Paulette said. She crossed her arms as the men hauled their luggage onto a cart.

With burning cheeks, Simone dashed onto the yacht, into the powder room. She had to compose herself. Sliding her hand against the cool wall, she pressed a switch; frosted glass sconces lit up the mirrored walls.

"Is this from him?" She raised fingertips to her cheek. It still burned from Marie's insensitivity. Her arched brown brows drew together. Her face beamed as if a star were exploding inside her. "My goodness, my eyes—"

They were glowing, and bigger than usual. And her lips—a deep rose hue bloomed where only traces remained of the mauve sheen she had applied during the hour-long limousine ride from the airport to the marina in Salvador. Her bottom lip trembled.

If Sonny Whittaker's eyes could make her radiate like this, what would happen if they actually touched? Or kissed?

8

Marie Cartwright's heart fluttered as she stared into the tender gaze of the man she loved. The festive beat of samba drums echoed from somewhere past the lush walls of foliage and flowers that created this private beach behind the honeymoon bungalow.

Despite the dizzying euphoria of seeing him after two weeks apart, and the Garden-of-Eden feel here at Sanctuary, maddening questions streamed through Marie's head: Was he marrying her for love? Publicity? Guilt?

"I missed you," Norris whispered over the lapping and fizzling waves between their toes. His brassy eyelashes came together against the bright sunshine. But even with lids at half-mast, his honey-brown eyes glowed with mesmerizing intensity. "Just twenty-four hours until we kick off the lifetime I've been wishing for."

"This feels like a dream," Marie said, loving the way the bright blue water and cloudless sky framed his height, the straight slope of his nose, the tanned hue of his complexion. His hair billowed over his shoulders, over the backs of her hands, as she kneaded his muscles.

"Mmm, my savior," he said, gazing down at her. "Your touch is my fountain of youth." He grasped her wrists, then raised them from his shoulders. "Baby, my sunburn, it stings. I want you to rub some cream on me when we go inside."

Marie gently kissed his shoulder. "Of course," she said softly, never wanting to pull away from his incensy musk or look away from his eyes. No, that was her connection.

"Just let me look at you," Norris whispered raspily. His eyes beamed down with such potency . . . Marie raised her fingertips to her pearl choker, making that soft *tap* sound. She could not stop the memory, even now . . .

Yes, he'll protect us, he'll save us . . . Jesus will save us. He'll save me—

"You got to," Marie prayed, staring up at the big painting of Jesus on the dining room wall. Her fingers felt hot and sticky at her neck. And the stinging pain, like the worst paper cut you could imagine, was starting to go numb. Even the beige carpeting under her back felt softer—

"Please, Jesus," Marie pleaded with her eyes at those big, brown irises, the white-painted tear in the bottoms of his eyes, the satin-smooth, tanned skin, the hair flowing over his shoulders as he stared up at heaven. "If you're crying for us, please ask God to save us."

A crash in the kitchen. The man was still here. The man with the scar that looked like a silver peanut stuck in the brown skin over his left eye. And now a big scratch down his whole face. His bloody skin felt mushy under her fingernails.

Marie closed her eyes. She had to play dead until he left with that big knife. The smell of paint stung her nose. A soft whoosh *sound filled her ears. No, stay awake. Just pretend for now, while Jesus works on saving us.*

"Please, Jesus," she prayed at a deafening pitch in her mind. "Please help Daddy over there." He was lying by the buffet, his shiny church shoes under the chair where he sat every night for dinner. Now, though, he was just staring up at the chandelier, eyes wide open and glazed. Mouth open, too. His booming voice, his angry words at the man who'd been writing the bad letters, still echoed in the room. Even though Daddy's throat was a river of red.

At least his head was resting on Momma's leg. She would shout to high heaven if she saw all those red spots on her favorite orange dress. How could she play the organ at church with her hands sliced up like that? And she'll be so mad, when she sees how that man spraypainted all over her walls . . .

"Please Jesus, why'd that man leave Momma sitting up like that, staring at me over here, with blood dripping through the choker Daddy just gave her for your birthday?"

Was that the back door slamming? Sirens, way down the street?

Marie told her eyes to open. They would not. They had to. She had just gotten her Sunday school certificate, for when you go into fourth grade.

"Open, eyes. Open. I have to look at Jesus." She saw darkness. So she made her mind re-paint the image of Jesus up there on the wall. Every detail, from the hair falling over the shoulders, the full, pink lips. And those soft brown eyes, which must have blazed when Jesus made his special request to God, to save the Reverend Rufus Cartwright Family—

"Yes, Jesus will save us. Jesus will. I can see it in his eyes . . ."

Norris came into focus.

"I promise to spend eternity," Norris said softly. He gently grasped her jaw. "Staring into your beautiful face, just like this."

Marie smiled. Those eyes, they made her feel closer to her parents. Safe. Like they had sent this man to her, to love her and protect her. To assure her that someone higher and more powerful was listening.

"And I," she whispered, "promise to spend the rest of my life staring back just like this."

He pulled her closer. "And I pledge, Doctor Marie Cartwright, to always kiss you like this." Norris leaned down, his bow-shaped lips parted, eyes closing.

Marie's head swirled as he pressed his hot mouth to hers. Her heart pounded. And Norris kept kissing her. Lips plying, his tongue sweeping over hers, his arousal pressing into her flat stomach.

"Let's go inside," Norris said, taking her hand.

Marie stiffened. Somehow, she had to make sure that Norris's love for her was motivated by sincere fondness for Marie Cartwright, the woman. Not for the ghosts she had helped him exorcise during five years of therapy. Not for her body, trimmed and toned now, thanks to his trainer. And not for her race, or the reputation repair that an interracial marriage could bring him and *The Colony*.

Right here, right now, this poor little black girl from Detroit—who'd made it on her own in big, bad LA—needed to know.

"Norris," she said. "Tell me why you love me."

He pressed her hand to the front of his safari shorts, now tented by a long, thick pole. He laughed. "For reasons far more profound than the fact that I want to make love with you all day, every day—"

"Seriously," she said.

"You'll know the score when you hear the vows I wrote for you," he said. "Tomorrow."

"Tell me somethin' good," Marie sang to the melody of that Chaka Khan song. "Tell me, baby. Tell me that you love me, yeah—"

Norris nuzzled her neck, above the choker. "I suppose you want to hear something more intelligent than the fact that I love the way your sweet skin reminds me of the most succulent crème brulée?"

"MMMhhhmmm," Marie said, combing her fingers through his hair, grasping his head. "Try again."

"Something sexier than the fact that I love your brilliant mind? How your insight and advice rescued me from the rotten pit of hell?"

"One more," Marie said seductively.

"Something about how if you ask me one more motherfucking insecure question like that"—his eyes were wide and sharp—"I'll ask you why you thought it acceptable to seduce your emotionally tormented client, in your office, *doc*-tor!"

Marie stepped back, her foot plunking in the cool water.

Norris snatched up her left hand. "Let this be your crystal ball, Doctor Cartwright. Anytime you have a question about me, let this Harry Winston special sparkle up the answers—"

"Norris," Marie said softly, her throat burning.

"I've had one fucked up morning," he said, resting hands on his hips. "And all I want is to lay in the arms of the woman I love. I need you to hold me, Marie, and tell me I'm gonna hit a home run. The movie. Erica's trial. All the pressure on Prism to prove I'm not my dad. And these threats—"

He lay his head on her shoulder; she stroked his hair. "Shh," Marie said, rocking him slightly. "Norris, baby, Mary's here for you."

"Mary, I'm sorry," Norris said, gently pulling her with him onto the warm sand. He lay in her arms, staring up at the sky. "Mary—"

"Yes, Norris," Marie said, stroking his forehead.

"Mary, I'm so sorry," he whispered. "All day, there's been this guilt trying to slam me into the end zone. My thoughts have been like a fucking ping-pong ball, back and forth, yes and no, right and wrong. Mary, tell me what to do—"

Marie's heart jumped to her throat. She focused on breathing slowly. After so many sessions about his dead wife, Marie had thought Norris had resolved The Voice, telling him what to do, how to do it. Even—he had divulged before they had become intimate—what women to sleep with, or cast in his films, and which ones to avoid.

"Norris," Marie said in the calm, steady voice she used while role playing with her patients, "what to do about what?"

"The wedding," he said. "I know you're still mad that I let Erica prance around the globe like a tramp, instead of taking care of her babies. And our son, I let him go to hell in a handbasket, too."

"I've told you, Norris, do what you can now to rectify that," Marie said.

"But Mary, the wedding tomorrow—"

"Are you in love?" Marie asked.

Norris trembled and smiled, still staring up at the sky with the same glazed look as when he had stared every week at the ceiling in her office inside the black high-rise office building on Wilshire and Fairfax in Los Angeles.

"Yes, I am so in love," Norris whispered. A tear rolled from his eye as he reached up, pulled Marie's head down, kissed her softly. His open palms and fluttering fingers traced her hips, her behind, the backs of her thighs.

"I love Marie Cartwright," he whispered, focusing on her. "And the final score in this match is love-love."

Marie inhaled him, pressed her body into his, and wished she could fast-forward to the moment when they would say "I do."

9

Sonny charged into his bungalow, through the airy entryway, across the rich wood floor. The theme song from *The Phantom of the Opera* echoed from the girls' loft off the vaulted ceiling, along with their laughter and Kindred's humming.

Now all Sonny wanted to do was sit at his easel for as long as it would take to paint every detail of that woman's eyes, her face, her body. With a silken canvas, he could immortalize that fantasy vision of womanhood.

"Don't you dare sit on that stool," Myles said as the door closed behind him. "You get into your paint zone, we won't hear from you for days. I told you, Cheyenne is about to come on GNN."

The scent of paint rising from the cluster of tubes and brushes and cans on the small table intensified Sonny's longing to lose himself in the deep concentration of creativity. He swept a hand over the white canvas, seeing the woman's face.

A feminine voice caressed his ears; Kindred's melancholy hum grew louder.

"My NASA bathing suit!" India exclaimed.

Sonny glanced up; Kindred leaned over, smiling and making her fingers into the OK sign. He chuckled; that sign here in Brazil was the equivalent of a raised middle finger. He always had to remind her not to do it in public. She flipped her long ponytail as she turned back toward the loft, saying, "Here, India, your barrettes."

"Where's my sarong?" Asia cried.

"Oh, little angel girl," Kindred said. "Here—"

"Hey Uncle Sonny," Jared said, rustling paper at the table. "We got some sandwiches."

"Not right now," Myles said, putting a hand on Sonny's shoulder, guiding him toward the double woven doors at the other side of the living room. "We got work to do—"

Delicious scents—salt, grease and spices—wafting from a picnic basket on the counter made Sonny stop. "Wait, Myles, I'm starv—"

"Sonny," Myles said over electronic static coming from a silver rectangle in his other hand. "There's a character assassination going on right now. As in, Cheyenne Moore, talking about you, on worldwide TV."

"My God, Myles," Sonny said, reaching for the basket. "Give me a moment's peace. I want to paint. The girls and I are having a picnic on the beach before Erica comes to make this bad day even worse—"

Myles's fingers clenched Sonny's arm. "Sonny, listen. Stop zoning out when I'm talking business. Let's go out back. I get the best reception—"

Sonny turned, stiffening as he stared into the face he had known and loved since first grade. Now, the tiny lines etched in the milky-white skin around Joseph Myles's brown eyes testified to the challenge and achievement of his fifty-five years. The trimmed hairs around Myles' Betty Boop pucker and plump jaw were like a dusting of brown and white sugar on an eggshell. He shook his head, making chestnut-hued hooks of hair dangle over his thick eyebrows and neck. His white fisherman's hat cast a shadow that accentuated the plum arcs of sleeplessness under his eyes.

"We both need a nap more than we need to hear Cheyenne's lies,"

Sonny said over electronic static as Myles's thick fingers grasped the palm-sized television.

"Better now than in court," Myles said. The bottoms of his rolled-up khakis swayed against his ankles like bells as he hurried toward the back of the bungalow. "Brett is calling her as a character witness in the trial."

"Why?" Sonny demanded.

"Brett wants to paint you as the biggest pussyhound ever to walk up the Avenue of the Stars," Myles said, leading Sonny through the airy, dark wood cavern of the bungalow.

"But that's not me anymore." Sonny savored one final sniff of delicious spicy-greasy food scents. Ever since his parents had taken Myles into their home back in Harlem, as if he were their own child, Myles had always helped Sonny by negotiating with the fourth-grade bully, Leonard Sykes, not to steal Sonny's lunch money. Or convincing Mrs. Richards to let Sonny clean her classroom instead of taking a detention for passing love notes to Nona Reese. Or convincing tattletale Mrs. Wilson up by the corner grocery that Sonny was allowed to have orange soda before dinner. Now Sonny felt a twinge of pride that Myles had turned his negotiating skills into a career, by putting himself through NYU for college and law school, then handling any and all of Sonny's legal matters.

"I don't get it," Sonny said, opening the double woven doors to the vast master suite. "Cheyenne has nothing to do with this divorce, or my children."

"Brett's motto is, if you can't dazzle 'em with brilliance," Myles said, "then blind 'em with bullshit."

Sunshine beamed through the high window on the knotty-wood balcony, illuminating the dark shiny plank floors and walls around the king-sized bed. On the vaulted ceiling, a fan whirred, stirring up the white mosquito netting draped over the pristine feather mattress and blankets. If only, right now, Sonny could escape the noise of Myles's television by letting the bed envelop him as softly as knee-deep, white powder snow in Aspen.

"This is supposed to be a Sanctuary," Sonny snapped as he hurried past the explosion of orange birds of paradise in a giant vase on the tradewind-style, clove-hued dresser. Slices of white sand, aquamarine water and teal leaves glowed through floor-to-ceiling wooden slats flanking the wide rattan doors. Sonny grasped the brass handles, swung them open, and inhaled the hot ocean breeze.

"Hurry up," Myles said. "It's about to start."

"I'm already burning up inside." Sonny's mind became one with the turquoise water and blinding white sand on his private, palm-shrouded beach. The porch, a large, dark-stained wood platform, burned his bare feet as he headed for one of two Adirondack chairs facing a hypnotic spectrum of green and blue.

He sat down, let his body slacken and inhaled deeply.

"Fome," he whispered into the hot air. Waves crashed on the beach about a dozen yards away. *"Fome—"*

"Sonny!" Myles shouted, his feet pounding the porch. "Let's settle a score right now." He stood in the shade of the spiral staircase draped by purple bougainvillea.

"Relax, man. You look like you're about to explode."

"No, Sonny, I'm sick of sweating through every crisis for you, while you talk about picnics or do this meditation shit! All my life, cleaning up your messes while you stroll down Easy Street—"

"How about 110th Street?" Sonny asked. "Where would you have gone without the top bunk in my bedroom to sleep in at night? And our kitchen table to nourish your body and do your homework?"

"I know I owe everything to your family," Myles said. "But—"

"Hours after your Aunt Claire took off for Arizona while we were at school, the Whittaker family was there for you. Starting with Mom's best Caribbean chicken and rice for dinner."

Myles's short brown lashes fringed his closed eyes.

"So now," Sonny said loudly, "be here for the biggest fight of my life, man—"

"I'm so dependent on you," Myles said, opening his eyes. He twisted the left side of his closely trimmed mustache. "I'm starting to resent that without the star power of Sonny Whittaker, the lights go out at my law firm. I never even took time to find a wife."

"If anyone should be whining right now, it should be the guy with armed bodyguards watching his children." Sonny snatched the poem from his pocket. "Read this, man. My eviction notice from Easy Street."

"Fuck," Myles sighed as he sat down and read, the tiny TV balanced on his lap.

"Rico called the authorities." Sonny fingered the velvety purple petals beside his chair.

"I'm sorry, man," Myles said. "But I need you to stop acting like you think I can pull magic solutions out of my ass and tell you everything is okay."

"That's why I write you big checks." Sonny pulled a flower from the vine, tickling his nose with it. "Did you see that woman? On the boat? When you so rudely interrupted—"

"There," Myles said. "GNN comes in clearly out here. Listen, the entertainment report is coming up—"

"I wonder where she is," Sonny said. "My God, she made me shiver—"

"No, Sonny." Myles extend the television. "I don't need you *shivering* in the courtroom Monday morning. So let's just place our bets on that vow of celibacy you made to your Buddhist spirit guide."

"There was something celestial about her," Sonny said.

"We're gonna need a little help from above," Myles said over the static, "when this wild card with the face of Cheyenne Moore comes into play. There's our Technicolor nightmare—"

Sonny focused on the screen, on the face he had kissed so many times: her small, intense onyx eyes, the sharp curve of her tiny nose, those high cheekbones set under flawless, roasted cashew-hued skin, the black Farrah-Fawcett-style hair. Dark lashes hiding the violent glints that always signaled a screaming tantrum.

The reporter said, "Global News Network caught up with Cheyenne Moore while autographing *Come Back* in a Los Angeles bookstore. The actress says she's hoping her book will convince silver screen romeo Sonny Whittaker that he's still in love with her—"

Sonny laughed toward the sky. "She is delusional. I haven't seen her in years—"

"Shhh," Myles said. "She's coming out with the book two months early, just to fuck up your trial."

"Her book is the *reason* for my trial," Sonny groaned. "Erica was perfectly content to galavant around the globe, until Cheyenne humiliated her—"

"—a romantic reunion," the reporter continued, "because the couple was a hot Hollywood item twenty-five years ago when they starred in the Oscar-winning romantic drama, *Come Back, My Love*. Filmed in the Brazilian jungle, it established Sonny Whittaker as an international sensation. But Ms. Moore's career fizzled and her personal life hit rock bottom—"

Deep voices inside the bungalow made Sonny glance back into his bedroom. But the sight of white mosquito netting spun him back to the set of *Come Back* on the Amazon. The sweet, heavy wood scent sucked from his memory images of limbs twisting, skin slapping, soaking sheets under the filmy curtain and bamboo ceiling fan stirring up the lusty scents of lovemaking. Her prominent pout, always painted red, was quick to pull back in a smile over the slightly curved white teeth that made her mouth look even more luscious.

Sweat prickled Sonny's skin; the memory was raw and fresh. He would marvel at voluptuous beads of sweat rolling down the caramel contours of her petite shoulder blades, down the valley of her back, plastering S-shaped black tendrils to her skin . . .

A molten gush of longing shot through him. That sensuous image morphed with the fresh memory of the woman on the boat. She became the female form twisting around him, panting, fusing their souls—

"My God," he whispered.

"Yeah, you'd better pray," Myles said. "Cheyenne has a royal flush worth of shit on you. My assistant who called, she read the book. Sounds like Cheyenne had a sign-in sheet on your nightstand for the past couple decades—"

"Sue her for slander," Sonny said.

"The problem," Myles said, "is that from what I remember, most of the stuff is true. It's just, we don't need every detail of your Casanova past broadcast to the world while we're trying to prove you're the most fabulous father ever."

"So convince the judge," Sonny said, "that the book can't be used in court." A bee buzzed on a red flower on the bushes between his and Jenn's cabins. Beyond that, streams of people bustled in the courtyard connecting the resort's club house, the swimming pool and waterfall.

"You think everything is just a matter of telling someone to do something, don't you, Sonny?" Myles snapped. "The book is probably not admissible. But we need to silence Cheyenne before—Look, there's Brett 'Half' Robinson. He'll have a field day—"

Sonny glared at the image of Brett's cornflower blue eyes glowing with arrogance from his golden-hued face.

"You'll be Brett 'None' Robinson when we get through with you!" Sonny said with a hard tone. "I know ten cats who've been reduced to bankruptcy by your samurai tongue. But you won't get me, pretty boy!"

Myles twisted his mustache. Sweat glistened between his eyebrows.

And a thousand flames of doubt poached Sonny's senses. If Myles was this nervous, how the hell could he prevail against the biggest, baddest divorce lawyer in LA? If he paled just seeing Brett Robinson on television, then could Myles dominate in what promised to be a week of lascivious and ludicrous allegations?

"Myles, man, stop that nervous habit!" Sonny said. "Stop twisting your mustache. And get rid of the cowardly lion look. You better roar like never before—"

"I'm saving my pit bull act for court," Myles said. "You can bet, we're about to bring Brett's cockiness rating down a couple notches."

"That's better," Sonny said. The buzzing bee whizzed between the bungalows, then disappeared against the lattice of green leaves and blue sky. Sonny groaned, "There she is."

The spellbinding woman from the boat was walking with two bellmen on the sidewalk in front of the bungalows, about fifteen yards away. So lovely in that white dress, like an angel.

"Sonny, pay attention," Myles said. "I'd bet big money Brett Robinson paid Cheyenne to publish this book. He is ruthless."

"No, we have to win," Sonny said, watching the woman traverse the pebbled path ringing the courtyard which all the bungalows faced. She disappeared behind the dark, rough-hewn wood corner of Jenn's bungalow.

"Wait," Myles said, turning up the volume on the tiny TV.

"Industry insiders tell us," the reporter said, "Ms. Moore's book is making tempers flare on the Brazilian set of Norris Haynes's provocative new movie starring Sonny Whittaker. The reason? Passages quoting Mr. Whittaker accusing Mr. Haynes of having an obsession with black, Asian and Hispanic mistresses. Even while his wife lay dying of cancer—"

"My God," Sonny said.

"Mr. Whittaker allegedly accuses the filmmaker," the reporter said, "of specializing in provocative movies with racial themes, to cover up the senior Mr. Haynes's reported refusal to hire black actors and crews—"

Sonny shot to his feet. "What could she possibly accomplish by—"

"I bet Cheyenne is Narcissus," Myles said, twisting his mustache.

"I don't like the look in your eyes right now," Sonny said. "You're scared to face off with Brett 'Half' Robinson—"

"I beat him in both cases I argued against him," Myles said.

"You settled the lawsuits behind closed doors," Sonny accused. "No courtrooms. No TV cameras." Sonny squinted in the sunshine, staring out at the ocean. He massaged the choking sensation in his throat.

"Speaking of TV," Myles said, "I think you should talk to Roxanne Jones—"

"Hell no."

"Tell your side," Myles said over the shrill cries of unseen monkeys in surrounding trees. "Paint Cheyenne as the jilted lover. You come out calm, cool and collected as always. Cheyenne? Unstable, crazy—"

"Roxanne is Erica's friend, she'll twist things around—"

"So decide how to roll the dice, man. This time, talking to the press might help."

"I'm under siege," Sonny said, pacing the porch. He could almost hear his nerves crackle like a string of firecrackers. "By women—"

Myles nodded. "Wife. Lover. Reporter. And if Narcissus is female—"

"But I just saw the one who can make up for a lifetime of mistakes," Sonny said, sitting on the edge of the porch with his bare feet on the burning sand.

"Sorry, buddy, but that would be me right about now," Myles said. "The last thing you need is another woman coming in and blowing down your fragile house of cards."

"Daddy!" the twins cheered in unison over the thunder of little feet. Two pairs of arms wrapped around his neck, from the back. Their curls crushed into his cheeks, over his ears.

"Come and have a picnic!" India said.

Myles tapped his shoulder. "You girls take care of this guy," he said playfully. "I'm gonna go make some calls, work on my opening statement. Call me if you need me." Myles disappeared inside the bungalow, just as Jared's Timberland boot struck the porch.

Worry roasted Sonny's limbs. This on-the-verge-of-exploding feeling would kill him if it intensified any more. He did not want to end up like Popa, dropping dead on a Sunday afternoon in the park. A heart attack at fifty-five. Two more months stretched between now and that morbid hurdle. And maybe that lovely vision of womanhood could help him.

"C'mon, Daddy!" The girls hopped onto the sand. Their happy faces set off a flame of fear through his gut; the stalker's words replayed in his head. They each pulled one of his hands, until he tumbled onto the hot sand. They climbed all over him, tickling him.

Upside-down, Sonny glimpsed the bungalow. Just inside the double doorway, Kindred stood in her pink outfit, the picnic basket hooked on her left arm. A swept-away glaze filled her eyes. She smiled up at Jared, who was whispering. Then she skipped onto the porch with the basket, her ponytail bouncing.

Lust burned in Jared's eyes as he watched her backside.

"Wait till you taste this," Kindred said, pulling back the orange and red plaid towel over the food. She jumped onto the sand; Jared and Josh followed.

A jolt of paternal machismo made Sonny shoot up from the sand.

"Daddy, tell them we can play on the beach," India said. Space-shuttle-shaped barrettes held back two poufs of black curls on each side of a center part. Her silver bathing suit with the American flag and USA across the front matched her shorts and astronaut bracelet.

Sonny sharpened his stare on Jared, then leaned close to whisper: "You touch Kindred, you'll be on the first plane back to 125th Street."

"Yes, sir, Uncle Sonny," Jared said with the standing-at-attention tone of a Marine.

"She's like a daughter to me, and neither of you need the distraction."

Kindred's jaw poked out slightly; she adjusted Asia's straw hat, the same chartreuse color as her bathing suit and floral-print sarong.

"They told Kindred," Asia said, frowning at Josh and Jared, "the beach is too dangerous."

Josh pointed to people on several blue and yellow windsurfers, a paddle boat and a pair of jetskis. "They look like vacationers, but—"

"I think we're safe here on the private beach," Sonny said. "Now, let's get to picnicking."

"Yay!" The girls gave him a high five.

"I'm so hungry, I could eat five steaks right now," Sonny said. And his soul could feast for a lifetime on that woman whose face was aglow in his mind. Was she married? Did she have children?

Kindred poked a finger into Sonny's stomach. "Grilled fish and fruit salad for you, Mister Movie Man." Her honey-colored eyes, her round almond face, beamed.

With a pear-scented swoosh of her ponytail, Kindred spun around, tickling the twins as they ran toward the water. She dropped the picnic basket on the sand, next to a blanket and towels.

"First one in the water!" Asia said, running toward the foamy line of wet, white sand. She dashed toward a clump of foliage near the water.

India giggled as her lanky, caramel-hued legs propelled her right behind her sister.

A red flare of panic exploded in Sonny's chest.

"Asia, stop!" He sprinted toward them. "India!"

But they kept running straight toward a man shrouded by leaves. Wearing a Sanctuary bellman's uniform, the ink-hued man had reddish dreadlocks sprouting from a straw hat. He faced the water, typing on a laptop computer.

"Hey!" Sonny's heart pounded, his skin burned with heat and fear. And that hateful poem crinkled in his pocket as he dashed toward his babies.

10

Sonny ran with what felt like bionic speed across the hot sand.

"I'm gonna jump in!" Asia giggled, running inches from the man's bare foot as she tossed off her sand-covered sarong. Her hat tumbled along the sand next to him. Her legs splashed into the water.

"Wait for me!" India shrieked, kicking up the surf alongside her sister. Her space-age maillot shimmered in the sunshine as she reached down, convulsing with laughter. She cupped up two handfuls of water and threw them at Asia and Kindred.

"I'm gonna get you!" Kindred said, running toward them.

Asia's little feet were heading straight for the man's hand on the sand.

Sonny grabbed her, one arm under her back, the other beneath her knees. Kindred's arm hooked around India's waist, pulling her close.

"Who are you?" Jared shouted down at the man.

"A bellman," the man said. "I always write my songs, for Carnival, during my lunch—"

"Show me some I.D.," Josh demanded, his boots submerged in the clear water.

Sonny and Kindred carried the girls to the nearby red blanket Kindred had laid out in the shade of almond and cashew trees. Together, Sonny and Kindred wrapped plush yellow towels around each girl, then sat them facing the water.

"We were just playing!" Asia protested, her amber eyes huge and bright in contrast to the dripping black ringlets framing her face.

"That was cool," India said. "Like you guys were ninja warriors!"

Kindred's hands trembled as she pulled the fabric from the top of the picnic basket.

"Triple hug," Sonny said. He placed a hand on her shoulder, pulling her toward the twins, who bowed their heads as he and Kindred embraced them. "That's better."

"No it's not!" Asia cried. "I don't want to be scared any more!"

"You're scared of the dark," India said. "Even at home—"

"Shut up!" Asia said.

"Asia and India," Sonny said, "with our Amazon warrior nanny here, and your cousins, you don't have to be afraid."

"Girls, look," Kindred said, pointing to two crabs climbing onto the blanket. "They're gonna eat your toes for lunch if you're not careful!"

The girls cringed back, giggling. Then they leaned forward, staring into the four black dots that were the crabs' eyes.

"I'd just die if anything happens to them, or you," Kindred whispered, her glassy eyes trained on the girls as they shed the towels and tumbled on the sand beside the crabs. "You're—"

"Shhh," Sonny said, pulling her close, hating the fear in her eyes and the quaking of her shoulders. "Kindred, you know you're like a daughter to me. We'll get through the divorce, the custody battle, the Narcissus drama."

"But it's so scary," Kindred said softly, beaming as the girls giggled. Yet, something strange glimmered in her gaze. Something he had never seen in the nearly eight years since he and Erica had first met her and interviewed her to become the nanny for their newborn babies.

"I see *saudade* in your eyes," Sonny said. "Rico says there's no transla-
tion—"

"Longing," Kindred said, resting her head on his shoulder. "Today I
tied this wish ribbon on," she looped her finger through a shoelace-style
yellow string around her wrist. "I made a wish that things will go back to
normal. Just you, me, the twins—"

Josh's and Jared's army green pantlegs billowed as they stood with feet
wide, one pair of eyes on the girls, the other constantly scanning the house,
the beach and the water. Jared kept glancing at Kindred, his eyes soft as if
he could feel her pain. Sonny cast him a warning glare.

"You're the only family," Kindred whispered, raising her hands to
cover her face. She sobbed, "the only family I have."

"Kindred, you're part of this family," Sonny said. "We're not related
by blood, but your name says it all. When we met you, we felt, you're a sort
of kindred spirit for me and the girls—"

"I feel like," Kindred said softly, "the plane crash took away my mom
and brothers. But they were replaced with you—a new father and two
sisters."

Sonny pulled her close, his throat burning with emotion. "We'll
always be here for you."

"Thank you," she whispered. She knelt before the picnic basket,
pulling out plates prepared by the resort restaurant. But her bottom lip
curled down, glistened. She spun toward the water and covered her face
with her hands.

Sonny's insides roasted with fear and anger. He had to put relaxed
smiles on the faces of his daughters and their nanny. Now. Without any
terrifying or upsetting interruptions.

He clapped playfully, then imitated a movie director's voice: "Everyone in their places. It's time for lunch action. Scene one."

The blanket was warm as Sonny sat down and crossed his legs. The girls
jumped with a spray of sand, then sat at his sides, facing the water and Kindred. She sniffled through pink-rimmed nostrils without looking up. She
placed the low-fat lunch in front of him—alongside a cheeseburger and
fries.

"Yes," Sonny said with a laugh. "You know me too well, Kindred.
Two weeks until I'm back on camera. Let me indulge with my family—"

"Daddy." Asia bit a french fry. "You'll be as big as the Nutty Profes-
sor—"

"I can't wait to retire and let myself go," he said, balancing the burger before his mouth. He made an exaggerated chomp, eliciting more giggles. "All I'm going to do is paint and eat and watch you girls grow—"

"No," Asia said, "Grandmama won't let you. She doesn't make junk food at the restaurant on Montserrat. Right, Daddy?"

"Oh, but the banana grits and conch bisque, and Grandmama's barbecued ribs." He held his fingers near his face. "Smoky, melt-in-your-mouth heaven on earth. The sauce drips down your chin. You get so full, you just want to lie around like a cat." He patted his stomach, making a *purr* sound.

The girls' laughter cooled his nerves.

"Daddy, tell us about when we move to Grandmama's," India said.

"Every morning, we'll wake up and feast on tropical fruits and her secret recipe cheese pastry." He inhaled loudly. "All day long, we'll enjoy the scents of thyme and allspice and garlic wafting from whatever's cooking on her big stove. Then at twilight, we'll eat on the terrace, watch the ocean swallow the sun, and make up adventures about the volcano—"

"*Pa-kow!*" Kindred said. "Just like in the story I read you girls about Zeus, remember?"

"Will it really erupt?" India asked.

"As a boy," Sonny said, savoring the french fry melting on his tongue, "I had my own seismology kit and a little safari hat. I used to sit and stare up at the lush green slope. Just wishing the Soufrière Hills volcano would shoot fire into the sky and ooze down toward me—"

"It would burn up the house!" Asia cried.

"Grandmama says she's putting up your big swing," Sonny said, "by the lagoon. She wouldn't do that if she knew lava would be coming down the mountain to ruin our fun."

"Can you find us a different mommy?" India asked.

"We have a mom!" Asia snarled. "And Kindred. So shut up."

Sonny's insides melted. That woman on the boat. He was sure she would treat him to emotions and sensations that he had never enjoyed with a woman. Especially not for the past five years. Since Erica took off with the amicable agreement that she just wasn't ready for marriage, and that he could take care of the girls, that's exactly what he'd been doing. There was no greater satisfaction or joy than watching them grow and laugh and love him back.

But in the meantime a whole side of himself had shut down. And with one glance, one intrigued parting of the lips, that woman had flipped the "on" switch. He had to find her, later, to hear her voice, look closely into her eyes, brush his fingertips to her cheek to make sure she was real—

"Mom!" Asia shot up from the blanket. She was a blur of chartreuse and black hair as she dashed over the sand.

"My baby dolls," Erica called with that deep, slow tone he had once found so sultry. "I came all the way from Bali to see you!"

Her voice made his blood bubble; he was sure it would burst right through his skin. Her wicked karma hissed across the sand, clawing up his legs, coiling around his neck.

But he had to stay cool. For the girls. For his own well-being.

Sonny stood, imagining a thick coating of teflon over his hot nerves.

"Mom, just in time for our picnic!" Asia said. "Stay with us for a while."

The pleading desperation in Asia's voice seared Sonny's heart. He focused on his little girl's narrow shoulders, her hair, the orange flower petal stuck to the back of her calf, as she ran toward her mother.

"Oooh," Erica moaned.

The well-nourished, Bohemian brunette he had fallen in love with now tossed a mermaid-like spring of loose white-blond curls over her bony shoulders. The hair covered the surgically enhanced chest that made Erica resemble so many stick-thin starlet clones. All that eyeshadow that accentuated the deep blue shade of her sunken eyes was almost as dark as the sheer black kleenex covering the V of her bathing suit bottom. The blue-and-black leopard-print fabric of her bikini matched the single, impossibly skinny strap over her toes and the gravity-defying spike heels that she balanced on, even in the sand. Her long toes—each nail a shiny pink square with a white strip at the end—fanned out over the black leather soles.

Sonny inhaled deeply. *I can't say it was a mistake marrying her, or I wouldn't have these two intelligent human beings who call me Daddy . . .*

He tried to snuff out the memory of the doctor saying the twins' dangerously low birth weight and potential for being born blind, could all have been avoided had Erica not dieted and exercised—and poisoned herself with drugs—during the pregnancy. He had not made love to her since that moment nearly eight years ago, out of fear of planting his seed in hostile ground.

Now, her boy-toy stood next to her: deeply tanned, mirrored sunglasses, a cowlick of dark hair sprouting from his broad forehead, hands as proportionately thick and muscular as his buff chest, arms and legs. He held her big straw bag and matching hat.

"Come here, baby," Erica cooed, poking out her bow-shaped lips as her white-tipped fingernails grasped Asia's shoulders.

"Mommy," Asia said, stroking Erica's hair over her shoulder, "will you stay and watch us sing for Grandpa and Marie? We've been practicing a special wedding song—"

Little fingers grasped Sonny's left hand; India stood at his side. Her brows crinkled as she watched her sister and mother.

"Daddy," India whispered. "I want to stay with you. She only came for the wedding. Not to see us."

Sonny kissed her between the space shuttle barrettes.

"India!" Erica called. "Don't you want to see what I brought you? This adorable shop in Rome had astronaut costumes! And you," she pulled Asia closer, "My little fashion plate, wait 'til you see the outfits—"

Her every syllable was a match lighting on Sonny's nerves. He did not even want her to touch the girls that he was raising, that he was loving every day, that he was answering questions about why Mommy hadn't called in three weeks, or why she had to spend months at a time on the Riviera, even on their birthday and Christmas.

"Asia, tell your sister she doesn't have to be scared," Erica said, holding Asia's hand as they stepped close. Her fake eyelashes did not raise high enough for Sonny to look into her eyes as she ran the backs of her fingers over India's cheek.

"Oh India," Erica purred. "This is a scary place. Can Mommy have a hug?"

India burrowed into Sonny's hip.

Erica trained her big blue eyes on Sonny. "Read any good books lately?" She smiled.

Sonny gazed upward, away from her, letting the green leaves and blue sky blur, just as Xavier did. He would not react in front of the girls. He would not let himself express the rage exploding inside him at the idea of Erica launching this divorce-custody war to save face after the embarrassment and humiliation of Cheyenne's book. Because the affairs he may have had during their farce of a marriage paled in comparison to what she had done to him and their babies.

"Were you girls eating *that*?" Erica asked, glancing toward the picnic blanket.

"We were having a picnic," Kindred said. "Their favorite."

"I don't want them eating that," Erica said.

"They eat plenty of fruits and vegetables," Sonny said. "Let them enjoy—"

Erica buried her face in Asia's hair, just above her ear. Asia frowned toward the picnic spread, fanning her hand over the girlish swell of her tummy.

"Okay?" Erica said softly, rising back up.

Asia nodded.

Sonny fought the urge to shout at her for starving them in utero.

"Erica," he said calmly, "I don't restrict—"

"I know," she said, raking him with her glare. "Come on, girls. Your father and I agreed, you would come visit with me for a while. I want to hear you sing."

"I'm gonna stay with Daddy," India said.

"It's okay," Sonny said softly. "You and Asia can visit with your mother for a little while. Kindred and the bodyguards will go with you. It's all right."

"Come on, Angel," Kindred said, stroking India's back. "Let's go let your mom listen while we practice our song for the wedding."

India jumped into Kindred's arms, wrapping her arms around the nanny's neck.

Erica glared at Kindred. "We don't need you," Erica said, grasping India's shoulders.

"No, I want Kindred to come with us," India said, holding onto Kindred's ponytail like a handle. "Daddy!"

Sonny imagined some awful visitation arrangement where Erica had custody of the girls and only let him take them once in a while. Where she had control over where they went, who they saw, what they did, what they ate. Terror burned in his veins; was his successful control of his temper a sign of weakness, that he would so peacefully give up the girls?

"Erica," Sonny said deeply. "If India wants to stay with me, she stays."

"No!" Erica said. "I haven't seen her in a month—"

"That's your own fault," Sonny said.

"No, it's yours, for bringing them to this island in the middle of nowhere!"

"Tell that to your father," Sonny said. "He loves it here."

"The Whittaker family!" a woman said loudly.

Josh and Jared strode toward the woman in a tight red dress. Why couldn't Roxanne Jones have just stayed up at the set?

But here she was, microphone in hand, trudging toward them. Right alongside the man carrying the *Entertainment Exclusive* TV camera.

11

The A-framed, dark-stained wood bungalow cast a cool shadow on Simone's face as she and two bellmen strode toward it. She clutched the damp, stained legal brief under one arm; she couldn't wait to get inside, change clothes and get to work.

With no schooners or ferries available because of all the guests coming for the wedding, Simone was trapped. For now, anyway. A security guard, according to Marie, was allegedly going to come to her bungalow. But she would go for a run, forget everything for a few moments, then figure out how to get the hell out of here.

"Bungalow Eight," said the first bellman as they walked along the pebbled walk lined by waxy green hedges and bright flowers. The sick-sweet scent made her queasy; her toes throbbed as she teetered in Marie's ridiculous shoes.

The bellman took two steps up onto the porch. He wore the same white bermuda shorts, safari shirt and beige straw hat as all the other employees here. A gold name tag glimmered on his shirt pocket. A few auburn dreadlocks fell over his sweaty sideburns as he jingled keys, aiming one at the door lock.

"No," Simone said over the rumble of the luggage cart being pushed by another bellman behind her. That, along with the samba drums rattling in the distance, made it hard to hear herself talk. "I'm supposed to be in Bungalow eighteen, not eight."

The bellman pulled a note pad from his right front shorts pocket.

"Here," he said. "Simone Thompson. Bungalow Number Eight."

"That's strange," Simone said loudly. "Marie told me I'd be in number eighteen, and our friend Paulette would be in nineteen."

"No, it says right here." He held out the white paper, which cast a blinding reflection into Simone's eyes. She barely focused on the heading "Haynes Wedding" over a column of names with adjoining numbers.

"This is correct," he said, opening the door. Sweat dripped down his sideburns.

"If you hadn't been lounging on the beach," the other man snapped in Portuguese, "there would be no mix-up—"

Simone followed the first bellman inside. He pushed back his straw hat, held in place by a black string at his neck, and balanced it on his back. He stopped to adjust knobs just inside the door. Bamboo fans hummed two stories above on the vaulted, stained-wood ceiling.

A washcloth and hand towel sat clumped on the kitchen island.

The first bellman dashed to the coffee table to straighten the magazines. "Housekeeping hasn't cleaned up from the last—"

He sighed. "This wedding is filling the resort faster than we can keep up. Here is your key," he said, clinking the brass on the counter. "Please, make yourself at home. And welcome to Sanctuary."

Simone forced herself to stand still and adjust her attitude as the other bellman hauled her suitcase up the open stairs. It thudded against the rail, made from polished, knotty tree branches arranged in a star pattern, all the way up and across the loft-style bedroom's upstairs balcony.

"What's that smell?" Simone wrinkled her nose.

"Sometimes," the bellman said, pointing toward the back windows framing sunbathers amongst palm tress, white sand and aquamarine water, "sea animals get under the house and—"

"It's really strong," Simone said.

"I'll send someone right away to check it out," he said. "I'm so sorry. I'll bring a fruit basket to make up for any inconvenience." The men left; Simone bolted the door.

"Ugh, this dress." She kicked off the shoes. She couldn't wait to switch into some running shorts and a tank top, and pound out her anger at Marie on the sand. She headed for the stairs—

That smell was stronger. Was it coming from the back bedroom?

Simone stepped closer, heart pounding. She remembered finding a dead rat in her dresser drawer as a girl once. Turned out Rosa had put it there, and had waited in the corner of the room to double over with laughter when Simone screamed. Now, with Narcissus—

"Stop it!" She moved toward the bathroom. Maybe the toilet was stopped up—

A shadowy form, on the floor. She flipped on the light.

"Oh God," she gasped. "What—"

Blood and beige clumps covered the white porcelain sink. Pink liquid splash marks blurred the mirror above. Reddish water, all over the floor.

And a woman.

Laying face down in a puddle of blood. A yellow ponytail, wicking up the red liquid. Her hands—melted pink wax.

Was she dead? All the blood—

Simone knelt, grasping the woman under the arms. She turned her over.

Simone gasped.

Went numb.

Heart hammering against her ribs.

The horrible smell—burning skin?—made her stomach lurch.

The woman's face was a big oval of pink and red silly putty, stretched and full of blood-filled holes. Even the lips and eyelids. Beyond recognition.

She wanted to feel for a pulse. The woman's wrists and neck were both bloody and raw.

With trembling arms and legs, Simone dragged her, under the arms, out into the living room. Her bare right foot swayed lifelessly as her thin legs trailed over the floor.

Her ears were splattered with blood, but intact.

"Can you hear me?" Simone shouted with a quavering voice. "I'll take care of you—"

Something gold glimmered in the swirl of flesh under the woman's chin; fresh blood oozed from the side of her neck—

If the skin dissolved over her jugular veins, she'd bleed to death right here. If she was not already dead . . .

Simone scrambled to the kitchen counter, grabbing the cordless phone and a white towel. She dialed zero, cradled the phone on her shoulder, and pressed the towel to the woman's neck.

A busy signal blared. With all the people arriving for the wedding, the front desk would be swamped—

She dialed again. The tip of the towel touched the crimson pool in the hollow of the woman's neck.

Tiny silver letters held by a chain appeared: JENN.

Simone gasped. "Jenn Ryder?"

Was *this* the face Simone had seen casting that come-hither smile from the magazine rack at the check-out at her local Ralph's grocery store back home? Or the woman rolling and laughing with a gorgeous man in a field of flowers in that perfume commercial that always ran between the eleven o'clock report on Channel 8 and *NightNews*? And gazing down on Wilshire Boulevard from a billboard for her latest movie near Marie's office building? Could this be Hollywood's hottest actress *du jour*, the female lead in *The Colony* with Sonny Whittaker?

Simone went numb. Did Narcissus do it? And was he waiting, watching . . .

"I've got to help her," Simone panted. She clutched the phone, praying for an answer.

Because Narcissus was here.

And he wants to kill Sonny Whittaker, Norris Haynes and—

Me.

12

On the beachfront deck of his bungalow, Sonny Whittaker faced the TV reporter, her big black camera on a tripod aimed at his face like a machine gun. Brown strings of frayed coconut palm bark hung behind the wooden Adirondack chair on which she sat, between the purple flowers on the spiral staircase and the giant ferns shrouding the edge of the wooden planks.

"I'll indulge you with fifteen minutes of my time and energy," Sonny said, squinting in the rays of sunshine shooting through the leaves. He leaned back on the warm boards of his own chair. Behind him, the sound of waves lapping the sand and the samba drums rumbling in the distance, sent a prickle across his already hot skin.

"Roxanne, I'm annoyed, sitting here with you while the rest of the island celebrates," Sonny said, sucking down a mouthful of salty heat. The platinum-haired cameraman leaned down to look in the viewfinder; the camera sat next to Myles, who was seated under the fruits and foliage carved into the dark wood around the open doors leading into the house. "You're vindictive, and I can't trust you—"

"Sonny," Myles said, crossing his arms. "Roxanne, no wild cards. Or you can bet, this interview will be over before it starts."

"I like feisty," Roxanne said. The let-me-fuck-you sparkle in her big brown doe eyes, ringed by a seductive smudge of makeup, glowed with the lust of destruction. Her red dress bound her thighs and breasts, forming two fleshy gorges at her chest and lap. "Makes for the best interviews."

Sonny would not be blinded by her sassy swoop of black hair, chocolate-hued skin and compact but curvy body. Norris once said she was like a petite gymnast who could be picked up, twisted and bounced every which way. There was no doubt, right now, she wanted to shove it to him, right here, and on televisions around the world.

But he was Sweet Sonny Whittaker. He knew how to play the game by staying as cool as any cat could. And he would not let the sex oozing from her every pore distract him.

"Let's get started already," Sonny said, shifting to break contact with her bare knees, which she posed at an angle. "I need to go check on my daughters."

His heart still pounded with the image, just a short while ago, of Asia skipping hand-in-hand with Erica as they retreated between the bungalows; following behind were the bodyguards, Erica's boyfriend and Kindred, carrying India, who buried her face in the nanny's neck. He hated the idea of them being all the way on the other side of the resort, in Erica's bungalow, which was near the honeymoon cottages where Norris was staying.

"It's a shame," Roxanne laughed, "you won't let me show all your fans how much you've changed. Sonny Whittaker. Who would believe this wholesome family man, the single dad of the century, is a reformed sex freak—"

"I'd be delighted to give your viewers some insight into your own past," Sonny said. "Freak doesn't begin to describe your—"

"Stop, both of you," Myles said, leaning forward. "The divorce, the trial and Narcissus are off limits."

Roxanne whispered to the thirtyish cameraman. He pushed a button on the camera. A red light glowed on its top.

"I'm trying to get my own talk show," Roxanne said, gripping the microphone and raising the metal mesh ball. "I don't leave gaping holes in my reports. Because your fans around the world want to know, how is Sonny Whittaker handling so much adversity—"

"Obviously," Sonny said with a bored tone, "it's worrisome—"

One of Roxanne's cheeks rose with the corner of her mouth. "That's it? Worrisome?" Her red lipstick glistened. "Someone wants to kill you, your children, your costar and your producer, and 'worrisome' is the only adjective that comes to mind?"

"At this moment, yes," Sonny said. "Listen, I'm going to have enough lawyers trying to drill me a new orifice next week. I don't need a Perry Mason act from you—"

"Well like it or not, you're the celebrity news *du jour*, thanks to Cheyenne Moore's book," Roxanne said. "Specifically, her claims about what you said about the most powerful producer in Hollywood—"

Myles put his hand over the round black rubber around the curved glass of the camera lens. "Off the record, Ms. Jones, my office is working on an emergency injunction right now, to stop that book from hitting stores on Monday—"

"Two months early." Roxanne turned to Sonny. "Are her claims the reason for the obvious tension between you and Norris Haynes on the set this morning? Do you think she's trying to hit you while you're down?"

"I am not down," Sonny said. "*The Colony* will have the most profound impact on moviegoers since *Roots*. Then, my painting will take center stage—"

"Sonny," Roxanne said, "your filming schedule and budget are disastrous. And it all leads back to Cheyenne Moore. When word was leaked about her book, Norris refused to go ahead with your project. The delays and budget blowout—"

"Shooting a movie is stressful," Sonny said. "In two weeks, my daughters and I and Norris will be back here to finish—"

"Come on," she said. Suddenly her expression, her impatient tone, evoked a déjà-vu memory. Nine years ago, at the *Vanity Fair* party. Roxanne had made herself comfortable with Sonny and Erica, Erica invited her back to the house for a nightcap, and the final result in Sonny's mind was *like father, like daughter*, as Erica wrapped her lips around the pointed tips of the giant chocolate kisses that were Roxanne's bare breasts.

"Stay there," Erica *warned as Sonny stepped closer to the edge of the swim-*
ming pool, glowing over the lights of Los Angeles like a giant aquamarine. "She's
mine."

"Now," Roxanne said, "Don't tell me you're not worried sick about
your film, your family—"

Myles leaned forward. "Enough, Ms. Jones—"

Roxanne's concerned expression and tone rang with insincerity: "Oh
Mr. Whittaker, back when I interviewed you in Cannes, when you were
promoting *The Rogue Brothers*—"

Sonny laughed softly. "I loved that movie."

"You were with Erica Haynes, just before you married her," Roxanne
said. "And you told me you've been spoiled by women all your life. How
you"—she deepened her voice—"love making love." She raised her dark
brows. "It must be devastating that women are now the bane of your
existence—"

Sonny made his eyes dance with amusement, to mask the rage shooting through his limbs. "Lust and love," he said with a matter-of-fact tone,
"are the two strongest human emotions. It's only natural, sometimes that
thin line blurs between love and hate."

Roxanne's eyes glowed with vengeance.

"Especially when the other person doesn't get from the liaison what
they were expecting," he said, staring back just as hard. Remembering
how Roxanne had, after that late-night swim with Erica, sauntered nude
into his paint studio, sat on his lap and asked for a cameo role in his next
film. "When motivations are driven by greed—"

"Hmm," she said. "Greed is one of the words Narcissus uses in the
L.A. Times editorials. What if someone were to call you greedy for—"

Myles stood. "Ms. Jones, you need a quick refresher course about the
definition of journalistic objectivity—"

"Actually," Roxanne said, "it's my past interviews with Mr. Whittaker
that help me appreciate what's happening now. He's about to climb all the
way out of that depressing career slump—he's doing his own movie, his
family is together, he gets his house back. But now he could lose everything and more—"

"I've been thinking, what's happening to me is the American Dream in
reverse," Sonny said. "You're supposed to work your way up to get everything you want. I did that, but lost it. It's much harder the second—"

"Sonny," Myles warned.

"Maybe I should send a message to Narcissus," Sonny said, turning toward the camera. "Whoever you are, wherever you are, don't blame your unhappiness on other people, or the movies, or TV. I found out the hard way, you have to face them head-on, deal with all the bad feelings by yourself, then——"

Myles stood in front of the camera. "Enough," he said. "Sonny, if she wanted a Shakespearean soliloquy——"

"It's alright," Roxanne said. "That was fantastic. Sonny Whittaker makes tearful plea to stalker: Leave Us Alone!" She laughed. "Get Therapy! Maybe Narcissus should make an appointment with Norris Haynes's bride——"

"I want to talk about my painting," Sonny said. "I have a gallery show next week, in Santa Monica——"

"I want to talk about your family," Roxanne said.

"I need to go check on them," Sonny said. He turned to Myles. "What time is it, man?"

"Three more minutes," Myles said. The white brim of his hat lowered as he tilted his left wrist upward to flash his multi-dialed watch.

"No children, period." Myles leaned forward. He shook his head, his wavy bangs shifting like meat hooks. "Nothing relating to the trial, including Sonny's relationship with Norris Haynes. So, Miss Jones, you'll have to hedge your bets on the movie——"

The reporter's fingernails tapped the shiny gold jacket on a hardcover book as she held it up. The frantic drum beat of samba music was getting louder, punctuated by shrieks and cries.

Come Back, My Love, the title said, scrolled in red letters across the top of a palm tree. Below that: *Cheyenne Moore's true tale of love, lust and longing.*

"Mr. Whittaker, have you read it?"

"I've been so focused on this character. I wrote this screenplay as a sort of elixir for the world——"

"Let's talk about the movie that made you famous," Roxanne said, "with the same title as this book."

Sonny chuckled. "I thought I had died and gone to heaven when I came down here to film *Come Back.* I've studied Eastern religions. And being back here, a quarter-century later, it reminds me of the Buddhist wheel of life——"

"But the way things are going . . ." Roxanne said. The samba drums sent a sinister charge through the air. She spoke with a louder, more urgent tone: "You may never finish *The Colony*. And if you lose custody of your daughters—"

Myles moved forward. "Ms. Jones, this interview is over."

"Wait, man, I need to defend myself," Sonny said.

"I'll say," Roxanne tapped the book, making it glimmer in the bright light. "There are some pretty lascivious passages—"

"Believe half of what you see," Sonny said with a grim tone, "and none of what you hear. That's what my mother always said."

The camera still hummed. Myles squeezed his folded arms against his chest.

"Let me read something from the advance review copy Ms. Moore gave me," Roxanne said, opening the book. "Here. Cheyenne Moore says you told her that while Norris Haynes was nursing his wife as she died of cancer, he quote 'still had to satisfy his appetite for dark meat. The guy's got a madonna-whore complex of mammoth proportions. He treats his wife like a virgin but becomes a frantic fuck machine with anything in a tight dress and heels.' Did you say that?"

Sonny sucked in the hot air, feeling as if his head were glowing red like the tip of a cigarette. My God, how he craved one right now. But that was just one more bad habit he'd given up, along with women.

"That's sensational. What do they say about a woman scorned? It fits the bill here." He reached for the book. "Let me see that—"

"Cheyenne describes wild orgies on the set of *Come Back, My Love*," Roxanne said, pulling the book toward her waist. "She writes, 'Every pillow and grass mat and hammock was a mass of naked people. At any given moment, I could have my pick of handsome men with perfect bodies. But after just one night with my costar, Sonny Whittaker, my insatiable appetite for men disappeared. He became the sole object of my affection, forever—'"

Sonny turned toward Myles. "And I'm supposed to be offended?"

"Wait," Roxanne said, squirming in her chair. She pointed to a line highlighted in yellow. "'Making love with Sonny Whittaker was like having a thousand beams of light shine down from heaven while a chorus of angels sang and lightning jolted and pulsated through me until my flesh melted, vaporized, and I floated up, through the white mosquito netting, to watch the greatest Adonis of all share his godly gifts—'"

"Get me a cold shower," Sonny said. "If every man could have a woman write a book about his lovemaking skills, what a happier planet—"

"The movie, Ms. Jones," Myles said. "Our time is almost up." He glanced toward the beach. "And that music is getting so loud—"

"Cheyenne claims that you once said, 'Norris Haynes hides behind the image of provocateur by making cutting-edge films about interracial friendships and romances. But he's just casting illusions over the white hood he inherited from his father's *Birth of a Nation* fantasies.' End quote."

"Time's up," Myles said.

"Sonny," Roxanne said, "Did you say this about your own father-in-law? The man who's producing the movie that you're hoping will change the way people relate—"

Sonny stood. The music, the cheers—

"Ms. Moore is planning to announce something incriminating about you," Roxanne said, "during your trial. She's giving me an exclusive—"

A piercing scream.

Goosebumps prickled his skin.

Was that a shriek of pleasure or pain? Fun or fear?

"What?" Roxanne paled. She turned to the cameraman. "Let's go!"

Sirens wailed nearby. Red lights flashed on the foliage between the bungalows.

Sonny's heart pounded.

"The girls," he gasped.

13

Kindred Germaine wanted to scream "No!" as she placed India next to her mother and Asia in the white crocheted hammock. But she had to stay calm and go along with the twins' visit with Erica here at her beachfront bungalow, because this was what Daddy Whittaker had ordered.

"Is that comfortable?" Kindred asked softly, adjusting the small pillow behind India's head, even though Kindred's every cell ached at the image of the girls stretched out on each side of Erica, who cracked open a blue hardcover Disney storybook against her raised, bare legs.

"I want *Cinderella,* Mom," Asia said. Her hair formed a black cloud at Erica's shoulder; her light caramel-hued legs pressed against Erica's, which were almost as tanned and just about as thin. "Then *The Little Mermaid*."

"Cool," Erica said. "We've got all afternoon to read every story in this big book. India, baby, pick one."

"*Peter Pan,*" India said, her arms crossed. "But you have to make the voices like Kindred does. A different one for Wendy and Tinker Bell and Captain Hook—"

Kindred started to smile. Until Erica raised her dark sunglasses and shot her daggers of hatred from her blue eyes. Kindred laced her fingers through the edge of the hammock, squeezing so tight that the rope burned her palms.

"We don't need you," Erica said. "I'm their mother, not you. And they'll be here the rest of the day. So—"

Kindred wanted to snatch a handful of Erica's hair, yank it and scream, "*You stupid bitch. I'm raising them. I'm loving them. So stop orchestrating this Narcissus stalker drama, just to make it look like they're in danger with their dad—*"

Kindred sucked down the hot, steamy air and exhaled slowly.

"These guys are all we need," Erica said. She twisted slightly, glancing toward her boyfriend, limp in the lounge chair he had dragged down to the water's edge to sunbathe in his flowered surfer shorts. Then Erica glanced toward Jared, who stood with arms crossed on the back porch, while Josh guarded them beside the coconut tree, to which the head of the hammock was secured with white rope. Josh continued scanning the lush walls of greenery around this private slice of white sand and light blue water.

"Go, Kindred," Erica said. "You're such a moose, making shadows on us."

Kindred gripped the hammock more tightly.

"She has to stay," India said, her big amber eyes pleading up at her mother. "Please."

"When you girls come live with me," Erica said, flipping pages, her lashes covering her eyes, "we won't need her anymore."

Asia and India both glanced up, their eyes wide with sadness and shock. Kindred stared back, letting her eyes radiate all that her aching heart wanted to say. That they would always be together. Always.

"I'll be inside," Kindred said. "Practicing my violin, for the wedding. Remember, little angel girls, we have to rehearse our songs tonight."

Erica glared at Kindred's fingers on the hammock. "Let go."

Kindred envisioned taking the girls and running away, after twisting

Erica like a piece of hard candy inside the hammock, leaving her for the seagulls and caimen and snapping turtles to eat . . .

"Have fun," Kindred said, smiling down at the twins as she gently released the rope.

Kindred spun toward the house, her insides quaking with resentment and hatred and rage. Moose? That bubble-headed slut had given birth to Asia and India, but that was about it. And no way was Kindred going to let Erica get away with this fake maternal act.

No, Kindred would not be robbed of one magical second, when people mistook her for the twins' older sister. She cherished Saturday mornings, shopping at Whole Foods Market, when the cashier would look across the gleaming wood floors and say, "Here come the Whittaker girls."

Kindred would grin for days after the husky-voiced waitress at Hamburger Hamlet on Sunset in Beverly Hills would say things like, "You could be triplets if it weren't for the age difference." And the strawberry vendor at the Farmer's Market: "I wish my oldest would make my little ones smile like you do these girls."

Yes, me, not their fake mother who's only out to hurt Mr. Whittaker. And us. I have to stop her—

"Long, long ago," Erica read from the story book, "in a land far, far away—"

Hot sand kicked up with every step of Kindred's pink leather mules as she strode toward Jared on the porch. She resisted the urge to stomp onto the shiny wood. She stepped lightly, staring straight ahead at the double glass doors. She slid one open, striding through the back bedroom. Right now, Kindred had to find something, or do something, to make sure Erica Haynes Whittaker would lose her contrived battle for custody.

"Kindred," Jared called behind her. "Wait up."

"He saw us, and didn't like it," Kindred whispered, without slowing her stride. "It's over." She gasped as Jared gently curled his fingers around her upper arm. Yes, those fingers, as long and firm as that other part of him that just last night had taken her virginity and her heart on Mr. Whittaker's boat.

Kindred yanked her arm away. She darted through the back bedroom, then the living room. Her spongy heels made a slight swoosh sound on the floor.

"We'll keep it on the down-low," Jared whispered. "Around him, strictly business. But away—" He cupped his palm over her ass.

Kindred dashed up the open staircase, two steps at a time. She had to find something incriminating in Erica's luggage. Something she could slip to Mr. Whittaker's lawyer to present in court, to prove Erica was as unfit as one of those evil stepmothers she was probably reading about right now.

Jared jogged up the steps behind her. Kindred stopped at the top of the stairs. She turned around, glaring at the masculine contours of Jared's model-perfect face.

"Every second you're looking at me," Kindred said, "Narcissus could be looking at Asia and India. And your uncle would strangle us both if something happened—"

"Josh is out there—"

"So is public enemy number one," Kindred snapped. "Their mother."

Kindred spun around, shot through the loft bedroom. A mountain of Louis Vuitton luggage sat next to the rustic bamboo bed. A matching toiletry bag sat open on the counter in the skylit bathroom. Kindred hurried in.

Jared followed. He closed the door. In the mirror, he towered behind her, his sexy-as-hell bald head glowing in the sunshine, his broad shoulders and the muscular ripples of his arms framing her, making her look petite. He nuzzled behind her ear, into her ponytail.

And pressed his hot hugeness into her backside. In the mirror, Kindred's full cheeks turned as pink as her outfit.

"Give me some more of this brick house," Jared whispered. "I promise—"

"You don't understand," Kindred said, leaning her head back into his shoulder, "how much this family means to me. Working for your uncle, I get to live the childhood I never had. It's like, every time I make Asia and India laugh, I pretend they're me, or I'm them, at their age."

Jared felt so good, so big and strong behind her. Until his gun, in a holster on his belt, pressed into her back. She stepped forward.

"We're all in danger," she said, her voice quaking. In the mirror, her honey-hued eyes were bloodshot. She loved feeling small next to Jared. She loved how Mr. Whittaker called her his Amazon warrior. They both appreciated her physique. She was not a moose. Better this than a scrawny, top-heavy X ray who needed a good meal or ten. "Jared, you have to promise me you'll protect us—"

"I have to," Jared said, "as a thank-you to my uncle. I told you when my pops died, I thought I'd be a statistic. But Uncle Sonny, he snatched me out of some very crazy shit back in Harlem—"

"Yeah," Kindred said, "I think he'll send you packing just as quick if he catches you trying to stir this honeypot once more—"

"Kindred, you ain't married to my uncle," Jared said, his hands fanning over the hips of her shorts. "You act like he's the end-all be-all of your life's happiness—"

Kindred glanced down at the open toiletry bag. Sleek lavender bottles with silver tops—the trademark design of the chi-chi Pour Vous salon in Beverly Hills—were marked shampoo, exfoliating facial scrub, lotion.

"I know she's got some aspirin in here for this headache," Kindred said, scanning a toothbrush. A hairbrush. And prescription bottles. A half-dozen, inside a ziploc bag.

Yes! Kindred's heart raced. She spun around with an open mouth. Hands behind Jared's thick neck. A hot kiss.

"Jared," she whispered. "He just can't think we're distracted by each other. So let's cool it down until we get back to LA." She kissed him again, with a flick of tongue.

"Yeah, baby," he groaned.

She pressed her hips into him. "Now go back down there and watch your cousins. Pretend they're me when I was a little girl, and you want to make sure I grow up big and strong so we can be together."

Jared licked her lips. "I'm there."

As he left, Kindred closed and locked the door. She grabbed the ziploc bag. The plastic rustled as she inspected each brown bottle. Claritin. Diet pills. Vicodin. Another Vicodin. Both Vicodin bottles said: *Take one tablet as needed for back pain.*

"Yeah," Kindred said. "That tiny back holding up those big boobs. That would hurt—"

One bottle said Dr. Dreyfus. The second bottle said Dr. Sims.

"Courtroom exhibit number one," she whispered. Her heart hammered with excitement; she could almost hear a judge telling Mr. Whittaker that he would keep custody of Asia and India. But—was that a siren?

"Kindred!" a pounding on the door. Erica screamed, "What the fuck are you doing up here!"

Yes. Sirens. In the distance. And getting closer.

14

On the front porch of Jenn's bungalow, the chiffon of Simone's white skirt snagged noisily on splinters as she inched away from a police officer. He kept scooting closer, asking the same questions.

"Clear the way," the paramedic shouted in Portuguese from inside the open door. The hollow clunk of gurney wheels on the wooden planks made Simone turn around.

She wanted to run away—to the boat, back home—to a place where she could forget what she'd just seen, and be safe from whomever wanted to mutilate her next. She stood, her leg muscles quivering the same way they had after running the marathon she had organized to raise money for

The Tree House last fall. Her head swirled; she sat back down.

"Again, Miss," the police officer asked, as he and two other men in white uniforms lifted the bright yellow gurney down the two steps to the grass. A white sheet covered Jenn's body up to the neck; black seat-belt-type straps stretched over her chest and thighs. "Was anyone else inside—"

Gasps and exclamations in English, Portuguese and French shot from the semicircle of gawking guests, most in bathing suits, who stood in front of the bungalow.

A chubby man with a sunburned bald head and a pink drink in his hand stood next to the headlights and grill of a yellow ambulance. A silver-haired woman with a necklace of fresh flowers wiped tears streaming down her crinkled beige face.

Their eyes followed the bloody swirl that was Jenn's exposed face and neck. She wore an oxygen mask, and her red-stained hair swayed on the white pillow, leaving small pink stains, as the paramedics maneuvered the gurney over the bumpy grass. As they passed in front of Simone, the breeze whistled in the trees, making a beam of sunshine illuminate the gory vision once again.

"No," Simone sighed. She raised her trembling fingers to her face, exhaling into the heels of her hands. She had to take off this dress, sticking to her stomach and leg under warm, pink and red stains.

"Judge Thompson," a deep voice said. She peeked at the grass; three pairs of black shiny men's shoes appeared, facing her. Each had black or navy blue cuffs with sharp creases.

Simone lowered her hands. The men in dark suits formed a semicircle around her. They were the kind of CIA/FBI types that had always clustered around Gregory Anderson during his official business here as American ambassador to Brazil. The kind of men who, when Simone was a teenager, would ogle her budding breasts and make crude comments in Portuguese about her, as if she could not understand.

"Yes," she said with a sober tone. She focused on their dark sunglasses, seeing only a cloud of her own tousled hair, her blood-stained dress, the terror glowing in her eyes.

"We are investigating," one man said with a thick Portuguese accent.

"I found her," Simone answered in their language. Then she told them what she'd just told this police officer five times. "She was threatened in the newspaper by the same person—"

"We know," the man said in Portuguese.

"Simone!" Marie cried, running. "They told me it was you—"

Marie wore canteloupe-colored capri pants and a matching sleeveless blouse. She broke through the men as Norris stopped to talk to an investigator.

"Girl, I would never forgive myself," Marie whispered with a quavering voice as she sat next to Simone, "if I convinced you to come down here and—"

Simone grasped Marie's shoulders and stared into her friend's blood-shot eyes. "Tell me you're sorry for talking to me like that."

"Oh, girl," Marie cried, "I have never been more sorry. I was trippin' and I apologize—"

"For heaven's sake, Simone," Paulette cried as she squeezed past Norris. Her feathery brown hair bounced under a wide-brimmed straw hat, over her bare shoulders. The ruffles on her mint green jumpsuit swayed. The silver camera, on a gray cord around her neck, dangled a good six inches in front of her cinched waist. Paulette wriggled to sit between Simone and the police officer.

"You scared the shit out of me," Paulette said. Pale and shaking, she raised trembling fingertips to the wooden bead securing the tan cord of her hat on her neck. She put her arm around Simone. "I've never been happier to see your face."

"Simone, I'm sorry—" Norris stepped toward her in beige safari shorts and a matching Prism vest and hat. He rested a warm palm on her shoulder; his light brown eyes glowed with empathy.

"Thank you," she said. "This is absolutely unfathomable—"

Norris looked toward the ambulance. The sunlight shot through the trees and his green-tinted aviator sunglasses, casting an emerald tint on the tears dripping down his smooth cheeks; he pinched his pink-rimmed nose. "The fool who did this, he wants to hurt me"— he focused on the crowd—"and you, too."

"Where is the witness?" A deep, distinctive female voice cut through the chatter.

Simone shook her head. "I know Roxanne Jones's voice anywhere. Paulette, may I borrow your hat—"

"Of course, honey." Paulette placed the wide straw brim on Simone's head, then held the cord and pushed up the bead, securing it at Simone's neck and tucking her hair inside.

"We have more questions," one of the suited investigators said, looking at Simone.

"I told you everything I know—"

A TV camera poked through the circle between the man's dark sleeve and Norris's bare arm. Simone pressed her chin to her chest; the straw brim shaded the V of her cleavage and halter top.

"Roxanne," Norris said. His white suede loafers sunk into the lush green grass, toe-to-toe with the points of Roxanne's red sandals.

"Did she see something?" Roxanne demanded. "Is she one of your guests?"

Simone's stomach cramped. No telling what PR spin Norris might be envisioning right now. Simone absolutely did not want Roxanne Jones doing reports broadcasting to Narcissus that she was here, or that she had found Jenn. For the past week, since the Narcissus threats had begun, Simone had avoided all media requests for interviews. Including Roxanne Jones.

As the camera hummed in the hand of the man wearing navy blue Birkenstocks, Simone had an even more intense feeling that one wrong move, and Roxanne Jones would be right there to document it for the world. Covering her gold scales of justice ring on her left ring finger, Simone leaned toward Marie's shoulder. Marie cupped a hand over Simone's ear and rocked her.

"Roxanne," Norris said, "please, go away. Not now."

"But the world wants to know what happened to Jenn Ryder," Roxanne demanded. "And what about your wedding—"

"Let me introduce you to Rico Miranda," Norris said, his voice trailing with the sound of feet slicing over thick grass. "He can—"

Sirens wailed. A cacophony of languages charged the hot, thick air. A throat-burning gust of exhaust mixed with the sick-sweet perfume of flowers and tropical plants. Simone's head spun; hot dots of sunshine shooting through gaps in the trees roused a feverish ripple of nausea. She shot to her feet.

"Simone?" Marie called after her.

"Stay with us," Paulette said with a pleading tone.

But Simone's limbs trembled with a torrent of horror, fear, panic . . .

"I—I'm going to be sick—" she gasped with her head down. She parted the wall of people, sliding past a woman whose hot pink bikini hugged curves the color of black licorice.

"Simone, wait." Paulette dove after her, squeezing her hand.

But Simone pulled it away. She bolted.

Yes, she needed to run. To pound out all these awful emotions by stomping the ground, one foot after the other, huffing and sweating until her mind was clear and her nerves were calm.

When her mother or Bianca or Rosa had yelled at her as a child in the carriage house, Simone would charge down the steps, dash into the garden, onto the wooden trail, and just run. Later, as a teen, she would run down Embassy Row, hop onto the Metro, get off at Union Station, then run up and down the Mall, from President Lincoln to the Memorial, up and down Constitution Avenue, around the White House. Always thinking, why, here in the capital of this land of liberty, was she born into such unfairness?

The run always burned off her anger and cranked up her determination to find answers.

Now, she bolted past the ambulance, dodging a paramedic in orange carrying a big red first aid kit and a mother shielding the eyes of a plump toddler in a frilly purple bathing suit.

She glimpsed the ten-yard space between two bungalows, toward a slice of white sand, skinny green leaves and endless turquoise water. Yes, she would run there, to the beach, to the marina, letting her pounding heart and pumping lungs, the rhythm of her running, wash away the image of Jenn's bloody face, and get her away from that reporter—

Simone closed her eyes, gasping as her hamstrings stretched, the dress swished above her knees. She dashed around the ambulance, where paramedics were just stopping the gurney.

"My God."

That deep voice . . .

Simone's toes gripped the grass. Her hot muscles froze. Her heart raced faster. She panted.

Because Sonny Whittaker stood right before her, close enough to touch. All around him, the people, the trees, the bungalows, everything became a kaleidoscopic blur. Her mind filled with cottony mist; the air felt softer on her face.

He was leaning over Jenn Ryder, reaching for her hand. But his long, elegant fingers stopped inches above white gauze mitts. His silky beige shorts fluttered around his long, muscular legs. He pushed up the sleeves of a thin, white cable-knit sweater with PRISM embroidered in beige on the left breast. His wavy hair met the back of his clean-shaven neck in a perfect row of curls, lined up like silky black question marks across the back of his head.

"*Senhor,*" a paramedic said, adjusting knobs on the gurney. "We must go."

Sonny Whittaker side-stepped close enough for Simone to inhale his spicy-musky-manly scent. Why did it feel so natural and familiar, here beside a man she'd never met? Why did she have the sudden sensation that she had known him forever, that their spirits were joining hands and twirling in a delightful reunion in the sun-dappled light? How could she—with this horror happening right before her eyes—feel like she'd just stepped into the warm, happy home she'd never had?

Goosebumps danced up and down her arms and legs, around her belly button. Her heart pounded so wildly, he had to be able to hear it. Yet he stood, seemingly unaware of her presence, as she beheld his celebrated profile.

If only she could reach out and stroke away the tiny lines of worry and shock and horror in the smooth bronze skin around his large, gentle eyes. Oh, her pulse raced as he gazed down at Jenn with so much tenderness and empathy, his lashes forming a black curtain that kept lowering, then rising, as if he were trying to blink away this gruesome vision. Simone wanted to run a fingertip over the dark arc of his brow, then trace the adorable apple shape of the front of his cheek. What would it feel like for her nose to bump the handsome slope of his as they kissed? Would the charcoal richness of his silky-soft-looking, trimmed mustache tickle her?

And the curve of his lips, parted now as he whispered his costar's name, just how hot would they feel pressed against her own? How luscious would the contrast of her own buttery complexion be against his bronze skin, deepened by the Brazilian sun?

Would she ever get treated to a flash of the immaculate, straight white teeth that she'd seen in so many movies? His shoulder, a good six inches higher than hers, radiated strength and brawn; she longed to grasp it, and the other, and crush herself into the comfort and security of his warm bulk.

His gently pointed ear faced her; if she were to whisper his name, to indulge in the sensation of those five syllables trickling over her lips, he would no doubt turn—

His shoulder pulled back. His strong jaw turned. He pivoted, facing her squarely.

Oh, yes . . .

His famous eyes—smoky and seductive, sensitive and serious—swept her a million miles away from this horror. The soft sunlight sparkled in his irises, tiny spokes of topaz and jade and brown velvet, spinning with intrigue and intelligence, flashing like the shutters of a camera. His lips parted—

He's making love to me with his eyes . . . Tiny waves of euphoria rolled up from her fingertips and her toes, soaking and tickling her limbs, her core, with numbing warmth.

Her mouth opened. A silvery haze wiped away everything but the mesmerizing presence before her. How could one man lure her spirit to slip from her flesh like a shimmer of heat—

"How—" The word billowed silently from her hot lips.

The seductive languor of his velvet-black eyelashes pulled back slightly. His eyes sparkled. He took one step closer—

"There he is!" Roxanne Jones exclaimed as she pressed through the crowd around the ambulance. "Sonny, talk to us about—"

No! Simone spun away. A cold splash of panic deluged her senses. She slipped between two young women in big sunglasses, thong bikinis and high ponytails. She jogged along the waxy hedge, away from that man whose face was still glowing in her mind, making her heart flutter.

"Take the cameras away," he said deeply. A dozen feet back, framed by the backs of two dark-haired men's heads, Simone watched him scowl at the reporter and say: "Show some respect."

God, if Roxanne Jones had gotten video of her staring with what could have only been a passion-swept glaze over her eyes, face-to-face with Sonny Whittaker amongst the tropical flowers and palm trees—

No! That was not the image she wanted broadcast over and over on national television. Ever. Especially if he'd be sitting in her courtroom Monday morning. She had to get far away from him, from this. Out of this blood-stained dress. And out of this country that was, yet again, scraping open old wounds and creating new ones.

15

"Excuse me," Paulette said, pushing past a woman in a taupe thong bikini, holding hands with a dark-skinned man with a huge sprouting of brown dreadlocks. Paulette grasped the camera around her neck. She had to find Simone in this crowd, comfort her.

"There," Paulette said, striding over the grass. Poor Simone looked like she was about to sprint toward the beach. But wait, just over her shoulder, Sonny Whittaker was watching the paramedics hoist Jenn into the ambulance. Roxanne Jones was already capturing the horror on his handsome face as he looked at his bandaged, bloodied costar. For heaven's sake, that picture was worth a thousand words.

And dollars.

"This is my chance," Paulette whispered into the hot air.

Her pulse raced; this camera around her neck could earn her a small fortune. One picture alone could probably pay off her way overdue and way overblown Neiman Marcus charge card. Two, or five photos—those could finance the note and insurance for her black Mercedes SUV. And if these pictures landed her steady work as a celebrity photographer, who knew? Maybe she'd make enough to actually buy one of the houses she'd been showing.

"I've got to get this," Paulette whispered, her heart pounding as she raised the camera. Her index finger stroked the silver button. She was just a click away from capturing Sonny Whittaker's heart-wrenching expression. With Simone in the foreground, just behind the two bare-chested resort guests.

Paulette peered through the hole, aiming—

A pink-beige palm blocked her view.

"Drop the paparazzi fantasy right now," Simone said, pulling the camera down. "Not only do I object to you trying to capitalize on this tragedy, but I'm telling you, Marie would be absolutely furious."

Paulette snatched the camera back. "Simone, stop! One of the most famous actresses in the world is lying there mutilated, and I have a camera. This is international news—"

"Don't intrude on his grief," Simone said.

Paulette raised the camera, aiming right back at Sonny. "Perfect," she said, clicking as he grasped the back door of the ambulance, resting his forehead on his hand, closing his eyes.

Simone used outstretched fingers to rake the camera down. "Do you have any idea how much that violates a person? Being photographed when they don't know it? Then seeing the pictures or video for the first time on television? It is absolutely dreadful—"

"You should know," Paulette snapped, pulling the camera back up. "Public figures aren't entitled to the same rights of privacy as regular folks."

"Paulette," Simone said, her silver-blue eyes wide and sharp, "don't sell us out like this. Show respect for Marie—"

"Maybe my pictures will help someone identify Narcissus," Paulette said over the click of her camera as Sonny Whittaker turned his back on Roxanne. "They catch him, then that helps you out, too. It's a win–win situation for all parties—"

"Paulette!" Marie's angry voice, and a cloud of her perfume, charged the steamy air as Marie stormed from between the hedges. "What are you doing?"

"I'm the only photographer here," Paulette said without lowering her camera. "Someone has to document this for the world."

"Not you," Marie said.

"I tried to tell her," Simone said.

"There's an unspoken rule I've learned from Norris," Marie said. "It's a sort of trust. When you're with people like this, you respect their privacy. Especially in this situation."

Paulette clicked some more. There, a great shot with Sonny facing the camera, his eyes full of worry as he talked with two investigators in dark suits, their backs to the camera, right next to the ambulance.

"Paulette," Marie snapped. "Put the camera down, and give me the film."

Paulette laughed, lowering the camera. "For heaven sakes, Marie. You sound like the Gestapo." Marie stood with a hand on her hip, the sun glistening in her giant diamond, and the other hand out, palm up. "Now."

"No," Paulette said. "You invited me here knowing I'm a photographer. Your famous friends wouldn't have become what they are if they didn't want to be in the spotlight. So leave me alone."

Paulette glared at Simone, who stood with her hands at her stomach, running her right fingertips over the knuckles of her balled left hand.

"Don't give me that look, your honor," Paulette said. "Squinting like I've committed a crime and need a punishment—"

"We're all a little tripped out," Marie said as her upper arm pressed Paulette's hair down on the back of her neck and back. "Now I'm going to the hospital with Norris. And I don't want you, Paulette"— Marie's face was just inches away, her brown eyes sharp and serious—"running around here like a mad shutterbug as our guests arrive."

Paulette withdrew from Marie's arm. "You said *People* and *In Style*—"

"Tomorrow," Marie said. "For the wedding. Which probably won't happen in the wake of this—"

Simone's hand wrapped around Paulette's free hand. "Come on, Paulette—"

Paulette stepped back. Her sandals made her taller than her friends. "For heaven's sake, you both have too many rules. I'll talk to you when you chill out."

"Take one more picture," Marie warned, "I'll have Rico confiscate your cameras."

"Go for it," Paulette said. She spun on a heel, then dashed back into the crowd. Ted would be so proud right now. Sure, his sports agency was doing well. But it was still new, and all the cash flow was going to cover the start-up costs. The lease, the furniture, the receptions, the airline tickets. It would be months before they even started to break even. And the boys' tuition was due *now.* The contractors who had just installed their new gourmet kitchen were already threatening to report her to a collection service. Not to mention the monthly bills.

"Paulette!" Marie called.

Paulette's breasts bounced, a big round curve of mint green, just under the little silver rectangle that was going to earn her a small fortune and send her flashing toward her own fifteen minutes of fame. She loved the way her red fingernails contrasted against the metal. A voyeuristic surge of energy made her tingle as she snapped away.

There—Norris Haynes on the blood-stained porch of Jenn's bungalow.
Click!

Action hero Lex Laurent walking up with a young blonde in black hot pants, cheetah-print mules and a sleeveless blouse tied above her bare belly. Definitely not Mrs. Laurent.
Click!

Sonny Whittaker's nanny with his two little girls and bodyguards, running toward him.
Click!

Forget Simone and her rigid rule-following. And Marie, acting like celebrities don't need publicity. All her life, Paulette had grown up around people dripping with money. All her life, being close enough to look at— but not touch—the glamour and wealth of Hollywood. All those times as a kid and adult, cruising the winding, mansion-lined streets of Beverly Hills. Staring in awe at the rich-looking people strolling out of Chanel on Rodeo into an awaiting Benz convertible. Driving past the Dorothy Chandler Pavilion, where dozens of limousines lined up to drop off stars in gowns that cost more than her parents' little house near Venice Beach.

Now, Paulette was closer than ever, ready to use her camera to join the ranks. Wasn't that why Norris wanted the wedding here, to promote *The Colony?*

For heaven's sake, yes. Marie got hers.

Now I'm gonna get mine.

16

"Daddy!"

The little girls' voices stabbed at Simone's heart as she and Marie watched Paulette traipse away.

"Paulette's blind ambition is maddening sometimes," Marie said. "As soon as Norris finishes talking to the police, I'll have him talk to girl-friend. You'd think she would have more respect."

Simone spun; she had to see the children who were crying the term of endearment that she had always yearned to say, but never had the chance to. A black police car and two Sanctuary employees stood behind her, along with a gray-haired couple with leathery skin and matching white short sets.

"Simone?" Marie said, grasping her arm.

"Yes," Simone sighed. Elbows and shoulders intensified the heat of bodies around her as she beheld Sonny Whittaker's profile about ten feet before them. His smoky eyes softened with a heart-melting, protective brawn. As the ambulance engine revved, he stepped forward, arms outstretched, as if he were looking at the very thing that made his heart beat—

"Daddy!"

Two little girls sprinted toward him, then leaped up. Sonny caught one girl in each arm. They rested cheeks on his shoulders; a beam of sunshine illuminated a tiny black pearl on each girl's ear, which were shaped with the same rounded points as their father's ears. He pressed a cheek into the pillowy poufs of their black curls, which hung in damp clumps down their backs and over their shoulders.

He closed his eyes and rocked them gently. A tall woman in pink, with long dark hair pulled back with a red ribbon, stepped toward them. Flanking them were two tall men with smooth brown skin, big muscles and bald heads.

Simone wanted to run away before he saw her. But the image of him holding his daughters so tenderly all but paralyzed her.

"Marie," she whispered. "Come over here." Simone ducked behind the broad-shouldered man with dreadlocks. With Marie at her side, she stared past the upper curve of his brown arm—tattooed with a sunburst—for an unobstructed view of Sonny Whittaker and his daughters.

"It's like he'd die before he let anyone so much as tangle their hair," Simone whispered. "Like nothing else matters but them."

Marie grasped her hand. "You should hear them sing."

Simone's breath caught in her throat. "Marie," Simone whispered. "That, right there. That's all I ever wanted. A daddy who looked at me like that—"

"I don't know what's worse," Marie said with glassy eyes, "never having it, or having it and watching a murderer steal it."

Simone put her arm around Marie's shoulder.

"I can't let it happen to Norris, too," Marie said deeply. "My whole life, working to catch and help people like that. Now it's happening again, to the only other man I've loved."

Simone stroked Marie's soft, copper-hued hair. "Shhh." She rocked her friend as the girls' voices drew her gaze back.

"We were scared, Daddy," one girl said, her amber eyes wide as her narrow shoulders pressed into his chest. Flashing red lights cast a crimson shadow over his cheek, the girls' dark ringlets, and their silver and chartreuse bathing suits. Their thin, light caramel-colored arms extended around his neck.

"We heard sirens," the other girl said. "Mom let us come."

Marie raised her head, wiping tears with her fingertips. "That's the nanny. I like Kindred. It's obvious she loves her work. Look how her eyes just light up when she looks at the twins—"

Sonny glared down at the young woman. "You shouldn't have let them come here," he said. The girls held out their hands, lacing little fingers with the nanny's longer ones of the same hue. Ambulance lights washed her shorts and shirt in red; her ponytail cocked to one side, secured by a red string.

"I hate those things." Simone massaged her wrist. "Brazilian wish ribbons. Rosa used to tie them on me with knots that made my hand veins bulge." She remembered, at age ten, playing on the wrought iron balcony at the Andersons' penthouse overlooking Copacabana Beach.

I wish dirty little Simone would fall off a cliff and die," Rosa said, pointing to the foliage-covered mountainous peaks above the high-rises and beaches of Rio de Janeiro.

"No!" Simone shrieked, running to her mother. Inside, Ruth Thompson was kneeling over a white satin Egyptian-style couch, rubbing aloe vera on Bianca's bare, sunbaked back.

"Get out, little brat," Bianca moaned. And rather than comfort on her mother's face, Ruth Thompson's cheek twitched, promising the wrath of words— and worse—when they were alone in the servants' quarters.

"I've seen them at the market," Marie said, "but what are they for?"

"You're supposed to make a wish, tie it and wear it until it falls off," Simone said. "I started carrying scissors in my Wonder Woman backpack, so my hands wouldn't fall off."

The ambulance belched a throat-burning cloud of exhaust. Deafening sirens wailed. Sonny's face blurred under her sudden sting of tears.

"Simone," Marie said, kissing her cheek as the ambulance roared away. "Norris is motioning for me to go. He and I are going to follow the ambulance. Be safe."

Simone closed her eyes. She had to get away—

"You're safe now, with me," Sonny Whittaker said. "Your angels are floating around—"

Simone opened her eyes.

"There, India," he squinted up at a wispy white cloud, "Your angel is making that swirl look like wings, and her gown is floating in the breeze. Just like in our painting—"

"I see her!" the girl said, her pillowy lips drawing back over tiny white square teeth.

"Angels for the little angel girls," the nanny said. She pivoted as she wiped sand from the child's leg. And she locked her gaze right on Simone.

Something in the woman's eyes flashed for a split-second, as if she were taking Simone's picture with her pupils. It aroused a visceral familiarity. Yet, Simone would remember the unusual color of the woman's eyes, like dollops of honey set in an almond-colored circle as dewy as the smaller faces in Sonny's arms.

The woman's narrow, tiny nostrils flared; her glossed lips tightened. She had the racially ambiguous look of so many young women in LA: Hispanic or black or Native American or even Polynesian. Could she have been one of the countless witnesses or plaintiffs or spectators who passed through Simone's courtroom every day? Someone on her jogging path along Santa Monica Beach? Another volunteer at the orphanage?

"Kindred," Sonny called. The woman flipped her ponytail over her shoulder to look at him as he said, "You see Asia's angels, don't you?"

The girl in the silver suit pointed up: "Asia, see?"

"No." The child in chartreuse rolled her eyes.

"That's because your guardian angel is there," Sonny said, pointing to sunshine slicing through long, finger-like leaves above. "Your angel is more discreet. Tonight we'll call Grandmama and she'll tell you all about—"

Sonny's gaze trailed down the beams of sunshine.

Simone gasped.

He looked right into her eyes. And his stare was whispering, promising, soothing her. God, just like the moment in so many of his movies, when he met a woman's eyes for the first time.

She could not look away. Did not want to. Ever.

Her flesh danced with a thousand times the intensity of her daily runner's high . . . a million times stronger than the heat of the sun that had stiffened her nipples and baked her skin a short while ago on the yacht. And made her lips part with the need to suckle every inch of him . . .

The ringing cell phone in her purse, strapped over one shoulder, did not break her stare; she reached in and grasped the gray metal rectangle.

"Yes," she said softly.

"Simone." The chief judge's deep voice sounded like he was a mile away, not on another continent and in a different hemisphere. "In case you were thinking about spending any extra days living the lifestyle of the rich and famous—"

"Hardly," she said somberly as investigators clustered around Sonny Whittaker.

"It's confirmed," Charlie said. "Food poisoning. You could shoot a cannon down the hallways here—"

Static blasted her ear. "Charlie, what?"

"Bad beef," Charlie said. "In the cafeteria. They served up a little *e coli* bacteria along with the burgers and fries. Judge Evans puked up his guts—"

Simone shook her head. "No, Charlie, don't even—"

"I know you don't like celebrity trials," Charlie said, "with all the media, but—"

Sonny Whittaker stared at her with tender eyes, framed by those adorable girls and the men in suits. How could she be impartial . . .

"Charlie, no—"

"It looks like I may need you to cover the Sonny Whittaker divorce trial Monday morning."

17

Marie Cartwright pressed Norris's left hand between her own clammy palms as they rode in the back seat of a chauffeured black Navigator whose outer doors said SANCTUARY in silver block letters.

"Norris," she said softly over the whine of the siren on the ambulance, just ahead on the narrow, tree-lined asphalt road. "I feel very strongly about this. It would be inappropriate—"

"Half of Hollywood will be here by morning," Norris said, staring straight ahead at the flashing red lights. "The way my schedule looks for the next six months, there's no other time—"

"But going ahead with the wedding," Marie said, "in the wake of this,

I just don't want to do it. It's hitting too close to home." She pressed her fingertips to her pearl choker. Dry and clean. Marie slipped a fingertip beneath it; the six-inch zipper of waxy-numb flesh was damp and hot, but healed. Physically. But the salty scent of blood burning her nostrils took her back.

Please, Jesus, save him . . . First Daddy. Now Norris.

"Look at me," Marie said.

Norris turned; his light brown eyes bathed her in reassurance as he squeezed her hand. "Marie, I think Jenn will make it. She'll recover, we'll resume filming—"

"If she lives through this," Marie said. "Those were not superficial wounds. She'll need years of surgery to get her face back. If that's even possible—"

Norris raised his fingertips to her cheek, stroking gently. "Marie, my savior, we can't cancel this day I've been waiting and wishing for."

"I wish you'd never made certain confessions to me," she said. "I can't separate the things you've said in my office from the things you've whispered in bed—"

"Such as?"

"Our wedding, this ordeal with Jenn," Marie said. "It feels like life imitating art. *The Colony* and *Avenger*." Marie recalled one grueling therapy session, when Norris had admitted to deliberately breaking his own leg during a motorcycle accident, on the eve of the premiere. As the media buzzed with rumors that he had died, he showed up on crutches, his leg bandaged up to his thigh. And, he liked to laugh, it was no coincidence, the movie about a Harley-Davidson-riding bounty hunter had subsequently spent six weeks in the number one spot at the box office.

She could still see the excited glint in his eyes as he lay on her brown leather couch and said, "One sharp left into the canyon wall! It hurt like hell, but dollar signs have a way of making the pain go away."

Now, something more sinister glinted in his eyes. "Strike two, Marie. There's a lot of shit on my mind right now, darling. If I want your brilliant analysis, I'll ask for it, every Thursday at two." He turned toward the window. Jungle foliage framed roadside vendors selling brightly colored fruits, sacks of earth-toned spices and strings of fresh fish.

"I can't hold this in," Marie said. "*The Colony* starts with a wedding, when Xavier marries Jenn's character. There's the bloody scene, where Jenn and the girls are killed by the World Council troops in their lavish oceanside mansion—"

Norris turned toward her. He drew his brassy eyelashes together, but his eyes still glimmered with something that made her stroke her choker.

"I'm starting to wonder if our wedding," Marie said, "is just part of—"

"Freeze frame, right there Marie," he whispered, raising a hand to his vest, covering the Prism logo. "That is below the belt. If you can't trust my motivation for marrying you—"

"I'm just making an observation," Marie said softly. "Let's just have a quiet, simple ceremony back home."

Norris's fingers pressed deeper into his vest, scratching the fabric. "Marie, when a movie is over budget, or a stuntman dies in a crash, we don't halt production. We keep going—"

"Our wedding is not a movie," Marie said.

"We've spent enough money for one," Norris said. "Starting with the check I wrote to Rico Miranda, to create the altar of *your* dreams. The band and dancers, the gourmet meal—"

"I don't care," Marie said, turning toward the window. She rested her hands in her lap, fingering the sharp, cold prongs around her diamond. "Remember how your dad flew off to Alaska to shoot a film, even when the doctors said that fifth childbirth could kill your mother?"

Norris pulled off his hat, rested it in his lap. "The bastard went anyway. Serves him right that Mom died."

"The point is, he could have waited," Marie said. "Maybe having him home, she would have survived. Just like you can wait. Because I'll be here—"

"We're getting married, Marie," Norris said, looking back out the window as the SUV pulled up to a helicopter in front of the clinic. "Tomorrow, as scheduled."

18

As the crowd dispersed from the courtyard, Sonny was sure his blood would freeze if he looked away from Her silver-blue eyes. My God, he had to make Her smile; no face that beautiful, no spirit that gentle, should ever pinch or pale with so much worry and longing. Or stand here in the stench of burning flesh, barefoot, in a blood-stained dress. No, Sonny's limbs tingled with the need to protect Her just as intensely as he needed to protect the little girls he was holding in his arms.

"Angel Eyes," Sonny whispered into two poufs of curls. "Go with Kindred and the fellas right now," Sonny said, nodding at Jared and Josh. "Finish visiting with your mom, and I'll come get you later."

His voice rang in his own ears more deeply than usual. The image of Jenn's bloody face tried to superimpose itself over his vision as he looked at Asia and India. "They do not," Sonny told Jared and Josh, "leave your sight for a single moment. Not one."

"Yes, sir," they answered.

Sonny locked eyes on Her as She dropped a cell phone back into her purse. During the call, Her *butterscotch cream* hue had paled to *mourning dove gray*, the name of a paint Sonny used to create faces of people who were ill. Now, Her intelligent eyes softened with maternal longing and love as She focused on him and the girls.

Sonny kissed Asia and India, then slowly set them down.

"Come on, little angel girls," Kindred said, taking their hands. "We'll sing—"

"Daddy." India turned back. "The space shuttle—"

"We won't miss it," Kindred said, flanked by Jared and Josh.

Asia smiled, waving. "Daddy, I want to call Grandmama later, too."

"We will," Sonny said. "Kindred, if the wedding is off, we'll all be on the boat to the airport in the morning. Back home—"

"Let me know," she said. "I'll get packing." Her large hands cradled the backs of each girl's head as she guided them down the hedge-lined path.

He turned back to Her. But a tree branch dangled in the sun-dappled light. A cloud of exhaust, blood and sick-sweet flora burned his throat.

"She's gone," he groaned.

He had to feel for Her, like Xavier, his character in *The Colony.* A blind man who had honed his powers of intuition so strongly, his sixth sense guided him with far more clarity than eyes ever could. The blue-green lattice of leaves and sky blurred as he concentrated on where She had gone—

The girls. Physically safe. Her *moonbeam gray* eyes appeared in the bright aura of sunshine inside his eyelids. And Her, on the boat, sandy hair blowing in the wind. The boat. Who wouldn't want to get the hell out of here after what had just happened?

Sonny sprinted toward the crowded beach. He squinted; a quarter-mile of white sand stretched in both directions, bookended by treacherous rocks, tall palm trees and foliage fanning over the turquoise water and waves. Was She here? Behind that red-and-yellow striped umbrella near the toddler crawling in a blue diaper? On the rainbow-patterned blanket amongst a half-dozen topless beauties soaking up the sun?

Sonny focused on the wall of jagged rocks leading to the marina.

There, a flash of flesh from a shell-shaped cove of feathery plants.

A flutter of white fabric, a bare foot on the sand.

"American movie star," a young man was telling several others as they sat on bright towels. "Jenn Ryder is destroyed—"

Sonny's heart pounded. Anyone on this beach could be Narcissus. And he or she could see him away from Asia and India.

He dashed over the hot sand, anxious to get back to them, after—

"Come, my nymph, let my arms be all the sanctuary you need." His lines from *Only in Xanadu,* some twenty years ago, moved his lips.

"My God," he sighed. Couldn't he think of anything normal to say? All these movie lines sounded corny. But it seemed like half a lifetime since he'd had a romantic encounter with a woman—

That toned calf. Two. Arms hugging raised knees, heels anchored in the sand, next to a straw hat. Her right fingertips were gently tracing the knuckles of Her left hand. Her long back arced slightly as her breasts pressed into the tops of her legs. Chin resting on knees, those unusual eyes gazed toward the baby blue waves rolling in, crashing in the afternoon sun, fizzing in white foam on the sand . . .

She was trembling. Even as he ran, now about ten feet away, Her whole body quaked as if She were cold. Her jaw chattered behind Her closed mouth.

In an instant, he could kneel before her, take her into his arms. He froze. What would he say? How would he introduce himself after this? He closed his eyes, breathing hard. What if Narcissus had sent her as a deliberate decoy, to distract him while a killer went after the girls?

My God . . . An icy-hot jolt shot through him. Sheer terror. The soft, salty wind tickled his cheeks, the same breeze that was stirring up a tangle of curls over her bare shoulders, and rippling her wispy dress, with its cinched waist and folds of chiffon cradling her full breasts, moving like frothy waves over muscular legs.

He had to hear her voice. Touch her. Kiss her.

He started to step toward her—

But now, his own torso was jittering. As violently as when he'd gotten robbed at gunpoint outside a party on Lexington Avenue as a teenager in Harlem. Then, some thug had demanded his cherished gold necklace, a gift from his father, and he never saw it again.

Was she yet another thief—like Cheyenne and Erica and Roxanne— trying to steal his children, his happiness, his future? The power emanating from her could pilfer his heart, his mind, his soul with one sultry whisper.

And he would hand it all over, on the most exquisite, diamond-encrusted platter Tiffany's could offer. The hot, heavy air smelled sweet with flowers, salty from the ocean.

A pelican screeched and splashed in the surf a few feet from him.

The woman turned as it snatched a fish in its claws, then spread vast brown-white wings and rose toward the sky.

She gasped.

My God, those eyes. . . .

An army of technicians could only dream of setting up kliegs or silver lighting screens to cast such a magical glow around her. Her eyes magnified the sunshine reflecting off the sand and filtering through the shell of feathery palm leaves around her.

"You're like *Birth of Venus* sitting there," Sonny said deeply.

"Then tell me"—her eyes shimmered but her face was stiff—"who does that make you?"

"I hope it makes me Adonis," Sonny said. "But as a painter, I'll settle for Botticelli."

Her eyes were like two moons, bathing him in silvery splendor. He set the hearing part of his mind on rewind, replaying her eight words over and over.

Silk on a soundwave. That was what her voice sounded like. Back home, he would name a painting that, then create a swirl of the softest colors, the silkiest texture, pouring like warm cream into his ears.

He stepped closer. "I would say, welcome to Sanctuary—"

"I will never come back to Brazil," she said.

Goosebumps danced across her bare arms and shoulders, as if someone had stroked velvet against the grain. He ambled closer to her bell-shaped nose, the soft sculpt of her cheekbones, the fullness of her lips.

"May I be so bold," he said deeply, extending a hand.

"I'm leaving," she said, staring at a palm-sized crab scurrying over a lump of sand. "As soon as I find clean clothes"—she glanced down at her stained dress—"and a boat—"

"You're too beautiful," he said, tracing the delicate bone of her jaw with his gaze, "to run away from paradise."

She turned to him, narrowing her eyes. "What I just saw doesn't happen in paradise."

"I'm sorry." He could sit next to her, digging his heels into the warm sand. But he would be like a moth, fluttering around a flame, wanting to land, knowing he would ignite if he did. "I was trying to forget—"

"When you learn how," she said, hugging herself, "let me know. That's an art I may never master."

Sonny focused on a pink streak on the fabric next to her collarbone. "Let me walk you to your bungalow," he said softly, "to change clothes—"

"A maid at the resort can have them," she said. "I'm not going back. In fact—" She clawed the skirt of her dress upward.

"What are you—"

"After I take off Marie's stupid dress," she said, hoisting it up, over her arms, her head. Her bare thighs—toned, smooth, pristine—framed what he imagined must be a golden gateway to heaven.

"I'm wearing a bathing suit," she said as she unfolded her long body and stood. White arches of fabric framed her bare behind; a bikini brassiere hugged her full breasts close.

A deep laugh—almost a lusty moan—passed over Sonny's smiling lips. From the side, her behind was a round, firm mound leading to the soft arc of thighs. His gaze trailed upward over the white triangle at the front leading to a smooth stomach, tiny golden hairs glistening in the sunlight around her belly button.

His tongue and the insides of his cheeks, watered. If only he could escape his worries by burrowing into all of that, starting with the succulent inner curves of her breasts. He would nuzzle in and suckle for dear life.

Her warm fingers wrapped around his damp hand.

"Run with me," she said, pulling him.

"No, I already had my brush with death this morning, right here, with my trainer."

Her legs pumped the sand as she jogged in place. Energy radiated from her bouncing hair, her glimmering eyes, her limbs. The painter and screenwriter in him marveled at how she was made for the cast of *The Colony*. No doubt this woman fit the bill for what the Brazilians lauded as *Mistura Fina*. But an "exquisite mixture" of what, exactly?

"Let's just sit here," Sonny said, "watch the sky, and talk."

"I have to run." She pulled a small purse from the dress crumpled on the sand; she draped the strap over her shoulder. "Come on, it's the best therapy."

Sonny could not move.

She bolted, long, legs stretching, pumping into the wet sand, splashing at the water's edge, her hair bouncing in the sunshine.

"My God," he whispered, watching the round curves of her behind and the smooth contours of her back, as she dashed away. "Is she real?"

A hot bolt of adrenaline shot through him. He took off, one foot after another, pounding the sand. His heart hammered, his lungs squeezed . . .

"I thought I gave up chasing women," he groaned. He had a few hours before he would get the girls back from their visit with Erica.

"Wait!" he shouted. She was a good ten yards ahead. The wall of sharp rocks separating the resort from the public beach loomed before her. "Stop!"

Fear injected his veins with adrenaline; his aching legs became turbo-charged pistons.

She ran alongside the rocks to the boardwalk leading to the marina and the public beach. Under the silver SANCTUARY arch she went. Two police officers stopped her, then let her pass. Her sandy hair and creamy shoulders disappeared over the bridge.

19

Paulette Barnes stood on the rocky ridge, camera in hand, watching people stream along the boardwalk from the marina to the little bridge leading to the resort. Her goal: recognize a famous face, snap their picture and shoot her career toward a more glitterati lifestyle. Marie and Simone would be proud, after the fact—

"Excuse me." A distinctive voice, a familiar one, made Paulette turn.

Her heart pounded. Rushing toward her were a sunbleached cameraman and a woman with a swoop of black hair, a skin-tight red dress, a silver microphone.

"I'm Roxanne Jones," the woman said, holding out a hand.

"Paulette Barnes," she said, shaking Roxanne's slim, soft hand and smiling. Her braces rubbed the inside of her bottom lip. She needed them adjusted, but she'd been putting off an appointment at the orthodontist. The thought of facing that grouchy, invoice-wielding office manager—

"Didn't I just see you with Norris Haynes?" Roxanne asked. "And you got some shots of Sonny Whittaker?"

Roxanne was even more gorgeous up close than on television. And last she'd heard, Roxanne was trying to get her own late-night celebrity show. Could she be Paulette's all-access pass to selling her pictures?

"Yes," Paulette said. "Isn't this horrible?"

"Were you inside Jenn Ryder's bungalow?" Roxanne asked.

What could Paulette say to impress her? That one of her best friends had found Jenn? Simone would never forgive her, but that was the truth.

"I only saw what you saw," Paulette said.

Roxanne flipped her hair, turning toward the marina. Her cameraman scanned the beach.

Opportunity was slipping away. Just like time, and her life, and her chance for fame and fortune. She had always been sure that someday she would get to live in one of those gated mansions on Sunset Boulevard, or pay the orthodontist bill on time, or walk into Fred Segal and buy anything without maxing out her credit cards, or drive a red Mercedes two-seater convertible without secretly raiding Ted's 401K investments.

"You met my husband last month," Paulette told Roxanne. "Ted Barnes, at the Lakers party—"

"I go to so many parties," Roxanne said. "What does your husband do?"

"He represents Jay Riley—"

"Rookie," Roxanne said with a dismissive tone. "Just off the pumpkin truck from Hicksville—"

Roxanne's eyes—lined with black on the upper lids, a few shades darker than her trimmed, shaped brows—raked over Paulette's body. Paulette ran her hands over her plump stomach—

I have to drop these twenty pounds. Finally. The boys are teenagers now . . . that little joke I always make about baby fat just doesn't work anymore . . .

No, to make it in Hollywood, a woman had to look as sleek and groomed as Roxanne, with her perfect make-up, her shiny-bouncy, just-styled hair, her curve-hugging, single-digit-sized dress.

Yes, looking that good could only help Paulette get rid of the gnawing fear that a big red BANKRUPT stamp would come slamming down on their heads.

No, I will not let my boys live like I did as a kid. Those humiliating tickets for lunch that only the poor kids had. Putting new school clothes on lay-away and not getting them until Halloween, if at all. Getting teased for having crooked teeth because Mom and Dad couldn't afford braces . . .

"Roxanne," Paulette said, raising her camera toward a young couple, in matching nautical white and blue pants and shirts. They stepped onto the dock from a long white sailboat. Rich, but not famous. "Wait till you see the pictures I got."

"What?" Roxanne asked.

"Lex Laurent. And the bikini babe on his arm was *not* Mrs. Laurent, I may add."

"Old news," Roxanne said with a bored tone. "They're separated. Heard any talk of Cheyenne Moore trying to crash this wedding?"

Something fast-moving on the beach caught Paulette's eye. She focused. A tall, brown-skinned man. Beige shorts and sweater. Running.

"Sonny Whittaker," she gasped.

"Get him," Roxanne said to the cameraman. "Why is he running—"

"Are they together?" the cameraman asked.

"Is he being chased?" Paulette aimed her camera, snapping. She zoomed past the colorful umbrellas, splashing children and sunbathers. Behind him, two men in Hawaiian-print shorts jogged side-by-side. And ahead of him, a woman in a white thong bikini, running.

"Look," Paulette said. "The women here are so sensuous, so comfortable with their bodies—"

"Figures," Roxanne said. "His life is being threatened, and he's literally chasing a piece of ass on the beach—"

Paulette gasped. Her insides got that crushing feeling that always came when she opened bills, or saw an abundance of parentheses on her monthly portfolio report. The heavy pressure of debt, of loss—

Because that sandy hair bouncing, the athletic build, the strong gait as she flew across the sand at the water's edge—

Simone!

No, Simone would never wear a thong bikini. Unless that was all Marie had given her—

"For heaven's sakes," Paulette whispered.

But Simone would certainly not run on the beach with Sonny Whittaker. Not after all she had said on the yacht and seen at the resort. But if they were, in fact, frolicking on the beach in the wake of Jenn's attack, and just days before he was scheduled to appear in her courthouse, pictures could be sheets of gold. And dollars.

No, Simone, don't put me in this position—

Paulette's heart leaped to her throat. Her palms became slick. Could she do this to the friend who'd loaned her money for books back in college, when Paulette blew her budget in the Nordstrom's shoe department? The friend who'd used her meager salary as a law clerk, right out of school, to help her and Ted buy a used station wagon to cart around two toddlers, with another on the way? Even now, Simone never hesitated to bail Paulette out of a sudden cash crunch, whether a surprise car repair or . . .

"I don't think that's him," Paulette said loudly, urgently, as the red light atop the black camera glowed and the lens aimed down at the beach.

"No," Paulette said. Loyalty to her friend's quest for anonymity was more important than this chance to impress *Entertainment Exclusive*. She could find other opportunities. But now, she had to get this *EE* crew away from whatever was about to happen down on the sand.

"Seriously," Paulette said. "I saw Sonny Whittaker go back to his bungalow with his daughters. You don't really think he'd leave his children while all this is going on—"

"I saw them walk away from him with their nanny," Roxanne said, squinting and nodding. "I know Sonny Whittaker when I see him. Believe me."

The cameraman's fingers adjusted dials as he swiveled to focus on Sonny. Was he zooming in for a close-up? Could he capture Simone's and Sonny's faces? Were they in fact running together?

Paulette stepped in front of the camera.

"Hey," Roxanne said. "Get out of the way."

"It's not appropriate," Paulette said, "with what's going on."

"*You're* not appropriate," Roxanne snapped. "Now move!"

20

On the public beach, Sonny huffed past a young woman with two boys building a sandcastle, two musclemen sunbathing in thongs, and a gray-haired man and woman holding hands and wading in waist-high water.

He sprinted past the impressionistic dotting of red, yellow and blue umbrellas covering the sand. His heart pounding in his ears rang with the frantic drumming of a samba band, a serpentine line of people dancing and shouting in the distance. He gasped air fragrant with bean cakes frying on an open fire next to a woman by the sidewalk. He drew energy from the vibrancy of the open-air market about fifty yards back from the water's edge, and the people in between.

There . . . he ran on trembling legs toward the water. Finally, she was an arm's length in front of him. How could she run so gracefully without even looking down at the clumps of seaweed, the scatter of kids' pails and sand castles . . .

"Thought you could get away—" he puffed.

She stretched out her arms. Tossed her head back. Her legs were like golden scissors, slicing so fast they blurred.

He sprinted in front of her, running backwards to see what in the world . . .

Her stiff nipples poked through the white, sweat-dampened fabric of her bathing suit. A light sheen glistened on her skin.

"There's nothing better!" she shouted. Her eyes danced, glowed, sparkled. Her shoulders twitched. And those beautiful, rose-hued lips parted into a bright grin. "Absolutely nothing better."

"I can think of a few things," Sonny said, still running backwards.

He held out his arms. The sunbathers, the cacophony of languages, the scent of coconut oil, made his head spin.

"See how it clears your mind," she said, sprinting. "Endorphins. Our body's opium—"

Sonny smiled. My God, this woman had more energy than ten people. A lightning rod of lust sizzled from the top of his sun-baking head to his sandy toes, then ricocheted back upward, lodging in an electric pulse in his shorts. To get in bed with her, to make love, to let her use those seemingly tireless muscles to please him—

His heel, a mound of sand—

Wham! The soft sand cradled his bare back, his behind. A gush of breath whispered toward the sky. A wave, as warm as bathwater, trickled over his left arm and leg.

And she began falling toward him. In slow motion, framed by brilliant blue and fluffy white. Her *moonbeam gray* eyes widened. Her full mouth opened. Her breasts, cradled in white, were coming at him. Her flat, toned stomach, all that *butterscotch cream* skin that he wanted to taste and kiss—

The momentum of her run thrust her hourglass shape onto him. Her toes lacing with his. Breasts crashing into his chest. Her open mouth, falling onto his. Lips interlocking like the round puzzle pieces cut from the same exquisite velvet long ago, now seamlessly reconnected. A droplet of sweat rolling from her upper lip, salting his tongue.

A warm wave lapped at their legs as the breeze fluttered down like the softest blanket.

It was a *From Here to Eternity* moment. Their karmic connection required no words. He would have forever to stare into her eyes, to taste her mouth. Oh how he wished, right now, he could reach around and stroke those two domes of flesh, resting on him like the steaming, golden-buttered tops of cornbread muffins.

The steel rod in his shorts, cushioned by her soft flesh, pulsed.

Her eyes widened. She gasped.

She sprung upward, cheeks rouged, hair wild. Two points poked through the white fabric of her bikini top.

"My God," he panted, sure that his racing heart would explode. "You are heaven."

"No," she whispered. "We're both running from our own personal Hells."

21

Simone could still taste him as she hurried along the crowded boardwalk, her bare feet burning with every quick step on the smooth, blue and white geometric-patterned tiles.

"Walk with me," Sonny called behind her. Sweat prickled his hot skin. "You can't be on fast-forward in this slow-motion paradise."

Simone dashed past pale green and yellow stucco arches framing merchant stalls packed with beachwear, wooden souvenirs and fresh produce. A chorus of romance languages exploded from open-air cafés teeming with suntanned natives and tourists in bathing suits. The bustling strip faced straw-roofed gazebos and tall coconut palms shading beachgoers on the white sand stretching toward the turquoise surf.

She had to get away from him. Before he learned her name. Before he could find out that she would probably be the judge deciding his family's fate starting Monday morning. And especially, before anyone—Paulette or Roxanne Jones or Narcissus or even a tourist who recognized Sonny—saw them together, and documented their sparking attraction with a camera.

"I just need to find something decent to wear," Simone said. His bronze chest, his towering height, his tender eyes, were a peripheral blur. She walked faster, coughing on the scents of spices and sweat on the fishy-salty ocean breeze. The distant rumble of samba drums, a tambourine and the shrieks of dancers charged the heat.

"Necklace for a lady!" A woman held out hands draped with a rainbow of beads.

"Fresh fish!" A man pointed to wooden buckets of ice showcasing crayfish-looking shrimp and sharp-toothed barracuda.

"Spices!" a shirtless boy called, standing over huge burlap sacks rolled down to display circles of red cayenne pepper, bright yellow cumin and white sea salt.

"Wait for me," Sonny said.

"After I find a boat, I'm going home—"

"Let's lose ourselves in the sensuous delights of Brazil," Sonny stepped in front of her. He grasped her hands, stared down into her eyes. "We'll forget everything, for a few moments of abandon. The bad stuff will be waiting, right where we left it."

"Leave me alone," Simone said, even though her heart was hammering. His gaze was swaddling her like brown velvet, covering the horrific filmstrip in her mind with cottony softness.

"Your eyes are asking me to stay close," he said softly.

Simone turned toward the ocean. A tangle of red crab legs sat on a table where a Bahiana in a white lace head wrap and dress poked a spatula into a black skillet on a white cube-shaped stove. Golden *acarajé* bean patties stuffed with shrimp paste sizzled in dark orange palm oil. The heat made the white sand appear as if it were melting; a bead of sweat rolled down Simone's neck, into the hollow of her clavicle. The heavy-spicy aroma wet her tongue.

"A hunger," Sonny said even more deeply, "for love, and answers to questions that your soul whispers in the darkness of midnight—"

Simone wanted to inhale him, to press her flesh right through him.

"Come with me." He put his arm around her shoulders.

Guilt gripped her stomach as they traversed the twelve-foot width of boardwalk. Surely everyone around them knew she was about to get herself into trouble: the three American-looking guys with bleached hair, flowered shorts and surfboards under their arms; the cluster of brown-skinned couples speaking French and petting a bright blue macaw; and the young woman pushing a stroller with a curly-haired toddler chomping a stick of yellow sugar cane.

"*Dois, por favor,*" Sonny said to a teenaged boy in front of a hut covered with palm fronds. On the sand before him sat waist-high bunches of fresh coconuts—bright green and yellow, as big as basketballs.

The wiry teen with corn-rowed black hair wore a tank top emblazoned with a soccer ball and RONALDO, Brazil's World Player of the Year for two years back in the 1990s.

"Years ago," Sonny said, "I met Pélé in the Maracana in Rio. It's sensational."

The teen pulled a machete from the hut's small arched door, placed two coconuts on a damp stump—

Whack! The tops of the shells thudded on the sand. The boy raised the coconuts before spilling a drop. He stuck a purple straw in each, then cupped each coconut in his palms, his leathery fingers extending upward around the yellow skins.

Sonny paid him four times what the sign said for each, then offered a coconut to Simone.

"No," she said, refusing to let the smell, the sight, spin her mind and memories back to that fateful moment by the pool when the ambassador's father keeled over, casting her deeper into her childhood hell. She had not eaten one cookie, or anything coconut- or cashew-flavored, since. "You don't understand—"

"What is haunting you, *fofa?*"

"Don't call me that. You don't even know my name."

"Our souls have already spent eternity together," he said, holding up the coconut. "Names cheapen the visceral bond I feel with you—"

"What movie is that line from?" Simone snapped. "I am a complete stranger—"

"Let me toast you with this syrupy nectar of the tropical gods. I made a wish to the goddess of the sea, and Iemanjá sent you."

The warm breeze tickled Simone's stomach. Someone behind her bumped her bare behind, in true Brazilian custom of standing much closer than Americans and not saying excuse me when they touched. She stepped forward. She clutched the small leather purse over her shoulder. "I would never walk around almost naked—"

"I see terror in your eyes," he said as the samba drumbeat grew louder, "but a craving for sensuous abandon in the rest of you."

The hot sun roused goosebumps from her shoulders to her sand-dusted toes. Simone indulged in the sensory extravaganza of his masculine scent, his tall solidness, and the way his shorts gathered and hugged his hips below his toned stomach and belly button just big enough to hold a cherry. A hot bolt of liquid fire zigzagged through her, igniting in a burning swell under the satiny sling of fabric between her legs. She closed her eyes . . .

I'm having a Sonny-gasm. . . .

"That's better," he smiled. "Here, you must be parched after that Olympic sprint on the beach. I should be running. After Jenn, maybe I'm next."

He held out his arms, a coconut in each hand, faced the sun, and closed his eyes. "I love Brazil. Even the air feels more sensuous—"

If only Simone could still the jitter in her legs telling her to run, or melt the guard against how this acquaintance could interfere with her work back home.

Click! Click!

"Sonny Whittaker," a youthful female voice cooed. Two tanned twentysomethings slipped next to him, smiling. A third woman snapped pictures, as one woman with two high side ponytails and a thin gold belly chain plucked a coconut from his hand and sipped for the camera.

Sonny's lust-glazed gaze rolled over swollen breasts, belly buttons, tiny triangles of fabric covering nipples and hairless vees between thighs.

"Adios," the woman with the camera whispered, blowing a kiss as the group of them sauntered away, the round curves of their bare behinds rising up and down around *fio dental*. Red lipstick on one of their rear cheeks said, "SONNY." The woman turned back, spanked herself, and kissed her fingertips.

"They'd give me a heart attack," Sonny said.

Simone stiffened. Why was she suddenly oblivious to the obligation she owed the court to maintain unbiased and fair regard for this soon-to-be defendant? And why were the women's lusty stares intensifying her arousal for him?

I have to tell Charlie, I will not oversee Sonny Whittaker's trial. Because I'm falling . . .

The throng of samba dancers and drummers was getting closer, their shrieks and music raising the tiny hairs on her body, making her remember the night she thought she would die . . .

Simone pulled away, hurrying toward a row of merchants' tables.

"Look," he said, lifting a foot-high wooden statue of the Afro-Brazilian deity Exu—said to mediate between humans and the gods—carved with an enormous erect penis. Another statue on the table was of a woman with babies carved in her round stomach, a tiny head extending down between her legs. "Think they got together?"

"I'll stop in DC," she said. "Surprise my mother—"

"The sadness in your eyes," Sonny said. "You're aching for something—"

"The court finds you guilty of life imitating art," Simone said. "You said that in *Promise Me Paradise*. I was only fifteen, but I was as mesmerized as the other women in the theater."

"I was thirty-five."

"Is that your secret?" Simone fingered a pair of beige pants with a matching blouse. "Making women worship you by reciting movie lines?"

"Katharine Hepburn said it best in *The Philadelphia Story*: 'I don't want to be worshiped. I want to be loved.' Grace Kelly said the same thing in *High Society*." He smiled, glancing toward the approaching samba dancers and ever-louder music. "I feel embarrassed—"

That would be the least of your emotions if you walked into court Monday and saw me on the bench . . .

"I'm a little rusty," he said, "talking to a beautiful woman. Lately, raising my daughters alone, I've confused myself with a monk."

Simone laughed. *Welcome to the first meeting of Abstinence Anonymous.*

"I don't know if I believe you," she said.

"The scales of justice," he said, taking her hand, staring at her gold ring. "Are you a Libra? Or married to one?"

"Cancer. There's an eclipse tonight, in Scorpio. And Mercury is in retrograde—"

"I suppose you've got a pack of tarot cards in your purse," Sonny said. "That 'what's your sign' astrology thing is as seventies as the ARIES sticker I put in the back window of the Corvette I bought to celebrate my first film."

"Cancer is water, Aries is fire," she half-whispered, savoring the sensation of her own breath passing over her hot lips as she gazed into his intrigued eyes. "And together, three things can happen."

He wrapped her hand in his long, elegant fingers, holding it close to his face. "Her water puts out his fire, or, his heat boils her away. Or—"

"They make an enticingly warm bath." The chief judge's voice rang in her mind, chilling the heat pulsing through her body. She turned to the merchant. "I'll take this. And those shoes, size eight." Simone fished a credit card from her purse, which was pressing against her passport and plane ticket. She took her package, then darted back onto the boardwalk.

"Wait," Sonny said behind her as the afternoon sun inched toward the watery horizon.

She walked faster, but stopped. A few feet away: a bolt of mint green and brunette tendrils, a silver camera. Paulette. And beside her, Roxanne Jones, in her tight red dress, cameraman at her side.

"What are *they* doing together?" Simone whispered.

Her heart pounded. Both their eyes glinted with a gossip-hungry sharpness that could only mean trouble. Paulette was really doing it—she was joining the ranks of the paparazzi. And Simone did not want to test the limits of their friendship by offering up herself in a bikini next to the movie Adonis they were no doubt looking for.

So she slipped into the ear-splitting, spinning, sweating throng of samba dancers.

22

Inside the light blue lobby of the Sanctuary Island clinic, Marie Cart-wright shuddered with a blood-chilling sense of déjà-vu as the doctor described Jenn Ryder's condition. If that wasn't heartwrenching enough, the chalk-white tension gripping Norris's face warned of the same reaction he'd had a year ago, when the hurricane destroyed the set and halted production of his tropical thriller, *Anywhere.*

"The burns are very deep," the doctor said, pulling back the blue surgical mask and cap that he'd worn to examine Jenn in the ER. He pressed a finger and thumb into his bloodshot eyes, obscuring his dark-stubbled face. "We've stopped the bleeding as best we can for now. Now the folks at the UCLA Burn Center—"

"When can she get back to work?" Norris demanded, crossing his arms. His soft brown eyes hardened, narrowed, just as they had during a therapy session when he had pounded the couch after Mother Nature had ravished his movie schedule. "A month? Two?"

"Norris," Marie said softly, "I think we need to call her family—"

"I told her father," the doctor said. "Ms. Ryder's condition is very grave. It appears the highly corrosive substance, probably acid, has gone far deeper than we initially believed."

"Christ," Norris said. He raised trembling hands to his muscular biceps, gripping his own flesh, shaking his head. "Whoever did this will *pay*."

"If Ms. Ryder survives," the doctor said, "she has a very long road to recovery ahead. And, Mr. Haynes, I think this was an attempt on her life."

"Marie," Norris's eyes softened. "I'm sorry this is happening on the eve of our day—"

"No, Norris," Marie said, "we're safe. And we need to make sure we stay safe. Like I said, I don't mind postponing—"

"My movie, my wedding, my life, will not be delayed by an acid-splashing stalker."

Marie grasped his shoulders. "Norris, baby. Don't be like my father. He ignored the danger. He gave a sermon the day Terrance said he'd kill him. And Daddy paid for his stubbornness with his life!"

Norris pulled away. He spun toward a painting of blue flowers over a row of plastic chairs where a mother was humming to a crying infant. "No one stops Norris Haynes."

23

On the beach boardwalk, the labyrinthine swarm of thighs and breasts and drums surged like a tidal wave of raw sex, and Sonny wanted to ride it to its awesome peak. But not without her. And especially not with a TV camera rolling. He would samba into the crowd, lose the media vultures, and find her—

"You make the sun," Sonny chanted in Portuguese along with dozens of men and women who were practicing for Carnival, which was still more than a week away, "rise and set on my heart." Inhaling the Babylonian perfume of sweat, he swayed his hips, becoming one with the frantic beat of brown and ivory and black hands pounding drums.

"I'll find her." He turned toward the ocean. There, by the two men shaking maracas, she stared through the round holes of a glittery butterfly mask on a stick.

Nearby, the TV camera was crawling like a black beetle along the top of the crowd, held up by a man's arms; Roxanne's black coif bobbed toward Sonny. A brunette with a silver camera followed.

But they got jostled toward the beach.

"Stop running away," Sonny said deeply, dancing close to the woman. Sandwiched by dozens of people, he grasped her trembling hands, dancing her behind a rainbow banner fluttering from a pole in someone's hands.

"Let go," the woman shouted. She tried to pull from his grip, her right leg poised to run.

"You make the sun," he chanted, staring into her eyes, "rise and set on my heart."

Sonny was dizzy amidst the carnal buffet: a yellow star tattooed on a supple, nutmeg-hued shoulder . . . a suede bikini, its beaded fringe bouncing on ripe thighs . . . bare breasts as pointy and beige as Egyptian pyramids . . . women riding men's shoulders, masculine hands clamped over juicy calves, the women jingling tambourines over bobbing heads . . .

The music pounded through him, convulsing his arms, legs, hips, shoulders. Even his stomach muscles were sliding and stretching. Sonny was a giant, oozing throb of abandon, thrusting deeper toward that peak of sheer ecstasy when a psychedelic spark sets fire to the mind, body and spirit. And in a flash—whether real or imagined, physical or mental—one glimpses heaven.

"Whatever is haunting you, let go!" He raised her hands—

Her pillowy lips pursed, eyes sharpened. She snatched her hands down. Crossed her arms, cheeks reddening as she scanned the impenetrable fence of shoulders and breasts and heads.

"You make the sun rise and set on my heart," he chanted, narrowing his eyes down at her, devouring her mouth with his gaze. With this woman, he would make a fresh start, paint a new picture of himself as the changed man that he was. *Yes!* He tossed his head back. He stared into the sun, wishing he could extend his arms, fall back and ride this float of humanity to the sky.

But not alone . . . He turned toward her. Tears welled in her eyes, but the mask obscured her face. Her bottom black eyelashes clumped over pinkened rims.

Sonny froze. His blood chilled. His lips ceased the chant.

Samba interruptus.

"I thought I could help you forget," Sonny said as he whisked her from the crowd. They passed about twenty men in orange pants doing a martial arts dance on the sand. His body still throbbed with the delights of that group orgasm. "It was insensitive of me—"

"Carnival makes me relive bad things that happened when I was small." Her voice was velvet against the metal twang of the dancers' music.

"Stay in this moment. The past is gone. Now is all we have."

Behind her, the men were doing cartwheels across the green grass. Resting on their hands, they snapped their orange-draped legs like scissors against a backdrop of blue sea and sky.

"Everything I say and do right now," she said, "can come back to haunt me next week, next month, next year."

"You can't live like that," Sonny said. "Xavier's troops in *The Colony* do the *capoéra* death dance. I admire that. Because I would die, before I would live by someone else's rules, if those rules are wrong or unjust. I am the master of my fate—"

"My track coach made us recite *Invictus* before our meets," she said, breaking a slight smile. "We always won. National NCAA champs."

"The men in my family, they ran away from slavery," Sonny said. "Escaped to the wild, wild west. Cowboys. My great grandfather, Wild Bill, he married an Indian—"

"You're lucky to know your roots."

"My mother's people came from Montserrat," he said. "They all met up in Harlem, and here comes Sonny Whittaker. What about your family?"

"It's getting late." The woman glimpsed a long table; palm-sized statues of ebony hands with gold fingernails prayed up toward her.

"Those ward off the evil eye," Sonny said.

"I have one on my desk." Goosebumps rose on her shoulders. "Ever heard the myth about the plantation owner's daughter who killed her family? She caused a bloody slave revolt?"

"Esmerelda," Sonny said. "Her mother was an African slave, and—I was doing research for *The Colony* over in Salvador. I still get chills when I remember the tour guide describing how she died on a pyre in the *pelourinho*—"

"The whipping post," the woman said.

"To think about the blood, the screams, as they punished runaway slaves. Where every slave that came into Brazil, five hundred years ago, passed through there, to the auction block—"

"I was only six," the woman said. "So small, and this old woman, during Carnival, she had on a shimmery green snake mask. She snatched me close, reeking of *cachaça*. She hissed the story about Esmerelda, with this hatred in her eyes—" She closed her eyes hard, then opened them. "Why am I telling you this?" She strode quickly toward the bridge.

"She never screamed," Sonny said, "but her eyes were like the full moon—"

"Everyone who looked at her died," the woman said, lowering dark lashes.

"It's myth," Sonny said. "Let go of the fear."

"*Senhora,*" begged a child with a small, angelic face. His dirt-caked toes and torn blue shorts and the dust on his matted black hair demanded a long, hot bath. Would this boy and his friends fall prey to police death squads who viewed homeless street children as pests who mugged tourists and blemished the country's mystic allure?

"Buy something to eat." The woman gave each child about a dollar in Brazilian reais.

"*Obrigado!*" the boys said. Their eyes brightened; Sonny imagined them running home to a *flavela*, dirt-poor slums ringing the city. Into a rusty tin shanty, and flashing the money to feed ten family members in a single, stinking room. If they even had a home.

"My heart breaks when I see these kids," Sonny said.

"Open a children's shelter."

"Back home," Sonny said, "we have a rule. No new clothes or toys unless we donate something to charity. Do you have children?"

"Veronica and Mia and Paul and Tyrone, to name a few. I've sort of adopted them, at a place where I volunteer. I give them the love that my own mother never—"

"Have dinner with me and my daughters. They would love to meet—"

"Thank you," she said, glancing at the marina, now shrouded by a golden glow. "But I can't." She turned, and walked toward the setting sun.

24

On the front porch of Erica's bungalow, Kindred glanced at her pink leather and silver watch: it was past time to get the girls and take them back to their own bungalow for dinner, a bath and the space shuttle launch on TV.

She'd been sitting here with Jared for hours, since Erica had told them to go away and come back later. But no way was Kindred going to abandon Asia and India, after what had happened to Jenn. Not to mention the psychological scarring that could occur with their mother.

"It's time," Kindred said, standing up, stepping toward the closed door. She knocked.

The door opened only wide enough to reveal the skinny width of

Erica's tanned face. Her hair was pulled back in a high ponytail around a cosmetic-free scowl. She squinted, her eyelids pale without the fake lashes.

"They're still sleeping," Erica snapped.

"Wake them up," Kindred said. "We follow a schedule every day. If they nap until dark, they'll never get back to sleep tonight. They need rest for the wedding. And we're about to change time zones—"

"Don't tell me what my children need," Erica said. She crossed her arms over a skin-tight white tank top and belly-baring shorts.

"Please," Kindred said softly. "If India misses the space shuttle launch—"

"She can watch it here," Erica said. "I'll call you at Sonny's bungalow if I need you to come back. Otherwise they can spend the night with me."

"That's not the agreement that you made with Mr. Whittaker," Kindred said.

"Go." The word shot with the force of a baseball through Erica's pillowy lips, slamming Kindred's senses. Erica closed the door.

Kindred covered her hot face with her hands. A sense of loss and terror swirled through her, making her feel cold.

"Hey, baby girl," Jared said, putting his arms around her. His warm chest, his Ralph Lauren cologne, comforted her. Until she remembered the twins, giggling on the beach earlier.

"I hate her," Kindred whispered. "She just wants to ruin our lives. The girls are happy the way things are, with me—"

"Let's go eat," Jared said. "Josh is in there. He won't let anything happen."

"I'm too mad," Kindred said, as they stepped off the porch. "You go to the restaurant, if you want. I need to go up to the set."

"For what?" Jared said, taking her hand.

"Stop," Kindred snapped. "I told you, no public displays." She scanned the hedges, the courtyard, the dark rose band of sky glowing over couples walking on the beach. "Even if Mr. Whittaker isn't around. He's been gone so long. I'm worried—"

"He's a grown man," Jared said with gentle eyes. "I'd need to take a walk if I were him, too. Or get some tequila shots. Or that *cachaça*—"

"I'll be back in a while," Kindred said.

"No," Jared said, striding alongside her onto the pebbled walk. "You're not goin' anywhere alone. I'll go up to the set with you. What—"

"India left her barrettes on the makeup table," Kindred said. "I told her—"

"Kindred, baby girl," Jared said as they approached the beach. "How long you gonna cut me off?"

"Someone wants to kill us!" she said, trembling. "So keep your brain focused on making sure they don't! If you've got sex on your mind all the time—"

Jared cupped his hands to his ears.

"That won't help either!" Kindred grasped his wrists, yanking his arms to his sides. "You need to hear. Now come on, if you're coming."

They trudged up the bluffside staircase to the darkened set.

"She said they're on the table, over by the barbecue," Kindred said, squinting at the tree-shrouded garden patio. "I don't know how to turn on the lights if the house is locked—"

A deep, lusty laugh echoed in the shadows.

"Shhh," Jared said softly. He froze, then raised an open hand to stop her.

"It's probably just some techies, hanging out," she whispered with an annoyed tone.

"Let's go," Jared whispered. "We don't know who the fuck—"

"Look," Kindred whispered. She nodded toward a flash of milky flesh in the shadows of the lush garden.

It was a man's bare butt, in front of the long rattan table where the twins and Jenn and Sonny had sat earlier. The man's khaki pants were bunched around his ankles. And female hands wrapped around his behind. Long fingernails glistened in the dim light of sunset glowing mauve and burnt orange over the balcony.

"Khaki," Jared whispered. "I *know* who that is—"

Dark thighs straddled the man's ankles, her knees pressing into the tiles. Bouncy black hair and a bare shoulder moved back and forth at his hip.

"You like that?" a deep, female voice cooed between tiny gasps and moans. "I know you want an exclusive piece of this ass, too—"

"Damn!" Jared whispered.

Kindred's heart pounded. There was no mistaking the brown hair flowing over the back of the man's muscular shoulders. Or the raspy voice, saying, "Yeah, baby, I'm about to come into the end zone—"

Norris Haynes and Roxanne Jones.

"The night before his wedding!" Jared said.

Kindred wanted to storm toward them, screaming. Her every muscle quaked with rage and a burning sense of unfairness and hypocrisy.

"No way!" she whispered through tight lips, as Jared put his arm around her to head back to the stairs. "Norris is financing Erica's war to destroy us. He's the one who's footing the bill for Erica to make Mr. Whittaker out as an unfit father—"

"Shh, c'mon," Jared said. "Let's not bust on ourselves."

Kindred felt sick. "I'll die before I let that sleaze take away my family."

25

The white wooden planks of the dock were warm and smooth under Simone's backside as she sat down. Her bare legs glowed golden as they dangled over the water, which shimmered like puddles of rose and orange and aqua all the way to the horizon. At her sides, rows of white Plexiglas hulls gleamed alongside sails and silver rails and polished teak. The yacht that had brought her was dark and quiet. As was Sonny Whittaker's boat.

"This is ridiculous," Simone said, pressing her heel into the dock to stand up. Narcissus could be watching, waiting, right now. He could sneak up, push her in the water—

Yet a lovesick languor made her stare toward the vast peach sky, with its feathery clumps of mauve, magenta streaks, and misty green zigzags.

She needed to take one of these boats. If she could remember all those lessons Brian had given her at the Andersons' homes on Martha's Vineyard and Fisher Island, where they would watch the purple haze of night envelop the Earth.

A fish splashed a few yards out. Simone jumped.

Until large, warm palms cupped her shoulders from behind.

No, a defendant isn't supposed to touch a judge like that.

Simone closed her eyes. She swallowed the moan that rose up from her soul. Sonny Whittaker's musky-spicy scent wafted around her; his heat tickled her back. And electric zigzags tingled down from his hot hands, around her heart, to her bare toes.

"You shouldn't be out here alone," he said, his deep voice vibrating through her chest. "After what happened today—"

"I'm looking for a ride," she said. "To get away."

He knelt behind her, then sat down, stretching his bare legs around her in a V. His warm stomach on her bare back provoked a gush of hot air from deep within her lungs that passed over her parted lips with a soft pant.

"You can scour the Met and the National Gallery and the Louvre," he said, his left cheek almost touching the right side of her face as he stared toward the sky over her shoulder, "and never find such a masterpiece."

His large, hot hand wrapped over the top of hers; he raised her right hand toward the horizon, lacing his fingers with hers, as if they were waving at the sky.

"My grandmother, in the islands, she can read the sunset," he whispered. "As a kid, I spent every summer with her and Grandpopa at Sunset Cove—"

Rays of creamsicle and lilac and crimson beamed between their fingers and streaked across the sky. His breath tickled her ear and her throat; his chin just touched the back of her head.

"They had a restaurant next to the house," he said. "We'd sit on the terrace while she peeled big buckets of garlic. Imagine, a volcano on one side, the most picturesque lagoon on the other. It's paradise. And the sunsets there—"

"I should get going," Simone said, pulling her hand away.

"Wait, please." He pointed her hand toward the huge red circle hovering over the dark horizon. "If you watch closely, and your karma is just right, there's a flash. A lavender flash—"

Simone laughed. "What do you have to smoke first?"

"No, no," he said, "Watch. If you see it, the universe is promising to smile on your future with peace and love."

"I used to sit on the beach believing things like that," Simone said, as swirls of marigold darkened to pumpkin.

"Believe now, with me," Sonny said. "As a painter, this is the most mystical time of day. And if you know anything about Buddhism, twilight symbolizes so many things. Grandmama said, what happens now is more momentous—"

Simone pressed her knuckles back into his palm. "You want to grasp it, but it's slipping away too fast—"

"All an illusion," he whispered into her hair. "The colors in the sky are changing and shifting by the second, just like our thoughts and feelings. We can try to hold on to the now, to the beauty—" He paused as the sun inched downward. "But all we can do is admire the shades and textures as they come."

Fast-paced drums and trombones and trumpets began playing back on the beach.

"In my movie, *The Colony*," he said, "twilight is a reflection of humanity."

A plum mist rolled over the horizon, fading up into pink and gold and blue. Great cotton-candy plumes glowed golden. The orange-red disc shimmered into the black arc of Earth.

And a sudden flash, like a lavender lightening bolt, cast a lilac glow over the water, the sky, their outstretched hands.

Simone gasped.

"My God," Sonny whispered. "I've never seen it so bright. It means—"

"I don't want to know," Simone said, getting up. Her pounding heart sent staticky throbs into her ears. The screeching birds, the lapping water, the samba drums, trombones, trumpets. . . .

"May I please borrow your boat?" The warm tropical air chilled her bare back. "I can drive it myself, I just need—"

"But we saw the flash," he said. "Together."

"I need to go to Salvador."

He took her hand. "Too dangerous, I won't allow it."

She glared at him. "No one tells me what they will or will not allow. Please, take me on your boat. I would be eternally grateful."

"I might hold you to that." Sonny took her hand as she stepped up onto the side of the boat, then down onto the beige carpeting, scratchy under her bare feet. He headed to the driver's seat, flipping on lights and switches.

"Sonny!" A man hopped off a nearby Sea Ray and jogged barefoot down the dock.

Sonny smiled, patting the man's back, chatting.

Simone grasped the red and black handles on levers next to the steering wheel. Her memory spun back twenty years, to when Brian had taught her to use the throttle, how to turn and stop by controlling the starboard and port side motors. Just turn the key and . . .

"Need extras for *The Colony*?" The sky turned from plum to eggplant.

"Don't know," Sonny said, pulling in the bumpers and ropes, freeing the boat from the dock. "Things may change."

Simone pressed the pads of her thumb and forefinger around the silver key in the ignition just beneath the big chrome steering wheel. The sky turned star-studded black.

Boom!

She froze. Icy terror gushed through her every cell.

Boom! Boom! The sky shimmered gold and red and orange. Simone stared up, stunned, at the blinding light. Fingers of fire arcing down, dancing on the black water.

Fireworks over the public beach. Just like those moments of terror.

The streetcorner. The gang of boys. Her screams. Running. Faster, faster. Then her mother, Bianca, Mr. Anderson, refusing to believe what had happened to eight-year-old Little Simone. Refusing to protect her, or assure her that she was safe. Making her sleep in that first-floor room with the open patio doors. She was sure the boys would climb in and finish what they had started . . .

Boom! Boom! Simone dove toward the steering wheel. The cool metal key turned between her fingers, she grasped the throttle, revved the motor.

"Hey!" Sonny shouted over the exploding sky and rumbling motor.

The bow pointed toward open water. She pulled the levers—

The engine roared. The boat shot over dark waves. The wind cut into her face; a salty spray stung her cheeks.

"Yes!" Adrenaline gushed through her.

But in seconds, Sonny was behind her, swallowing her knuckles in the huge fleshy grasp of his palms over the steering wheel.

"Only I drive this boat," he said, his lips tickling her ear.

She closed her eyes, her every cell soaked with guilt. Her memory spun back to ethics class back in law school. What had she learned about tumbling on a beach, wearing only a thong bikini on top of a defendant?

And feeling his manhood throbbing under her thigh? What about driving his boat?

"I said, only I drive this boat." The dark choppy water stretched before them, dotted with red and white lights on faraway boats.

"Too late," she said, gripping the wheel. "I've got it now."

He reached for the levers, gunning the motor. The wind forced her back into him.

"I've never let anyone touch this steering wheel," he said deeply. "Never."

"You've got a new driver now," she whispered, not sure if he could hear her against the wind. She gripped the wheel so hard her fingers ached.

26

Sonny Whittaker turned the steering wheel, making the boat curve sharply to the left. The force pushed the woman back, cradled in his body, as the bright lights of Salvador glowed to their right. The pastel colonial-style buildings, the lighthouse, the elevator shaft connecting the clifftop part of town with the bustling bayside street and shops—it all became a watercolor blur, silenced by the wind and roaring motors.

"Turn back," she shouted.

"No," Sonny said, "I'm taking you to a *pai de santo* I know. He's got a place, on a tiny island just a ways back."

"I'm not going to some quack priest in the middle of the bay!" the woman shouted. She pulled at his hands, but he steered away from the city.

"He's the best spirit guide around," Sonny said. "He can take us to a *candomblé* ceremony. You can face your fears—"

The woman turned around, her eyes inches below his, her body pinned between him and the steering wheel. "I'm facing *you*! And I want you to take me to the mainland. Now!"

Sonny fought a biting sensation in his jaw and lips. Her mouth and her bare shoulders were just a bend of the neck away from being devoured. He tightened his fingers around the wheel. "Come back to the resort with me. There are no flights until morning—"

Her hair blew into his mouth; he sucked on the saltiness.

"I don't need to watch a priest drip chicken blood on someone's head," the woman said, "to feel better. The pipes, the chanting, the dancing, it's not for me."

"I love it," Sonny said. Even though Grandmama had warned him, communing with spirits during *candomblé* was no game. She'd said the trance-style worshiping practiced by the followers of the Umbanda religion was very powerful. "It's sensational."

"No," she said, "All the women in white lace, they reminded me of the old lady in the *Pelourinho*, who told me about Esmerelda—"

"That's myth," Sonny said, still turning away from the city. "Entertainment. But *candomblé*, it's chic now. Besides, if Brazil is the place that hurt you, then Brazil is the place that will heal you. But leaving alone, it's dangerous—"

"Take me to Salvador!" the woman shouted. "Now!"

"I don't want to let you out of my sight," he said. "But I don't even know your name."

Something mysterious glimmered in her eyes as she stared at him. Her lips parted.

He had to kiss her. Now.

The boat struck a small wave, the bow going slightly airborne, then slamming back onto the water. The impact pressed her head back into his shoulder.

He leaned down slightly. But something somber flashed in her eyes.

"I'll ride in the taxi with you to the airport," he said over the gentle splash and humming engine as he steered back toward Salvador. "It's too dangerous—"

As he turned into the marina, she pulled away to retrieve her shoes from the floor. Two hot, damp spots marked the steering wheel. He grasped them, absorbing her energy and heat.

"Bring it over here," a marina attendant called in Portuguese, pointing to a slip between a towering yacht and another cigarette boat. Music, voices and clinking dishes charged the air.

"Sonny Whittaker," a woman called down from the upper deck of the yacht. More women laughed and blew kisses. Sonny guided the stern toward the dock.

The thud of feet on the dock made him spin. The woman, she was sprinting away.

"Wait!" Sonny tossed the keys to the attendant. "Watch the boat."

He ran after her, bounding over a coil of white rope on the wooden planks, weaving through a cluster of people. Sonny sprinted up the stairs. On the crowded platform adjacent to a busy street and row of ancient, colonial-style buildings, he dodged a man in a shiny maroon suit, thrusting little red bottles of what he promised was a magic potion for eternal youth.

The woman flitted like an apparition past voluptuous ladies with heavy eye makeup and lipstick who were leading foreign men toward narrow alleyways.

Sonny started to call out to the police officers, like those on every corner of the cobbled street, to stop her. But they would never hear him over the ear-blasting rhythms of the *trio eléctrico*: three men playing drums on the back of a flatbed truck parked at the curb. A man using a box of kitchen matches as a tambourine turned to watch the woman run.

She wove around people clapping and singing and helping themselves to the band's barrels of sugarcane liquor. Sonny dashed past them, ignoring one shirtless reveler who offered a clear plastic cup as his sweaty face broke into a grin.

She was at the taxi stand. Getting in one.

Sonny ran faster.

She closed the door.

He grabbed the handle, knocking on the glass.

She looked up, *moonbeam gray* eyes full of tears, glistening like pools of mercury. Thick lashes came down, like black fringe against the smooth buttercream of her cheeks.

And the cab sped into a sea of red taillights.

27

Through the rain-blurred window of a taxi, Simone Thompson watched familiar mansions whiz past on Embassy Row in Washington, DC. Waves of dread and determination washed through her as the high spiraled towers of the Andersons' chateau-style palace appeared, just beyond a sprawling, pine-shrouded colonial.

"The next one," she told the driver.

He started to turn at tall hedges where antique lamplights illuminated the foot of a brick-patterned drive.

"I hope they got a coat for you in there," the driver said, pinching the bill of his brown tweed cap that matched his corduroy jacket. He pushed a dashboard lever into the red zone; the heat roared. "When I seen you at the airport in that summer outfit, sheesh! I thought, wherever she come from, she didn't watch the Weather Channel."

Simone rubbed goosebumps on her arms. "This is an emergency trip," she said. She hoped by now a maid back in Brazil would have found her luggage, abandoned twenty-four hours ago at Sanctuary, and made good use of her clothes.

"I've been too distracted to think about clothes," Simone said. She had to excuse herself from the Sonny Whittaker case. Her feelings now were absolutely too strong to conduct an impartial trial involving him.

"What are you, tryin' to get killed!" the driver shouted as the tires screeched.

Simone clutched the back of the shiny vinyl seat.

"Watch it, guy!" the driver shouted.

A valet squinted in the headlights. In a rain-slicked yellow jacket and hood, he held up a hand. Behind him, limousines and luxury cars curved bumper-to-bumper in front of the beige stone mansion. High windows cast golden rectangles on a white tent at the double front doors. A valet helped a woman in a fur coat and a tuxedoed man slip into a Mercedes.

Simone's gut ached; crashing one of Bianca's parties would hardly put her mother in the mood to share the secret she'd kept for thirty-five years.

"Hey, guy!" The driver's breath plumed into the darkness through his rolled-down window. "I'm not just droppin' the lady off in the rain."

The valet opened the back door. His eyes widened as he peeked in. "Oh," he said. "I'll be right back." He sprinted to the front doors, then returned with an oversized umbrella. He paid the driver, then shielded Simone as they dashed between parked cars.

"Didn't know you were coming home, Judge," the valet said.

"My home is in LA," Simone said with a tone as icy as the puddle sloshing into her beach shoes. Under the tent, two men opened the front doors that had been off limits to Simone when she had lived here.

"Welcome, Miss—?" A woman with silver hair and a champagne-colored gown frowned at the capri pants and shirt that Simone had purchased on the beach. The woman spoke over live jazz booming through the crowded hall with a high, gothic-arched stone ceiling. "Are you with the Committee to Revoke Judicial—"

"Simone! How brave, stepping into the stream of *pirañas*."

Bianca's deep, sultry accent made Simone stiffen and turn. Then, Simone stared up into the large, wide-set moss-green eyes that had made her cry so many times as a child. The way Bianca had always had her dark eyebrows sculpted into a sideways apostrophe shape only accentuated the meanness in her eyes.

Bianca's small, sharp nose pointed slightly downward; her crimson lip liner enlarged her thin upper lip, making it proportionate to the full lower one. A tiny black mole dotted the rise of her left cheek. And neither her smooth skin nor the dark mane spiraling over her left breast revealed that she was fifty-five.

As she stepped close, her burgundy satin spaghetti-strap gown swished about her curvy hips and strappy rhinestone sandals, which tapped the stone floor.

"You have to leave this party," Bianca said, grasping Simone's shoulders and bending down to air-kiss each of her cheeks. Her Bulgari perfume stung Simone's nose. "Our guests, they think people like you are the scum of the earth. Little Simone, what are you wearing?"

"Where's my mother?"

Bianca glanced toward the wide archway to the dining room. "She is meeting with the head of the—" Bianca raised her left hand, causing her inch-wide ruby bracelet to shimmer. "Ruth, you didn't tell me—"

"What are you doing here?" Her mother's voice cut through the music and festive chatter. Her tone slapped up a lifetime of sadness.

Simone's cheeks burned. Her mother's thin hand grasped Bianca's outstretched fingers. Bianca pulled Ruth close.

Simone's blood turned to ice.

My mother. Still a homely miniature wannabe Bianca, the former Miss Brazil. Starting with the burgundy lace inlay of her mother's black velvet cocktail length dress. It cast a reddish hue over the olive oval of her face. Her nose still resembled a man's work boot; perhaps because of the way her mother would nod slightly, her nose rising and falling with a repetitive kicking motion, as verbal kicks shot from between the lips that rarely kissed her only child.

Though she and Bianca were the same age, wrinkles etched Ruth's upper lip, the tiny sacs of skin above the corners of her brown eyes, and the cheeks that shook and reddened when she screamed. Clearly, a professional makeup person had painted the perfect shadows of wine and silver on her mother's eyelids, with the black liner and mascara. But the coldness and disgust glowing in her dark pupils—that was raw Ruth Thompson.

"Let's go in the study." Simone looked down into her mother's eyes. "You have to answer a question."

Rose-shaped, antique garnet earrings shook as her mother looked around; a matching barrette held her shiny black plume of a ponytail. "I have obligations—"

"Exactly," Simone said, taking her mother's other wrist.

"There are guests to greet," Bianca said, yanking Ruth's hand.

"I'm not going to lose at tug of war tonight," Simone said. "Let's go."

Simone's fingers were like a wrench around her mother's wrist, and her thigh muscles flexed as she fought her mother's backward pull. She did not look back to see if Bianca followed them past the towering buffet of cheeses, breads and fruits.

"Excuse us," Simone said loudly, pushing through the crowd. A goateed man and a woman in sequins parted in front of the double doors to the study. Simone pulled her mother inside. She slammed the doors, pushed the bolt, then blocked them with her body.

In the soft recessed light, Brian's image stared down from a gilt frame, his dark eyes aglow with the only tenderness she had known in this luxurious prison. Next to him, the Andersons' only daughter, Rosa, "the warden," stared down with Bianca's wide-set green eyes and dark hair, Mr. Anderson's fleshy nose and round chin.

"She's my servant," Rosa would boast, grinning to the spoiled, rich daughters of other ambassadors and lawmakers and lawyers. As they waited for the fourth-grade teacher to check on their reading group in the library of the Academy, Rosa would pull on Simone's tam that matched her uniform, identical to the other girls' crisp red wool skirts and vests.

"My mom bought her and her mother," Rosa said. "Because they don't have a dad. She lives in my garage. I can make her wipe my nose if I want. Little Simone, my dirty chore girl."

The other girls would shriek, pulling their books and chairs away from Simone.

"She's bad luck, too," Rosa said, "She was the last person who talked to my grandpa when he died. She's poison—"

"I need this job," her mother would answer later in the carriage house, after Simone's tearful retelling of that typical scene.

"Be grateful, girl," her mother would say, wearing her usual crisp white dress shirt and black trousers. "I couldn't afford to send you to private school on my own. We'd be living in the slums—"

"Then I'll go live with my father. I'll go to school where he is."

"Simone, the judge said you have to be with me. He doesn't want to know about you."

Now, Simone glared down at her mother's loveless face.

"Tell me my father's name," Simone demanded through tight lips. "Where he lives. And the truth about why I've never met him. Now."

Her mother's eyes blazed; her skin turned chalk-white.

"Were you raped?" Simone asked flatly.

"God no," her mother sighed.

"Was he married?"

"Bianca is waiting—"

"No, I'm waiting. For answers."

"Yes, he had a wife, but—"

"Was it Mr. Anderson? Did you make some kind of deal, that you could raise me here and be Bianca's slave, to make up for his affair?"

Her mother's earrings shook as she snapped, "You ought to be grateful, Simone. Maybe you wouldn't be where you are if the Andersons hadn't—"

"What? Treated you and your bastard child like indentured servants?" Simone glanced up at the arched windows facing the back yard. She pointed to the lighted carriage house, remembering the odors of car oil and exhaust fumes wafting into her tiny bedroom at all hours. "You live over the garage! Does she still pay you a hundred dollars a week?"

"I did it for you, Simone. I dropped out of school, nowhere to go. With a baby, I couldn't—"

"My secretary is a single mother," Simone said. "Two kids. Law school at night. So don't make excuses—"

"If I had taken a nine-to-five job as a secretary, you couldn't have gone to the Academy, or traveled all over the world—"

"I would've traded all that for a real mother and father in a heartbeat," she said, closing her eyes over burning tears. She remembered Sonny Whittaker, kissing the tops of his daughters' heads, paternal love glowing in his eyes . . .

"I want answers." Simone leaned closer; her mother's face darkened in the soft light. "Your parents. Is what you told me—that your college fund was used up after they were sued for that fatal car accident—is that true? Is that why they moved to your grandmother's house that we visited every summer in Italy?"

"Yes," her mother said, closing her eyes.

"What about my father? Who is he? What's his ethnic background?"

Her mother sharpened her gaze on the brass-plated plaques lining the wall, all engraved: Gregory Anderson, American Ambassador to Brazil.

"Some things are better left unsaid," her mother said.

"Like 'I love you?' And 'your father's name is—' "

"Simone, it would shock—"

"Little Simone," Bianca shouted, pounding the door. "Ruth. Let me in.' "

"Is he really a judge?" Simone asked.

"Not—"

"Ruth, is she hurting you?" Bianca demanded.

Simone rolled her eyes. "She never asked that when you were whipping me with a belt."

"You are impossible," Ruth said, her thin shoulders quaking. "Let me out."

"You started to say 'not,' " Simone said. "Not what?"

Ruth's eyes widened. They were bloodshot, glassy. She placed a palm on Simone's cheek. "He didn't—" Her voice cracked. "He didn't know I was—he doesn't know you were born."

Simone fought a numbing geyser of shock. She stepped forward, grasping the sides of her mother's arms. "Why didn't you tell him?"

The lock clinked; the doors burst open. "There," Bianca said, holding a key.

"What's his name?" Simone cried over the party noise. "Tell me!"

Two men in dark blue suits appeared at her sides.

"Don't touch me," Simone said without looking at the men. She stared into her mother's eyes. "You will not rest until I get an answer."

Sadness glinted in her mother's tear-glazed eyes. Bianca put an arm around her, but Ruth crossed her arms and strode to the window, staring out at the carriage house.

"Ruth, honey," Bianca called. She snapped her fingers toward the young men in blue suits, both clean-shaven with military-style crew cuts and angry eyes. "It's time for Little Simone to leave."

With a final glance at the back of her mother's trembling shoulders, Simone stepped between the two men and headed for the door.

"Little Simone." Gregory Anderson's deep voice boomed from the doorway. He crossed thick arms over his tuxedo, holding a martini glass at his elbow. His suntanned face was more plump, like his middle, than the last time Simone had seen him, when he'd made a surprise visit to her courtroom a year ago. His dark gray curly hair, parted at one side, skimmed his collar; one ringlet dangled between his eyes, which roved her body. "Er, Judge Thompson I should say. On the run from Narcissus, are you?"

As she had done so many times as a child, Simone studied his thick, capillary-marbled nostrils that ended in a bulb, then his flat, circular earlobes, and his U-shaped chin. She had none of the above.

"Thought I'd drop in on the judge haters of America you're entertaining here tonight," Simone said. "Interesting company you keep, ambassador."

"Hey," he said, sipping his drink, "I owed their lobbyist a favor. Any excuse for a party, right? Speaking of party gone bad, my buddies at the CIA have some leads on who melted Jenn Ryder's face."

"That's why I'm here," Simone said, glaring at him, Bianca and her mother. "I've been on the run all my life from your cruelty," Simone said with a sharp tone. "But no more. It's time for all of you to make amends to me, by answering some questions."

"Little Simone," the ambassador mocked. "Relax, have a drink—"

"No," Simone said. "I want to know who my father is. Tonight."

"That's in the past." Her mother strode forward, tears in her eyes. "Just live your life now. Forget—"

"No," Simone said. "Being in Brazil made me realize that I can't forget! I can't forget that you"—she glared at Bianca and Gregory—"blamed me for an old man's death to appease your own guilt—"

"Get out!" Bianca screamed.

"That's quite a weighty accusation, judge," Gregory said, clinking his ice cubes. "You left town before we could make you pay for killing our son, too."

"No!" Simone said. "Brian died because you sent him away from me. His death was fate punishing you for your aristocratic snobbery. You couldn't handle your son being in love with the servant's daughter!"

"I am not a servant," her mother gasped.

Simone raised her palms toward them, shaking her head. "I'm here for one reason: the truth. So tell me, and I'll leave."

Gregory turned down the corners of his mouth, shaking his head.

"Sometimes the truth isn't what you want to hear," he said. "My sources say Jenn was seeing a local guy. She told him to get lost. He got revenge. Happens a lot in India. A girl rejects a guy's marriage proposal, he says fine, if I can't have you, nobody can." Gregory made a tossing motion with his glass. "Boom, acid in the face."

"This was not random," Simone said. "And if you know so much, have your sources find Narcissus and arrest—"

"Nothing is that simple." Gregory stirred his drink with a finger. "We have to find out exactly why Narcissus is after you, Norris Haynes, Sonny Whittaker—"

Bianca cursed in Portuguese.

Gregory laughed. "Little Simone. A grown-up woman, full of sass. Boy, if Brian could see you now. But," he said, watching the clear liquid in his glass swirl around the rim, "you'd better be careful of a Hollywood Lothario like Sonny Whittaker. 'Else he'll twist you around his finger like a diamond pinkie ring, and you'll feel as cheap and used as—" The ambassador cast a piercing stare at his wife.

"Shut up!" Bianca shouted. She darted past them, out of the room.

Gregory stared at Simone. "And hey, Sonny Whittaker will be a free man after the divorce. A poor man, after Brett Robinson gets through with him, but a free man all the same."

"Simone," her mother said softly, stepping to her side. "Don't get caught up in—"

"Ruth, Ruth," Gregory said. "Little Simone has blossomed into full-blown womanhood now. She can handle—"

"Simone," her mother said with a sharp stare. "I said don't get caught up with any of those men. You don't know—"

"You're right, I don't know. And you're going to tell me."

28

Marie Cartwright carefully placed one stiletto wedding slipper in front of the other, forcing her trembling legs to carry her up the aisle. Despite the hundred pairs of eyes and the TV camera watching, she had to tell Norris she could not go through with marrying him.

"My savior," he mouthed, his soft brown eyes glowing with rapture. He stood about a minute's march ahead, on the tropical altar she had designed herself. The platform, built over the resort's swimming pool, placed Norris and the plum-robed minister in front of a two-story waterfall over boulders adorned with vines of fuchsia flowers. From nooks in the rock, feathered and sequined Carnival-inspired masks stared out at guests in gilded bamboo chairs lined up around the patio.

The hot air sparkled with the satiny sound of Asia and India Whittaker singing the wedding march as their nanny played the electric violin. The trio stood just behind Norris, three manes of flower-adorned black ringlet curls flowing over gauzy peach gowns.

Norris's brown waves shrouded the broad shoulders of his black tuxedo as he looked at the girls. He slightly closed his eyes, then opened them wide back toward Marie. It was the same way her father would gaze at her mother, and the way Sonny Whittaker had stared at Simone yesterday as the yacht approached him.

She's not here. Yet another reason Marie could not go through with this—

"Ah," Marie cried softly as her heel caught on the poufs of opalescent tulle softening the aisle. The tulle extended forward like a cloudy plank that linked the patio to the altar, as white orchids and vanilla candles bobbed in the cobalt-blue pool.

She stumbled.

"Whoa there," said trainer-to-the-stars Len Rone. He leaned forward in his chair, grasped her elbow with a thick hand, and pulled her upright. "You okay?"

She nodded, coughing on spicy cooking scents wafting from the candlelit patio on the other side of the pool, where round tables draped in white mosquito netting held huge centerpieces: a crown towering with real fruit à la Carmen Miranda, sparkling silver samba drums, a gold-green-black snake mask framed with white feathers.

"Relax, honey," whispered actress Marlene French, sitting next to the aisle in front of Len. She tilted her teased-up bouffant of salt-and-pepper hair, which complimented her black-and-white striped dress, and winked. "I've never seen Norris so happy."

Marie gasped; the maternal glint in Marlene's eye made Marie envision her mother, in her bedroom back to her childhood in Detroit, inside their small, Cape-Cod-style house on Oakman Boulevard:

"You can rise the highest in this world if you marry a white man," her mother said, raising a clump of tissues to her sharp, freckled nose. She sneezed again, then rattled the lock on a trunk set on the flowered carpet. "Ooh, this old thing is so dusty. Excuse me—"

"Then why didn't you, Momma?" Marie asked, stepping toward the gardenia-scented cloud rising from her mother's dress.

"It's a new world," her mother said, pulling a cream-colored satin gown from the open cedar box. "A world of opportunities—"

"*I'll be Detective Marie Cartwright,*" Marie said, "*I'll hunt down the bad guys and—*"

"*This here,*" her mother said, holding the shimmering column against herself, "*is my wedding gown. You take it, Marie, and wear it when you meet the right man. Take it now, just in case—*"

"*Momma, I'm only eight. I don't need a wedd—*"

"*Just in case,*" her mother said with tear-glazed eyes. She laid the dress over Marie's pink plaid bedspread. "*Find you a good man, with the virtue of Jesus Christ and your daddy's passion for his work.*"

Her mother's pearl choker caught the soft afternoon light coming through the ruffled pink curtains over the window seat full of stuffed animals. "*An important man, who'll protect you from the likes of that man.*"

"*Momma, why can't the police catch him?*"

"*Child,*" her mother said. She tossed her tissues into a butterfly-shaped waste-can, then faced the mirror, pointing toward her choker. "*When the time is right, you'll wear this, too—*"

"*Momma, answer me.*"

Her mother spun around. "*You're old enough to understand, the police have better things to do than find some crazy man who's givin' a black preacher the blues—*"

Now, Marie kept stepping forward, toward the important white man who was getting the blues from some crazy person whom the police had yet to catch. The soft rustle of her mother's wedding gown seemed louder now with each step. The column of ivory satin hugged her breasts, cinched her waist, and curved around her hips and behind.

As if the dress were made for her.

If Momma could see me now . . . Marie's chest squeezed.

 . . . *all those red spots on her favorite orange dress* . . . *blood dripping from the choker* . . .

And Daddy . . . *lying by the buffet, his shiny church shoes under the chair* . . . *staring up at the chandelier, eyes wide open and glazed. Mouth open* . . . *throat* . . . *a river of red.*

She looked forward toward the man in the tuxedo under the waterfall.

 . . . *those big, brown irises, the tears in his eyes, the satin-smooth, tanned skin, the hair flowing over his shoulders* . . .

Yes, Norris. She stepped faster. Her crown of white orchids slipped slightly, scratching her forehead. She tilted her chin, her shoulders, higher.

"Dazzling," Sonny Whittaker whispered as she passed the front row. In beige linen pants and a mandarin-style shirt, he sat on the end, angled to watch the twins sing. Next to him, Rico Miranda, the swarthy owner of this resort. Then Erica and her boyfriend.

"Gorgeous," Paulette mouthed, smiling, snapping a picture. Her long fingernails gripped the silver square as her wispy brunette tendrils fell over her shoulder, bared by a strappy lemon yellow dress.

Marie smiled back.

But the buttery-smooth planes of Simone's face should have been turned around right now, glowing with approval, as her silver-blue eyes sparkled with assurance. Her sandy-hued waves or tight French roll should have been right there, next to Paulette.

Marie's chest squeezed; she had been way too hard on Simone yesterday. All that talk about finding a man, being happy. Was Marie being true to herself? She looked at Norris.

I cannot marry a man who told me he killed his first wife . . .

First the wedding proposal. Then the confession. It had burst from his bow-shaped lips in a stream of consciousness as he lay a year ago in the darkness of her plush, stained-wood office. She could still hear him describing her agonized moans, her sleepless nights, her pleas to end her suffering. Giving her more and more morphine. And finally, staring into her gaunt eyes, watching a tear roll past her once-beautiful ear . . . over her bald scalp. So ugly, like a plucked chicken. Norris had told her that the syringe felt cold in his fingers as he watched one push of the thumb, a peaceful sigh, a serene glow on what was left of her skin-on-skull face.

Now, Marie gripped the satin-wrapped stem of a single white calla lily.

I can't marry a killer. A man who did what God was supposed to do, in due time . . .

How could she and Norris celebrate tonight with a bulky bodyguard standing every five feet around the perimeter of the pool and patio? How could they smile as Jenn Ryder was being flown, unconscious and in critical condition, back to Los Angeles? How could she let Norris force her into going ahead with the wedding tonight? And how could she do it without her very best friend in the world?

Simone would tell me to listen to my heart, stop this before it's too late . . .

Marie stopped just inches before Norris. They faced each other with the guests on one side, the minister and boulders on the other.

She would call it off right now. But the words created a raw sensation in her mouth. She tried to bite down on them, to force them between her lips, but they slid back down her throat . . .

"My savior," Norris said softly, grasping her hands. "I pledge to you eternal love, as I cherish you, a gift from God, until my dying breath."

Marie stared, silently, her eyes burning with tears. Norris raised a gentle thumb to her cheek, wiping them away. He ran his thumb over her glossed lips.

"Speak," he breathed, "sultry sentry of my soul."

Her insides melted at the memory of the sweat-soaked passion they had shared last night under the tropical stars. In her wildest dreams, she had never envisioned a bed in the middle of a private beach in Brazil! Especially with her fortieth birthday looming not too far over the horizon.

Now, her left hand felt heavy under the weight of her diamond. The constant stream of clients in her office came to mind, sent by all the publicity of dating, then getting engaged to, and now marrying Norris "Midas Touch" Haynes. And his image, the hair and eyes and face that made her feel safe, inspired her to squeeze his hands.

"And I pledge to you," Marie said over the crash of water into the pool, "my undying devotion as our love bonds us forever."

29

Sunday evening, Sonny Whittaker sat on the edge of his king-sized bed, sinking into the jewel-toned silk stretching between four carved mahogany canopy posts. The soft light of sandalwood-scented candles glowed from the black wrought iron swirls of an arabesque-style panel, hinged in two places and set against one of the limestone walls.

"Myles, man," Sonny said into the cordless phone cradled on his shoulder. A crisp gust from the double set of terrace doors made him turn; far below, Los Angeles sparkled like a million diamonds tossed on black velvet. "I only have a minute before we videoconference Grand-mama."

"Sure thing," Myles said over rustling paper. "I need a break from reading all these depositions—"

"Just reassure me," Sonny said, shooting up from the bed. He descended three limestone steps, then strode across the cavernous room. He grasped the brass handles on the double doors; the night air cooled his burning cheeks. "That at the end of the week, I can lie in this room and close my eyes, knowing the girls and Kindred are down the hall."

Sonny closed the doors, then locked them. Tomorrow, the security company crew would install sensors on every window and entrance in the house. He should have updated his old alarm system long ago. Sonny stepped toward the huge carved wood dresser that he'd purchased years ago in Tibet. The poem from Narcissus was a white paper ball under the large mirror.

"Sonny, man," Myles said, "The stakes in this case are as high for me as if this were my own divorce, my own children's future on the line."

"You don't have kids," Sonny said.

"Have I ever let you down?" Myles asked. "Ever?"

"I have this sensation," Sonny said, turning toward the voluptuous brown velvet chairs facing the fireplace, "this image of Erica and Brett Robinson. They're building a pyre of lies, throwing me on top and setting it on fire. But no matter how hard I kick, how loud I scream out in pain, you can't put the fire out—"

"No chance," Myles said with a laugh, "I got a fire hose the size of the Alaska pipeline. You'll be swimmin' in victory before you know it, but—"

"No buts." Sonny returned to the bed, sat down and bent to remove his black loafers with silver buckles across the tops.

"Sonny man," Myles said, "Lady Justice is dealing us a wild card. Half the courthouse is out sick with food poisoning—"

Sonny started to slip; he grasped one of the bedposts, carved with finger-length gods and goddesses amongst ivy and arrows.

"What—" he focused on one of the faces that was staring down at the fringed and beaded velvet pillows where he rested his head every night. It was Her. A nymph with flowing hair and big, haunting eyes. Sonny stroked the polished wood, poking a thumbnail between her lips.

"You'll be saying more than that," Myles said, "if Evans doesn't show up in the morning. We could get reassigned to Johnston. I bet Brett Robinson thinks he's on the road to riches right now—"

Sonny clawed his collar. One of the candles made a sizzling sound and glowed brighter.

"Johnston," Myles said, "he's got a grudge against fathers. He was caught up in the big mafia scandal, and a nasty custody case years ago. He makes it no secret, he thinks children should be with the mom no matter what."

Sonny's blood pumped harder, hotter. But his tone was cool. "I trust you'll keep my family out of his hands."

"The odds are in our favor," Myles said. "The chief judge is a very 'better safe than sorry' kind of guy, especially since three of his judges are in the slammer right now."

Sonny grasped the heel of his loafer. "My God, I've had these shoes on for twenty four hours. That twelve hour plane ride home, then the doctor's office. Oh, that feels good—"

"Are you hearing me, Sonny?" Myles snapped. "This is no time to tune out on me, man. And don't you dare stay up all night painting. You need sleep, so you'll be alert and ready when Brett Robinson gets you on the stand—"

"All this time I've waited," Sonny said, pulling off his other shoe. "India asked for a new mommy. And Asia is sick. She threw up six times, starting with the moment she had to say good-bye to Erica down at Sanctuary."

Through the candlelit grill, across the room, Sonny glimpsed the beige marble fireplace. "What am I doing here? All my films, my paintings, Asia and India, *The Colony*—I want to leave a legacy in this world."

Myles laughed. "Sonny, drift into your philosophy zone *after* the trial."

Sonny clawed the bed, wondering how it would feel to have her fingernails raking down his back. "I have to find her," Sonny said.

"Stop," Myles said over the sudden drone of a television. "Remember that trip we took to Thailand, when we were, what, twenty years old? On the beach, having the best weed—"

"That was a lifetime ago," Sonny said. He quickly slipped off his pleated black trousers and crew-necked short-sleeved knit shirt, and the black leather belt with the silver buckle that matched his shoes.

"Anyway," Myles said, "you looked up at all those stars and said, 'what's it all about, man?' I said, 'death, taxes and women. The rest is a crap shoot.' But this week, we'll be shouting 'Yo Eleven!'—Hey, turn on channel 8."

"My television is not on," Sonny said, glancing at the closed center doors on the huge armoire that matched the bed. He walked toward it, opened it, scanning shelves holding his neatly folded collection of silky kimonos. He chose a black one, slipping it on over brown flannel pajamas and shearling slippers. He opened another door on the cabinet to expose the television.

"The housekeeper can turn it on for you," Myles said.

"Guadeloupe is downstairs with the girls, getting ready for our call." Sonny picked up the black remote; two dozen buttons, some black, some red, winked up at him simultaneously. "I don't know. God, if it weren't for Kindred and Guadeloupe, I would never watch TV—"

"Try POWER, Sonny. Nine times out of ten, it's usually red."

Sonny pushed the sole green button. The TV clicked on.

"My God. There's the woman I met in Brazil—"

One succulent bare shoulder and arm extended from a curve-hugging black dress. Hair flowing, arm hooked with a guy in a tux in front of a green sign that said dot-com something. But the picture was silent. "Myles, look at this."

"Yeah, Cheyenne, on Channel 8. See her?"

"Where's the volume?" All these arrows and numbers—

His own face looked back, then Jenn, Norris, the trailer from *The Colony*—but all silent.

"Shit!" Sonny shouted. He could craft an Oscar-buzz screenplay, paint beautiful portraits and still lifes that were now on display in the National Gallery in Washington and sold for small fortunes around the world, but—

"I can't make this fucking thing work!" He hurled the remote across the room.

Smash! It struck the large looking glass over the long dresser.

Shards of mirror and black plastic rained down on the half-dozen pillars of sandalwood candles set on the black square plate he'd bought in Tokyo, painted with the Japanese characters for peace and love. A single shard caught in the folds of the Narcissus poem.

"Sonny, you better cool that fiery temper of yours. I know you're stressed, man, but you can't just explode in court. When we walk in there tomorrow, you will be the epitome of Sweet Sonny Whittaker. Calm, in control. Got that?"

"Don't give me any reason not to be," Sonny said.

"Mister Whittaker!" Guadeloupe cried as the double doors opened. Worry crinkled the dark skin between her close-set eyes and the silver waves of hair that were pulled atop her head and secured in a bun. She wiped her hands on the beige apron tied around the slim waist of her forest green trousers and matching blouse. "We heard the noise—"

Jared, now in a red long-sleeved T-shirt and black jeans, towered behind her, his right hand on the holster at his waist.

"Calm down," Sonny said, striding toward the door. "You know technology brings out the worst in me." He nodded toward the mess on the dresser. "I'll clean it up later. Let's go talk to Grandmama."

Sonny followed them through the long upstairs hallway, with its lighted alcoves displaying a gilded vase he'd bought in Beijing, ornately painted chimes from India and a wooden warrior sculpture from Nigeria.

"Uncle Sonny," Jared said, "the alarm crew is coming tomorrow. I moved the installation up a day, so you don't have to sit in court and worry."

"A blaring alarm won't stop a killer if they're bound and determined," Sonny said as they hurried to the open front upstairs hallway.

"We'll be here," Jared said. The smooth planes of his face turned cobalt blue and crimson and maize as the outside yard lights illuminated the geometric pattern in the stained glass above and around the massive double wood doors that opened onto the huge foyer.

"Myles will give you the phone number of the courtroom," Sonny said as they dashed down the open, curving front staircase. His slippers made scraping noises as he clutched the ornately carved wooden banister that matched the Moroccan-style shutters inside the windows.

"I want you to call me at the slightest sign of trouble." Sonny led them through the jade cobblestoned foyer, which led to a cross of hallways. One stretched from the family room to the garage door and back staircase. The other led from the foyer to the kitchen.

Sonny turned right, through the short tube that he'd painted like Van Gogh's *Starry Night*, with brilliant cobalt splashed with yellow sunbursts. All he wanted right now was to enjoy this last evening with Asia and India before the trial, and let Grandmama's words of wisdom guide him through the rings of fire he would have to jump through inside the Santa Monica Courthouse.

As he approached the family room, loud static was coming from the television. Asia said, "That hurts my ears."

"Hey," Sonny said, stepping down three steps, where the girls and Kindred stood in front of the mahogany cabinet centered by the six-foot TV. Snow danced on the screen.

"I don't know what's wrong," Kindred said, staring down at a white remote in her hands. She wore head-to-toe yellow fleece sweatpants and sweatshirt, her hair a dark cape of waves over her broad shoulders.

"You look like a giant baby duck," Sonny chuckled as Jared stood by the tall French doors leading to the terrace on the left, while Josh sat on a purple velvet stool at the long countertop bar leading into the kitchen.

Kindred adjusted a knob on the television. "I pushed teleconference—"

"We're on the wrong frequency," India said, as she and Asia dove into the middle of the plush sapphire chenille couch. It matched the oversized armchairs around the low, carved wood coffee table that Sonny had purchased at an estate sale in Morocco. Circular recessed lights in the ceiling cast soft light on the gold walls.

Beads of sweat broke out on Sonny's forehead as he walked past the two-story wooden mantle that he'd salvaged from a Parisian mansion. It felt chilly enough for a fire, but he did not want to stare at flames. Sonny sank between the twins, putting his arms around their little shoulders. He raised his feet to the tapestry ottoman, between India's moon-boot footies and Asia's soft blue slippers. "Feel better?"

Asia's cheeks were sunken and pale; her eyes dull.

"Kindred made me eat soup," Asia said, crossing her arms over a fuzzy blue bathrobe. "And Guadeloupe gave me Pedialyte—"

"Remember, the doctor said, lots of liquids," Sonny said.

"I'll make her drink water," India said. The silvery robe over her shoulders crinkled; her white, princess–cut nightgown swayed around her ankles. "Kindred, does it work? I want to see Grandmama!"

"Mom says we're not going there," Asia said with a teasing tone. "She says we're moving to a castle far away—"

Sonny's heart skipped a beat. "Daddy won't let his Angel Eyes get away." He tickled their tummies. "Kindred, work some technological magic for us."

"Don't let Daddy near it," Asia said playfully. "The last time he tried to make me a fruit smoothie," she giggled, "the blender exploded and sprayed the ceiling with strawberries!"

"Ugh," Kindred exclaimed. "Guadeloupe, why did you get this new remote when the other one worked perfectly fine?"

"That one," Guadeloupe called from the kitchen, "puts everything at your fingertips."

India shot up from the couch. "Let me see," she said, "Remember, Kindred? On NASA's website, we saw how mission control keeps in touch with the astronauts. First link to—"

"Grandmama!" Asia cheered as Grandmama's face lit up the television screen.

"Yes," Kindred said, smiling. "Right on time."

"Sweet Sonny." Grandmama's silky Caribbean accent boomed through the room. "Are you takin' good care of those babies?"

"Yes, Grandmama." The rich brown skin of her heart-shaped face was like ancient but well-oiled leather; the tiniest lines marked the delicate skin around her wise, black eyes. A head of silver braids adorned with cowrie shells dangled over the shoulders of a flowing lavender dress. She stood on the terrace overlooking the pristine beach, lush greenery and the Caribbean sunset.

"The volcano is actin' up," Grandmama glanced up and back at the lush green slope behind the contemporary, stained-wood house. "They say it's threatenin' to blow. If it does, I'm going with it. All my neighbors left. Smells like sulfur somethin' terrible."

"Grandmama, leave the house until it's safe!" Sonny cried. He wanted to kneel in front of the screen, to wrap his arms around her sturdy shoulders.

"Mother Nature will not run me out of my own home." She raised an arm toward the blaze of orange and magenta shimmering over the watery horizon. "Me and your Grandpopa's grave, we'll be right here."

"No," Sonny groaned.

"Sonny, we got more to talk about. I see her." Grandmama turned toward the sunset. "You see those fingers risin' like fire?"

"I see them," Sonny said.

"That means you're about to walk through the flames," she said. "But there'll be plenty of water to keep you safe. Might scald a bit, but you and those babies will not get burned. She will make sure of it."

"Grandmama," India said, "I'm scared for you."

"No, baby, you just give your daddy all the hugs he needs, you hear?"

Four little arms wrapped around Sonny's neck as the twins said, "Yes, Grandmama."

"We got some cotton candy clouds for you girls," Grandmama said. "I'm savin' 'em up, for when you come stay with me."

Asia crossed her arms.

"Kindred, you take care of my babies."

"Yes, ma'am," Kindred said. "Please tell us we'll be safe—"

Grandmama turned toward the sky. "You're in for a fright. Sonny, your Grandpopa, he's sayin' you got to watch your back. Don't trust anybody, 'cause there'll be wolves creepin' about in sheep's clothing."

30

Note to self: next time, wrap the spray paint cans in paper towels, *then* put them in the duffel bag. All that clinking could be a dead giveaway. If anyone were home, of course.

"What a rush! I'm in!" Laughter echoed off the shiny pine floor that stretched forever, its walls showcasing a museum's worth of framed movie prints. All those famous faces and titles dotted the white wall between countless pine doors and built-in cabinets. They faced the high glass panes and white square columns overlooking the turquoise rectangular pool glowing in the dark yard.

And the security cameras—easy enough to duck under the one in the kitchen, and those idiots installed them facing out to the pool.

Another note to self: can the sneakers. Too squeaky.

"If I come back to send him for a deadly dip in the pool, I can't make all this noise."

Squish, squeak. Squish, squeak.

A quick pat on the pocket of this white painter's jumpsuit. Thanks to the security keycard, there was an open invitation. Another door, this one with a wooden handle and a tiny square window. A redwood sauna, Finnish stove included. Now there was a hot idea . . .

Squish, sque—

Beeping sounds, a deep voice. *Beep.*

Oh, just a distant answering machine. But hurry up, they would be home soon.

Inside the last door. Yes! The screening room, where he probably sat jacking off while watching all the anorexic actresses with fake boobs pretending to act in his movies. Then he probably patted himself on the back for casting the blockbuster hunk of the month, with equally bad acting skills but a pretty enough face and deep enough voice to keep the women wishing and wanting an impossible dream like that at home . . .

"I'm gonna teach them all—"

The little metal ball bearing rattled against the inside of the can. Red, very appropriate.

SSSSSSStttt. Big letters, all across the vast white screen and padded walls. How 'bout some marks on the white leather couches and recliner chairs, set on all these levels like it's a damn stadium or something—-

SSSSStttt . . .

A deep, distant rumble. Garage door . . .

"Oh, wait, my calling card."

From the duffel bag, two dozen daffodils . . . tossed in the air. Stomped into the white carpeting. Doors closing.

Squish, squeak, squishsqueak . . .

And laughter into the night.

31

"Oh, help me," Marie cooed playfully as Norris scooped her into his arms, as she stepped out of the white limousine. His strong arms pressed into her back and below her bent knees as he raised her high enough to see the distant lights of Los Angeles, twinkling far below the tall, ivy-covered fence and gate ringing their Tudor-style mansion at the top of a winding street in Beverly Hills.

"May I carry you over the threshold, Mrs. Haynes?" Norris whispered as he pressed his warm lips into her forehead.

"Only if you take me directly to the bedroom," Marie said, closing her eyes, wishing the security guards' walkie talkies would stop crackling and reminding her of the fear. "And promise a night of erotic indulgence."

"A candlelight massage," he whispered raspily, "your delicious skin, drinking up warm oil under my fingertips."

His eyes sparkled with tenderness in the soft glow of gold and glass lanterns on the arched brick portico; a half-dozen security guards dotted the mauve stone drive. In black trousers and matching satin jackets, knit caps and coiled earpieces, they were closing limo doors, raking their sharp eyes over the underlit foliage of the vast, sloped front yard. At the double front doors, the mauve, iris-shaped stained glass reflected their dark reflections in two tall panels framed by shiny teak.

"All clear, Mr. Haynes," said the lead security guard, Lance, as he pulled the gold knobs and swung open the doors. His eyes were hard as blue marbles, showcased in a ruddy, upside-down triangle of a face. His cheeks were as sharp and round as if they had been set in place by an ice cream scoop. His black workboots straddled the brass strip between the stone outside and the black and white checked marble tile inside.

"Mmmm," Marie whispered, "all the flowers—"

The chandelier, its oblong crystals extending from two stories above, spotlighted huge rose and lily and bird of paradise arrangements, each tagged with cards showing wedding bells or congratulations, lining the base of the enormous curved wood staircase.

"Would you like to inspect the new control room?" Lance asked, raising a hand toward what had been the cloak room before Marie had left for Brazil. A wall of television monitors cast an eerie blue glow from the doorway. "We've got a bird's eye view of every entrance," Lance said.

"Just keep this place tight as a drum, so we don't have to think about it." Norris's hair fell over his cheeks; he clenched Marie more tightly into his beige Prism sweater as they approached the red carpet of the staircase. "We do not want to be disturbed."

Marie inhaled the flowers which almost obscured the usual cedar-pine scent of this house built by Norris' grandfather in the 1920s. This mansion that she had called home for the past two years, after selling her condo. This grand palace that was a universe away from the dingy apartment in the projects . . .

Here she enjoyed imported gorgonzola and goat cheese, not the orange government rubber that had bound her guts into an aching knot. Calamari and Kristal, not fish sticks and Kool-Aid. English and Egyptian linens and downy pillows, not tattered and stained sheets pulled over a pee-stained mattress on the floor. Norris's love and affection, not Aunt

Zola's cranky weariness from raising six kids alone. Silence and serenity, not five other kids shouting and bickering and making fun of her for studying and using verbs and complete sentences.

"Mmmm, nothing like home," Marie whispered.

Norris buried his nose in her neck, just above her pearl choker, as he took the first step up. "You are sweet as crème brulée," he said.

Marie stiffened. "Wait," she said, inhaling more deeply. "Paint. Do you smell it?"

"That's just from the new surveillance room," Norris said.

Lance closed the front doors, nodding. "The crews just finished yesterday—"

"No," Marie said, extending a leg toward the floor. "It's fresh—"

"Christ, Marie, let's just go upstairs, take time out in a bath together," Norris said. "This week in court is gonna be—"

"Norris," she said, "it smells like spray paint." The smell took her back to the long, dark corridors in the projects, the brick-walled lobby, the layers and colors of gang symbols on the once-blue elevator doors. "I know spray paint when I smell it."

Marie's heart leaped to her throat. She strode away from Norris, following the smell that wrenched up the images of her parents bleeding to death on the dining room floor.

"Mrs. Haynes," Lance called. "The house is secure."

Marie hurried through the paneled hallway, to the huge Mediterranean country style kitchen, with its gourmet stainless steel appliances and pale yellow cabinets. To the modern, back hallway.

Red footprints dotted the shiny pine floor.

"Norris!" she screamed. She had to see him, in the flesh, to know this was not happening again. That someone was not killing the ones she loved, right in front of her. "Norris!"

"Code six," Lance said deeply into his walkie-talkie. He was a tower of black, holding out a long arm to stop her. "Back gallery. Code six."

"Christ!" Norris shouted, his white suede loafers screeching on the floor. He joined Marie in pushing past Lance's arm.

"The screening room," Norris said, as he dashed past the glassed-in gallery to the last door on the left.

"Norris, wait," Marie called with a trembling voice. Her mind swirled with red, blood gushing from throats. "Norr—" she coughed.

"Mr. Haynes!" Lance ran to his side as Norris opened the door. "Let us secure—"

"Mother fuck me!" Norris shouted. He turned as white as the gallery walls as he stared into the room.

Marie stepped behind him, looking into the home theater where she had joined him in watching his last four movies, as well as all their favorites like *Gone With The Wind, The Godfather, Lady Sings the Blues* and *Casablanca.*

"Oh Lord help us," Marie cried.

Across the white screen in dripping red block letters: HOLLYWOOD KILLS. The far wall said: NORRIS, YOU'RE NEXT. And the back wall: THE NEW MRS, TOO.

Marie pressed her fingers to her choker. A bitter plant smell rose from yellow daffodils crushed into the white carpet. There, a white paper tied with a yellow ribbon. She picked it up, opened it, and read aloud:

Norris Haynes
Who gave you the power to dictate how we should look and feel?
By making movies about love that in real life is never real.
You stroll the red carpet to collect awards like you're a big, bad Zeus,
Brainwashing the world, trapping everyone in some beauty myth noose.
Your star actresses have bones jutting from sequined designer gowns,
Making young girls look in the mirror, starve, throw up and frown.
You torture actors with crazy pressure to look just as young and lean,
Trapping real men in hellish insecurity, inferiority or vanity that's obscene.
But now Norris Haynes, it's a wrap for your perverse, trend-setting ways,
So be warned, from me, your movie mogul madness has seen its final days.
Narcissus

"Fuck!" Norris shouted. He struck the wall near the door.

"No," Marie gasped. Dizzy, she stroked her choker. It would kill her to lose yet another loved one to the violence of a stalker.

32

The gray bag from the video store crinkled on the front passenger seat of Simone Thompson's dark blue BMW SUV as she turned off Sepulveda Boulevard into her eclectic neighborhood in the Westwood section of Los Angeles.

She couldn't wait to get home, pop the movies into the VCR in her bedroom, and stare into Sonny Whittaker's eyes once again. Then in the morning, she would have to tell Charlie she could absolutely not oversee his divorce.

As Tennessee Avenue curved into Lauriston, red and blue lights flashed on her Spanish-style ranch. Police cars crammed the street. Neighbors watched from palm-fringed porches and pastel-tinted windows in close-set stucco homes.

"What?" The sultry song "Stranger" by LTD played in the CD deck; she had sung along with Jeffrey Osborne at least a dozen times since she'd pulled out of LAX. The rear-view mirror reflected the headlights of the undercover squad car that had met her at the airport. Charlie Rhodes was overreacting, ordering this round-the-clock protection until Narcissus was caught. But why were a half-dozen black and white police cars angled at her driveway?

"Don't tell me they're at my house."

Simone's fingers trembled against the dark blue steering wheel. Her foot pressed the accelerator; she sped past the speckled trunks of honeysuckle trees between the sidewalk and street. A police van hummed at the end of the indigo petunia-lined walk leading to her front door.

She pulled into the driveway, behind two police cars whose headlights lit up the lacquered wood panels of the two-car garage. Lanterns on the ivory stucco walls illuminated a cluster of officers writing in notebooks and talking in walkie-talkies, near the wrought-iron rail of the porch.

Simone bolted from her SUV, slammed the door. Her stomach cramped as two police officers stepped from behind the waxy box hedges close to the two shuttered windows on the left. Stake lights cast backlight on them and the baskets of fuchsia petunias hanging over the porch.

"The boys are checkin' the point of entry," an officer said as he stepped outside, through her open front door.

Simone stormed toward him. "What is going on? How did you get inside my house!"

"Judge Thompson," he said, his warm eyes squinting as he ran long fingers over his clean-shaven chin. "I'm sorry. There's been a break-in. Looks like Narcissus."

"Oh my God," Simone cried. Behind him, in the soft yellow light of the sponge-painted harvest gold entrance hall, chunks of white plaster coated with chrome littered the clove-colored tile. "No, not my statue!"

Simone bolted inside. Three pillars of freesia-scented candles perfumed the air, untouched on the long, black lacquered table to the left of the door. Above it, silver moon-crescent sconces on the wall illuminated the chrome and plaster carnage of what had been a man cradling an infant, his palms wide and neck bowed protectively as the tiny face shined up at him. She had purchased it years ago at a UCLA student art show. How dare someone violate her home and destroy one of her most cherished images.

"Who did this?" Simone shouted.

The tall officer in the doorway stepped close.

"I'm sorry, Judge Thompson," he said, his smooth face beaming compassion. "We're searching the premises for clues. But considering the threats—"

"Catch this person," Simone said. "Now."

Rage roiled in her eyes, in her reflection in the sun-shaped, brushed-gold mirror over the table. The deep chop of helicopter blades rumbled overhead; van doors slamming on the street drew her attention to a TV news crew rushing up the lawn.

The officer closed the front door.

"What else did they do?" Simone demanded, turning around to face the arched entryway to the living room. The hallway light glowed on the sunken expanse of ebony carpet, furniture and a tiled fireplace. The open top of the baby grand piano gleamed in front of the tall, arched window.

Simone took about six quick strides to the end of the hall, turned right, and dashed past walls lined with Academy and UCLA track ribbons, certificates and trophies. The door to the garage was closed. A yellow warning light glowed on the security system alarm pad on the wall. Below it, her navy blue Nike running shoes sat on a carpet square.

She turned left, into the all-white kitchen. The countertops were clear except for a coffee maker and tall glass canisters of brown rice, whole wheat pasta, brown sugar and oatmeal. A green plant was draped in front of the window over the double sink. A glass bowl of bright green Granny Smith apples sat on the island.

"The mud tracks stop there," a female voice said over the crackle of a police radio in her family room. The woman stood just beyond the four-chair dinette, down two steps, where the white bear rug guarded the fireplace in the brick-walled family room.

"What happened?" Simone demanded. On the left the vertical blinds were open, as were the two doorwalls leading to the back patio.

"It appears," the woman officer said, nodding toward the green leaf-print cushions on the patio chairs and umbrella table, "the suspect jimmied this door open—"

"What about my alarm?" Simone asked, she gripped the back of one of two cozy beige couches, tossed with animal-print pillows, angled around a square coffee table and the large television to the right of the ornate black metal fan-shaped grate blocking a charred log.

"The alarm worked," the officer said. "That's when we came. We think it's Narcissus because of this. Here." The officer held out a scroll of paper; a yellow ribbon secured it to the stem of a single fresh daffodil.

Simone unrolled the paper and read:

Simone Thompson
Despicable, self-righteous hypocrite of the law,
The thought of you, the sight of you, makes my insides bloody and raw.
I'll shove my pain and suffering back to you, ram it through your gut,
You'll beg for mercy, say you're sorry, for being an unscrupulous slut.
Those big pretty eyes of yours, I thought were so tender and sweet,
But you used them against me, betraying me with gruesome defeat.
I'll speak for all the others I imagine you've cloaked in similar shame,
As you play with our lives from your high bench, like it's some fun game.
No more, Simone Thompson, I'll soak your robe in blood,
And smile as your dead body falls to the floor with one tremendous thud.
                                                              Narcissus

An icy wave of numbing fear washed through Simone's limbs as she read the poem again.

"Who is this?" she asked through tight lips. "And what case are they referring to?" Her mind spun back over the dozens and dozens of trials she'd conducted over the past six years. The ones she'd tried as an assistant prosecutor before that. The briefs she wrote as a clerk to Appeals Court Judge Ray. Even the work she'd done as an undergraduate and law student.

"Who could hate me this much?"

33

Hours later, after a second pair of officers was assigned to watch her house, and the story had aired on the eleven o'clock news along with the vandalism at Marie and Norris's home, Simone pulled her SUV into the garage. And she retrieved the gray bag of videos.

As she pushed 0-7-1-2 to reset the alarm, then dashed through the center hallway toward the bedrooms, Simone hoped that watching Sonny Whittaker movies would relax her. She stepped into her apricot-walled bedroom, which smelled fresh and floral from her basket of bath salts in the master bathroom.

"I'm so tired," she sighed as she strode past the king-sized cherry sleigh bed. She just wanted to lay back on the fluffy pile of pillows and blankets and gaze at his face, across the apricot carpet toward the twenty-inch television. It sat on a stand in the corner, next to the long cherry dresser and under a long window shrouded by womb-like folds of ivory taffeta.

"I can't believe I'm doing this," she whispered, fingers trembling, as she pulled *Destiny* from the clear plastic case and shoved the video into the VCR under the TV. She jammed the play button. She fast-forwarded through the red, white and black FBI warning, the title—

The phone rang. She stepped toward the nightstand. The black phone with a built-in answering machine sat on a cream-colored crochet doily, next to a Tiffany lamp with gold beaded fringe; an identical nightstand and lamp sat on the other side of the bed, near the open door to the master bathroom and walk-in closet.

Simone picked up the receiver; the red message light was flashing. "Yes?"

"Simone, it's Charlie. Are you alright? The police just told me—"

"I'm more mad than afraid," Simone said. "They got into my house, Charlie!" *Destiny* flashed across her TV. In just moments she would see his face. "But I have to tell you, under no circumstances can I take the Whittaker divorce tomorrow—"

"It's not up for debate," he said. "Things are worse than we thought. Evans, he's sick as a dog. Definitely need you to fill in for him tomorrow—"

"Absolutely no," Simone said, staring into Sonny's eyes. "Charlie, I have to tell you—"

"Simone, the media is going to suck up every salacious detail of this trial. And with the Narcissus threats, I just need to play things straight and narrow. Without Johnston. I'll see you in the morning."

Simone exhaled loudly as the dial tone buzzed. She pushed the black PLAY button. The electronic feminine voice said, "Message one."

"Simone, it's Paulette. I'm so worried about you and Marie. Call me at home."

Simone crossed her arms. Her stomach cramped with distrust. What the hell had Paulette been doing with Roxanne Jones on the beach? That could only mean trouble. But had they recognized her, or worse, photographed her with Sonny, before she had slipped into the dancing crowd on the beach?

"Message two."

"Simone," Marie said. "The cops told me you're home safely. We had a break-in, too. Narcissus. The house is . . . Oh honey, I know you're upset, but I understand why you left. Just call, let me know you're okay."

Simone squeezed her arms even tighter across her chest. Had Marie and Norris gone ahead with the wedding? Would Marie now turn back into her sensitive friend? Simone reached for the phone.

But she froze.

"Tell me I'm not really doing this," she whispered. Her heart skipped a beat as she glimpsed her reflection in the big mirror over her dresser, washed in the silver glow of the television. A fiendish desperation glowed in her wide-set eyes; her hair was a wild cloud about her shoulders. Two points poked her plain white cotton t-shirt; the crotch of these blue jeans rubbed just the right way. "This is crazy."

His face filled the TV screen. He wore a white suit and fedora, as he took long, confident steps past huge willow trees dripping with Spanish moss, toward a New Orleans-style mansion.

"Yes," Simone sighed, falling back on the bed she'd inherited from her grandparents in Italy. "Here, with me, now."

A close-up—brown eyes smoldering as the heroine answered the door. He held out a dozen red roses.

"Are you going to make me stand here all day?" he asked with the sexiest masculine bass ever to grace a movie screen. "I would, you know, if it meant seeing your beautiful face."

Simone smiled. This was where her mother and Bianca, and every other woman she knew, would sigh and glaze over, fantasizing that they were opening their front door to see him.

"A woman like you"—Sonny's deep voice drew her attention back to the screen—"the world should bow down and kiss your toes every morning."

She smiled. A week of that voice, that face, that awesome karmic extravaganza of his presence.

"No!" Simone dove toward the VCR. She would hit STOP/EJECT, then return these five movies to the video store, tonight. "Be a professional about this."

But that intelligent magnetism glowing from his eyes, the *joie de vivre* radiating from his beautiful mustached mouth parting over sturdy white teeth in the most enchanting smile—

She had to watch just a minute longer, as he stepped into that grand house in the movie. And the love scene, it was just a few minutes away. Yes—

There he was, the broad, bronzed muscles of his chest, those long, strong arms that had wrapped around her, his narrow waist . . . trousers falling to the floor, long strong legs twisting with the heroine on her big bed . . .

Simone peeled down her jeans, kicked off her white sneakers, pulled off her shirt. She was drawn to the dresser, to the drawer full of things she had bought a year ago while dating Clark, but was never in the mood to wear for him. Even on the rare occasions when he stopped working long enough to get romantic, his over-in-a-minute libido wasn't worth the effort of embellishing the experience with a negligée or . . .

Yes, these wine-colored satin panties with the ribbon ties on the sides. Simone slipped them on, along with the filmy camisole. Her heart pounded. What if he were to somehow find her house, and come knocking on the door right now?

"He doesn't even know my name," she laughed. "But he will in the morning." Simone modeled the satiny ensemble in the silvery light of the television. A deep moan—

Yes, he was kissing her, making love to the woman on the screen.

"That's me," Simone sighed, falling into the rose-patterned comforter on her bed. "I am Her."

Then, her fingertips slid down, down past the silky scalloped edge of her camisole. His hands were her own hot, damp palms, following the smooth curves of her hips, the slope of her waist, the round swells of her breasts, the firm peaks that ached for the heat of his mouth.

If only her fingertips tracing the velvet throb between her legs were him. Every inch of him, starting with his forehead, his nose, his lips, his elbows, knees, toes. Stroking her into the sort of carnal delirium she could only imagine would result from an attraction this instinctual.

Over and over. Day after day. Year after year.

But for now, she would have to settle for rewinding, fast-forwarding, movie after movie. Until the first rays of dawn shot through the slatted cherrywood blinds on the window.

"What . . ." she gasped toward the mirror. "What's happening to me?" She collapsed back on the bed, staring wide-eyed at the shadowy ceiling.

34

Sonny Whittaker's chest squeezed as the lemon yellow elevator doors opened to the noisy, crowded second floor of the Santa Monica County Building.

"This way," Myles said, nodding toward a shoulder-to-shoulder crush of people cramming the speckled brown tile floor. Straight ahead, recessed lights illuminated several people in jeans and business suits sitting on a rust-colored pew set inside a long, moss-green cove. Several copies of the *Los Angeles Times* flashed the page one headline: STALKER PUTS HOLLY-WOOD ON HIGH ALERT, then in smaller print: TIGHT SECURITY EXPECTED AT HAYNES–WHITTAKER DIVORCE TRIAL.

"There's Sonny Whittaker!" a female voice cried over the din. Others whispered his name; eyes and faces turned toward him.

"This isn't a movie premiere, it's a trial," Sonny said with a dry tone as he focused on the back of Myles' head. "Who are all these people?"

"Lawyers, reporters, spectators, cops," Myles said over the shoulder of his navy blue suit. "Excuse me," he said, angling his thick body and black briefcase past two young men. "Lots of cops. Just like the ones at your house right now."

Having those squad cars on the street, as they had pulled away this morning, was the only way Sonny would leave the twins, Kindred, Josh and Jared, and Guadeloupe alone while he was in court all day. If they needed him, the cell phone clipped to Myles's navy blue leather belt inside his suit would vibrate.

Sonny stiffened. A sign on the courtroom door said PHONES AND PAGERS MUST BE TURNED OFF.

"Myles, man," Sonny said close to Myles' ear. "What if the girls—"

"I gave Kindred the clerk's number," Myles said. "And I've already given the clerk and the bailiff explicit instructions to interrupt proceedings if we get any calls from home."

A few strands of gray skimmed the starched white collar of Myles's dress shirt. They appeared brighter and more abundant in the sixty-degree February morning haze glowing through the large windows behind them, windows that overlooked the media battalion that had just tried to attack as they had approached this boxy, two-story, white building.

"Sonny, right here." Myles nodded at four sets of sheriff's deputies flanking double wood doors marked ROOM 202.

"Shouldn'ta married that white woman anyway," a young female officer sneered to another. "Don't matter whose daughter she is."

"Keep your gossip to yourself," Sonny said deeply as other officers opened the doors.

"Oh," the woman said, her rattan complexion turning ruby. "Mr. Whittaker—"

Sonny returned his gaze to the back of Myles's head as they entered the courtroom. Hushed chatter rose from four crowded rows of people on each side. And Sonny's eyes stung under the fluorescent rectangles of light beaming down on the vast, redwood-paneled chamber.

"The Evil Bride," Sonny whispered with a harsh tone as he strode behind Myles up the shiny tiled aisle. Straight ahead, the meringue-like whip of Erica's hair hung over her pink suit jacket as she sat at a long table next to Brett Robinson. "With her Doberman ready to bite my balls."

Erica leaned leftward, her petite left shoulder pressing into the pad of Brett's navy blue pinstriped suit. The starched top of his white shirt collar contrasted with his smooth, golden-hued neck. His round head of close-cropped, sandy curls, reminded Sonny of a painting technique in which he dragged a wide-tooth comb through a thick layer of paint to make squiggly lines.

"The best-dressed Doberman in America," Myles said into his hand as he twisted the side of his mustache.

The image of Erica and Brett turned on a blowtorch that hissed violet-blue through Sonny's mind and body. How could he sit this close to Erica for a week and keep his rage and resentment in check? How could he not call her out for the vicious user that she was? And how could he subject himself to days and days of whatever legal tormenting Brett had up his French-cuffed, gold-cufflinked sleeve?

And Myles—doing that nervous habit that he'd never had during previous trials that he'd won for Sonny.

Sonny projected a cool mask of calm. He would—no matter what flaming canons were shot his way—keep his nerves on ice until he reached the end of this barefoot walk over hot coals.

"All these pews," Sonny whispered, scanning all the faces that turned toward him. He walked toward a waist-high wooden banister with a gate in the center. Just past the long table, a podium stood, its silver microphone rising like an antenna. Above it all, the judge's pulpit-like bench— a six-foot-high, redwood cube between two smaller boxes. "I feel like I'm facing the altar in the church of the damned."

"Sonny, this way." Myles pushed through the gate. He plunked his briefcase on the floor next to the redwood table; his manicured fingernails brushed over the branded initials *JM* by the handle as he opened the flaps. "Have a seat."

"It's hot as hell in here." Sonny clawed the damp collar of his olive cotton dress shirt under the matching tweed jacket. "Don't they have air conditioning? This is California." As he sat on the blue tweed chair, he glimpsed Roxanne Jones sitting amongst the shoulder-to-shoulder strangers. "I don't see how this could be of any interest—"

"A lot of them are journalists," Myles said, "and spectators."

"It's the opposite of a wedding," Sonny said, recognizing Erica's relatives behind her. That empty spot at the end of the front row was no doubt reserved for Norris. "Myles, why didn't you warn me before I fucked up my life?"

"I did," Myles said softly. "I told you even in the 1990s, Norris Haynes was not ready for a black son-in-law."

Sonny crinkled his brows, shaking his head. "I don't remember you saying that—"

"You were too busy cussing me out," Myles whispered. "Like you did in twelfth grade. I said, 'They call her Bust-'em-and-Burn-'em Brenda Sykes for a reason.' But you wouldn't listen. Until you came running with your dick in your hand, trying to hunt down some penicillin."

Sonny's insides ached as he remembered the way his mother would use the skirt of her rose-print apron to wipe the scent of fresh-chopped celery and onions off her elegant cocoa-brown fingers. *"Hard-headed Sonny Boy,"* she would say, shaking her head, *"always learning lessons the hard way. Lord, I hope it never catches up with you."*

"Pull up to the table, man," Myles said, placing two yellow note pads before them. "It's gonna take awhile to play our winning hand just right."

"All this chair needs," Sonny said, his insides humming like an engine ready to roar, "is wrist straps and a silver helmet. So these folks can't see the smoke shooting from my ears when Erica tries to fry me—"

Myles leaned down to fish something from his briefcase.

Brett Robinson, sitting about six feet away, turned. Through shiny, half-dollar sized rimless lenses, Brett's cornflower blue eyes radiated superiority and nonchalance. As did the golden disc of his clean-shaven face— from the broad forehead framed by combed-back waves, wide but prominent cheekbones marked by an almost chiseled shadow between his strong jawline and the blondish bristles of closely trimmed sideburns. His full, deep rose lips pursed; a barely perceptible nod made the delicate gold stem of his eyeglasses glimmer.

Sonny projected his most confident countenance: chin raised, eyes wide and sharp, even a slight smile like Buddha. Because in Brett's face and eyes was a reflection of himself: that pretty boy charisma that worked magic with women. Just sit, look good, and they'll fawn all over, spoil you rotten . . .

A sudden blaze in Brett's eyes reciprocated his understanding of their membership in this unspoken elite. But it was the type of kinship that was the last thing Sonny wanted to share with his wife's divorce lawyer.

"Nine out of ten times," Myles said, sitting upright, "what you need in your briefcase is at the bottom."

Brett's gaze sliced to Myles. The corners of Brett's mouth rose with I've-won-this-hands-down arrogance.

Myles pulled a pen from his breast pocket and wrote on his note pad. A hot waft of cologne tinged with nervous sweat rose from his suit jacket; sweat glistened on his neck just below his ear as he focused on the yellow paper.

"Myles, man," Sonny whispered over pangs of doubt shooting through his gut. "You better stare down that loathsome motherfucker like you've got the biggest, baddest balls this side of hell. Now!"

Myles squinted, then turned toward Brett, who nodded slightly.

"You've never let me down," Sonny said. "So don't start now."

He wanted to relax. Myles usually had everything under control, like when he had successfully defended Sonny against a dozen or so frivolous lawsuits filed by former housekeepers or actors or that woman who claimed he'd stolen her screenplay. Now, Sonny would have to trust his friend, this man who had risked his own life to save him from an undertow off Baja California.

"He's all huff and puff, and we're gonna blow his house down," Sonny said, leaning toward Myles. "Handmade suit and all."

"All rise!" bellowed a bailiff at the front of the courtroom. The thirty-ish tawny man with a crew cut wore the same army green pants, short-sleeved, tan shirt, and black leather holster as the officers by the door.

Sonny rose as feet thundered on the floor behind them. He leaned toward Myles. "You're sure this guy's fair?"

"Face forward, man," Myles whispered.

The gold block letters E PLURIBUS UNUM above the judge's bench strengthened his resolve to trust that this person would do the right thing.

"Quiet, please." The bailiff's voice boomed through the packed courtroom. "The Honorable Simone Thompson presiding."

"I thought it was a man," Sonny whispered. Where had he heard that name—

"I called this morning," Myles said. "The clerk said Judge Evans would be back—"

Sonny wanted to tune out, then turn back on a week from now when the judge, any judge, was telling him that he could have sole custody of his daughters. He didn't care about whether Erica got the house or even the money. If he had to raise Asia and India in a tent, then so be it.

"Sonny," Myles said. "Face forward. Judge Thompson is good news."

"That name is familiar," Sonny whispered. "Where—"

"Shh, she likes stillness and silence," Myles said.

A column of black fabric swooshed in a doorway to the right of the bench. The light shined on her smooth sheen of hair, pulled straight back like golden threads, twisted up in a French roll. Only her left side showed to the courtroom; two thumps sounded as she rushed up behind that first wooden cube. The silver stem of wire-rim glasses supported rectangular lenses on a delicate bell of a nose.

"So pretty for a judge—" Sonny whispered.

She had smooth, flawless skin, the color of—

Butterscotch cream.

She took another step up, to the center of the highest cube, facing the court. Her slightly tinted glasses did little to dim the glow of her eyes—

Moonbeam gray.

"Good morning," she said, sitting down. Her voice—

Silk on a soundwave.

"My God," Sonny gasped. "That's . . . that's Her."

35

Seated at the defense table, Joseph Myles stroked his mustache, wishing
Sonny would obey the rules of the court by keeping quiet like everyone
else. He wanted this duel to move as swiftly and smoothly as possible.
Because the last time things got out of control in Judge Thompson's
courtroom, Myles had ended up walking out with a hefty ticket for contempt.

"Sonny, man, sit down," Myles whispered. To his right, in his peripheral view, Brett Robinson and Erica Haynes were facing them. Why the
hell was Sonny glazing over like he'd just bet his life away? Why was he
turning three shades lighter, as if Judge Thompson—up there shuffling

papers on the desk part of the bench—had just dealt him the news that he'd lost everything?

A fresh prickle of sweat broke out as Myles angled his hand over the right side of his mouth. "Sonny!"

Sonny's knees folded; he slowly lowered to the chair.

Something burned in Sonny's eyes as he leaned close. Something that made Myles's heart gallop.

"Myles, man, I gotta tell you somethi—"

The air hummed with the drone of a silver electric fan on a gray file cabinet in the left corner. A cough. The rustle of fabric behind them.

Myles shoved the yellow pad in front of Sonny. Pressed a pen into the soft paper. He could feel Judge Thompson watching—

"The matter before me," she said, "is case number 02-6645, Whittaker vs. Whittaker, a dissolution of marriage and a petition for full custody."

Sonny's fingers trembled as he grasped the black Mont Blanc pen. With shaky letters he wrote: WE MET.

"What?" Myles asked.

"Thursday. In Brazil."

Shit!

"Sonny Whittaker," Myles whispered forcefully, "do not tell me *she* is the woman you were talking about last night—"

Sonny's eyes sparkled.

"Counsel, are you ready to proceed?" the judge asked.

Brett Robinson stood, a pillar of navy blue in Myles's peripheral vision. "Yes, your honor."

Myles rose. "Your honor, one more moment, if I may, please." He gritted his teeth, leaning so close to his friend that his bottom lip touched Sonny's hot earlobe. "*Don't* tell me you've broken your vow of celibacy with Judge Thompson."

Sonny smiled. "Not yet."

Motherfuck! How should Myles proceed? He was obligated to disclose to the court what Sonny had just said. Yet, was it the full truth? Would he be placing a velvet-lined pandora's box right in Brett Robinson's hands, so that every day of the trial Erica's lawyer could pull out another scandalous tidbit and hammer them as hard as the nails he wanted to drive into Sonny's coffin? Because taking away Asia and India would, without a doubt, kill him.

"Mr. Myles," the judge said, "Mr. Robinson, are there any matters that need resolution before we begin?"

Brett stood. "No, your honor."

Myles sat down, leaning toward Sonny. "What exactly happened?"

"We met at Sanctuary. After the attack."

"And?"

Sonny shrugged. "We were both so shaken, I didn't even ask her name. She left. I didn't know she was a judge or the same person in the paper. Completely innocent."

Myles stared into his client's eyes long and hard. "Lay it all on the table right now, Sonny, or it could trip us up later—"

"That's all." Sonny's black eyelashes swept leftward, as if brushing off any more discussion on the matter. He glanced back up at the judge.

Myles ignored the questions still flashing in his head. He just wanted to get on with winning. After all, having Judge Thompson was a best case scenario for Sonny; in the dozens of cases he and his associates had tried in front of her, she had always been fair, and always awarded custody to the most deserving parent.

"Mr. Myles," the judge said, crossing her arms. "Perhaps you'd like to share with the court what your client is telling you?" She cocked her head. "We've got a lot of ground to cover. I will not tolerate stalling."

"Yes, your honor." Myles stood quickly, resting open palms on the table. "Your honor, there is a significant matter that I need to address. May we approach?"

"You may," she said.

Myles put on his best poker face as he strode across the gray Berber carpet toward the wooden bench; he and Brett were like two climbers angling up the sides of a pyramid where she sat at the top.

"Your honor," Myles said with a strong voice just low enough for her—not the courtroom—to hear, "my client has just informed me that you and he had a brief encounter in Brazil three days ago."

Brett Robinson closed his eyes hard, kept them shut for a few seconds, then opened them, flashing a stunning expression at the judge.

"Your honor," Brett Robinson said. "I'll not have my client's rights compromised. Surely a renowned Romeo like Mr. Whittaker coming in contact with a woman such as yourself, would be far from an innocent tête-à-tête."

"Mr. Robinson," Judge Thompson said. "Let that be your first and last insulting insinuation toward me and this court."

Myles let out the cool-and-controlled chuckle he'd learned from

Sonny. He turned to Brett. "I'm afraid their meeting was not quite so tit-illating."

Judge Thompson's left hand sat balled into a fist on the desk; her gold scales of justice ring came in and out of view as she stroked her right fingertips over the knuckles of her left hand. He'd seen only one person doing that, but he couldn't remember who.

"Mr. Myles," she said, "what exactly did your client say?"

Myles stared into her silver-blue eyes, wondering how any man could look into that face and *not* fantasize about—

"My client," Myles said with his best lawyer-in-control tone, "simply said that he spoke briefly with you in the aftermath of the Jenn Ryder attack. He did not know your name or your position, and was quite concerned with the welfare of his daughters at the time. End of story."

Brett Robinson's eyes blazed. As if Myles had just tossed that Doberman an enormous lambchop that Brett would lick and smack until all that remained of Myles, Sonny and even the judge, was a blood-stained bone.

36

As Simone Thompson sat cradled in the contours of her well-worn black leather chair, she stiffened with resolve. She was not going to let the condescending and pompous glint in Brett Robinson's eyes shoot down the control and confidence she emanated here atop this judicial zenith. Nor would she allow Joseph Myles's eyes to roil with worry for one more moment over whatever Sonny Whittaker had just divulged about their acquaintance in Brazil.

And until I find a way to get off this case, I will not let Sonny Whittaker dazzle me into getting his way.

Even though triumph twinkled in his smoky eyes as he gazed up from the long table, with his olive tweed and combed-back black waves framing his sun-bronzed face. The corners of his mouth began to rise—

Absolutely never. Simone tilted her chin higher, relishing the tight pull of her twisted-back hair and the weight of the rectangular, silver-rimmed glasses on her nose. She savored the sensation of her black gabardine robe yoking her chest and draping from gathers at her shoulders. The inch-wide cuffs hugged her wrists as she rested her elbows on the bench.

"Gentlemen, we will not be distracted or delayed," Simone said firmly over the low hum of the fan, "by tangential discussions about a chance meeting between myself and the defendant."

"Your honor," Brett Robinson said, his words flowing as smoothly and deeply as a saxophone solo, "Mr. Myles describes a Sonny Whittaker movie of the week, starring you!" His straight brown brows raised like a drawbridge. He stared up with unblinking eyes that glowed brightly against his light caramel complexion that was as smooth and clear as if he were modeling designer skin care products in a glossy magazine.

"And you want me to believe," Brett said, the fine lines around his eyes deepening as if he were making a deliberate display of the life experience that his sixty-plus years had chiseled into his pampered face, "that your rescue mission rendevous was strictly business?"

"That's a ridiculous exaggeration!" Mr. Myles whispered angrily, his wavy chestnut bangs shaking over his forehead.

Simone cocked her head as she leaned forward. Words shot through her lips like ice pellets: "You will respect this court, Mr. Robinson."

"I respect my client's right, your honor," Mr. Robinson said the last two words with a mocking tone, "to a fair trial, unbiased by a tropical tryst."

"Your honor!" Mr. Myles said. "That is inaccurate, offensive—"

A tumble of blond and a form-fitting pink suit flashed on the left as Erica Haynes Whittaker shifted in her chair at the long wooden table. Behind her, Marie's copper-hued hair almost grazed Norris's flow of brown waves, the shoulders of her orange blouse touching his beige suede, as she leaned toward him to whisper. Dark arcs puffed below their eyes.

"Mr. Robinson," Simone said, raising an index finger toward the back of the courtroom and the door to her left which led to a hallway and her chambers, "perhaps you're feeling a bit off-kilter due to the multiple sets of sheriff's deputies guarding us this morning?" The sarcastic edge in her voice hung in the silence.

Fluorescent rectangles in the white-tiled ceiling illuminated the red dress and raven-black coif of Roxanne Jones, sitting in the first of five wooden pews of reporters, spectators and family members.

"Nor will this case be tried in the media," Simone said, as a single TV camera focused on her from a tripod in the empty jury box on the right, to provide pool video for all media. "Any inappropriate conduct will be strictly sanctioned."

Mr. Myles nodded, but a bored glaze covered Mr. Robinson's eyes.

Yet, something glinted in his gaze—he had not forgotten, nor let go of the need to avenge the embarrassment and expense of falling prey to the conscientiousness of a college student.

"By the way, Mr. Robinson, did you notice the title before my name?" Simone pointed to the name plate on the outer edge of the wood cube between them. "The governor and the voters of Los Angeles County believe in my ability to protect children, to place them, and marital assets, with the right person."

"Precisely," Brett Robinson said. "As Erica Haynes Whittaker believes in me, to protect her rights as a mother and wife. Poetic stalker not withstanding."

"Your honor," Mr. Myles said. "May we proceed?"

"No." The milky spikes in Brett Robinson's blue eyes seemed to shift, like the glint of silver knives. "Your honor, I respectfully request that you recuse yourself from this case."

"I have considered it," she said flatly. No, she had begged for it. But her persistent plea to Chief Judge Charlie Rhodes a half-hour ago in his chambers had only netted a firm order that she would remain at the helm of this case until she had navigated it safely and smoothly to a fair conclusion.

"Your request for my recusal is denied," Simone said with a steady, strong tone.

"I demand to see the chief judge," Brett Robinson said. "Now."

"You have that right," Simone said. "But you could potentially delay this trial for months. As we speak, Judge Rhodes is frantically trying to staff our courtrooms. With half the building out sick—"

"I prefer justice delayed," Mr. Robinson said, "over justice denied."

"Gentlemen, please step back," Simone said, focusing on the thick, orange-brown braid down the back of her court reporter's herringbone blazer. Sitting to the right of the bench, the otherwise casual-dressing grandmother from South Central had joked this morning at her desk, applying red lipstick instead of her usual Chapstick, that if Sonny Whittaker were *anywhere* in the building, she was going to look her best. And when Simone had told her they were getting the Whittaker case, Johnetta had shrieked playfully, making a typing motion. "Hallelujah! These fingers are going to type the words from his pretty mouth. Just fan me if I start to swoon."

Now, as Brett Robinson cast a defiant glare, and Mr. Myles stepped back to the defense table, Simone said, "Madame Court Reporter, we're going on the record now."

Johnetta's sharp nose slanted toward the oblong beige machine that parted the pleated skirt between her knees.

"Let the record reflect," Simone said over the click of Johnetta's new blue-green-swirled acrylic fingernails over the rows of keys, "that the court met Mr. Whittaker in Brazil, three days ago, after a shocking attack. Our exchange was anonymous and innocuous in regards to this proceeding. After discussing the horror of what happened, Mr. Whittaker and I went our separate ways."

Brett Robinson stood. "Your honor, please allow me to reiterate my request that you step down from this case. The fact," Brett Robinson said, "that both you and the defendant are targets of threats right now, may inspire some unspoken bond or sympathy—"

"Mr. Robinson, please sit down. We will pursue this through the proper channels—"

In the audience, a deep, masculine voice and the rustle of a newspaper punctuated the continuous hum. A sheriff's deputy took long, quick strides toward a young man with a buzz cut, then leaned to whisper.

"Ladies and gentlemen," Simone said sternly, "I will have quiet in this courtroom, or I will have my court officer clear the courtroom. As for you—"

Simone turned to Brett Robinson. "Mr. Robinson, the court has no such sentiment for either your client's father or the defendant. Now, the court rules provide that you may make your request to the chief judge."

Simone did not look away from Brett Robinson. *You're so stupid and wrong*, his eyes projected now, just as they had during a good dozen trials before her, and just as they had as he stood over her on the witness stand so long ago. He sat, leaning to whisper to Erica Haynes.

At the defense table, Mr. Myles huddled with—

I tasted him. I touched him. I shuddered with need last night, for him . . .

An agonized gasp burned Simone's throat.

Sonny Whittaker raised his thick lashes at her.

Humility. It radiated from his face as if his forehead were stamped with the very word. Simone wanted to scream with frustration, anger. She hated that she agreed with Brett Robinson, that she should step down from this case. But perhaps after Charlie heard it from Brett, he would agree to deliver her from temptation.

37

In the red glow of her dark room, Paulette Barnes tapped tongs in the trays of developing fluid, as the pictures came into focus. It had been months since she'd been down here in the basement. And usually, if she were working on pictures, they were ones she had taken of the boys playing soccer, or Ted barbecuing out back.

But now, this little room below their four-bedroom ranch in the San Fernando Valley would be her passcard to flash her own name across the HOLLYWOOD sign. Her stomach rumbled; how she was going to get through enough days and weeks of diet shakes to pare off these twenty pounds was anyone's guess. But willpower was the key word, and keeping her eyes on the prize. Along with developing—and selling—just the right sensational pictures.

Anything, and anyone, but Simone.

"Is that her?" Paulette squinted. The woman behind the sequined mask looked like Simone—and half the other women dancing along the beach.

"I know that was her." Paulette ignored the ringing phone upstairs. She had to show a house in an hour, but she wanted to get these pictures ready ASAP. Her bills were waiting.

Paulette smiled as she studied the pictures of them running on the beach—from behind, no one could prove that was Simone. What were they doing?

"Where are the ones of Sonny by the ambulance, with Jenn?" Paulette whispered. That phone again. "For heaven's sake!"

Paulette dashed up the stairs, into the kitchen, which still smelled like fresh-cut wood from the new pine cabinets. Sunshine splashed through the new French doors in the nook, gleaming off the white ceramic tile. The swimming pool glimmered on the other side of the white-paned glass.

Paulette picked up the cordless phone on the built-in desk, piled high with bills and unopened mail. "Hello?"

"Paulette Barnes?" It was a deep, familiar female voice.

"Yes." Paulette fingered the overdue invoice for the boys' tuition. The dollar amount was a few digits longer than her bank balance.

"This is Roxanne Jones, *Entertainment Exclusive*. A friend of mine at *Famous* magazine wants to meet you. She might want some of the pictures you took in Brazil—"

Paulette gripped the phone as if she were holding a winning lottery ticket. "Sure. I've got rolls and rolls—"

"We're hoping you can help us identify the woman who found Jenn Ryder, and possibly that Brazilian woman we both saw later with Sonny Whittaker—"

No, that was Simone. *I can't do that to my friend . . .*

Paulette spun; from the hanging basket of bills over the desk, the red print of Nation's Collections came into focus. The aftermath of last year's Christmas shopping, still haunting her . . .

"Ms. Barnes," Roxanne said through the phone that Paulette was squeezing with damp fingers. "I'm sure you know, *Famous* doesn't mind paying top dollar if you've got what they want."

38

Simone Thompson charged through the redwood-stained door to her chambers; the chief judge's footsteps followed hers on the gray Berber carpet. White miniblinds along the wall of windows straight ahead cast a gloomy gray glow over the black leather couch with animal-print pillows, the television in the corner, the sleek wooden desk on the left, and the walls of shelves holding leather-bound law books.

"Charlie," Simone said, unzipping her robe. She yanked the garment back, pushing each shoulder forward. Peeling out of the silky black fabric, she exclaimed, "Take me off this case!"

"I cannot do that," Charlie said. The closed door framed him as he crossed his arms over the chest of a brown wool suit. He raised an oar-like hand, latticed with raised blue veins and speckled with age spots. He exhaled, grasping the tops of his ruddy cheeks with a thumb and forefinger. A downward pull revealed the red underlids of his eyes, like a sleepy saint bernard. "There is no suitable replacement—"

"Then get a visiting judge or two to fill in," Simone said, charging past two leather chairs facing her desk. She perched on the front of it, feeling the heat of the pearlescent apricot-hued Tiffany lamp through her body-hugging, camel-colored, turtleneck sweater dress.

Charlie shook his head. "You're overreacting."

Simone exhaled loudly. "You're not hearing me, Charlie! I'm telling you, I have this feeling that I've known Sonny Whittaker forever. This electricity—"

"So feel electricity, Simone. As long as you didn't—and don't—plug it in." The bristles of his mustache—dyed brown except for silver roots, just like his crew cut—rose as he smiled.

Simone shook her head. Charlie had guided her with level-headed reason since her first trial, six years ago, as the youngest woman ever appointed by the governor to this courthouse. But now, doubt seeped through her gut.

"I was feeling exactly as you do, decades ago, when Raquel Welch sauntered into my courtroom." Charlie's brown eyes sparkled. "I was a ball of putty on the bench, watching my own *Fantastic Voyage*. But after an hour of proceedings, she was just another witness—"

"But you hadn't met her first." The scent of Irish Cream-flavored coffee rose from the cold mug on her desk, mixing with the citrusy fumes of furniture polish.

"Movie stars." Charlie turned down the corners of his mouth. "One introduction feels like much more. This person has been on the television in your living room—"

My bedroom . . . Simone's cheeks grew hot with the memory of Sonny Whittaker's face and voice last night on her television; she turned toward the windows. Beyond the parking lot below, palm trees swayed around a large peach and white shuttered hotel on the beach about a half-mile away.

"Simone? Christ, I think this stalker is making you paranoid. Just relax. If I had to reassign cases every time a judge knew someone in front of them—in this town—I'd spend all day playing musical courtrooms."

"Two people in my court are targets—"

"One on each side," he said. "Even."

"Charlie, you know it's bad if I agree with Brett Robinson—"

"I think you're shaken up by the break-in last night," he said. "I'll review the transcript. But until Judge Evans gets out of the hospital, you are in charge."

"I'm telling you, Charlie, I cannot do this trial."

"You have no choice. I appreciate your honesty, but under the court rules, your brief encounter with Sonny Whitaker is not grounds for recusal. The integrity of this court is protected. And certain of your colleagues cannot be trusted the way I trust you."

Simone crossed her arms over her burning stomach. Leaning over her desk, she scanned pink message slips. The top one: Sister Margaret at the orphanage. Her ex, Clark. None from her mother, though. On her big calendar under the glass desktop, red letters said SACRAMENTO on Wednesday of next week; she was supposed to testify at a legislative hearing for a bill that, if passed, would create more strict guidelines for judges to use in determining which parent should get custody.

"Simone." Charlie stepped close, smelling of coffee, Old Spice and pipe tobacco. He grasped her hands. "Your passion for doing the right thing, that's what makes you the best judge for this case." He turned toward the wall over the couch; hardly an inch of beige paint showed for all the plaques and awards.

"You're one of the youngest judges in this court, with more accolades than a veteran like Judge Johnston."

Simone let out a dry laugh. "Wouldn't he love to get me back for the Katie Moore case. He'd yak to the media for time immemorial about"— she lowered her voice to imitate him— "'that sacred bond between mother and child.'"

Charlie ran his hand over his face again, then picked up today's *Los Angles Times* from the coffee table.

"Read today's letter to the editor," Charlie said, pointing to a headline: NARCISSUS TARGETS JUDGE.

"Why *not* make my day more torturous?" Simone took the paper. She read aloud:

"Just as I made Jenn Ryder fade to black for tormenting women with an unattainable standard of beauty, I will convict Simone Thompson for letting her incompetence crush a family. Her evil deed laid open the gruesome carnage for the vultures of society to pick to the bone. Her judgment day is coming soon. The sentence? Death."

The paper rustled in Simone's trembling hands.

"Investigators are interviewing everyone remotely connected to the Cheyenne Moore case," Charlie said. "It's no coincidence that her book and this trial and her daughter—"

"No one has seen or heard from Katie Moore since she ran away from the orphanage," Simone said. "She could be anywhere, or dead."

"Maybe she's somehow connected," Charlie said. "The whole tragedy is coming full circle—"

"One more reason," Simone said, "to take me off this case."

"Let me go talk with the lawyers right now," Charlie said. "I'll review the transcript. Then I'll decide."

39

Brett Robinson took his seat at the long wooden plaintiff's table. Straight ahead, to his left, the judge was settling into her chair. He just wanted to get through this trial in time for the birth of his first grandchildren–triplets. But enduring a week beside Norris Haynes's daughter—with her cloud of perfume and hair just as big—would be a study in patience and feigned grace.

"The best case scenario," Brett whispered to her as he had done so many vengeful wives, "is to get transferred to Judge Johnston. We'll walk out with everything we want, within a day. Guaranteed."

"So what's the wait?" Erica demanded, her black lashes rising like awnings as she glanced up at Judge Thompson. "Why doesn't she just go—"

"She's got the chief judge's decision in her hand right now," Brett said. He squared his loafers on the floor, knees wide enough to stretch some of the tightness from his hamstrings, which still burned with the vigor of this morning's crack-of-dawn workout.

"Well," Erica said, "If she doesn't say something already, I'll just go up there and read it myself."

"Didn't your dad ever tell you," Brett said, "patience is a virtue?"

Erica's suntanned cheeks twisted into a scowl. "Didn't my dad ever tell you, my impatient, do-it-yesterday attitude is even worse than his? I just want my kids. It seems like we've been sitting here forever—"

"Plaster a more pleasant expression on your face," Brett said. "And use a more pleasant tone. Your body language is shouting anger and insincerity."

"I just don't like that chick," Erica said, crossing her fingers on the lap of her short skirt. "She's too severe. Like I want to go up there and give her a make-over. Let her hair down, pitch the glasses. Dust more makeup on her, in peach tones—"

"Judge Thompson has an impeccable reputation as a jurist," Brett said. Something about the judge reminded him of his own daughter. She and Sheila were around the same age, and seemed to apply the same intelligence and sensitivity to their work. He almost smiled; this morning Sheila had called from her Santa Barbara firm saying her staff had surprised her with a cake on her ten-year anniversary of trying personal injury cases.

"They're all convinced once these babies come," Sheila said, "I'll be so busy changing three diapers at a time—oh . . ."

"Sheila?" Brett stiffened, held his breath.

"They're doing tae-kwon-do in there," she said. "All that sugar. I had three pieces of cake. One for each."

Brett studied Erica's eyes—thank goodness Sheila never felt possessed to wear so much makeup or tease her hair so high or trace and gloss her lips outside the lines. He was so tired of dealing with spoiled, greedy women who had no concept of the work he'd put into his practice since coming to Los Angeles half a lifetime ago. Or the profound weight of carrying on with opportunities that his own father never had as a young black man barred from law school in segregated Washington, DC.

If only Dad could see him now, as reputation, not race, elevated him to the highest heights of the American Dream denied his own father, who had toiled as a railroad porter.

Dad, it's your name, Brett Robinson, that people say along with "dynamite divorce lawyer." Not Brett Robinson, "a black lawyer who does divorces."

Now all Brett wanted was to secure his family's future. And winning this highly publicized case would catapult him to national stature, even bigger fees, and an ever more shining example that a man of color could truly "transcend" race if fate smiled brightly enough. Now, being hired by Norris "Midas Touch" Haynes was the latest and the greatest affirmation that leaving an admirable legal post on the East Coast for this 1960s-born California dream—driving cross-country with pregnant Agnes and little Scott—had been well worth the risk.

And that striking and overly serious young woman directing this trial was not going to stop this cat's shooting star from blasting all the way through the legal stratosphere. No, he would not let her stop him from winning, as she had some seventeen years ago. Who would've guessed, a snot-nosed college student named Simone Thompson could take the stand with such an air of credibility, and the articulate description of Cheyenne Moore's abuse of her little girl, and convince the jury to rule against him. Never again. Even though she was the judge and the jury during this bench trial.

"If she's so great," Erica demanded, tapping her fingernails on the table, "then why fire her? I mean, even if she met Sonny, she is definitely *not* his type—"

"Quiet," Brett said softly. He had not had a case before Judge Thompson in six months or so. Yet a pang of indignation gripped him inside at the memory of that divorce trial for actress Jade Meekes. At the most hectic point of the trial, a dispute arose over evidence; Judge Thompson demanded that he produce a brief within twenty-four hours. He worked through the night to do so—

And she ruled against my ass anyway. But I'll get her back, somehow, starting with this case that wasn't even hers.

Even though, at the end of the week, Sonny Whittaker would be a mere lump of carnage bleeding on the tracks behind the sleek, high-speed train Brett had expertly engineered and navigated so many times through a secret and treacherous route that only a Hollywood divorce could take.

Whether deserved or not.

Not, in the case of Sonny Whittaker. Six private investigators working this case, and not one hint of indiscretion on that brother. Not one woman. Not one party. Not one drink.

Just trips with his daughters and the nanny to the Getty Center. A boat ride and picnic on Catalina Island. Roller-blading along Santa Monica's oceanside South Bay Bicycle Trail. Even the PIs down in Brazil had gotten so bored with his monotonous routine—early-morning workouts, grueling shooting schedule, playing with the twins on the beach and late-night painting—Brett had almost called them home a week ago. But, as suspected, the flocking of guests for Norris Haynes's wedding may have proven even more tempting than the natives.

"We're back on the record," Judge Thompson said, "with case number 02-6645, Whittaker versus Whittaker."

Brett rested his forearms on the edge of the table, then laced his fingers together. He could only imagine Sonny Whittaker pulling his most mack daddy *Come Back, My Love* routine on Simone Thompson down in the land of butt-naked Carnival dancers, African voodoo and jungle heat.

"We had a one-hour adjournment," Judge Thompson said, her silver-blue eyes bright against her yellow-tan skin that always made Brett wonder if there were a couple sister-drops in her ethnic mix. But he'd never seen her at any black lawyer functions, nor had any of the reports about her appointment and subsequent re-election to the bench cited race. Was she passing? Or did her roots extend to Cuba or the Creoles of New Orleans?

"The chief judge," she said with no hint of ethnic twang, "has reviewed the request of Mr. Robinson that I recuse myself after I disclosed on the record that I met Mr. Whittaker."

"Why does she take so many words to say it already?" Erica whispered.

"Shh."

"Now," Judge Thompson said, her gold scales of justice ring glimmering on her left hand, "I am going to read into the record the order of the chief judge—"

Brett tuned out, listening only for a yes or a no. The judge had a wonderful voice, but this courthouse would be a lot easier to get along in without the likes of her pulled-back hair, stern expression and hardline attitude. She just took herself too seriously.

" 'Therefore,' " the judge said, " 'I support her decision to deny Mr. Robinson's request that she recuse herself.' "

Brett laced his fingers more tightly. His relaxed face showed no trace of the disappointment bludgeoning his senses.

Erica whispered: "Are we totally screwed now?"

"I would call it invigorated," Brett said softly, as the judge set down the sheet.

"This order is signed by Chief Judge Charles Rhodes," she said. "Gentlemen, any further discussion?"

Joseph Myles stood. "No, your honor."

Brett rose to his feet. "No, your honor, with all due deference, counsel reluctantly accepts the decision of the chief judge."

And it would be with great bravado that he would hunt down tangible evidence that their encounter was far more salacious than either she or Joseph Myles were disclosing. In the meantime, he would present his case with even more fervor to show her that Sonny Whittaker was a despicable pussyhound. And should she rule in Sonny's favor anyway, Brett would have grounds to forever pluck this pretty thorn from his side, from this courthouse, once and for all.

40

"Opening statement," was all Sonny heard from the judge's mouth as Brett Robinson strutted between them. A theatrical air radiated from the lawyer's trim, six-feet-plus frame, starting at his gleaming oxblood lace-up wingtips to the sharply creased pantlegs, the burgundy silk tie to the powder blue shirt that accentuated the wide pinstripes in the body-hugging suit jacket.

"I humbly request that the court focus on one word," Brett said with a voice as deep and smooth as a Coltrane sax solo, "as I prove that a generous divorce settlement should be awarded to my client, Erica Haynes." He swept his right hand toward Erica; a gold cufflink glinted.

"And that word," Brett said, "is acting. Acting. It's a word we hear every day. It's the very engine that drives the multibillion dollar machine called Hollywood. But what does acting mean?"

With that last word, he pinched his thumb and fingers of his right hand—a large, elegant hand that made the eyes marvel as if studying a Rodin sculpture at the Met—at waist level, as if Brett were sprinkling salt into the wounds he was no doubt intending to slash on Sonny's back.

Like opening lines in a play or film, whatever that scoundrel was about to say could set the tone for tragedy or triumph, for the rest of the performance. Now Sonny cast a pleading stare at the singular critic whose pen had the power to swipe away his meaning for living.

Simone, beautiful angel of justice, please reserve judgment until the final act . . .

But those big *moonbeam gray* eyes remained fixed on Brett Robinson.

"Our fine friend Mr. Webster defines 'acting' as, quote, 'temporarily assuming the duties of another,'" he said. "Another definition: 'to behave insincerely.'"

Brett spun on a shiny wooden heel, focusing on Sonny as he accused: "To behave insincerely."

Without blinking, Sonny let his eyes bore through the charismatic potency of Brett's stare.

"I am going to prove that this man," Brett said, sweeping his left hand toward Sonny—a plain gold band glistened on his wedding ring finger—"this man is a master of insincerity. Sonny Whittaker has made a life of pretending, yet failing miserably in every role. As husband. Father. Actor. Painter. And as a human being worthy of anyone's respect."

Sonny scribbled on his notebook: "Make him stop lying."

"Wait," Myles wrote. "I pick my battles."

"Now," Brett said. "Given Sonny Whittaker's stature, the court may be asking, how can that be?"

Brett unhooked the single button on his suit. His right hand grazed his body-hugging waistband; the dark fabric contrasted with his fingernails—manicured and polished, clipped so that no nail grew past the wide, rounded nailbed.

"*Sweet* Sonny Whittaker." Brett imitated a swooning woman. "This man has three Oscars for lead roles in important films that helped shape our popular culture. He is an icon of romance and swashbuckling adventure. He is a pioneer for African American men in Hollywood. And his latest endeavor, as painter, has hung his creations on walls from Chicago to Copenhagen to China."

Brett continued: "There is no denying that the prevailing image of Sonny Whittaker is that of a superstar—adored and admired by people of all ages and races around the world."

He stepped back to center stage, about six feet in front of the judge.

"However, I am here this morning to perform the unfortunate task of pulling back the velvet curtains that shroud the dark side of Sonny Whittaker." Brett cocked his head slightly, gesturing back to Sonny.

"I am going to expose the real man behind the mask of fame and fortune, of charm and charisma. A man motivated by greed and lust for money and women, who feeds off the bravado of whatever role he may choose to play from day to day, whether on stage or off.

"I am going to prove," Brett continued, "with my client's testimony and that of other witnesses, that Sonny Whittaker is at heart a despicable villain, the ultimate bad guy, a godfather of deception."

Myles shot to his feet. "Your honor, I object to these slanderous—"

She pried her gaze from Brett, flashing a glimmer of annoyance.

"Mr. Myles," she said with a slight scowl. "Sit down. Wait your turn. You'll have plenty of time to state your own case." She looked back at Brett.

"I will show, in effect, that this court should punish Sonny Whittaker. For bombing in his role as a husband. For making all the wrong moves as a father. For getting a double thumbs down for squandering money, whether for business or pleasure. For wasting his artistic talent on a caché of erotic paintings that illustrate his perverse obsession with the female form."

Sonny scribbled: *No!*

"Not admissible," Myles wrote back.

"I will show," Brett said, "that he has instead chosen to spend inordinate amounts of time rehearsing his favorite role: a sex hound on an X-rated stage in an escapist orgy of women, booze and drugs. In effect, this whoremongering hedonist—"

Myles was a navy blue blur shooting up on Sonny's right. "Your honor!"

"Mr. Robinson!" she seethed. "Tone down your language!"

Brett paused. "Mr. Whittaker should be officially stripped of the precious possessions that he has, in effect, already relinquished by his despicable behavior. First and foremost, his children."

The words slammed Sonny's chest. He raised his hand to his throat, massaging away a choking sensation.

"Where was Sonny Whittaker on his daughters' third birthday? Where was he when little Asia was rushed to the hospital with a fever so high it caused her tiny body to convulse in her screaming mother's arms? Where was Sonny Whittaker when his terrified wife and children huddled inside their hilltop home as a mighty earthquake rocked Los Angeles?"

Sonny sucked in the stuffy air.

"Sonny Whittaker was on stage, as international sex symbol. And with that, the court must indulge the question: how many of our seven continents are home to forgotten children spawned by Sonny Whittaker—"

Myles stood. "Objection, your honor, it's irrelevant and immaterial what my client has done in other countries. And as you allow these questions to proceed, you're creating a mockery—"

"Overruled." She did not look away from Brett.

"After all, shooting in exotic locales such as Brazil, Paris, the African jungle, and Polynesia, surrounded by beautiful women, Sonny Whittaker has sprinkled his seed the world over, never staying in a woman's bed long enough to find out if a human being was growing in his wake. He may never know if a Sonny Junior is preparing to graduate from high school in Osaka, Japan, or a girl in Toronto, Canada, is gazing out her front door, wishing her famous daddy would walk up and introduce himself."

Sonny faced forward; Simone's *butterscotch cream* was now *mourning dove gray*—

"Now," Brett said. "It's well been documented in the media that Sweet Sonny Whittaker's performances have earned him a fortune. But what has he done with that income?"

Myles had better have made sure to have covered their tracks.

"I would like the court to envision a story board with a few sketches detailing just how Mr. Whittaker has squandered millions," Brett said. "First, picture him in a chef's hat, standing over the grill at Calypso, his Caribbean-style restaurant on Melrose Avenue."

The restaurant had been as trendy-hot as his grandmother's secret jerk chicken recipe. But the flash of popularity lasted about as long as it took to prepare another house specialty, spicy pan-seared scallops.

"Another picture might show Mr. Whittaker," Brett said, "pulling up to the valet in his Ferrari at the luxury high rise on Wilshire Boulevard in Beverly Hills, indulging in an afternoon tryst with one of several mistresses he housed in apartments around the city."

Only once. But Cathleen had gotten so demanding, with the credit cards . . . Well, twice. Dorian moved in. Until her pro-boxer husband came calling . . . Sonny's jaw ached even now at the memory: *opening the white door in his black silk boxers, Dorian a luscious curl of long legs and elegant arms in the bedroom. "Flowers for Mr. Whittaker," a deep voice said on the other side of the door. The blur of a big fist, the cold marble floor slamming up to meet his cheek. And when he came to, she was gone.*

"It goes without saying," Brett said, "one of these pictures would show him being fitted for custom suits or the latest designer shoes in boutiques up and down Rodeo Drive."

Yeah, right alongside you. Brett took a step close enough to send a waft of very light, clean-smelling aftershave through the air.

"One more picture might show Mr. Whittaker in a secret meeting with various *associates*—using sophisticated tricks of the rich trade to hide money and assets from his wife and from Uncle Sam."

No! I always had my accountants and money managers follow the law to the letter for investments and taxes.

"Next question," Brett said. "How did Sonny Whittaker earn that money? How did a starry-eyed boy from Harlem luck out on all the fame and fortune of Hollywood legend?"

Brett cocked his head in the spotlight of the judge's stare.

"Only one name rolls on the credits here: Norris Haynes. The most respected and powerful producer in the world. The golden-hearted man who saw raw talent, who gave Sonny Whittaker his first lead role in *Come Back, My Love.* Who introduced him to the movers and shakers, promoted him, built him up—"

Brett raised his voice: "Only to have Sonny Whittaker become the ultimate backstabber. Sneaking off to marry his only daughter. Slandering him on the pages of a scorned woman's kiss-and-tell book. And now, bullying him with the help of a powerful civil rights group into producing a controversial film, *The Colony.*"

Wrong. Norris came to me.

"A film and set," Brett said, "that one might conclude has made his daughters targets of a vicious person who is publicly sharpening an ax to grind into the very neck of Hollywood. Leaving the Whittaker children terrified, under the constant watch of bodyguards."

Brett shook his head full of slick, blond-brown waves as he faced the judge. "What kind of life, I ask the court, is that for innocent seven-year-old girls? And what kind of torture might that inflict on their mother, thousands of miles away, worried sick about her babies?"

The judge focused on Brett, but her eyes glazed like Jenn's had as

Xavier's wife, Aurora. Simone Thompson was watching her own mental film strip. Could that include the image of him holding India and Asia in his arms, watching from the crowd as Jenn was rushed away?

"All this," Brett said, "on top of Sonny Whittaker's repeated sullying of the respected name of Norris Haynes, by disrespecting his daughter with unchecked adultery and abandonment. All this is building toward the climax of this drama:

"I want this courtroom to light up in a moment of epiphany—that Sonny Whittaker's fame and fortune do not belong to him. They were given by, and should be returned to, his father-in-law. And nothing would compensate Norris Haynes more graciously than the security and comfort of knowing his daughter and precious grandchildren will forever be provided for by the investment this movie mogul made in Sonny Whittaker.

"And so, as this court contemplates how to equally divide the Whittaker's marital estate, in a way that will give Erica Haynes the alimony and child support to continue a life to which she is accustomed, I humbly request that you remember the word *acting*."

Brett did another gold-glimmering hand-sweep back at Sonny.

"That Sonny Whittaker is *acting* in the doting daddy role. That Sonny Whittaker is acting as if he were *ever* a good husband. As if he ever loved the daughter of Hollywood's most powerful producer. That Sonny Whittaker is acting when he claims he is a changed man. I pray the court will believe none of these desperate acts of deception.

"No," Brett said, shaking his head. "Instead, please help me direct this final act of Sweet Sonny Whittaker's life. Because I will produce evidence that he is a master of illusion. A man who thinks he can always get his way with women and with work by using his good looks and acting talent.

"So I humbly request that the court join me in this intriguing character study," Brett said. "In the end, there will be no doubt about how we, together, will write the final scene for Sonny Whittaker's failed role as father and husband, and we will craft a punishment of Shakespearean proportion. Thank you."

Sonny could not breathe. He had never felt so powerless.

41

Simone rested her elbows on the bench with her fingers laced together. The courtroom was silent, except for rustling fabric and creaking chair springs as Brett Robinson strode back to the plaintiff's table and sat beside Erica Haynes Whittaker.

"Mr. Myles," Simone said, focusing on his eager eyes. "You may begin."

"Thank you, your honor," said Attorney Joseph Myles, whose chesnut hair bounced on his forehead like silent, dangling hooks. Perspiration glistened under the close-cropped beard that fringed the bottom half of his plump, eggshell-white face.

"I choose not to titillate the court with sensational word play," Mr. Myles said, a column of neat, navy blue about three feet in front of her. "Instead, I am going to keep things plain and simple. And real."

His steady voice clashed with Brett Robinson's words, still ringing in her mind: *character study*. All these strangers, journalists, lawyers, Mr. and Mrs. Whittaker, were judging her character. They could reach only one verdict: that Simone Thompson let nothing interfere with her responsibility to make fair and just decisions for the embattled family before her. And that meant turning off all she had seen, all she had felt, and using only the information being presented on the record, within the redwood paneled walls of this courtroom. Nothing more.

"Because real," Mr. Myles said, half-turning with his back to Brett Robinson and Erica Haynes, "real is the best way to describe my childhood friend and favorite client, Sonny Whittaker." His eyes glowed with affection toward Sonny.

"Because when we peel away the layers of image and reputation," he said, "what lies beneath is a genuine man with a heart of gold and a gentle spirit. However, before we can delve into just why a model citizen and father such as Sonny Whittaker deserves full custody of the daughters who are his meaning for living—"

Simone shifted in her chair, trying not to remember that paralyzing moment in Brazil, when she had witnessed in him all that she had longed for in a father of her own—

"—we must first deal with the sad disappointment and devastation," Mr. Myles said, "he has endured while mourning the loss of marriage to Erica Haynes Whittaker."

Marie's copper coif and thin, maple-hued face came into focus behind Erica. Simone's insides twinged with anger; Marie had been so callous in Brazil. But with her here in court, caught up in this trial, Simone certainly was not going to confess that she indeed had made a love connection with Sonny. What was that strange expression in her eyes? Norris's unnaturally smooth face was tense. And not one spark of wedded bliss was coming from that front row.

"In a nutshell, Erica Haynes Whittaker is a rich, spoiled temptress," Mr. Myles said, turning toward the plaintiff's table, "who used empty promises and mind-numbing sex appeal to trick my client into marriage."

How much time and hairspray did it take to create that fountain of platinum hair flowing in corn-cob-sized curls over Erica's shoulders? And the pink suit? Any innocence implied by the color was nixed by the very miniskirt, low V-neck collar and bare legs. Not to mention the pink patent leather strappy spike sandals that made Simone's toes throb. The unnaturally plump lips, the high-maintenance fingernails . . . It was hard to think *anything* when looking at Erica. No telling what went through a man's head when he laid eyes on her.

"Erica Haynes Whittaker contradicts everything Sonny Whittaker stands for," Mr. Myles said. "Specifically, romantic love and devotion, and the rare ability to unite people across color, culture and religion. The court must understand—"

Something in Erica's big blue eyes, past the black mascara, liner and the dark arcs of shadow, sliced at Simone's heart. A glint of something—

"She lured my client to a wedding chapel in Las Vegas," Mr. Myles said, "for one reason: defiance. She sucked Sonny Whittaker into her own twisted power play against the most influential man in Hollywood, and is now holding her husband up to face the wrath wrought by her own malice."

Erica glanced down and scribbled a note to Brett Robinson.

"Erica Haynes Whittaker rarely saw Norris Haynes as she grew up," Mr. Myles said. "Because he was always off shooting in some exotic locale, or holed up at the studio here in Los Angeles, working long hours to earn the golden Oscars that line his office walls.

"Erica Haynes hated that her father sent her to the rigorous Dorchester Prep School, virtually ignoring her and her mother and her brother. She hated having an absentee father who thought hiring an entire circus for her fifth birthday party would make her happy, instead of being there himself."

Simone's breath caught. The pain and resentment flashing in Erica's eyes was exactly what Simone had seen in her own bathroom mirror this morning. But which was worse—living with your father, never seeing him and feeling second place behind his work? Or not knowing his name, his whereabouts, or whether he even knew you were alive?

"All the while, Erica Haynes was spawning a plan of vengeance," Mr. Myles said. "At boarding school, amongst students from India, Europe, Africa and Japan, she grew to loathe the racist legacy handed down to her father by her filmmaking grandfather. And she despised his strict rules on what she could wear, where she could go, and with whom.

"So after graduation, Erica Haynes set off on a decade-long rebellious streak—dating only men of color, wearing only enough clothing to keep from getting arrested. Filming a few adult movies. Trying her hand at modeling in Europe, only to get fired by her agency for using heroin before hitting the runways in London and Milan—"

"Your honor," Brett Robinson said calmly. Something in his eyes seemed hauntingly familiar. "That is false and inflammatory—"

"Please, Mr. Robinson," Simone said with an irritated tone. "Mr. Myles, continue."

"Meanwhile, Norris Haynes was trying to prove to the world that he was not his racist father, that he instead endorsed Dr. Martin Luther King Jr.'s dream of racial unity. And he was doing that by making a flamboyant show of nurturing and showcasing the awesome talent of a young black actor, Sonny Whittaker."

Mr. Myles ran a thumb and forefinger over the edges of his mustache.

"Erica's anger at her absentee father intensified as her mother lay dying of breast cancer, a tumor over her heart, broken by the absence and abandonment of her childhood sweetheart."

Simone's stomach cramped; over the weekend she had seen in her own mother's eyes a new softness. Regret, or perhaps even a willingness to tell the truth.

"But here," Joseph Myles said, "Norris Haynes's plans for Sonny Whittaker, and Erica Haynes's vengeance, cross. Her *coup de grâce*? Marrying her father's protégé. A black man. An older man. A reputed ladies man. Sonny Whittaker, the last man on the planet that Norris Haynes would choose for his daughter.

"And she did this by promising him that by becoming Norris Haynes's son-in-law, Sonny Whittaker could achieve still more fame and fortune. But he wanted to enter into marriage with caution. Sonny Whittaker would settle for nothing less magical than the twenty-five-year union he witnessed between his own parents, whose spiritual bond was so profound, his mother mysteriously died in her sleep just six weeks after leukemia claimed his father."

A hot lump burned Simone's throat as she imagined a gray-haired woman asleep, her husband's wispy spirit swirling over the bed, taking her hand, pulling her up . . . now enjoying eternity together. And Sonny actually believing that was possible.

"Sonny Whittaker also feared losing his friendship and partnership with Norris Haynes. He was forever grateful to this movie magnate for giving him the big break that all actors envision when they wish upon having their own star on the Hollywood Walk of Fame. Obviously, Norris Haynes was the last man in the world that Sonny Whittaker wanted to cross. But—" Mr. Myles turned toward Erica.

"I pray the court will consider the bewitching power of Erica Haynes. The influence of her father's name. The allure of her promises. The hypnotic effect of her dazzling beauty, all the more enhanced by seductive behavior and sexy clothes."

Simone stiffened. Shouldn't he give Sonny more credit? To boil it down to the fact that Erica was so sexy she numbed his mind of all rational thought was insulting to such an intelligent man. Then again, *did* he let his sex drive control him so profoundly? Could he have known in Brazil that she was a judge, and that a semi-seduction in the tropical heat might help his case right now? Was his apparent ignorance of her name and position just an act?

"Yet," Mr. Myles grimaced, "Erica Haynes's promises of storybook success quickly became Sonny Whittaker's worst nightmare."

The image of Sonny making love to that woman, wanting to share his mouth, his tender gaze, the gentleness of his large hands that she had felt on her own shoulders on the dock at Sanctuary, and that burning rod in his shorts—No, that image was too incongruous. Yet, two little girls blended Erica's bow-shaped lips, Sonny's bronze complexion and wavy hair . . .

"Even the joy of knowing his new young wife was carrying life they created quickly turned to terror," Mr. Myles said. "Because Erica Haynes refused to nourish the lives growing inside her. And to my client's horror, she continued to drink champagne, and revealed her years-long flirtation with street drugs—"

"Objection!" Mr. Robinson said.

"Mr. Myles, unless you can document criminal activity," Simone said with a hard tone, "don't waste our time with slanderous allegations."

"Yes, your honor. Once the twins were born," Mr. Myles said, "Erica's disdain for motherhood became apparent. Midnight feedings? Have the night nurse do it. Diapers? The nanny knows where they are. Soothe their crying in the rocking chair in the nursery? No, that would mess up the pretty arrangement of lace pillows. Dress them in expensive outfits and show them off? You bet!"

Simone could not look away from Erica Haynes; the regret in Erica's eyes was sincere.

"Meanwhile," Mr. Myles said, "Norris Haynes blackballed his new son in law. No studio would hire the man who crossed the most powerful man in Hollywood. And that forced Academy Award winning actor Sonny Whittaker to support his family by doing humiliating television commercials. Bit parts in B movies. A few plays."

Mr. Myles shook his head. "He was forced to rent out the only home his children had ever known, while they lived in an apartment. Still, even bankruptcy would not defeat him. Under the strong spiritual guidance of his Caribbean grandmother, he found faith in her assurance that everything happens for a reason. And his Buddhist beliefs assured him that this new round of suffering was preparing him to rise to a higher state of enlightenment and enjoyment. And so, Sonny Whittaker began to follow his first artistic passion: painting.

"All while cherishing the miracle of his daughters' birth," Mr. Myles said. "That moment in the hospital, when he first held them seven years ago, changed his life. He shunned the parties and pleasure-seeking that had almost robbed him of this most precious gift of healthy children. Instead, he cherished every moment of soothing their tears, reading nursery rhymes, watching these human beings grow and smile and look up at him with eyes as loving and unique as his own mother's.

"Sonny Whittaker tried to give his daughters the peaceful home that he had known as a child," Mr. Myles said. "And that was easy, when Erica spent months at a time visiting the world's most exclusive spas or yachting in the Greek Isles with boyfriends or visiting relatives in Scotland."

For a moment, Erica's Barbie-doll face morphed into Simone's mother's thin, sharp-nosed image. Her wispy hair darkened, shortened. And she was Ruth Thompson. Gone. Leaving her little girl to choose between another peanut butter sandwich or the last box of macaroni and cheese in the carriage house kitchenette, while Ruth dined with Bianca on melt-in-your-mouth Brazilian beef, beans and rice, and coconut cake . . .

"Erica Haynes was abandoning her family," Mr. Myles said, "scarring her children with the same cycle of pain and disappointment and emptiness that her father had inflicted on her."

The tip of Erica's slender nose glowed pink. Black crescents of lashes, as she scrawled on white paper, hid her eyes.

"Four years ago, Erica Haynes called her husband from Vienna, saying she would not be back home. Ever. That she had made a mistake marrying him. That she was not ready for motherhood, but that she trusted their nanny, Kindred, to take care of them. And that as long as he agreed to the split, she did not want to bother with all the lawyers and paperwork involved in a divorce or formal custody arrangement—"

"Your honor—"

"You had your turn, Mr. Robinson."

"At the same time," Mr. Myles continued, "Sonny Whittaker was literally pouring the angst over his failed marriage and its disastrous impact on his acting career, onto canvas after canvas. He supported his family by selling his paintings at shows and galleries around the world. Always taking his daughters with him.

"At one point, he was invited to teach a painting course at the art school on the Caribbean island of Montserrat, where he spent summers as a child with his grandparents. There, his grandmother took care of the twins while Sonny not only inspired young painters, but on the terrace overlooking the sea, he wrote the screenplay that would catapult him back to the top of Hollywood's A List."

Mr. Myles shook his head. "Not for the fame and fortune that had motivated him the first time. Now, it was Sonny Whittaker's intention to use *The Colony* to heal hearts and minds the world over of the prejudice that had tarnished his own sterling reputation.

"And now with Oscar buzz growing ever louder," Mr. Myles said, "*The Colony* promises to enlighten the world like no film has ever done before. Because its very inception onto film is being done at the hands of the man who had once set out to destroy Sonny Whittaker. Under pressure from civil rights groups accusing production houses like Prism Films of bleaching Hollywood, Norris Haynes offered to produce *The Colony*."

Mr. Myles paced. "But just as my client caught a glimpse of this glorious possibility, Erica Haynes tries to strike a deadly blow—taking away his children. And that is why we are here now, interrupting a rigorous production schedule in Brazil, for this trial. But why *now*?"

Erica let out a bored sigh. Her elbows thumped the table; her thin shoulders slumped.

"Erica Haynes Whittaker is going after her husband with the same malice that she inflicted on her father. This time? Her motivation is not monetary or maternal. She simply wants to punish Sonny Whittaker for another woman's vicious lies."

Erica shook her head. Brett touched her back; she sat up straight.

"Erica Haynes Whittaker is humiliated by a new book that's being released today. A book in which a woman makes hurtful claims about my client, and things he did not say about the Haynes family. A book that is the only reason Erica Haynes Whittaker is here today, a book that may have something to do with the fact that the lives of four people in the courtroom are being threatened—"

"Your honor," Brett Robinson said angrily, "it is inappropriate to interject that—"

"I recall you brought it up first," Simone said. "Mr. Myles, continue please."

"The bottom line," Mr. Myles said, "is that we are here today to talk about something far larger than decisions about dividing property and assigning custodial parents. Sonny Whittaker is in the midst of leaving a profound legacy on the world. A message that he believes in so strongly, he has cast the Whittaker twins as his character's children. But he cannot present this healing salve to the world without his daughters."

Simone's breath caught in her chest. And the desperation in Sonny's eyes clawed her senses.

"In essence," Mr. Myles said, "a defeat for Mr. Whittaker in this court-room would be a cruel defeat for mankind. Because without the inspiration of watching his own flesh and blood smile and blossom into womanhood, Sonny Whittaker would all but shrivel up and die."

42

Kindred Germaine hummed along with the jazzy theme song of *Entertainment Exclusive* as she stirred a steaming copper pot of chicken noodle soup. The vast expanse of the cobalt blue kitchen blurred—from the shiny countertop tiles to the sleek U of cabinets to the appliances. Standing over the burnerless stove on the kitchen island, she faced the breakfast nook, with its wall of windows overlooking the terrace, the table and chairs, and the television mounted in the corner.

"An *EE* special report," the male anchor's voice said as a graphic showed a picture of Mr. Whittaker, Erica, and the girls. Zigzagged edges broke the image in three parts: Sonny on one side, Erica on the other, the girls in the middle above a gold question mark.

"No," Kindred cried, raising her trembling fingertips to her face. "Just take out Erica, and keep us all together—"

"We will continue to bring you the very latest on the Sonny Whittaker divorce trial," the anchor said, as Roxanne Jones appeared on the screen in front of a boxy beige building. "Our reporter is live right now at the Santa Monica Courthouse, with a shocking report."

Roxanne Jones gushed with a *can-you-believe-this!* tone: "Controversy rocks the court this morning, as the judge in the Sonny Whittaker divorce trial admits she met the sexy movie star on a tropical island, just days ago!"

Kindred sniffled as she swirled the soup more quickly with a big spoon. Roxanne Jones's swoop of dark hair bounced over the shoulders of her red dress as she stood, gripping her silver microphone with the yellow *EE* logo in the hazy sunshine.

"Flashy divorce lawyer to the stars Brett Robinson is fuming," Roxanne said, as video showed him standing in court. "He's demanding that Judge Simone Thompson step down immediately from this case—"

"Kindred?" The housekeeper's angry tone made Kindred jump. "You do not finish math lessons until twelve-thirty—"

"The girls are hungry," Kindred said, taking note of how skinny and suntanned Roxanne Jones looked today. "They're watching *The Little Mermaid*. Josh and Jared are upstairs, so—"

"Go up with them," Guadeloupe said, smoothing her apron and stepping toward the stove. "I'm in charge of lunch."

"You weren't around," Kindred said, without looking away from the television. "There's grilled cheese in the oven."

"I was taking chicken salad to the police outside," Guadeloupe said. "Sitting in those cars all day, God bless them. But now—"

"Wait," Kindred whispered. "There he is—"

"Sonny Whittaker leaving the courthouse just moments ago," Roxanne said as video played of him—flanked by two brown-uniformed sheriff's deputies—slipping into his lawyer's navy blue Mercedes, "reportedly to visit Jenn Ryder in the hospital. His costar is still in critical condition."

The tension tightening his face around dark sunglasses stabbed Kindred's heart. "I hate this," she said. "If it weren't for that book, Erica wouldn't be lashing out—"

Guadeloupe whispered in Spanish and fingered the ivory crucifix on a chain around her neck. "I hope she makes it. And the monster who did it is punished, before anyone else—"

"The security people are coming any minute," Kindred said, glancing down the dark hallway toward the front foyer and the door to the garage.

"Meanwhile," Roxanne said, as video showed red spray-painted HOL-LYWOOD KILLS on a big white screen. "LA cops hot on the trail of a vicious attacker named Narcissus, while Norris Haynes cleans up threatening vandalism in his own highly guarded fortress."

"I hate him," Kindred said, glaring at the televised image of a man with a golden complexion, wavy hair, and a navy blue suit.

"An exclusive chat now, with Brett Robinson," Roxanne said, tilting the microphone up toward his mouth. "What does this mean?"

The oven rack rattled as Guadeloupe peeked in at the sandwiches.

"The canons of law state that a judge must," he said, "maintain unbiased objectivity toward everyone before her. Lawyers, wives, husbands, witnesses included."

Kindred let out a dry laugh, remembering what she'd seen Roxanne doing to Norris on the darkened set. "Yeah, let's let Roxanne define objectivity. There's a reason she gets so many exclusives."

"Kindred!" Guadeloupe dove toward the stove; the soup was bubbling over and sizzling.

"That man is the devil," Kindred said, "If Brett Robinson gets his way, the girls—"

A soft, floral scent lingered around Guadeloupe as she set the pot on a cooler part of the stove. "Oh, *señorita*," Guadeloupe murmured. "Your imagination—Mr. Whittaker will keep his babies. We'll all stay—"

"We have to," Kindred said as video showed the judge. The judge with big blue eyes who had devoured Daddy Whittaker with a single look, as he held their little girls. "They're my life. My life. It can't happen."

"No more reports," Guadeloupe reached and pushed a button; the TV went blank and silent. "Just like the girls, you should not watch."

"I don't have a mother," Kindred said. Unquenched curiosity surged through her so strongly, it prickled a hot sheen of sweat under her canary-yellow, scoop-collared cotton shirt and cigarette pants. "So don't talk to me like you are."

Kindred strode away as Guadeloupe whispered something in Spanish.

She had to know what was going on, how the lawyers and that judge were casting her fate. And she would find out, even if she had to set the VCR to record the news and special reports—along with the usual *EE* taping at seven-thirty every night—so she could watch later, up in her room.

The clank of plates in the kitchen subsided as Kindred dashed through the center hallway, toward the door leading to the garage. She rested a hand on the post at the base of the cube-shaped staircase, lit by a two-story-high stretch of jewel-toned stained glass. The banister felt slippery—the cleaning crew must have just oiled it—as her leather loafers took two steps at a time. In the long upstairs hallway, she ran along the plush cream carpeting.

"Hey, Kindred," Jared called, standing about twenty yards away, on the balcony overlooking the foyer and vaulted living room. To her left, Josh glanced up from a sports magazine; he was sitting on a red-cushioned bench in the soft glow of recessed lights.

Kindred put her hand on the cold doorknob leading into the girls' room. The television was still on. But it didn't sound like *The Little Mermaid*. Kindred leaned close to the door:

"Channel 8 giving you an exclusive look right now," a man said, "as the stalker scare brings super-tight security to the Sonny Whittaker divorce trial—"

Kindred's heart pounded. She swung open the door, stomped to the right, toward the white cabinet holding the big TV. She slapped the POWER button. The word stalker made goosebumps ripple down her back as she scolded: "Your dad said no TV today!"

To her right, Asia stared down at her toes as she pulled her knees to her chest. In silky blue pajamas, she sat in the center of her pink bed, over which a giant bow secured sheer fabric that draped around the gathered satin headboard.

"Where's India?" Kindred asked, looking at the mini spaceship on her left. The glossy wooden tube, about six feet wide, stretched about twelve feet high. Red, white and blue paint on the side said USA and pictured the American flag. A large oval about two feet off the floor opened onto India's bed.

"In the cockpit," India called from a small window near the top. "Finishing my math problems." In an instant, she slid down a firehouse-type pole onto the lower mattress, and stepped out, waving a sheet full of numbers and pencil marks. "I need more work."

In jeans, a GIRLS RULE T-shirt and a high ponytail of curls, India stared up, then knitted her little brows. A framed and autographed poster of astronaut Mae Jemison loomed on the wall behind her. "We're sorry, Kindred." India wrapped her arms around Kindred's hips, pressed her cheek to Kindred's stomach. "Don't be mad. We wanted to make sure Daddy's okay."

"It's his rule." Kindred said, stroking India's curls. White sheers billowed in from the back wall of floor-to-ceiling doors. Kindred stormed toward them. "Why are these open!"

Calm down. Calm down. She tried to take a deep breath, but the fear, and the uncertainty of everything—their safety, their future—it all exploded up into a hot lump in her throat. But she could not let Asia and India see just how worried she was. Kindred closed her eyes, inhaled deeply. She pulled the terrace doors shut. The hazy sun warmed her face; she inhaled the dusty sage scent of grass and mountain vegetation shooting up from the treacherous rocky slope just below the ornate stone banister.

Click. The TV turned back on.

"There he is!" Asia jumped up, pointing.

Kindred turned; Mr. Whittaker was dashing into the courthouse past a media mob.

"I want them to leave him alone!" Asia said, crossing her arms. The remote control slipped into a swirl of pink covers. "All those cameras look like guns aimed at him."

Kindred snatched up the remote. "Asia," she said softly, "this is why you're in bed with a tummy ache. Worrying so much. We don't need to watch." Kindred aimed the white rectangle at the TV.

". . . taking the stand this afternoon," a female reporter said, "Erica Haynes, who is challenging Sonny Whittaker for full custody of—"

"There's Mommy!" Asia said.

"She only wants us to make Daddy mad," India said.

Asia gripped her stomach, then pulled the comforter over her face. India hopped onto her sister, yanking up the blanket. Asia's face twisted in a sob, tears clumped her lashes together.

Kindred perched onto the edge of the bed, drawing Asia's head onto her lap; India burrowed between Kindred's ribs and arm.

"Somewhere, over the rainbow," Kindred sang. The twins joined her.

Kindred froze. Shattering glass? Maybe the AlarmTech crew was here to install the new alarm system, Guadeloupe let them in, and they had to break a window to put in the sensors.

Crash. Kindred's heart pounded as they sang. Yeah, that had to be it.

43

In her chambers, Simone Thompson's hand trembled as she scrawled her name across the bottom of a beige check. Her knuckles scattered a thick stack of pink message slips across the glass desk pad.

"Here," she said, ripping the check out, handing it across her desk to her secretary. "Just let me know when the next one is due. I wish I had enough to bail out The Tree House—"

"Judge," Yolanda said softly, grasping the check. Gratitude glowed in her onyx eyes; her round cheeks rose as her frosted cinnamon lips broke into a smile. "I don't know how to thank you—"

"Just graduate and pass the bar," Simone said, glimpsing a message slip that said "Marie" and "CALL ME." "Somebody's got to replace me someday."

"Judge, I won't let you down," Yolanda said, raising pencil-thin brows toward a side-parted bob. Sudden brightness through the windows illuminated prune-colored puffs under her eyes.

"Another late night with Mr. Tort and Mr. Tax Law?" Simone asked.

"One more year," Yolanda sighed. "Every time I yawn, around midnight, I think of you, and I'm good to go another couple hours."

"Hope I never disappoint you."

"No, everybody in my study group thinks you're the bomb," Yolanda said. "We meet tonight. The black lawyers association hooked me up. Our tutors—a prosecutor, a defense lawyer—"

"I always envied their close-knitness," Simone said, remembering nights when she would pass the BLA's student meetings in the law school lounge. "But mystery-ethnic folk like myself—"

The phone rang on Simone's desk. Yolanda answered; the dramatic webbed sleeve on her long green dress swayed as she handed over the gray receiver.

"It's your mother." Yolanda's chunky silver necklace and matching earrings swayed as she hurried out and closed the door.

"Simone!" Her mother's voice was like a sharp claw digging into Simone ear. "I am incensed by your behavior over the weekend."

"That's how I've been feeling all my life. Do you have an answer for me now?" Simone shuffled message slips: two corporate donors, Judge Caroline Drew, the *Los Angeles Times*, Sister Margaret. On her desk, the Tiffany lamp illuminated a newspaper with her name in the headline. Simone slammed the paper into the silver garbage can under her desk.

"Simone, do not call me about this anymore," her mother quavered. "The past is the past. You've done just fine, so let's—"

Bianca's voice boomed in the background.

"I can't talk now," her mother whispered. "The charity dinner is Friday—"

"You're pathetic," Simone said. Disgust and disappointment cramped her stomach. "Tell me who my father is, and I'll never interrupt you again. Ever."

"Simone, I want to tell you, but—"

"Was it Mr. Anderson?" That heartless, shady bastard could not be. No, not a man Simone had watched thirty years ago, *taking the podium in the Brazilian sunshine, drawing applause from the fancy crowd. By the street, as a girl not much older than Simone was snatched off her bike by a group of men . . . her dirty yellow hair ribbons fluttering over dark ponytails as she screamed . . . one man's hand covering her mouth as they shoved her into a car.*

Then, *Simone's frantic efforts to tell her mother, and Bianca, then later Mr. Anderson.* "Those were probably her parents," he answered, "or the police, taking away the dirty street children during our ceremony."

Her mother—silent.

"Ruth Thompson," Simone said, shooting to her feet. "Is he really a judge?"

Her mother sobbed. "He was—"

Bianca whispered something.

"Is he here in LA?" Simone asked.

The dial toned buzzed.

"Damn her!" Simone slammed down the receiver. "God, I need to run—" But not with police in tow. And the clock on the credenza facing her desk showed she had just over an hour before she had to resume the trial. As she dashed out of the office, Simone cast a longing glance at her running shoes by the door. Usually, at lunchtime, she would lace them up, slip on running clothes, then sprint two blocks to Santa Monica Beach. She would pound out her emotions on the winding path alongside rollerbladers, bikers, even film crews. Sometimes, when jogging on the Pier after work, she would pass the ferris wheel, vendors and fishermen just in time to watch the giant red sun touch the ocean.

"Judge, the media—" Yolanda warned.

Simone shook her head. "I'll use the judges's door."

"But the chief wants the police—"

In minutes, Simone was whizzing through lunchtime traffic, up Pacific Coast Highway, to the sprawling Mediterranean-style mansion on the beach. A flower-shrouded sign said THE TREE HOUSE. The orphanage had been donated to the Sisters of Saint Theresa by an anonymous Hollywood millionaire, rumored to have been an orphan found in a park by an actress who raised him and made him a star.

A Channel 8 News truck pulled out of the long gravel driveway as she turned in. Why were they here? Her heart pounded as her tires crunched toward the small parking lot at the side.

Behind the house, dozens of children—in coats, windbreakers and hats—sat at picnic tables on the grassy sprawl overlooking the water. Two kids in red parkas raced down the ladder from the adorable stained wood playhouse in a tree. They ran toward a nun serving plates from a smoking grill.

"What are they doing outside?" Simone asked, stepping into the biting, damp air. She dashed up the steps onto the wrap-around porch.

"Simone." Sister Margaret pushed open the screen door. The unusually chalky hue on her wide face accentuated the pink rims of her gentle blue eyes and her slightly humped nose.

"Thank God you're safe," she said, clutching a gray scarf draped over her short, salt-and-pepper bowl cut hairstyle. A charcoal-colored wool coat hung to the hem of her black habit; thick white socks hugged her thin ankles above white athletic shoes.

"Sister," Simone said, hugging her and taking note of the perpetual scent of graham crackers and Play-Doh. "Why the coat, and the barbecue? It's freezing—"

The nun stepped back into the shadows of the panelled hallway. "They turned the heat off. No lights." Her voice echoed up the wide oak staircase; the nicks and crayon marks on the well-worn steps and banister testified to decades of children's energy and mischief.

"Those developers," Sister Margaret said, handing over a business card, "they are trying to scare us into moving."

"But the bills are paid through the end of the month," Simone said, reading the card, which had only an 800 number on it. "Lindo Designs. That's 'lovely' in Portuguese. Who brought this?" Her mind spun. If this were Rosa Anderson's company—

"We can't cook," Sister Margaret said. "If it weren't for the ladies auxiliary bringing breakfast—"

"I'm meeting with the loan officer at my bank, tomorrow at five," Simone said. "You and these children will not lose your home."

"Miss Simone!" Little feet thundered across the floor. Four pairs of arms wrapped around her legs; hands grabbed her fingers.

"Have lunch with us!" Veronica said, her eyes sparkling from behind overgrown straight bangs. Her two ponytails bounced over the shoulders of her puffy red coat; her milky round face crumpled, her tiny point of a nose wrinkled. She sneezed. "Can we go to your house? It's cold here!"

Simone smiled to mask anger at the coldhearted bastard whose money-hungry greed was making these poor children shiver.

"Miss Simone!" Tyrone tugged at her hand. "Did you bring some more licorice? The blue kind?"

She pulled tissues from her purse and wiped his runny nose. She pressed a palm to his broad brown forehead. No fever, yet. She pulled his LA Raiders ski cap down over his ears.

"I'm going to take all of you home with me tonight if—"

"Channel 8 is working to get some buses," Sister Margaret said, "to take us to a hotel for the night. But tomorrow will come—"

Simone swallowed over a hot lump as she bent her knees and hugged Veronica and Tyrone, Mia and Paul, who wore matching red coats. If one child had to feel as unwanted and uncared for as she once had, it was one too many.

"We're going to make everything okay," Simone said softly. Sister Margaret wiped a tear as Simone glanced up from the huddle of little heads. "I promise."

"We saved you a hot dog!" Mia said, wild yellow curls shooting around ear muffs. "I couldn't bite mine. See, no teeth." She grinned; her two top front teeth were gone. "Come on!"

The children pulled Simone through the wide hallway through the center of the house. She usually turned away from the right wall, painted to look like bricks, a window flower box and shutters framing a mirrored observation window to the playroom.

But now, facing Brett Robinson in her courtroom, and expecting Cheyenne Moore to take the stand, possibly tomorrow, Simone flashed back. She had been a college student volunteer, along with psychology graduate student Marie Cartwright, in the experimental program for kids whose parents were going through divorces.

Peering through the window, Simone almost dropped the bowl of pretzels she'd gone to get to ward off her and Katie's pre-dinner hunger. She could not believe what she saw inside—

Cheyenne Moore's long burgundy fingernails clawed Katie's mop of brown curls. The sound of hair ripping from her scalp . . .

"Get away from that!" Cheyenne shrieked, yanking Katie from the metal Erector Set she and Simone had been using to build a miniature crane. "I will not raise a fucking tomboy!"

Katie's eyes became enormous as she laid her cheek on the shoulder pad of her mother's silk dress.

"I'm sorry, Mommy. I'll play with my dolls when we get home. Please love me, Mommy."

Simone watched, heart pounding. Just minutes ago, they'd been waiting for Katie's mother to return from court where she was suing NBA star Peter Moore for divorce and custody of Katie. And according to news reports and Sister Margaret, the actress who played on a weekly, glamorous nighttime drama, would probably get to keep her daughter, thanks to doting dad Peter's travel schedule.

But now Simone was seeing a side of Cheyenne Moore that no one—including the judge—seemed to know about.

Even as Cheyenne stroked Katie's back, hatred twisted her perfectly made-up face. She grabbed another handful of hair, snapping Katie's head back so they were face to face. Cheyenne's brown eyes grew bigger as she hissed, "Your real father, when he comes back, will want a perfect little girl, Katie. Not a boy!"

Katie smiled, as if she were acting on cue. "Don't be mad, Mommy. I'll be perfect."

"You'll never be perfect, you miserable little—get your coat!"

Trembling and still out of sight, Simone knew exactly what she had to do . . .

"Miss Simone is here!" Veronica shouted to the scores of kids as they stepped onto the huge back porch with cozy swings and little tables with crayons, games, books. A little boy approached with a plate, a hot dog rolling out of the bun, splattering mustard and ketchup in the potato chips and a plastic cup of peach slices.

"Thank you, Mark. I'm starving." Simone bent down, taking the plate, marveling at pudgy fingers letting loose, the big eyes and face searching hers for approval. She bit the hot dog. "Mmmm, delicious."

Another child handed her a dixie cup of red punch. "Here, Miss Simone." Several kids shouted, "Sit with us!" Simone squeezed onto the wooden picnic bench with them. Her mind spun over how these children could keep their home. Someone like Sonny Whittaker or Norris Haynes could help in a matter of minutes, and never miss the money. But those men were off-limits during the trial.

"Boys and girls, Miss Simone has to get back to work," Sister Margaret said.

"No!" they shouted.

Mia burst into tears. "But it's dark in there."

Simone hugged the little girl, who smelled like ketchup and mustard. She glanced up at the house, to the window that little Katie Moore once called home.

"I think tonight," Simone said, "you get to stay at a hotel and go swimming!"

The kids cheered as Tyrone asked, "And we'll go to the zoo with you again?"

"Universal Studios!" Veronica shouted.

Simone smiled, but a chill snaked down her back. Narcissus's words blared in her head. Was she being watched right now? And was that putting these children at risk?

44

An antiseptic smell filled the teal-and-white room at the UCLA Medical Center as Sonny Whittaker stared down at the mummy wrap of bandages obscuring Jenn Ryder's face and neck.

"What monster would do this?" Sonny asked deeply.

"The same one who wants to do it to you," Myles said as the doctor entered between the two police officers guarding the door. Myles had objected to them trying to leave the courthouse during this lunch break, having to dodge the media outside and risk getting stuck in traffic on the 405 freeway. But Sonny had to see his costar, to combat this sense of powerlessness against Narcissus, who could be anywhere, plotting the next attack.

"Myles, try the house again. I don't know why the line would be busy for so long. It worries me—"

"You bet," Myles said, reaching for the phone. "The security company is probably jamming the lines while they install the high-tech stuff. Relax, man."

"We should've gone home for lunch," Sonny said. "All these break-ins. It bothers me, being away from the girls."

"They'll be fine." Myles dialed. "With cops out front and your bodyguards inside—"

"I don't care," Sonny stroked Jenn's thin upper arm beneath the green hospital gown. Her hands were wrapped in gauze. "Jenn, it's Sonny."

A woman in a white lab coat, with a cameo pin at the collar of her white blouse, and a short pouf of maroon-hued curls, stepped to Sonny's side. "Mr. Whittaker, I'm the doctor. Jenn has not been conscious since we flew her in from Brazil."

"Can she feel it, the pain?" Sonny asked.

"We're keeping her comfortable and safe," the doctor said. "We don't know yet whether we can repair—"

"Get him out of here!" a man shouted. "It's his fault!" A tall, slender denim-clad man with a full white beard stomped through the door on brown suede hiking boots. "I told Jenn not to do that film! America is not ready for that interracial love bull—"

The doctor grasped his shoulders. "Mr. Ryder, lower your voice. Jenn may hear—"

He pulled away, shouting: "Sonny Whittaker, you and that we-are-the-world talk you're always givin' to the media. My ex-wife, convincin' me this was a good career move for our girl."

The man's eyes were the same shade and shape as Jenn's, but they lacked her compassion and forward-thinking glimmer.

"Well, buddy," the man shouted, "the only thing in the world this movie is changin' is my daughter's face. She's ruined! If she lives to ever look in the mirror again!"

The doctor strode to the door. "Officers, come in! Mr. Ryder is out of control."

The man grumbled: "The crazy guy who did this is probably in the fuckin' KKK. Pissed off about all those love scenes they kept previewin' on TV. You wrappin' your lips around my daughter! Her actin' like she loved it!"

Sonny shook his head.

Two police officers hurried in.

"Escort him out," the doctor said.

The officers took the man's arms. As they led him to the door, he turned. "I hope they melt your daughter's face, too, Sonny Whittaker. So you'll see how it feels."

45

Kindred held the twins' hands, the three of them singing "Over the Rainbow" at the tops of their lungs, as they spun ring-around-the-rosie style. They tumbled to the carpet, laughing.

"Let's remember those words," Kindred said, poufing their curls. "Anytime we get sad, we'll sing that."

"Okay," they said.

She savored their smiles, wishing she could keep them this happy, this distracted from all that was going on, forever.

"But you have to promise, no more sneaking the news," Kindred said, aiming the remote up at the TV. "It only upsets you."

The sound of more shattering glass echoed from downstairs.

"What's that?" India asked.

"The security crew," Kindred said. "They must have to break some windows to install the sensors."

"Another story involving children," the anchor said, "just coming into the Channel 8 newsroom—"

Kindred balanced her finger on the POWER button as video showed a Mediterranean-style mansion framed by a rolling green lawn and the ocean behind. A big sign said "The Tree House."

"At this orphanage," the reporter said from the long covered porch, "boys and girls and the nuns who take care of them, could be homeless in just a few days."

Kindred's heart pounded. Homeless. Without the twins, she would have nowhere to go.

"A cash crisis leaves the house cold and dark," the reporter said, "as a developer tries to seize the property to build luxury condos—"

"That's where we take our toys and clothes for all the kids!" India said.

"But it's *not* like Little Orphan Annie," Asia said, as video showed children having a picnic in the back yard and running around, playing tag and laughing. "An orphanage is where mean people take you from your parents. You mop the floor. And sleep with a thousand other kids."

The twins stared up, looking perplexed and sad.

Click! "This is why Daddy Warbucks said no more TV." Kindred set the remote on the shelf next to the TV, but it clicked back on.

"Kindred!" Guadeloupe's stern tone shot into the room. She hurried in with a wooden lunch tray. "You are upsetting them!"

"No, I—"

Guadeloupe set the tray on a small table by the windows. Then she jabbed OFF on the television. Her dark eyes focused on the twins, then back at Kindred.

"Is the security company here?" Kindred asked. "I heard—"

"No," Guadeloupe said, "I took the police some soda out front, I would have seen them." She glared, then glanced quickly at the girls. "Just relax—"

The housekeeper hurried from the room, closing the door, with the remote in her pocket.

"Come on, little angel girls," Kindred said playfully, leading them to small chairs, where they sat before three bowls of soup and grilled cheddar on wheat sandwiches. "Eat. Asia, you have nothing in your system—"

"If bad guys come to our house," India bit her grilled cheese, "we need energy to run!"

Kindred swallowed a mouthful of sandwich. "There will be no bad guys—"

"Then why are they outside our room?" Asia demanded, crossing her arms. "Don't treat us like we're stupid little kids."

"Eat," Kindred said, spooning up her own soup.

"I only want soup," Asia scowled at melted cheese oozing from between the golden-brown bread onto the plate. "Mom says cheese gives you fat legs."

Kindred stopped chewing. If she could force-feed Erica with a huge, greasy pizza and three chocolate shakes, right now . . .

"Come here, girls," Kindred said, leading them into their walk-in closet with the floor-length mirror. "Remember at your last checkup the doctor said you were just the right height and weight for seven years old?"

The girls nodded.

"And how he said it's important to eat well so you'll stay healthy?"

India curled her right arm like a bodybuilder. "Protein for muscle." She pointed to her bright grin. "Milk for teeth." She jumped up. "Bread and cereal for energy!"

"Exactly," Kindred clapped.

India put a hand on her hip. "Asia won't eat peanut butter," she said in a tattle-tale tone, staring at her sister. "Or ice cream. And those oatmeal cookies last night, she—"

Asia crossed her arms as she glared at India.

"She gave them to her doll," India taunted.

"Why?" Kindred asked.

Asia shrugged. "I had a stomachache."

"Show me," Kindred said. India led her to the play corner, where shelves held books, puzzles and toys. In the driver's seat of a pink, kid-sized Barbie Jeep sat a huge porcelain-faced doll. India lifted its lacy skirt, revealing a napkin and three cookies.

Kindred took Asia's hand. "You know better than that. Guadeloupe will have a fit if she finds bugs up here—"

"Mom was already mad—" Asia's face crumpled; tears shot from squeezed-shut eyes.

"Why, honey?"

" 'Cause we ate fried manioc and chocolate at Sanctuary," India said. "It's against mom's rules. No fat, no sugar."

"Those grown-up rules are not for you." Kindred took their hands. "Let's eat before our soup gets cold."

Asia gripped her stomach. "I wanna go back to bed."

"Just a few spoonfuls," Kindred said. "And some juice."

"Asia, Kindred is smarter than Mom." India slurped a spoonful of soup, sucking in noodles that speckled her chin with yellow droplets. "Mmmm!"

Asia took a few spoonfuls and a sip of juice. But then she slunk onto Kindred's lap, resting her head on Kindred's shoulder.

"India, we'll work on more math problems," Kindred said, as she tucked Asia back in bed and ran her palm over her forehead. "Then we can read."

That shattering glass sound again. The security system installers, they would not need to break so many windows. Would they?

Kindred strode toward the bedroom door. Josh and Jared would know—

A smash, then a shower of shards on stone.

Kindred raised her hands to her face for a moment. Think . . . was someone breaking in? And if so, wouldn't Josh and Jared come in *here*?

Someone was breaking out every window . . .

Downstairs, just below them, on the terrace. The hairs on the back of Kindred's neck rose. She lowered her hands.

"The stalker!" India shrieked in a whisper.

Asia pulled her comforter around herself and wedged under the ruffles of her bed.

Kindred raised a trembling finger to her puckered lips.

"Come on, angels," Kindred said. "We have to hide."

46

In the courtroom, Sonny Whittaker squared his shoulders as he sat next to Myles at the table. Erica sat about a dozen feet before them, in the witness box, tapping the silver mesh ball of the microphone. Her glossy, bow-shaped pink lips poked out, her brows drew together and her hair tumbled over the shoulder of her suit as loud bursts of static shot through speakers around the courtroom.

The noise scraped across Sonny's steaming nerves as he leaned toward Myles.

"Let's try the house one more time," Sonny whispered, trying to shake the panicky heat that had sparked back at the hospital with every call that met a busy signal.

"At the break," Myles whispered. "All the cops at your house right now, they're fine."

Ear-piercing static from the microphone made him freeze. A groan rose from the spectators behind them.

"Mrs. Whittaker," the judge said, "it's working. Mr. Robinson, let's get started."

As Brett stepped toward Erica, Sonny whispered, "Whatever garbage comes out of her mouth up there, do not let her describe my erotic paintings."

"You bet," Myles said.

Sonny bristled at the memory of Erica finding his caché of secret canvases. He could still hear the frames splintering on the jade tiles in the foyer, his years and months of expression cracking and crumpling, as she pitched the paintings over the balcony, screaming—

"She went crazy, man," Sonny whispered. Of the hundreds of images Sonny had painted, the dozens that delved into his darkest, most private thoughts were off limits to his wife, the media, and any discussion of him being a full-time dad to two little girls. Besides, in this bizarre twist on "courtship," with Simone Thompson, keeping the paintings a secret would be as much damage control as he could do while his ex-wife, her lawyer, Cheyenne and God knew who else, would try to tarnish the judge's impression of him.

"Mrs. Whittaker." Brett stood at an angle, facing Erica and Simone. "Tell me how you felt when Hollywood legend Sonny Whittaker asked you to marry him."

"Ohmygosh," she cooed. Erica's lipstick glimmered as she smiled. She clasped her hands in the lap of her tiny skirt and glanced his way, her eyes sparkling.

"What girl wouldn't be just dizzy about it? He was the most charming, I mean, he always opened doors and quoted philosophers and really cool lines from his movies, and he told me I was beautiful and—he was just so sophisticated and cool—"

Sonny let the corners of his mouth curl up. But a sudden hot flash made him lean toward Myles. "Something's wrong at home," Sonny whispered. "I can feel it, man, in my gut. Why can't we get through?"

"We'll try again at the next break," Myles said.

Sonny turned back toward the judge. Her profile was stiff as she sat in her leather chair, swiveled to the left as she watched Erica and Brett.

"I think," Erica said, "he was kind of a father figure, too. I mean, my dad worked a lot, so my love for Sonny, with our age difference and everything, it meant more."

Brett nodded. "Tell me, Mrs. Whittaker, about how your husband proposed marriage."

Sonny pressed the pen to the top line of the notepad: *She proposed!*

Myles nodded slightly.

"Oh, it was a dream," Erica said. "We were both really into this fantasy of him being the sultan and I was like, his one-woman harem. I had a whole bunch of sexy costumes, and names, and I would pretend I was a different concubine every night—"

The judge's head moved forward slightly.

Sonny's heart pounded. What was Simone thinking?

"Sonny would go wild, man!" Erica said. "Making love for *days*. The housekeeper brought food to the room. I mean, you can't live on each other's body fluids alone—"

Sweat soaked Sonny's entire length. He did not want Simone to hear this. Then again, maybe it could work to his advantage.

"—and Sonny was, ohmygosh, he was the best lover." Erica smiled at him. "Lust didn't begin to describe our attraction. We were sure we had known each other in a past life, and our house, we designed it like a palace so we could play—"

Sonny wrote: *I designed it, after Lawrence of Arabia.*

Brett said, "Mrs. Whittaker, the proposal—"

"Oh yeah," she said. "We were in the Jacuzzi on our terrace overlooking LA. All of a sudden I heard all these tiny bells, like the kind I used to wear around my ankles when—" She shook her head. "Anyway, Sonny poured me some Dom Perignon, and smeared my favorite Beluga caviar over my lips. He liked to lick off every tiny little egg, one by one—"

The judge was so still—the black shoulders of her robe, her bell-shaped nose, her wide-open eyes. Was she even breathing?

"So this music," Erica said. "I turned around, and, like, dozens of belly dancers came twirling out of the house. Long hair, sheer fabric. Orange, green, yellow. Really cool chains and gold coins dangling everywhere on their foreheads, around their waists."

Erica's voice cracked; her eyes filled with tears. "This really gorgeous woman spun toward me. She held out a velvet pillow with gold fringe. And on top"—She exhaled loudly—"a pink diamond set in platinum.

Sonny put the ring on my finger, and he said, 'Spend another eternity with me.'" Erica sobbed. "I've never been happier than that night."

Brett Robinson's cufflinks glimmered as he pulled the white silk pocket square from his upper left pocket, and placed it in Erica's outstretched, ringless left hand.

Sonny's heart pounded red-hot. The tip of the pen carved into the paper as he wrote: *She hired dancers, my birthday! She had two rings made, and she proposed!*

"Hold your horses," Myles whispered.

"What about a break," Sonny asked, that ominous sensation burning through him. "The girls—"

"With all the cops and bodyguards, your house is as secure as this courthouse," Myles said. "Relax. They're fine."

Brett Robinson said, "Mrs. Whittaker, please describe the wedding."

"Sonny was going to Australia," she said, "he was about to shoot *The Quest*, in like, a week. So we thought it would be fun to go to Vegas, to Caesar's Palace. He wore his costume from *Julius Caesar*. I dressed up like Cleopatra. It was so cool—"

"Were you happy?" Brett asked.

"Ecstatic."

"When, Mrs. Whittaker, did you start to get clues about your husband's true character? Clues that began to erode your love and trust?"

"Oh," she said, "there were so many. First, every week, he would get love letters from Cheyenne Moore. But—"

Erica's bottom lip trembled. "Sonny and I were going to celebrate that I was pregnant, with a picnic by the ocean—"

Sonny's heart pounded. They had to call the girls, right now—

"I was looking," Erica said, "for this basket that had a special slot for a wine bottle, and matching plates. Anyway, I opened a closet in the hallway by his paint studio"—she dabbed her eyes—"I found his perverted paintings—"

"Stop her!" Sonny whispered to Myles.

47

Simone had to shake this sense of intrigue—even a twinge of envy—that charged the warm air over the polished partition between herself and Erica Haynes Whittaker. She had to stop her mind from trying to spin a fantasy about the man, just a dozen feet away, whose very presence was threatening to simmer and steam away her cool mask of composure and level-headed judicial temperament.

As long as I don't look into Sonny's eyes . . .

"This is so embarrassing," Erica said, glancing up. Her dark makeup accentuated the visual plea for sympathy, radiating from her sapphire eyes. She was just a few feet below, in the witness box on the left. The fluorescent light caught the white-blond streaks in her hair as it cascaded onto the blue tweed back of the chair. Her eyes grew ever wider as she repeatedly glanced from Brett Robinson to Sonny Whittaker, and—

Me. The woman who's dreaming about picking up where you left off . . . the woman whose body is hot and damp, right now—

"Mrs. Whittaker," Brett Robinson said softly, "I know this is difficult, but remember, we're describing for the court the true character of the man who wants custody of your little girls. Please describe the content of the paintings."

"Your honor, I object," Mr. Myles said, "The themes of my client's paintings are broad and diverse. To focus on only one aspect is misleading—"

"Overruled." Simone ignored the stomach-cramping pang of conscience, telling her to stop this potentially inflammatory testimony. She nodded at Erica. "You may proceed."

"Okay," Erica said, clamping her pink fingernails into a geometric pattern on her bare legs. "Sonny says every woman has a special feature that he kind of obsesses about. But when I saw these paintings—Oh . . . my . . . gosh!" Erica exclaimed. "What a sicko!"

Myles shot up. "Your honor, I object. This is irrelevant and misleading. Her descriptions are highly subjective, and only portray a small fraction of what Mr. Whittaker has spent his life painting—"

"Mr. Myles, I will stop testimony when I feel it's inappropriate," Simone said as Sonny shifted in his chair.

"Mrs. Whittaker," Brett Robinson said. "Please tell the court what you saw."

"The canvases, they're about waist-high, all leaning against each other. I turned on the light, and the first one, it was called 'blood kiss'—"

Her lips parted; her eyes widened. "It was me!" Her head drew back slightly, sending up a waft of perfume. "Well, just my birthmark. A strawberry patch"—she lowered her voice—"kind of in the shape of a red mouth, at the edge of my pubic hair—"

Erica's eyes grew wider. "But, this other one—'tangle.' It was like, a whole bunch of women's bodies lounging on a giant tongue sticking out of Sonny's mouth. And 'dew drop.' It was him, laying back, naked, lounging in—"

"Your honor!" Myles shouted.

Simone had to stop this. Erica could be making it up, and unless the court actually saw the paintings—

"It showed," Erica said quickly, "Sonny laying inside these purple petals, that were, like, covered with dew drops. At first I thought it was a flower. But it was long and— it was a vagina. It showed him lounging on a giant purple vagina. How perverted is *that*?"

Mr. Myles leaped up. "Your honor!" he shouted. "I vehemently object! Mrs. Whittaker's interpretation of what she sees in these paintings is irrelevant and inaccurate."

"Sustained," the judge said.

Simone cast her best mask of judicial indifference at Sonny. Was he obsessing about a part of her body? Had he painted her? Could he see that she was feverishly imagining herself in the scenarios his wife described?

"Mrs. Whittaker," Brett Robinson said, "around the time you became pregnant, how would you describe your husband's personality?"

Sonny shifted; his sunkissed bronze complexion paled. The skin around his eyes crinkled.

"He was sweet, usually," Erica said, "but he had this streak. He had to show who was boss. Like he would ask me to do little things for him, that he could easily do for himself."

"Share an example with the court, please," Mr. Robinson said.

Erica imitated his voice: "Oh, *fofa*—"

Simone stiffened.

"—that's like, a term in Brazil," Erica said. "It means, honey or sweetie. Anyway, '*Fofa*, will you get my slippers?' or in his bath, '*Fofa*, can you scrub my back?' And, when we made love, he would never let me be on top, even if he was tired—"

Erica sighed. "Here, this is like what I'm trying to say: imagine a whole bunch of different women attached to strings, and those X-shaped marionette sticks. And Sonny's giant hand is making them dance. That was his painting, called 'dominate'—"

"Mrs. Whittaker," Simone said with a hard tone. "Do not make any more references to Mr. Whittaker's paintings."

"But that's how Sonny expresses himself," Erica said. "If we got in a fight, the next morning I'd go in his studio and see these really twisted explosions of colors on the canvas—"

"Mrs. Whittaker," Simone said. "Please speak only when you are questioned."

Brett Robinson grasped the polished wood in front of Erica. "Mrs. Whittaker, how would you describe your pregnancy?"

"I was sick, constantly," Erica said. "I had the worst morning sickness.

Everything came up, even crackers and water. I couldn't gain weight until the end. It was horrible."

"I am submitting medical records to the court," Brett Robinson said, setting a folder on the bench, "detailing that Erica Whittaker did everything her doctor ordered throughout the pregnancy."

"Now," Brett said, "Mrs. Whittaker, please tell the court how you felt about the issue of race."

"At school," Erica said, "I had close friends from Bangladesh and Tokyo. I visited their countries. It was so beautiful. I always thought it would be cool to have daughters named Asia and India. I loved Sonny's ideas about us all being human, and that our children would symbolize that."

"At what point," Brett Robinson asked, "did things begin to sour in your marriage?"

"Well the paint—" Erica cast a quick glance up at Simone. "I mean, it was hard being married to him. Everywhere we went, waitresses would write their numbers on the bill. One chick climbed into the moon roof of our limo. I would open the mail, and lingerie would fall out of envelopes!"

"Did these incidents strain your marriage?"

"Of course. We would argue. But then we'd have the hottest sex ever, when we made up. I think I kind of got excited about all these women wanting my hus—"

Simone turned slightly, toward Sonny. The heat in his eyes . . . she sucked in a sharp breath. The voices, the people, faded under the fierce pounding of her heart, and the blinding phantasm of Sonny Whittaker's aura. Just like when she'd first seen him on the boat . . . *his smoky-brown eyes . . . luring her soul to flow toward him like molten gold and pour into a cast of embracing lovers . . .*

Yes, just imagine for a moment, now . . .

Simone steps down from the bench, her robe fluttering around the stiff leather of her pointed black stiletto boots. She pulls the pins from her hair, shaking her head, big waves dancing down her shoulders. The intensity of their attraction elevates them to another dimension where all these people and questions and rules melt away . . .

She stands before him; he unzips her robe. It slides into a black puddle at their feet. His long fingers clasp her thighs, pushing up her dress, curling his fingertips into her bare buttocks, the black lace tops of her thigh-high stockings.

He presses his cheek into her belly, then begins to stand . . .

She pushes him down . . . straddles him on the chair, claws his belt, the hook, the zipper . . .

Yes, that huge throb that had electrified her on the beach, it snakes upward from a nest of black silk and olive tweed. Panting, she pulls aside her satin thong, her dew drops ready to soak and tangle and dominate . . .

He tilts his head back, eyes glazed with surrender. She leans down, sucking his lips, savoring that familiar taste of Him . . .

She hovers . . . lets his hot, throbbing tip lap the thick cream boiling up from her soul to nourish his carnal craving for her . . .

She rises, then—

Her body sucks him in with the same breathtaking, heart-pounding power that he is wreaking on her life—

He reaches up—

No . . . she pumps up and down, up and down, her knees grasping the sides of his hips in the chair. She needs the fierce friction of their flesh fusing, their minds melding into an oozing opiate of oblivion. Over and over, harder and harder, hammering her feminine heat, tossing her head back, shoving an aching nipple into his mouth, letting him suckle as if it were fueling his very heart beat. Screaming . . .

". . . a really cool guy, into a total jerk," Erica's said, "so now I have to make things right, officially, with my daughters—"

Simone gasped. A courtroom full of eyes, all turned toward her, came into focus. Strangers, Roxanne Jones, sheriff's deputies, the lawyers, Erica. And Sonny, eyes sparkling.

"You okay, judge?" Johnetta mouthed from below. Her fingers were motionless over her keys on her stenography machine.

"Judge Thompson?" Brett Robinson asked with a mocking tone.

"Your honor," Mr. Myles said. "I request a short recess—"

"Excuse me," she coughed. "Proceed, please."

She would not look at Sonny Whittaker again.

48

Joseph Myles rested a hand on the waist-high, wooden witness box, and peered into Erica Haynes Whittaker's eyes. With a sex-kitten pout, she sat with bare knees together, hands clasped in the lap of her pink skirt, chin high. He had to make his throat stop burning with resentment that Sonny had taken such a high-stakes gamble by marrying this woman, against Myles's advice, and created this colossal mess to clean up.

Now here I am, as always, busting my ass to make things right.

Now, to win, Myles would push things to the absolute farthest limit without pissing off the judge.

"Mrs. Whittaker, please think back, about eight years," Myles said, "to the car accident. How did it happen?"

"We had just left the restaurant." Erica's tanned face was stiff. "Me, Sonny, your girlfriend and you. After dinner at a romantic restaurant on a cliff. What does this have to do with anything?"

"Mrs. Whittaker," the judge said. "Please answer the question."

Myles had to focus on the next question, but the judge's striking face made him twist his mustache. She was yet another symbol of Sonny always upping the ante.

"Sonny was driving his white Jag," Erica huffed. "Another car, all of a sudden—" Her voice cracked. "It came out of nowhere. We rolled down the cliff—" Her bottom lip trembled.

"Who was driving that other car?"

"My dad had just confronted us at dinner. It was dark. Nobody proved anything!" Tears smudged bits of black as they carved pink-beige squiggles down Erica's cheeks.

"As a matter of fact," Myles said, slapping a piece of white paper on the judge's bench, "this police report confirms, Norris Haynes was driving the Bentley that cut off Sonny Whittaker's Jaguar."

"They didn't prove Daddy was driving!" Erica shrieked.

"Here," Myles handed over two more stacks of paper, "are affidavits from witnesses who described the driver. Your father—"

"Your honor, this is irrelevant," Brett Robinson boomed behind him.

"Mr. Myles, please step to the bench," Simone said.

The faint scent of mustard and soft floral perfume wafted as she leaned forward. Her eyes sharpened. "Mr. Myles, please steer your questions into more relevant territory."

"Your honor," he said loudly, "I need to establish that Sonny Whittaker was entering into a marriage at great risk to his own life. That Erica's father disapproved so vehemently, his actions put his own daughter's life in jeopardy—"

"Mr. Myles," the judge said softly. "Tread lightly."

Myles twisted the side of his mustache as he turned back to Erica. "Mrs. Whittaker, tell us about the deal you just signed to pose nude—"

"Objection!" Brett Robinson shouted.

"—completely nude, for Video Vixens."

"It's not posing," Erica snapped. "I'm a spokesmodel for a new line of clothing. They're starting, like, this shopping channel—"

"Spokesmodel?" Myles mimicked. He stepped toward the defense table, where Sonny sat, feet planted squarely on the floor, straight posture, forearms resting on the table, fingers laced, as if praying, eyes sharp on him, and Erica. Myles picked up *Famous* from the table.

"This gossip magazine," Myles said, holding up the paper, "has photographs of you taping a nude video on a beach in Cabo San Lucas. Tell me, Mrs. Whittaker, what part of 'sex kitten' do you think qualifies *you* to raise two intelligent and self-confident young girls?"

Erica crossed her arms. "I'm not going to answer that."

"As you know, the children's devoted father is encouraging India's interest in the non-traditional pursuit of aeronautical science," Myles said, "and Asia's passion for reading. Now—"

Erica raised her eyebrows.

"You accuse Mr. Whittaker of objectifying the female body," he said, "while you are attempting to make a career of it. Do you want to brainwash your daughters into thinking that a woman's worth is her sex appeal?"

"The talent in life that I have," Erica said, "is acting. Our higher power made me to look like this."

"Isn't it true, Mrs. Whittaker," Myles said, "that since you left my client, your appearance has been drastically altered?"

"I don't know about drastic," she said. "Every woman is entitled to improve herself."

"Isn't it true that you got breast implants," Myles said, "for the sole purpose of posing nude for a men's magazine?"

"I object," Brett Robinson shouted. "Your honor, women do this every day for whatever reason."

"Your honor, what is in evidence is," Myles said, "she posed after the breast enlargement."

"Overruled. Continue, Mr. Myles."

"Mrs. Whittaker," Myles said, staring down at Erica, "You were describing your *talent*?"

"I'm studying with an acting coach, so I can hopefully get some good roles, to support my daughters."

"By writhing nude on a beach!" Myles said. "What impression, Mrs. Whittaker, would you make on the two girls you claim to love . . . if they walked into a store and saw you sprawled on the cover of a men's magazine?"

"Objection!" Brett Robinson shouted. "Inflammatory and prejudicial."

"It goes to her credibility, your honor," Myles said.

"Overruled. Proceed."

"Mrs. Whittaker, you claim that during your pregnancy, you were afflicted by severe morning sickness. Would that have anything to do with"—he raised his voice, glaring down at her—"the *heroin* in your blood!?"

"I did not!" she screamed.

"Are you clean today?" Myles shot back. "Do you want to adjourn the trial for a urinalysis to prove it right now, Mrs. Whittaker?"

"Objection!" Brett Robinson shouted. "He's assuming facts not in evidence."

Myles held up a stack of papers. "I have in my hand a report subpoenaed from Mrs. Whittaker's doctor. The morning sickness was so severe, the doctor took blood tests. The report reads like a *Just Say No to Drugs* brochure."

"Overruled," the judge said.

Brett Robinson snatched up the folder. "That is not on the evidence list. It is not admissible."

"It's proof!" Myles nearly shouted. "Proof that Erica Haynes is a wild, drug-using party girl with pornographic aspirations whose sole motivation for this divorce and custody is to further torment my client!"

"Gentlemen!" the judge shouted.

Brett Robinson pressed his palms on the bench.

"Your honor! Strike that slanderous babble from the record or I will *carry* you"—he held up his palms—"to the Judicial Tenure Commission!"

Judge Thompson slammed the gavel. The crack echoed through the silent, still courtroom. She shot up. The chair bumped the wall behind her. Her chest rose and fell quickly.

"Mr. Robinson, get out your checkbook," she said through tight lips. "Pay to the order of Los Angeles County. Five hundred dollars. On the memo line: Contempt."

Brett Robinson took heavy steps back to the plaintiff's table.

"Mr. Myles," she said, pointing the gavel. "Go do the same."

49

Sonny forced his face to project a calm coolness—despite the indignation sizzling over his nerves—as Myles approached the table. The actor in him was loving this melodrama, but this was real. And what the hell was Myles thinking, enraging the judge to the point that she stormed through that wooden door behind the bench, letting its slam punctuate the shocked silence of the courtroom.

"Get a fucking grip," Sonny said deeply, standing behind the table. "I don't know what is going on with you."

"You never have," Myles said, lifting a beige file. "Always too caught up in your own issues. That's why we're here."

"Whatever trip you're on, man," Sonny said, with a piercing glare, "you better take a quick detour back to a more rational state. Or live with the guilt of killing me."

Myles held his stare. "I'm trying to win for you, man."

"She said we have twenty minutes," Sonny said. The panicky feeling over the girls' well-being gripped his gut. "Let's go in the hall and call home. We should've asked the judge to have someone call or go check on them already."

"Why don't you just go back in her chambers and ask her yourself," Myles snapped.

"What is your problem, man? It's me, Sonny. The guy whose family took you in when you had nothing and no one. You were lost and unwanted. Don't inflict that on Asia and India. Now, give me your phone—"

"Sonny, I want more appreciation," Myles said. "I've basically spent my life at your beck and call. But when it comes to my needs, you're as blind as Xavier—"

"You could have walked away at any moment," Sonny said. "You've got your own reasons for sticking with me."

"Your dalliance with the judge," Myles said, twisting his mustache. "It set off this warning signal inside me. I feel like we're reeling toward yet another example of me getting battered and bruised, while you end up sitting pretty, oblivious to what—"

"The world is out to get me," Sonny said, "and you're joining the party—"

Myles slipped into his chair, shaking his head. "I'm sorry, man. I love you like a brother. I just, I need to shuffle my emotions back in order." Myles pulled his cell phone from his pocket. "Let's go call—"

"All rise!" the bailiff bellowed. Judge Thompson dashed back in—

She was ashen. Not *mourning dove gray*. More like *chalk white*.

"Ladies and gentlemen," she said. "Due to an emergency, court is adjourned until tomorrow morning."

"Mr. Whittaker," the officer said. "We need to take you home, right away."

A chill slithered down Sonny's back. Narcissus. His family, home without him. The LAPD . . . wasn't that enough?

"What," he said with a tinny tone. "Are my daughters—"

"We're not sure what's happening, sir," the officer said as they bolted down the crowded aisle, toward the swinging double doors flanked by more sheriff's deputies.

An officer's walkie-talkie crackled: ". . . weapons drawn, now searching the premises for an intruder at the Whittaker residence, Mount Olympus area . . ."

Sonny's chest squeezed. He went numb.

50

Simone hurried back to her chambers, where her staff gathered around the color television in the far right corner, next to the couch. Gray haze pouring through the white mini blinds highlighted the silver roots of Charlie's hair. Simone's lips tightened, her insides hummed with rage, that he was making her stay on this case.

Now it was even more important that the full extent of her interaction with Sonny Whittaker in Brazil never saw the light of a television news report. Because after today's explosive testimony, and what was unfolding live on TV, Simone did not want to be the focus of any sensational reports about the Sonny Whittaker saga.

She wished they would avoid mentioning her name or showing her face at all.

"Have they said if the children are safe?" Simone stepped close to the television, between Johnetta and Charlie.

A reporter inside a helicopter was narrating video of a Middle Eastern-style castle on a mountain ridge. "We're here live in the news chopper over a very tense, very dangerous, very frightening situation at the Whittaker residence," the reporter said. "It's located in the very exclusive neighborhood known as Mount Olympus—"

The U-shaped home embraced a two-level terrace with a stone banister over a sheer drop, a pool, a tennis court, all overlooking Los Angeles. The ocean glimmered in the distance. The chopper showed the back of the house; orange and yellow sheers billowed past shards of glass in tall windows. Broken pieces of window shimmered on the terrace.

"The file says the girls are home-schooled," Simone said, cringing at the idea of the stalker confronting those precious children. "But are they there now?"

"Looks like Narcissus tried to break in," Charlie said. "And look, several cars in the driveway." He pointed to the front of the gray stone house. A gleaming driveway stretched from a multi-car garage on the left, across the front of the house, and out to the wrought iron fence that ran the length of the yard at the road. Its tall, black arrows pointed toward the gloomy sky.

"All those SWAT guys are on it," Yolanda said, pointing to men in black with rifles scattering across the vast green lawn. "The LAPD doesn't play—"

"Let's just not have another Darius Dayne," Simone said, her throat burning. Just months ago, she had handled the trial for the police officer who had fatally shot the actor inside his own home, after the wife reported a burglary. It was dark, chaotic. "Or the children."

"Hmmm," Johnetta said. "All that money, and you still can't be safe."

"Right now Channel 8 is trying to find out if the intruder, or intruders, actually made it inside the Whittaker home," the reporter said. "You recall, Narcissus recently vandalized the homes of Judge Simone Thompson and filmmaker Norris Haynes. Now sources tell us, the Whittakers's nanny made a chilling call to 911 from the children's closet—"

Simone's heart pounded.

Johnetta gasped. "I know that fine man is a mess tryin' to get home to that—"

"Take a look at this exclusive Channel 8 video of the actual intruder rappelling down the sheer rock—" The screen showed someone in climbing gear, gripping a rope attached to the stone banister on the terrace behind the house, clouds of dust kicking up from boots as they hit the cliff every twenty feet or so.

"Looks like something out of one of his movies," Charlie said.

"As Channel 8 has been telling you, the Narcissus stalker is targeting Sonny Whittaker and his family. A landscaping crew in the area is helping police artists compose a sketch of this rock-climbing suspect, possibly linked to the attack on Jenn Ryder, still in critical condition—"

"Look at all that broken glass," Simone said. "If the break-ins are just a scare tactic, let me tell you—" Simone shivered. "I'm still getting chills."

"Sonny Whittaker and Erica Haynes Whittaker were not home, of course," the reporter said, "facing off in a very public and very ugly divorce trial at the Santa Monica Courthouse."

Charlie snickered: "Can she say 'very' one more time? See if the other channels—"

Yolanda pointed the remote. The same image popped up on the following three channels.

"Roxanne Jones just now getting to the scene," a male anchor said, "after explosive testimony in the divorce trial—"

"How did she get there before," Simone asked, "Sonny Whittaker—"

"Helicopter," Yolanda said, rolling her eyes.

"While Roxanne sets up," the anchor said, "we want to show our viewers exclusive video we shot in Brazil, just moments after Jenn Ryder was attacked—"

Simone stiffened.

"Here we see the legendary actor looking distressed as he sees his badly burned costar," the anchor said over video of Sonny leaning over Jenn's gurney. Simone's heart pounded. If Roxanne's cameraman had shot her standing there, and showed her now, all the world would see that they had been there together—"And now, watch as the ambulance pulls away, Sonny Whittaker is obviously worried about his daughters' safety, even though he has hired round-the-clock security."

Simone wanted them to go back to the aerial shot of the house. Now.

"Then," the man said, "unbelievably, Sonny Whittaker goes for a jog on the beach!"

Simone held her breath.

"Is somebody chasin' him?" Yolanda asked.

"They musta shot that at another time," Johnetta said, "now they're just tryin' to make him look bad. It's so far away, might not even be him—"

"Take a look at this!" the anchor said, "Sonny Whittaker appears to be chasing a Brazilian beauty in a skimpy thong bikini!"

No!

"Due to the graphic nature of this video, you can see *EE* has digitized the woman's backside," the man said.

"They need to blur all that!" Yolanda said.

Dizziness . . . Simone struggled to inhale.

"But watch how the couple tumbles affectionately on the sand," the man said.

"Whew!" Johnetta fanned herself. "Looks like that scene in *Come Back, My Love*—"

"No word yet," the anchor said, "about this mystery woman's identity. But *EE* is working to make it an exclusive scoop—"

"Simone," Charlie said, "has Brett Robinson tried to use this? Simone, you look ill—"

51

Cheyenne Moore watched the yellow flame dance at the tip of the long match. It hissed alongside the white wick sprouting from a thick forest green pillar of wax, the twenty-fifth on glass shelves filling her secret place, her favorite place, with soft yellow light.

"This rainforest scent is so lovely," she said, smiling at the memory of buying all fifty candles on the shelf in that little shop down in La Jolla. "So authentic, I'm there. And one last dress rehearsal is all I need."

Tomorrow, when she would be close enough to touch him, her future would begin again. She closed her eyes, humming along with the theme music playing from the television.

"I didn't know if—" she mouthed along with herself on the screen. She spun, making her gauzy lace gown flutter in the light of bamboo torches. Someday, they would return to the Amazon, to that beautiful log cabin on the misty white creek, the thick green leaves of every shade and size, shading their love nest.

They would eat their reunion meal again, which now awaited on the screen—at the rough-hewn table under the gazebo. The aphrodisiac piranha soup, the buttery Brazilian beef—

"I didn't know if you'd come back for me, like you promised," she recited along with a younger version of herself in the video. Then, and now, she tossed her long hair.

But what was wrong with the picture? Those police choppers overhead were always so disruptive, noisy. And it was too bright—

Above, a beam of hazy sunshine, coming through a three-inch scratch in the dark green paint covering the glass dome, was distorting the picture on the television. It even washed out the red digits telling time on the VCR.

She leaned closer. Yes, the rewind and repeat functions were activated to keep their love alive, beaming over Los Angeles to his palace all night, all day, for as long as she could remember. That was why she kept this special place up here, on a flat part of her roof reached only through the locked trap door in the bedroom she used to share with Peter.

Until the idiot blew his brains out. My poor little Katie . . .

The images started to rush back—

"Oh, my favorite scene," she sighed toward the screen.

Sonny Whittaker wrapped his large hands around her slender waist, as he'd done countless times in her trailer, away from the camera crews, or Norris Haynes barking directions.

"Cheyenne, I never break a promise," he said raspily. His smoky eyes flickered with passion as he gazed down, about to kiss her, eternalizing their love on screen for millions around the world to witness.

"If you hadn't come back," she panted, "I would have died of heartbreak."

He inched his lips closer. "The only thing I want to break here is bread," he said, glancing at the table.

"I knew you'd come back, my love," she sighed, pressing her cheek into his chest.

"Yes," Cheyenne now declared, spinning, bumping the antique chest of drawers holding the original script, newspaper clippings about the movie, reviews, posters, a ball of hair from his brush, a lipstick-stained pillow case from the first time they made love, Katie's birth certificate.

She stopped just long enough to shove the corners of pictures sticking out of a small drawer. Pictures from his latest gallery showing, and the set of the new movie, and him shopping in Rio, and Norris's wedding in Brazil. She stacked them neatly next to a plastic-covered jungle bloom he'd given her long ago, during a blissfully erotic swim in a moss-green pool under a waterfall near the set . . .

"I will return to heaven with him! Yes!"

Cheyenne froze. She sniffed. Rainforest . . . something burning.

A hot burst against her right wrist.

A yellow flash hissing from the long lace of her sleeve. The original gown she'd worn a quarter century ago in the movie.

"No! I need this. For him! When we re-enact—"

Her left hand grasped the burning fabric, squeezing out the flame. She felt nothing as steaming black flakes fell from her open palm. A charred smell made her cough.

She held up her right arm, looking straight through a doorknob-sized black ring in the fabric, at the television. There, she and the man of her dreams, the man who would love her again, were embracing, kissing, promising to return to the United States for a life together, forever.

Cheyenne smiled. Until she saw her reflection on the dark glass dome around her. She willed her cheeks to flatten.

"Keep grinning like a lovesick fool," she told her reflection. "You'll have laugh lines deep enough to plant corn in by the time you take the witness stand. But I *am* lovely for forty-five."

If she could bottle all the time and energy she'd put into preserving her youth, for him, she would have a fortune. Power yoga, the nutritionist, the facials, the high colonics, the writing partner for the book, the publicist.

If Norris had only understood her plight, and cast her opposite Sonny Whittaker in the new movie. How perfect that would have been in *The Colony* . . . the two of them, in another love story, back in their beloved Brazil.

And now that Jenn was out of the picture—

"I might get my casting call after all," she said, spinning.

Stupid Norris. Still ignoring calls, letters, notes.

"Not to worry," she said. "He'll come to his senses, too."

And once the judge edited Erica Haynes and those brats out of the nightmarish film strip that his life had become without her—

"You'll realize, dear Sonny," she sighed toward his handsome face on the screen, "that I'm the one for you. We can be one big happy family, forever and always."

52

As the squad car pulled up in front of his house, Sonny had to get out, run inside, and make sure Asia and India were safe.

"Stop!" he shouted from the back seat as an officer slowed to pass dozens of police vehicles and media vans jamming the road in front of the black wrought iron fence guarding his home. "Let me out!"

"Sonny, man," Myles said, seated on the back seat next to him. Red and blue lights flashed, sirens blared and helicopter blades thumped overhead. "Relax a minute," Myles said. "Let them handle this. It's not safe for you to—"

Sonny slid toward the door, scratching for a handle. There was none. And, looking through the window, he froze.

"Why is there a tank on my front lawn?" he demanded.

"It's routine," said the officer driving. "In case we encounter a barricaded gunman situation—"

"I knew it, Myles," Sonny said, scanning the house. Officers stood in and around the open, twelve-foot-high double front doors. The stained glass above and around the carved wood was intact. His gaze trailed the length of the house's façade, with its dozens of rectangular windows adorned with Moroccan-style carved wood panels, to the decorative towers at each end. "I could feel that something bad was happening—"

"There's Kindred's SUV," Myles said, as the car pulled past reporters speaking into microphones. In the driveway were two AlarmTech trucks, a red ambulance and media vans with satellite dishes on top. And the silver Nissan that he'd bought for Kindred to drive the girls around in.

"They're home," Myles said.

"Open the fucking door!" Sonny shouted.

"Mr. Whittaker," said the officer in the passenger seat. "The SWAT personnel are securing the area—" Men in black with rifles dashed around the house, from the cluster of trees to the south, to the sheer rocky drop on the north side.

Guadeloupe, pale and trembling, ran to the car. She opened Sonny's door.

Sonny shot out of the car.

"Where are the girls?" His voice sounded high-pitched. He was numb except for his heart exploding against his ribs.

"They're inside," Guadeloupe gasped through trembling fingers raised to her mouth. "With Kindred—"

Sonny ran across the grass, toward the open double doors.

A half dozen men in black with guns drawn were aiming—

Sonny bolted onto the porch, past the tall waxy trees, whose great pots spilled orange flowers onto the gray stone rectangles under his feet.

"Mr. Whittaker!" An officer grabbed his arm.

Adrenaline propelled him toward the door.

"I'm going in!" Sonny's throat was as dry as sandpaper.

"Stop, sir! You'll be arrested!"

Sonny ran into the cavernous foyer. Hazy light poured through the stained glass above the door, casting blood-red hues on the jade tile.

Muffled crying . . .

"Asia!" Sonny shouted. "India! Kindred!"

He shot up the steps, two at a time.

A man in black with a long black rifle appeared at the top of the steps.

He raised the gun.

53

"Asia, fight the ninjas!" India screamed, kicking and pounding the invaders who had pulled them from the closet. There was an army of them. "You can't take us!"

"Let me down!" Asia shouted, grabbing the hood over the man's head and face. "Daddy!"

"Who are you!" Kindred screamed behind them.

The men were carrying them out of the bedroom, pulling Kindred. They were heading down the hallway, three or four guys in front, three or four more behind.

"What are you doing?!" Kindred shouted. "Where are Josh and Jared?"

India aimed a balled fist at the man's eye, all that showed through his black mask. His long thick arms pinched the backs of her legs, as her stomach and chest pressed over his shoulder.

"Put me down!" she shouted. But he was taking giant steps down the hallway. "My Daddy won't let you take us! Put my sister down!"

Beside her, Asia was like a blue airplane on the guy's shoulders.

"Kindred!" India turned back. "Make them put us down!"

"They're the space soldiers from Daddy's movie!" India shouted.

"He's the emperor of *The Galaxy*!" Asia cried.

A few of the men laughed as they reached the balcony leading to the foyer.

"It's not funny!" Kindred shouted.

Asia's eyes grew huge as she turned to Kindred. "Is this 'cuz of Mommy and Daddy in court? Are they taking us to an orphanage?"

Tears streamed down Kindred's cheeks.

"No!" India imagined mopping floors with kids like the ones she'd seen begging on the beaches in Mexico and Brazil and Vietnam. The bright light of the foyer stung her eyes.

The men stopped.

Another guy in black was pointing a gun down the steps.

At a man.

"Daddy!" India screamed.

54

A guttural cry surged from Sonny's parched lips, making his jaw chatter even more violently. Standing still as a statue about three steps above, he stared up, watching Asia and India kick and claw the SWAT officers. The men who could blow him away, right now.

"No!" His scream echoed through the cavernous foyer.

"That's our daddy!" India screamed. "Put us down!"

"Ace!" one of the men shouted.

The round black tip of the rifle lowered.

They set the girls down . . .

A blur of silver and blue and dark curls shot toward him, little legs pounding the stairs, giant amber eyes.

A silent, double jump.

Sonny grasped one girl in each arm, sobbing into the soft, coconut-scented poufs on top of their heads. Their faces buried into his sweat-soaked shirt; they quaked.

"I will never," he groaned, pulling them closer as the SWAT men passed, "ever let anything happen to you. Ever."

"We're sorry, Mr. Whittaker," one of the officers said. "We didn't know—"

Jared, in blue jeans and a brown cashmere turtleneck, came around the upper hallway corner; a black gun glinted in his hand. He followed Kindred as she descended, her face pink and swollen and wet with tears. She crumpled at Sonny's feet.

"I can't take it," Kindred sobbed into her hands. "I can't—"

Sonny bent under the weight of the twins, pressing close so Kindred could lay her cheek on his shoulder.

"I'm taking all of you far away," he said. "The moment I finish this ridiculous trial—" Sonny's insides were a molten swirl, bubbling up searing flashes of frustration and powerlessness.

No! How could he protect the girls during the rest of the trial? He couldn't leave them here, again, without him. He couldn't take them to the courthouse; they did not need to see the battalion of media—the trucks, the satellite dishes, the rabid reporters—out front. Could he send them to Montserrat with Grandmama? No, the active volcano . . .

Could they somehow call off the trial? What would Judge Simone Thompson think about this?

"My babies!" Erica shrieked as her footsteps made hollow sounds on the tile below. She ran up the steps, embracing the girls, pressing her face between them, sealing the gap with a bleached cape of hair.

Her face was inches from Sonny; he closed his eyes to block out the ghoulish image of her tear-smudged makeup, her lips that were speaking so many lies, maybe causing this unbelievable scene right now. He held his breath to escape her choking perfume.

"They can't stay here while we're at court," she said.

The girls' arms tightened around him.

"I'm taking them home with me," Erica said, "to Daddy's house—"

Never.

55

At home in her family room, Simone Thompson held her left palm to her burning stomach as she sunk into the oversized brown chenille couch. Still in her sweater dress, she rested stockinged feet on a giraffe-print pillow on the ottoman; a ceramic cup of ginger-peach tea steamed within arm's reach on the lacquered coffee table.

"Tell me those little girls are okay," Simone demanded, clicking the remote toward the large television. The smell of a charred log wafted over the bear rug in front of the brick hearth; the odor obscured the soothing scent of tea.

"Chaos in the courtroom of Judge Simone Thompson today," a news anchor said, "as Sonny Whittaker's estranged wife reveals lurid details of the movie star's—"

"No!" Simone clicked to another channel.

"—*Entertainment Exclusive* still trying to identify this woman," Roxanne Jones said over video of Simone's exposed backside as she ran on the beach in front of Sonny Whittaker, "seen romping nearly nude with the embattled movie star—"

Simone closed her eyes. She pushed the OFF button. And cringed in the dim silence.

"I want this all to be over," she whispered toward the brick walls. She ached to talk to someone, to hear a comforting voice or lay her head on the warmth of safe shoulders. But right now, she felt more alone than ever. Her best friends had acted strange, caught up in their own dramas, in Brazil. Sonny Whittaker's face flashed in her mind; he was more off-limits than anyone. Charlie was not taking her seriously. She could call Judge Caroline Drew for advice, but she did not want to divulge the extent of her angst to a person she admired and never wanted to disappoint. And her mother—

"I know it's bad if I want to call *her* for comfort," Simone sighed, reaching for her tea. She inhaled the ginger-peach steam, closing her eyes. She had gotten this far in her life, alone, and she would get through this difficult week, and be stronger—

The doorbell rang. Simone dashed up the front hallway, the clove-colored tiles cold under her feet. Through the gold-tinted square window on the wooden door were the blurred faces of Marie and Paulette, framed by the two police cars parked on the street.

Simone opened the door; deep down she hoped they could help her relax and forget.

"We're worried sick about you," Marie said, sweeping through the door in an ankle-length burnt-orange leather coat with an oversized collar turned up against the back of her head and ears. A gust of her expensive perfume whooshed in with the pine-scented, cool evening air.

"Why haven't you returned our calls?" Paulette demanded, stepping in and raising a big white paper bag. "Dinner. Your favorite—Thai Palace."

The strong spicy scent made Simone clench the knit fabric over her waist. "I'm too stressed out to eat right now."

"Just a little rice, then," Paulette said, "it'll calm your stomach. You guys go sit down. I'll get everything ready." The black ruffles on her jacket swayed around her shoulders as she hurried straight back down the hall toward the kitchen, where she flipped on the lights.

"Simone," Marie whispered, clutching her elbow as she closed and locked the door. Marie guided Simone into the living room. Simone flipped on the track lights over the fireplace; she dimmed them.

"Simone," Marie said, glancing toward the hallway, as she peeled out of her coat. She wore a satin, burnt-orange-colored blouse and camel wool trousers. The sharp heels of her pointed leather boots dug into the fuzzy black rug under the sleek coffee table.

"Marie, you look terrible," Simone said, sinking next to Marie, into the soft cushions of the L-shaped couch. Silverware and plates clanked in the kitchen. "You and Norris, in court, I could tell you're upset—"

"Simone," Marie said, her eyes sharp and nervous. "Everything I said about Sonny, on the boat, about the two of you getting together—"

Simone's right fingertips skimmed the knuckles of her balled up left hand in her lap.

"I hope what came out in court was all there was to it," Marie said, "for your sake." She squinted. "I mean about your personal involvement—"

"There is no involvement. Why are you saying this like he's Narcissus or something?"

Paulette's footsteps and the sounds of cupboards and drawers opening and closing echoed from the kitchen.

"I'm worried about the professional complications, for you," Marie said.

"Oh," Simone said with an annoyed tone. She tossed her head back, her hair twist hitting her neck. "*Now* you're worried about it!"

Marie's French-manicured fingernails tickled Simone's fist; her diamond ring glimmered.

"Simone, I know it was you on the news," Marie whispered. "I saw you running. In my bathing suit, with Sonny. Who's now in your courtroom." A grayish pallor dimmed the usual glow of Marie's maple-syrup-hued complexion.

"Marie," Simone said with a warning tone. "It would ruin me if—"

"My lips are sealed." Marie stroked her pearl choker. "But take it from me. Don't do it—"

"I don't know what you're talking about," Simone said.

"Romance," Marie said. Her usually fluffed short copper hair lay flat. Her lips were pale and chapped as she said, "Love."

"Marie, why do you look so—"

"Norris," she whispered, over the tap of her fingernails on the pearls, "is my client. Has been for five years. That's how we met."

Simone stared into her friend's worried eyes.

"What about the movie?" Simone asked. "I thought you met when you consulted on his script, and when he found out you helped catch your father's killer, he decided to do the TV movie about your life?"

Marie shook her head. "That's the official story. But he learned about me while I was counseling him. You're the only person on the planet who knows. But I need help. Today in court, I could see when you looked at Sonny, you're heading down the same treacherous path—"

"Tell me what—"

"Simone!" Paulette called. "Wine or Diet Coke?"

"White zin," Simone said.

"Me, too." Marie squeezed Simone's hand. "It sets off really strange, almost demented dynamics in the relationship. You don't know where the professional barriers end and the personal ones begin—"

"Is he still a patient?" Simone asked. "Even now?"

Marie nodded. "Standing appointments, Thursday at two. Even when he's on location, in Brazil. We do it by phone." She exhaled sharply. "It goes two ways. Help me figure out what—"

"The rumor," Simone said. "Are you still worried about the race factor?"

Marie shook her head. "The vandalism, the threats, that's overshadowing everything. He's trippin', girl. He is trippin' out on me, like—"

Paulette dashed into the room, carrying a tray with steaming bowls, glasses, a bottle of wine. She set it on the coffee table. "Dig in," she said, sitting next to Simone.

"This is for the Simone Thompson Savings and Trust," Paulette said playfully, leaning back to reach into the front pocket of her lemon yellow stretch pants. The ruffled sleeve of her matching blouse rippled as she handed over an envelope and said, "Thank you."

Simone peeked into the envelope. An accordion of hundred dollar bills whispered back. "What's this for?"

"You probably forgot about the loan." Paulette twisted a silver corkscrew into the wine bottle. "For the boys' tuition." She shrugged as the cork popped. "Anyway, there it is, with interest."

"Did Ted sign the number-one NBA draft pick, or what?" Marie asked, pointing a wine glass toward the bottle.

"I got a new job!" Paulette shrieked as she poured. "My dream—"

Simone stiffened.

"What?" Marie asked.

"*Famous* magazine!" Paulette said.

Marie's brows drew together. "Don't tell me you used pictures from the wedding—"

"Nothing unauthorized," Paulette said. "Just Lex Laurent and his girlfriend, and—"

Marie shot up. "I told you not to! How could you cash in on our friendship?"

"You're cashing in on your marriage," Paulette shot back. "You could've bought a car for the price of your Oscar gown."

Marie snatched up her coat. "You are so low, girlfriend. Simone, be careful." Marie spun and strode toward the front hallway.

"Marie, wait," Simone said, following. She grasped Marie's hands, aching at the sight of her friend's puffy, bloodshot eyes. "Are you alright?"

Marie shook her head. "Just remember what I said," she whispered, "about Sonny. Norris keeps throwing it back on me, that I seduced him, that if I ever tell anyone—"

"Are you in danger?"

Marie shook her head. "Narcissus, he was in our home, Simone."

"Welcome to the club," Simone said, glancing at her now-empty hallway table. The statue was in her garbage bin in the garage; the very air in the house felt different, violated.

"You guys," Paulette strode toward them. "I want your support in what I'm doing. It is so exciting to me—"

"Your timing is really appalling," Simone said. "We're both going through a lot right now, and the media is partly to blame. We can't trust you—"

"For heaven's sakes," Paulette said. "I would never jeopardize our friendship."

Marie opened the door.

Simone made sure not to focus on the police cars out front.

"My first assignment is tomorrow night," Paulette said. "Sonny Whittaker's art show at that hot new gallery on the Third Street Promenade. Not far from court. All this stalker stuff is sure to make it the place to be—"

"Simone, watch your back." Marie's coat swept up behind her as she strode down the porch steps, the front walk, toward her red Kompressor Mercedes, parked just past the LAPD squad cars.

Simone's limbs hummed with disappointment and anger as she glared at Paulette. "Tell me how you can thrive off someone else's trauma?"

"How can *he* dance on the beach after his costar was attacked?" Paulette cast a sharp, knowing stare. A threatening glint lit up her eyes.

Simone pushed the door open wider.

56

As Sonny Whittaker sat on the couch in his family room, the grainy image of Grandmama on the television screen immediately softened the rock-hard tension in his shoulders.

"Kindred is getting us plane tickets right now," Sonny said over hammering and drilling and electronic beeping, as crews installed new windows and a state-of-the-art security system throughout the house. "We're going to come as soon as—"

"No, Sonny," Grandmama said. "The volcano is smoking—"

"Then I want you on the next helicopter to Antigua," Sonny told her as she rocked on the terrace, framed by the dark orange sky over the Caribbean. "We can all go to New York, or Brazil. I want you safe, with us—"

"I belong here, Sonny. I'll tell you the same as what I told the government folk. This is my home, with your grandfather. Long after I leave this body, my spirit will stay right here by the ocean—"

Sonny knelt before her. "Grandmama, please. If they're saying you should leave—"

"My neighbors, they left and came back. Wait." Her boxy, gray dress fluttered as she raised her arms. The picture zigzagged. "Tremors. We've had them all day."

Sonny's heart thundered. Without her, he would have no elder family members. No wise words to turn to anymore.

"Grandmama," he said. "Tell me what—"

"You'll be put through the rings of fire," she said, pointing toward a ruby band across the horizon. "I saw the flash tonight. Bright as the day I met your grandfather. 'Cept for the green vapors. Treachery—"

SSSStttt. Electronic snow danced on the screen.

"Kindred!" Sonny shouted. "Come and fix this!"

"—as long as you believe," Grandmama said. "And I may be watchin' over you soon."

The screen went blank.

"No!" Sonny groaned. Was that the doorbell? He glanced through the terrace doors, whose wispy sheers were pulled back to allow the security crews to work. Shards of glass reflected the sky, pointing toward him like pink knives.

"What is it?" Kindred cried. She was a flash of yellow, kneeling at his side in her jeans and fuzzy sweater. Her arms curled around a phone and notebook. "The twins are asleep. I've ordered all the tickets to Mont—" She stood up, grabbed the remote, and pushed a few buttons.

Grandmama's face was close to the camera. "Sonny?"

"Yes," he said as Kindred whispered about packing.

"Remember, Sonny, I love you," she said, reaching toward the camera's OFF switch. "Don't let them put out the fire in your eyes, Sonny. You got to share your gifts—"

"Mr. Whittaker," Guadeloupe said, her eyes still wide with sorrow.

After the police had left earlier, the housekeeper had confessed to having dropped the phone in terror as the windows were being smashed.

That explained the busy signal. The police were still looking for the intruder; they said it would make sense if it had been Narcissus, since he had already broken into Norris Haynes's and Simone Thompson's homes.

"The police are here," Guadeloupe said. "And Mr. Myles is back."

Two officers stepped down from the front hallway.

"Sonny, man," Myles said, coming close in jeans, a purple Lakers sweater and a matching baseball cap. "They've got some news."

"Did you catch the bastard who took a bat to my house?" Sonny asked angrily as he rose to his feet. "I'll play judge and jury for the miserable—"

"No, Mr. Whittaker," said an officer with a small, round nose set in a square face. "It's about Jenn Ryder."

Sonny sunk into the couch. The hammering and drilling and workers shouting were torching his already charred nerves.

"She died, man," Myles said. "The substance ate into her neck and—"

"Bled to death," the officer said.

"My God."

"Now we need to ask you," the officer said, framed by the dark fireplace, which emitted a smoky scent. "Is there anyone who's given you trouble? Disgruntled employees?"

Sonny raised his fingertips to his throat. "There's always been an obsessed fan or two. Writing letters, waiting outside hotel rooms." He envisioned Jenn, thick red blood gushing onto white hospital linens. The light caramel perfection of the twins' necks . . . Simone Thompson's delicate collarbone . . .

"No!" Sonny said. "But when I go back to court tomorrow—"

"Rest assured, Mr. Whittaker," the female officer said. "We are deploying a special security unit." She pointed to the terrace, where two officers strode back and forth.

"They're assigned to your home indefinitely, covering every possible entry, during your trial, per the chief judge's orders," the male officer said.

"The judge," Sonny whispered. "Myles, I need to talk to you, in the kitchen—"

A hot bolt of distrust sliced Sonny's gut as Myles twisted his mustache; his eggshell complexion paled. Sonny needed to straighten his friend out, now. Because for the rest of the week in court, Sonny wanted his lawyer on his usual even keel. Not that off-the-rocker BS he had pulled today.

"About tomorrow," Sonny said as they strode into the kitchen. The aromas of garlic and tomato still hung in the warm air, from the spaghetti that Guadeloupe had served for a dinner that he and the girls and Kindred, Jared and Josh, had been too shaken to eat.

"Listen, man," Myles whispered over the sudden scream of a drill in the back hallway. "Norris wants to make a deal. A settlement."

"If Erica is ready to walk away from this ridiculous soap opera," Sonny said, "I'm listening."

"Not quite," Myles said. "You know tomorrow, Cheyenne takes the stand."

"She's crazy," Sonny said over the *rat! tat! tat!* of a hammer. "The woman has no credibility. I don't care if she does have a book—"

"She and Brett want to make you look like the biggest pussyhound ever to strut through Hollywood," Myles said.

"Eh!" a deep voice shouted. "String those wires through here!"

"Quiet down," Sonny said, leaning around the corner to look at three power-tool-wielding men in workboots, jeans and denim shirts. "My daughters are sleeping."

"Sorry, Mr. Whittaker," said a man with a bristly mustache. "This is a big job. We want to do it right."

Sonny stepped back into the kitchen, softly lit by six cobalt blue domes, hanging on skinny silver wires over the island.

"Anything they say," Sonny said, "you blast away. Dazzle them with my painting and humanitarian awards, my undeniable commitment to keeping my children happy and healthy—"

"Sonny, man, listen," Myles said with a shaky voice. "We can avoid that entirely—"

Sonny crossed his arms. "Myles, I don't like that look in your eye—"

Myles twisted his mustache, closing his eyes. "Just listen to the offer Norris and Brett Robinson put on the table. My dinner table, as a matter of fact—"

"They came to your house?"

Myles nodded. "For twenty-five million dollars," he raised his brows. "Let me repeat, twenty five million dollars, Norris is asking that you walk away from *The Colony* and let Erica take the girls, at least until things die down."

Sonny clawed the ribbed purple and yellow of Myles's collar. Myles's bangs shook, his eyes grew huge. The sound of ripping fabric filled the air as Myles's back thudded against the tile of the kitchen island.

"You sorry spineless motherfucker!" Sonny shouted through clenched teeth. "We are not for sale!"

"He's giving you twenty-four hours to consider it—"

Sonny twisted the collar. "My family! My flesh and blood. Myles, how could you even—"

Saliva bubbled on Myles's lip. He coughed. "Says he'll set you up with a paint studio in Copenhagen, Rio, Maui, wherever—"

Sonny shoved Myles back.

"Disgust," Sonny said over a burning throat, "does not begin to describe how I feel right now."

"I'm just relaying a message," Myles said.

"What'd he promise you? A signing bonus?"

Sonny spun away from the guilty glaze in his friend's eyes. He clutched the cold lip of the countertop. Red and yellow peppers, the starfruit, blurred in the tall jars against the blue tiled backsplash.

"Myles," Sonny said, turning back around, catching a flicker of shame in his friend's eyes. "Go tell Mr. Haynes, Lincoln shut down the auction block back in 1863."

57

In the nighttime dimness of her bedroom, Simone Thompson craved the oblivion and serenity of sleep and answers to so many questions. But even as her cheek hit the peach flannel pillowcase, and her aching limbs sunk into the plush sheets, the soft harp rendition of *Moonlight Sonata* playing on her stereo did little to quiet the voices or erase the images of the day.

"Tomorrow will be worse," she whispered into the freesia-scented air. After all these years, Cheyenne Moore would be sitting an arm's length away, in the witness box.

The phone rang. The bathroom night light cast a soft glow as Simone reached out of her warm coccoon for the receiver. "Hello?" The blare of a samba band made her sit up.

"Si-Simone, I—"

"Have you been drinking?" The only time she knew of her mother getting drunk at one of the ambassador's banquets—shortly after Grandma Thompson died—her mother had said something about Bianca being "so gentle and loving."

"Some cham-champagne is all. What do you want, Simone?"

"Answers. Call me in the morning, when you're sober."

"You need to know." Her mother blew her nose over the sound of a door closing. The loud music faded. "You should know when your father is close . . . close enough . . . to touch."

Simone's heart raced. "Who?"

"I'm sorry. I didn't want to say on the phone. But you look so sad—"

"Please tell me," Simone said softly.

"I saw the news. Your trial. Sonny Whittaker," her mother slurred. "Stay away from that man, Simone. I don't want him touching—"

Simone's eyes widened. The shadowy room blurred as her mind flipped on a mental calculator: Sonny Whittaker was twenty years old when she was born. So if he was in Washington thirty-five years ago . . . or her mother had been in LA or Brazil—

Simone closed her eyes, laying an arm over her cramping stomach. "Please, don't tell me that."

"Heartbreaker," her mother said. "Ladies man. Pick you up. Put you down. Always laughing—"

Had they had a one-night fling, and he never knew about the pregnancy? But if a brown-skinned man were her father, how could she have come out so white-looking? And how could her mother have committed the unforgivable act of not telling her child that she's half black?

Her trembling hand made the phone shake against her ear. "Please," Simone cried.

Her mother sobbed. "Can't do it anymore. My baby—"

"Tell me!" Simone slid out of bed.

Her mother let out another loud sob, several slurred words.

"I saw him today," her mother sniffled.

"Joseph Myles?" Simone asked. A New Yorker, according to reports about the trial, who grew up with Sonny Whittaker. Former Marine. No wife, no kids. No link to Washington or Brazil.

"Brett Robinson?" Simone demanded. "No—" She remembered

turning fifteen, hearing her mother say: *"He ran off to California to be a star. Doesn't want to be bothered with us."*

Simone gasped. Brett Robinson was a former judge in Washington DC. No! The ethical offense of a romantic liaison between a defendant paled in comparison to overseeing a case involving one's father. Whether he were a lawyer, defendant, anyone. It just was not allowed. Period.

And Brett's work was the antithesis of hers.

"Which one?" Her quaking voice echoed off the ceiling.

Music blared through the receiver again, as if someone had opened the door to the room where her mother was talking. A plunk, like a drink set on a coffee table. Rustling fabric, like taffeta. "Ruth, I need you," Bianca said. "Greg is an ass. I need—"

"Tell me!"

Her mother sobbed. "B—"

"Hang up," Bianca whispered.

"Tell me now!" A scream and a sour heave collided in Simone's chest.

"He didn't know I was preg—"

Simone's insides spiraled with shock.

No way could one of the men in that courtroom be her father.

Sonny Whittaker?

Brett Robinson? There was no denying the similarity of their eyes, hair, complexions—

"No, that can't be right," Simone cried. "Absolutely never."

58

Now alone in the darkness and silence of midnight, Sonny had to burn off the adrenaline still pumping through him from the day's terror. He had to escape the soul-smashing gamut of emotions he had endured today.

The security crew's power tools buzzed and whirred as Sonny closed the door to the girls' bedroom. He had just kissed them, both asleep in the glow of ballerina- and spaceship-shaped nightlights. Jared and Josh sat on the red velvet bench in the hallway.

"Uncle Sonny, we tried," Josh said, his eyes wide and looking just like his father. "I even shot at him, but—"

"I wasn't lettin' nobody through this door," Jared said, shaking his head. "But when them SWAT dudes came, I was like, what the—"

"Both of you, go to sleep," Sonny said, patting their backs. He did not even want to think about leaving them alone again tomorrow, even with the high-tech security.

"Might as well," Jared said, "Between all these wires and drills and the LAPD, this place'll be more secure than the White House by sunrise."

As Sonny descended the back staircase, through the kitchen and family room, his fingers trembled with need. He had to indulge in his ultimate escape, the best therapy he knew.

"By myself, anyway." He hurried into his paint studio. As the seductive jazz of Charlie Parker wafted from his CD player, Sonny yanked the black sheet draping his huge easel.

Yes. A larger-than-life image of the woman he'd painted last night. Had only twenty-four hours passed since he'd sat here, not even knowing her name?

"Simone Thompson," he whispered, grasping the smooth wooden handle of a paintbrush from the riot of jars and tubes and empty coffee cans on tables flanking the easel.

"I want you to feel me," he said, thrusting the brush upward to even out the dark background. He ran a fingertip over the smoothness of the *butterscotch cream* paint curving and swirling to form delicate shoulders, full breasts with taut nipples the same amber rose shade as her lips, a beautiful neck—

A splash of red, gushing from Jenn's neck, then Simone's, blood soaking invisibly into her black robe . . . No!

He lowered his gaze to her bare, hourglass waist, hips with enough curve to give him a perfect handful of flesh, to ground himself as he plunged her molten depths . . .

Her presence enshrouded him like mist as her image mesmerized him. Her soft floral scent, the taste of her hair in the salty wind on the boat, the fear and questions on her face. Her eyes, glowing from behind the sequined mask amidst the Carnival dancers. He squeezed the orange and white tube of *moonbeam gray,* then dabbed a bit onto a brush. With small circular motions he made her eyes even brighter, deeper, so they were smiling yet seductive.

Sonny fanned his fingertips over her full mouth. A dab of *mauve dream* on a Q-tip, to contour the bottom curve, the pillowy sides highlighted with *carnation pink,* contoured with *burgundy blush.*

My mouth should be there. . . . Tasting the flavor that he'd been craving for so many years, without even knowing it, the essence of what could nourish his soul like no other. He shifted on the black stool, resting his feet on the chrome circle about a foot off the floor. Someday, he would ply her lips with his own as he was now doing with a small brush. Just a tickle of *ripe cranberry*. He would knead her thighs with *butterscotch cream*.

Oh, to paint her there—should he use soft, slow strokes? Or should he jab with fast, hard ones? Should he close his eyes, and use Xavier's intuition to guide his body as he captured her spirit? Or should he take visual delight in all the shades and textures of creams and corals, browns and butters.

He sighed, no longer smelling paint, but the Babylonian perfume that had swirled around him and Her on the beach in Brazil. The bare bodies, swiveling and shrieking, acting out what he hoped to do one day with Her—

With a long, thick brush, he made frantic strokes up the long runner's muscles of her legs. As his chest rose and fell, he ran the cream-dipped, black bristles over the soft curves of her breasts. He languished with excruciatingly slow strokes over the stiff peaks.

Sweat prickled his hot skin as he dabbed a staccato of dots and downward dashes—tiny sandy-hued threads embroidering the golden temple where he would one day worship. He moaned, lunging forward, grasping the top of the canvas, pressing his cheek just a kiss above hers . . .

His every cell ached for the moment, in a matter of hours, when he could behold her again.

59

Under the pre-dawn haze, Marie Cartwright Haynes's heart pounded in her ears as she sliced through the heated blue water. She wanted every muscle-burning lift of her arms, and every fluttering kick of her feet, to dissolve the textbook of worries streaming through her head.

Norris's nude body passed in the next lane. He had insisted they swim here without guards, in the Olympic-sized pool, before another day in court. But was it safe out here this morning? In the house, the new security system would alert them of trouble. But out here, under water—

"Ah!" A tight vice around her thighs. Water filled her mouth. She went under. Flailing arms. Kicking for dear life. Heart exploding.

The stalker came for Norris and is getting me, too. No!

Marie's foot struck firm flesh. Hard.

The hands released her.

Norris doubled over, big bubbles exploding from his open mouth. He floated upward, motionless . . .

Panic sent her pulse racing. She grabbed his shoulders. She would put him on the patio, do CPR . . . but where was the attacker?

"Gotcha!" With a great splash, Norris shot to his feet in the five feet of water. His laughter boomed over the steaming pool.

"You scared me to death!" Marie splashed him.

He lunged, kissing her, pulling her onto the stairs, where his lips melted her chills into hot shudders.

"My savior," he moaned, pressing an open palm to her stomach. "So sexy when you're all wet and slippery. Let's do it again in the sauna." Norris's wet hair draped over his smooth, muscular shoulders as he glanced toward the house. Just inside the glass-walled gallery, a cedar handle marked the white entrance door to the redwood chamber.

"If I'm already pregnant, it could be dangerous," she said. "And if I'm not yet, you need to stay out of that heat. It kills sperm, you know."

His lips tickled her ear. "Can't we just hit one home run before court?"

She kissed him back. "I'd love to. Let's drive separately; at the lunch break I'd like to sneak to the office."

"Did you talk to our friend the judge?"

"Norris," she pressed her fingertips into his wet chest. "Simone and I don't share secrets if it means breaking our professional—"

"I come first," Norris said, sloshing up the steps toward a stack of towels on the umbrella table.

"I am offended, Norris," she followed, "that you would insult the integrity of my commitment to—"

"Don't be a hypocrite, Marie." His eyes sharpened.

She threw a towel at him. "You're being impossible."

"I'm going to the sauna."

A short time later, after Marie had dressed, she returned to the kitchen. "Norris, aren't you ready yet? Don't tell me he's still in the sauna—Norris?" She turned toward the gallery. "What's—"

Her heart raced. Her pumps pounded the shiny bleached wood floor.

"Norris!" she screamed.

Silence. Only a two-by-four board, wedged at an angle. The low end rested on the gallery floor against the baseboard. And the other end was jammed under the handle on the sauna door.

60

Tuesday morning in the courtroom, Sonny Whittaker sat ramrod straight at the long wooden table, anxiety crushing his chest. The creases of his thin black wool trousers bunched as he grasped the tops of his thighs.

"Mr. Robinson," Judge Thompson said. "You may call your witness."

Sonny closed his burning eyes to savor her *silk on a soundwave* voice. If only right now he could stroke away the dark circles under her *moon-beam gray* eyes that he had painted until the first rays of dawn had beamed like spotlights over the canvas, forcing him to shower and dress to come here.

"Your honor," Brett Robinson said as he stood in a double-breasted brown pinstriped suit with a pearlescent tie and starched stiff-to-his-neck ivory shirt. "I call Cheyenne Moore."

A hot burst of rage hissed through Sonny's limbs. He sucked down the coffee-and-perfume scented air. No matter what that woman would say or do this morning, Sonny would stay cool. Because Cheyenne's malice was the reason he was here.

"You may approach, Ms. Moore," the judge said with a firm tone as she looked toward the silent, still audience. Her eyes were sharp through silver-rimmed glasses. Could her ashen hue have something to do with this morning's paper? A page-one story had detailed how Simone, as a college student, had testified against Cheyenne during her divorce, causing the judge to give custody of Cheyenne's little girl to the father, who then mysteriously killed himself. And the girl found him—

Trust no one, Grandmama's voice whispered over his thoughts. *You'll pass through rings of fire.* Starting with the twins' desperate tugs around his neck in the back hallway at home as they cried: "Don't leave us alone, again, Daddy!" But he had closed the door between himself and India in her silvery astronaut pajamas, Asia in a frilly yellow nightgown, and the scent of Guadeloupe's bacon and apple cinnamon crêpes wafting from the kitchen.

Erica, in a custard-colored suit and flowing hair at the other end of the table, flashed disgust in her sapphire eyes, even though she had instigated this battle for Sonny to continue sharing every morning with his daughters, waking up and laughing with him, under his roof. At least for the next eleven years.

With a sweep of his arm, Brett reached back toward the swoosh of fabric coming up the aisle; delicate heels tapped the tiled floor.

"Sonny." That husky female voice raised the tiny hairs on the back of his neck. Cheyenne's pheromone-charged musk stole Sonny's breath, even before Cheyenne sashayed toward the bench. The top of her black feathered hair, which bounced softly about her petite shoulders, barely reached Brett's bicep. And that dress—

"She wore that in our movie," Sonny whispered to Myles, seated at his right in a dark blue suit and red tie.

Her breasts bounced with each step, ever so bouyantly. Just as they had when she would come toward Sonny, nude, in the candle light of his bungalow, so long ago—

"Sonny," she mouthed toward him. Tiny lines of red lipstick leached through hair-like wrinkles around the edges of her full mouth. Her bright onyx eyes glimmered through thickly mascaraed lashes, over the chiseled cheekbones of her caramel-hued face. Her sharp, tiny nose tilted upward. On sharp-pointed shoes with cream ribbons criss-crossing over her ankles, Cheyenne stepped around the stenographer and into the witness box.

"State your name for the record," the clerk said.

"Cheyenne Moore." The voice was as deep as a chain-smoking sailor.

Myles stood. "Your honor, Ms. Moore's legal name is Gertrude Michaels."

Brett Robinson, standing before Cheyenne, bowed slightly to Myles. "Thank you for the attention to detail, Mr. Myles. But Ms. Michaels became Mrs. Moore when she married, after legally changing her first name nearly a quarter-century ago."

"Cheyenne was the heroine's fictitious name in *Come Back, My Love*," Myles said.

Erica's dark lashes were motionless, aimed straight at Cheyenne. The two seats where Norris and Marie had sat yesterday were empty.

"Ms. Moore," Brett Robinson said, after several monotonous questions. "Please tell the court about the first time you and Sonny Whittaker made love, after he married Erica Haynes."

"On their eight-month anniversary," Cheyenne said. "We were in New York. Erica was home, too pregnant to travel. He said she hadn't let him touch her for months."

Brett said, "Did he try to explain away his marital status?"

"Oh, no. But I could tell it was old hat for him," Cheyenne said, "by the way he was saying little things like, 'This is just between us,' or 'I trust your confidence.' "

"In your book," Brett said, "you list at least a half dozen sexual liaisons he's had with women while living with his wife. Would you—"

"Objection!" Myles shouted. "That's double hearsay."

"Sustained," the judge said, "Unless the plaintiff can produce the women who made these allegations—"

Sonny's chest squeezed as his head filled with the image of a parade of women streaming into the court, taking Cheyenne's seat, one after another, making up more lies about him.

"—we will focus on only this witness's interaction with Mr. Whittaker."

Cheyenne turned slightly, staring up at the judge with a glint in her onyx eyes. It was a shimmer that was captivatingly beautiful, and may have signaled some brilliant comment she would make over a candlelit dinner. But that glint, he later learned, would always come before Cheyenne screamed in her sudden fits over Sonny choosing the wrong restaurant or signing a leather pants-clad woman's autograph at a Lakers game or refusing to carry on their sick affair after he'd realized just how emotionally unstable she was.

"Yes, your honor," Cheyenne said with a sweet tone and a sharp stare at the judge.

The golden threads of Simone's pulled-back hair caught the fluorescent light, her lips pursed slightly, and her dark lashes angled down at Cheyenne. The air between them was so charged, Sonny imagined a hissing sound or blue-white sparks.

"Continue, Mr. Robinson," the judge said as she tilted her chin upward.

"Ms. Moore," Brett Robinson said, nodding slightly. "I believe you have something to tell Mr. Whittaker today. Something that will have profound bearing on the court's opinion of the true character of Sonny Whittaker as a father."

"Sonny," Cheyenne said deeply, her eyes glinting like never before.

Sonny grasped the tops of his legs. He breathed deeply. He would not show a reaction—

"There's something I have to tell you," Cheyenne said with a syrupy purr; she leaned closer to the silver mesh ball of the microphone.

"It's not in the book," she said, looking toward him with love-glazed eyes. "And it's not hearsay. We have a daughter."

Her sentence hung in the silent, still air for a few moments. It was like fire snaking along a detonation cord, sizzling and racing toward four dynamite sticks—one for each word she had just spoken.

With a red flash, rage exploded inside Sonny's head.

His blood boiled and burned through shaking limbs.

"That son of a bitch!" Myles whispered angrily as he glared at Brett. He shot to his feet, making his bangs shake.

A deep buzz spread through the courtroom behind them.

"Your honor," Myles shouted. "I request an immediate adjournment."

The judge paled. Her brows drew together slightly as she looked from Cheyenne to Brett—standing tall and proud before her.

"An adjournment is granted, Mr. Myles," the judge said with a hard tone. "Until after lunch. Counsel in my chambers." Her lips tightened as she demanded, "Immediately."

Hushed voices shot from the back of the courtroom.

"No!" a young female voice shouted. "I'm tired of waiting! I want to meet my father now!"

Sonny's heart hammered. He turned back, toward the aisle.

A tall, curvy woman took long, hard steps toward him. In a black skirt-suit and heels, she was Cheyenne twenty-five years ago. Feathered hair. A small, striking face with tiny, chiseled features and sharp, dark eyes. A prominent, red-painted mouth whose pout poked out slightly over curved teeth. And amber eyes. Just like the twins.

61

Simone cringed into her leather chair, holding her breath as Katie Moore took long, colt-like steps toward her. Was that really the girl whose face, whose laugh, whose sadness, had influenced every legal decision Simone had ever made regarding children?

Does Katie recognize me? Does my face morph into her father's bloody grimace as he lay dead on the bedroom floor, custody papers and birth certificate in one hand, a gun in the other?

No matter the shock deluging her senses right now, she had to keep control of her courtroom. Especially with that TV camera to her right, watching everything from the jury box. Not to mention Roxanne Jones in the first row, her eyes wide with an orgasmic glaze.

"No!" Sonny shouted as he shot to his feet. "She is not my daughter!"

"Come here, Katie," Cheyenne cooed. Her lacy dress draped over the wooden partition as she stood and raised her arms toward the young woman. "The three of us are finally together again."

"Your honor!" Myles said, striding toward the bench and Brett Robinson. "This is taking my client totally by surprise. And to interject this kind of information—"

"I did not know she would walk in here," Brett Robinson said loudly.

"I've waited twenty-five years," the young woman cried through trembling lips as she extended a long arm and elegant caramel-hued fingers, toward Sonny. Her voice was deep and syrupy. A sheriff's deputy blocked her from passing through the wooden gate. "I won't wait any longer," she said.

"I've been telling Katie," Cheyenne boomed through the microphone, "since she was a little girl, that someday we'd get to be with her real daddy." The corners of Cheyenne's mouth curled up slowly. She closed her eyes for a second. "That Sonny Whittaker would come back for us. Well—"

"No!" Sonny shouted.

"Order in this courtroom!" Simone slammed down the gavel.

Sonny's face took on a green pallor as the woman stopped in the aisle and cast pleading eyes at him.

Simone swallowed hard as a sour heave rippled up her throat. Could Sonny have committed the same despicable act as her own father, and set this woman's tragedy into motion?

"What more abomination of humanity could there be," Brett Robinson whispered deeply, "than a man letting his own child wonder and wish—every morning, every birthday, every Christmas—for the father who's never smiled at her? Never hugged her? Never tucked her in bed with a goodnight kiss?"

His cornflower blue eyes glowed with tenderness as he held Simone's gaze. Her heart pounded. Was he trying to tell her something to confirm her mother's drunken riddle?

A hot bolt of rage squelched the tears stinging Simone's eyes.

Rage at Brett Robinson's blatant disregard for courtroom decorum. Rage at the way his words were making Sonny Whittaker quake. Rage at the idea of him committing the very sin he was condemning. And mostly, rage at herself for allowing this . . .

"You son of a bitch," Myles whispered to Brett loud enough for her to hear. "You got any other unscrupulous surprises?"

"Katie, give your daddy a hug," Cheyenne purred.

"Sit down, Ms. Moore!" Simone spat down to the witness box.

"Stop this already!" Erica shrieked. She glared at Sonny with wide eyes. "Is this true?"

"She is not my daughter!" Sonny shouted.

Simone slammed the gavel so hard, her arm vibrated.

"Everyone!" she said angrily. "Silence. Or jail. Your choice."

The sound of rushing blood in her own ears was all Simone heard as the courtroom hushed and stilled.

"Gentlemen," she said through taut lips. She glared down at Brett Robinson and Joseph Myles. "My chambers! Now."

62

Sonny Whittaker grasped the wooden arms of the chair so tightly, he was sure they would crumble. With Myles in the judge's chambers right now, Sonny had to hold on, to stop himself from storming over to Cheyenne Moore and—

He raised his chin, squared his shoulders. Just as Xavier chose the high road when put on trial before the brutal and biased World Council—

Fome. Sonny inhaled and exhaled. Slowly focusing on his breath. *Fome.*

Especially with his chest squeezing more brutally than ever—even the day Erica set this nightmare in motion. He would not let this drama kill him.

The courtroom buzzed behind him. Roxanne Jones' eyes were boring holes into the back of his head. And that young woman . . .

Sonny turned toward Cheyenne; her affectionate gaze seared his senses.

"Sonny," she said, her eyes sparkling.

The courtroom hushed.

"Sonny—"

"No talking, ma'am," said a deputy standing in front of the witness box. He moved his feet farther apart.

But her lovesick stare continued, as if she expected him to scoop her into his arms and carry her off into the fucking sunset. Sonny unhinged his cramped fingers from the arms of the chair. He rose, turned and faced that young woman who could *not* be his daughter—

"Sonny," Cheyenne said on the red carpet outside the premiere of Come Back, My Love. *"We're pregnant," she said, placing her new husband's huge beige hand over the still-flat belly of her beaded gown. "You wouldn't marry me, so I finally told Peter yes—"*

"Congratulations," Sonny said awkwardly to her and the towering NBA star she'd just insulted. "Good luck with the baby—"

Sonny strode past the flashing lights and paparazzi who were calling his name. He smiled with relief that he'd always used condoms with Cheyenne during their on-set tryst. He had several in his wallet right now, for whatever indulgences the night promised.

Because now that he was getting so much attention, so many scripts and offers for exciting projects, being tied down with a wife, baby or sexually transmitted disease was nowhere on his storyboard.

"Sweet Sonny Whittaker!" Norris called, patting his back. As they posed for countless flashes, Norris said, "Hold on tight. Your star is about to shoot to infinity!"

Now, if this young woman were his flesh and blood, he had to touch her, smell her. See if her fingernails had the same distinct oval shape that he, the twins, his mother, and Grandmama had. See if her ears had flat, smooth lobes and almost pointed tops . . . if her hairline at the temple and back of her neck had the same fine, golden fuzz as the twins. If her left ankle crackled, as his had done all his life, every sixth step or so.

And he had to see if her spirit felt like it had sprung from his.

Sonny stepped from behind the table and opened the gate.

"Mr. Whittaker, you'll have to sit down," a sheriff's deputy said. "Until the judge gets back."

Sonny stepped through the gate, staring down into her pleading face.

And he knew.

63

In her office, Simone charged toward the two lawyers, who were standing in front of the long window. The gray sky glowed through the mini-blinds.

"This is an outrage!" Simone shouted. "I will not allow either of you to make a circus of my courtroom. And I will not stand for a trial by ambush."

"I demand a mistrial, immediately," Joseph Myles said calmly, twisting the side of his mustache. "Mr. Robinson should be sanctioned. Severely. His bush-league trial tactics are an abomination. My client is—"

"Your client," Brett Robinson said calmly as he studied the painting behind Simone's desk, "was simply being informed of his own irresponsible—"

"Gentlemen," she stood before them, her lips tight. "This is some of the worst lawyering I've ever seen. I *am* on the verge of granting a mistrial."

"That's the only appropriate thing to do," Mr. Myles said.

"It's not necessary," Mr. Robinson said.

"As of now," Simone said, "I want to avoid the publicity and delay. But mostly, I do not want to prolong the uncertainty for the children. Have those two little girls crossed either of your minds for the past two days?"

Her face felt stiff and hot as she glared into Mr. Robinson's bright blue eyes.

"No matter how important this information is," she said, "it is absolutely improper to introduce it in this way."

"I didn't know she'd come into the courtroom," Brett said.

The door blew open.

"Judge Thompson!" Charlie stormed in, his brow furrowed. "Can we expect jugglers and clowns to join the carnival in your courtroom this afternoon? Every reporter in LA wants to know."

"Charlie," Simone said with a hard tone. With her eyes she shot at him all the anger surging through her; he had forced her to stay on this case. "I can handle this."

She faced the lawyers. "Unless you want censure and a mistrial, no more docudramas in my courtroom. In the meantime, both of you, keep a toothbrush in your briefcase. One more split-second of these antics, and you'll both be sleeping in jail."

Her robe rustled as she strode toward the door. "As for right now, I'm ordering an immediate paternity test."

64

In a private hospital room at Cedar-Sinai Medical Center in Los Angeles, Marie stared at Norris's swollen face. It appeared all the more crimson against white hospital linens and the glow of a deep rose curtain just beyond several silver IV poles. A bank of shelves above the bed held monitors that beeped and flashed red numbers.

"Why?" she cried, gripping the bed rail. "Why would someone do this?" She stroked his hair over the pillow, then straightened the blue hospital gown around his ruby-hued neck.

"We'll keep things peaceful and quiet," she whispered. Now, Marie just wanted him to use this break in production for *The Colony* to get better, and avoid as much of the chaos of Erica's trial as possible.

"Marie?" The scent of floral perfume soothed her; solid-sounding steps came closer.

"Simone," Marie sighed, slumping into the soft shoulder of her friend's black trench coat. "We'd both be dead if I'd taken a sauna, too—"

"Shhhh," Simone whispered over the *hoosh* of the machine.

Erica strode into the room. Worry crinkled her face as she took quick steps toward her father. But she froze when she saw Simone.

"I'll go," Simone said, kissing Marie's cheek. "I'll call you."

"You leave the room when I come in," Erica snapped at Simone, "but you stay and visit with Sonny in Bra—"

"Quiet, Erica!" Marie whispered loudly as Simone left the room.

"She is so against me," Erica's bloodshot, black-smeared eyes focused on the door. "Yesterday someone tries to kill my kids. Now someone gets my dad. And you and she are right in the middle of it!"

"He promised my mom he would never get married," Erica shrieked. "Daddy!" she cried inches from his head. "But then those civil rights groups and their protests, he took Sonny's project, then married you—"

A doctor hurried in. He was dark-haired with small glasses, sallow skin and small, bright eyes. "Please," the doctor warned. "Keep quiet and still. Mr. Haynes suffered quite—"

"Will he be alright?" Erica grasped the doctor's hand. "Tell me he'll be fine."

"Dr. Zachs," Marie said, "this is Norris' daughter, Erica Haynes Whittaker."

"Please," the doctor said. "Your father needs peace and quiet."

"Nobody would be after him if he hadn't married the stalker queen here," Erica hissed. "You make me sick, Marie. You're just one more distraction that keeps my dad from paying attention to me. So don't even say the word daughter-in-law—"

"If you don't quiet down," Marie choked, "neither of us will be getting any attention from him."

65

In the courtroom after the lunch break, Sonny sat stiffly at the table, his blood boiling ever more fiercely, as Myles strode toward the bench.

"Your honor," Myles said, stepping close to Cheyenne Moore in the witness box. "I will be succinct."

Myles looked down on the woman who had forced Sonny to forfeit his blood and his integrity back at that lab during the noontime adjournment.

"Ms. Moore," Myles said with a matter-of-fact tone. "You've been a bad actress all your life. You're being a bad actress now. And we present this charade, your honor, as Exhibit A. No further questions."

66

Kindred Germaine settled into the lumpy tweed chair in the witness box. She hooked her left index finger into the sunshine-yellow wish ribbon tied around her right wrist. It was the same color as the fuzzy cuff of her cashmere turtleneck, which was making her sweat under her trim gray pantsuit and loose hair over her shoulders and back.

"Ms. Germaine," Brett Robinson said, clenching the wooden partition with his manicured hands, staring down with superiority in his blue eyes. "I'm curious, what in your tender age of twenty-five, qualifies you to raise and educate two children?"

Kindred stared back at him, hard. Part of her wanted to cover her face with her hands to block out his handsome face, the judge, and that bitch Cheyenne Moore. All of them were torturing Daddy Whittaker, the twins—

"I graduated third in my class from Dorchester Preparatory School," Kindred said, twisting the ribbon. "Then the Whittakers worked out my schedule so I could earn an undergraduate degree in early childhood development. As the twins get older, I'm still taking classes to keep up."

"Keep up," Brett Robinson mocked. "What, exactly are your duties in the Whittaker home?"

Kindred glimpsed the gray flannel rectangle between her high heeled black loafers. When the time was right, she would open her purse, and retrieve her own evidence to prove Erica's unworthiness as a mother. That was her duty here, today.

"My duties," Kindred said. "They change as Asia and India grow and mature. As newborns, I did everything, including night feedings. When I went to class, they hired a replacement for those hours, but the girls screamed when I was gone."

"How did you and Mrs. Whittaker get along?"

"Great." Kindred shrugged, ignoring Erica's sharp glare. "If I were leaving for class, she would stand in the foyer with a baby in each arm and say, 'Hurry back.' But she's very impatient, and I think the way I took my time reading or doing puzzles or singing with the girls, it made her jealous—"

"Ms. Germaine," Brett Robinson said, "Tell us about your own family."

"I don't have a family," she said flatly, twisting the bracelet.

"Everyone has a family," Brett Robinson said. "What happened to yours?"

Kindred turned upward, to the right, peering over the wooden box at the woman with the pulled back golden hair, the silver glasses. She wanted to ask the judge if she had to tell the story of the plane crash, of the horrible loneliness and emptiness that she had endured ever since.

"Ms. Germaine," Mr. Robinson said, "Please answer—"

"I did. Mr. Whittaker is like a father to me—"

"Does he hug and kiss you when you're upset?"

"Sometimes."

"Does he tuck you in bed?"

Kindred looked up into Brett Robinson's handsome, pampered face. "I won't justify that with an answer."

"Did he tell you to say that?" Brett snapped back.

"I have my own brain," Kindred said. "Mr. Whittaker has never made even the slightest gesture or comment to make me uncomfortable."

"Certainly you must admit, Ms. Germaine, your excitement over Mrs. Whittaker's departure from the family home. How you envision replacing her as the lady of the house, mother of two beautiful children, and you, the young trophy wife to a world-famous movie star!"

"Objection," Mr. Myles said. "Mr. Robinson is badgering the witness."

"Sustained."

"Ms. Germaine," Brett said. "Be honest, now. Have you ever even fantasized about the life of luxury that you could enjoy, as Mrs. Sonny Whittaker?"

Kindred turned toward the judge. "Do I have to answer that obnoxious question?"

"Your honor," Brett Robinson said, "I need to establish that Ms. Germaine's adoration for her employer and his family erodes her credibility. In addition to making her a potentially hostile witness."

"Ms. Germaine," the judge said. Her shiny silver glasses magnified the tough-tender glow in her eyes. "Please answer."

Kindred held the judge's stare, then squinted at the lawyer before her.

"Mr. Robinson," Kindred said, "You've read too many gossip magazines. Mr. Whittaker's behavior is the epitome of respect."

"Did he and his lawyer coach you to say that?"

"Do I look like I don't know the definition of perjury?" Kindred tilted her head slightly, widening her eyes up at him. "I have my own brain, and a nice vocabulary list to choose from."

"I want to ask you, Ms. Germaine. Given your lack of a family yourself, does it hurt to know you're being paid to be part of the Whittaker family?"

Kindred steeled herself—stiff face, unresponsive eyes, arms and legs and torso just as poised in this chair as they had been before his words had stabbed her heart. "Of course not," she said with a steady tone. "I am the nanny. I get paid every week. And?"

"And," Brett said, "given the familial void in your background, perhaps you would do and say anything today to maintain your privileged position. Living in a mansion, driving an expensive SUV, traveling to exotic lands—"

"Objection," Mr. Myles said. "Enough of this insulting speculation. Mr. Robinson is badgering—"

"Overruled."

"You are his employee," Brett said, "and that bothers you, doesn't it? If you love those girls and him as your own family, something deep in the pit of your stomach just doesn't feel right, being on his payroll—"

"Objection," Myles said. "Your honor, he *is* badgering the witness."

"Sustained." The judge's voice raked over Kindred's nerves.

"Has Mr. Whittaker promised you anything," Brett Robinson asked, "any perks or rewards, for helping him win custody of little Asia and India?"

"Of course not," Kindred exhaled loudly. She reached down, grasping the gray flannel purse between her feet. As she rose up, the warmth in Mr. Whittaker's eyes gave her a jolt of determination.

And the disgust pinching Erica's perfectly painted face, and just behind her in the audience . . .

Cheyenne Moore.

That demented diva who'd seen much better days, staring up here with her fiery eyes, as if she hated that anyone else dared take the witness stand after her pathetic and hurtful melodrama. It had made Kindred gasp as she had watched the lunchtime news reports. Along with the sadness in Mr. Whittaker's eyes as he had dashed past dozens of cameras, into a waiting car—

I have to make things right for him. I have to keep us all together . . .

Kindred turned toward the judge. "Your honor," she said, unsnapping the purse. She pulled out two prescription bottles—the ones she had plucked from Erica's Louis Vuitton toiletry bag in the bathroom at Sanctuary.

"I have evidence of my own," Kindred said, placing the bottles on the wooden bench in front of the judge. "Erica is still on drugs."

"Objection," Brett shouted. "Hearsay, inadmissible, no foundation laid. We don't know where Ms. Germaine obtained that.'"

"They were next to the other bottles of drugs I found in Erica's bathroom—"

"Objection sustained," Judge Thompson said firmly. She cast those bright silver-blue eyes down: "Ms. Germaine, you are here to answer questions. Only."

Kindred bit down a smile. *That's exactly what I just did. I helped everyone reconfirm that Erica is a druggie, not a mommy.*

67

Simone Thompson's every muscle clenched as Brett Robinson stood before Sonny Whittaker in the witness box. One inappropriate tone of voice and she would take swift and decisive action. Because this morning's chaos still throbbed raw on her nerves, making, she feared, a permanent stain on her reputation.

She scooted her chair so close to the bench, it pressed into her burning stomach. She rested her elbows on the wooden desk, and inhaled Sonny Whittaker's spicy musk.

He was close enough to touch, just a few feet below on her left. But rather than the hot tropical sun warming their faces, a hundred faces and a

TV camera burned her cheeks. And instead of the warm ocean breeze, the rigid rules of conduct chilled the air between them.

As did Brett Robinson, who was training those eerily familiar blue eyes that made her insides ache. But she had to concentrate, not contemplate whether her mother's drunken babbling had any truth. And she would not allow herself to filter Brett's questions about paternity, or Sonny's answers, through her own haunting lens of questions.

"Before the children came," Sonny said. "Erica and I ate, slept and breathed each other. We were inseparable. Until—"

"Until," Brett Robinson said, "you remembered the other women you loved to eat, sleep and breathe—"

Laughs rose from the audience.

"Objection!" Joseph Myles said. "Your honor, he's badgering the witness."

"Sustained." Simone studied the shape of Brett's eyes, the fullness of his bottom lip, the sharper points of the top lip, the buttery hue of his skin.

"Mr. Whittaker," Brett said, "while we await the results that prove you have at least one illegitimate child—"

"Objection!" Myles shouted. "Your honor, I request that we make no reference to that until the lab results are in."

"Sustained."

"Have you, Mr. Whittaker," Brett asked, "ever wondered if you've fathered bastard children in any of the exotic locales around the world, where you've filmed movies?"

"Objection!" Myles said. "Badgering."

"Sustained," Simone said. "Mr. Robinson, I've just turned on the contempt meter."

"Do you know if you have any other children?"

"I have two children," Sonny said firmly. "Asia and India."

"Enjoying a beautiful woman and making a baby only takes a minute," Brett said.

"Speak for yourself, Mr. Robinson."

The audience let out snickers and muted laughter.

"Gentlemen!" Simone snapped. "Quiet in this courtroom."

"Mr. Whittaker, you're deep in the doting father role right now, but what about the night you were half a world away in France for the Cannes Film Festival, while India was in the hospital with a one-hundred-five degree temperature?"

"No, even when I called to check, Erica didn't—"

"What about the time when you were entertaining lady friends at your family's estate on Montserrat, while your wife and children huddled in Los Angeles during the earthquake!"

"I was painting! And I had the house built with special fortifications. I couldn't—"

"That's right, Mr. Whittaker. You *couldn't* make it home. And sending Erica and the twins to Disneyland cannot replace a father's kiss and voice singing 'Happy Birthday.'"

Simone's cheeks burned. Was the man before her the person who had made the thirty-some birthdays Simone could remember mere tear-stained smudges on the timeline of her life?

"That's not fair," Sonny said. "Everything I do is for them—"

"Would that include," Brett asked, "skinnydipping threesomes in the pool after you think they've gone to bed?"

"Of course not."

"How about developing a rather intimate relationship," Brett said, "with your attractive young nanny who sleeps just down the hall from your bedroom?"

"That's disgusting," Sonny said. "You heard Kindred. She's like a daughter to me. We consider her family."

Sonny looked up, meeting Simone's gaze. Pain and anger roiled in the topaz and gold and olive spokes of his pupils. "How long do I have to be subjected to this?" His combed-back black and silver waves moved back and forth as he shook his head and radiated disgust toward the man before him.

"Tread lightly, Mr. Robinson," Simone said.

"Certainly a man of your experience," Brett said, "would be used to a pretty young woman performing whatever duties you desire—"

"Objection!" Myles shouted. "Your honor, he continues to badger the witness."

"Sustained. Mr. Robinson, get out your checkbook. Your thousand dollars will be put to good use by the County of Los Angeles."

Brett Robinson removed his gold-rimmed glasses.

Simone could not breathe. Because the resemblance between the barrister glaring up at her—and the reflection she had seen in her bathroom mirror this morning—was undeniable.

68

Marie Cartwright Haynes hurried into her high-rise office, in the corner of the tall black glass building on Wilshire Boulevard. She had to take her mind off Norris for a while—

"Hi, Miss Cartwright."

Marie's heart pounded as she ran her hand over the light sensors just inside the double doors, on the smooth polished wood. She sniffed clove cigarette smoke and patchouli oil.

"Tabitha?" The lights flickered on. "How did you—"

"Your secretary was at lunch." Soft tendrils of long brown hair framed her bloodshot blue eyes and red glasses. A too-dark shade of makeup covered the circles of acne on her almond cheeks. "Hope I, uh, didn't scare 'ya."

Marie strode to her desk. She pushed a button to open the curtains lining the windowed walls. Tabitha rose from the chair in the far corner. Her black skirt and bulky sweater swished against her thick, round middle as her lace-up granny boots plodded over the carpet. She sunk into the leather chaise by the window. And she sobbed.

Marie sat next to her, stroking her back. "Tabitha, honey—"

"I uh, I can't come here anymore." Her mouth twisted behind a curtain of hair. "My dad says it makes me more retarded. He flushed my medication. He uh, some guys at his job saw the insurance records. They started teasin' him that his kid is a loon. Said he wouldn't be surprised if I'm that stalker 'cause I'm so ugly."

Tabitha sobbed into open palms.

"Shh, shhh," Marie said, laying her back. She went to the stereo and played soothing music. "Tabitha, I want you to close your eyes. Relax. And help me understand what started this."

"Oh uh, Miss Cartwright, I needed, I needed to talk to you so bad since all this stuff started. But I uh, I had no, no way to get here."

"Since what stuff started?"

"That stalker. My uh, my dad said only an ugly girl like me would hurt someone as beautiful as Jenn Ryder—"

"That was in Brazil. If you can't even get a ride here—"

Tabitha shot up, staring out the window. "'Cause when they got her last week, and we saw the news, I uh, I said it kinda made sense, ya know? All the pressure on girls to be pretty and skinny, ya know. And I said—" she sobbed.

"I said I uh, I was glad somebody was finally speakin' up for the ugly girls. My dad slapped me." Tabitha's blue-polished fingertips covered the blemish. "He said I wouldn't be ugly if I uh, if I didn't sit on my fat ass all day at my job and—"

"Enough of what your father said," Marie snapped.

Tabitha turned to her.

"I agree with you," Marie said, acknowledging her own preoccupation with maintaining her trim shape, tinting her hair to just the right shade to complement her complexion, and getting weekly facials to ward off wrinkles.

"That stalker," Marie said, "in a sick sort of way, does have a point. But violence is not the solution. What we need to do, Tabitha, is find ways for you to feel good about yourself. Regardless of your father, or TV or magazines. Does that make sense?"

Tabitha nodded. "Dr. Cartwright, I uh, I can't afford to come without my dad's insurance. This is my last time—"

Marie sat at her desk and flipped through Tabitha's file. "Tabitha, you've been paying cash since you started coming to me two years ago. I don't see any record of insurance here."

Tabitha curled up on the chaise. "I uh, I admit I lied. But I prefer not to continue coming here. I despise what I see when I look inside myself. And you, uh, you make me look, Dr. Cartwright."

"That's the only way we can heal," Marie said.

"I don't want to heal," Tabitha said, snapping her head. "I uh, I want everyone to know how much it sucks! How much it sucks to be *me*!" She shot to her feet. Her fists slammed into the sides of her thighs. "That's what Tabitha Yates wants!"

"Tabitha, here's more medication," Marie said, handing over two small boxes. "I want to see you again this week. Friday afternoon. Don't worry about money."

"Dr. Cartwright, you don't understand. I can't come back."

Marie grasped her arms. "Tabitha, I will see you here, Friday at three." Fingerprints and smudges on Tabitha's glasses caught the light in a way that obscured her eyes.

Suddenly, something seemed strangely familiar about Tabitha. But what?

69

The courtroom was silent and still as Sonny Whittaker vowed to remain graceful under fire throughout the rest of this humiliating and insulting attack here in this godawful little witness box. The toes of his rust-colored suede loafers bumped the wall again, the lumpy blue cushion irritated his back, and the silver mesh ball of the microphone, suspended inches from his face, was a phallic symbol that he was getting screwed.

"Your honor," Brett Robinson said, stepping to a TV and VCR on a roll-in stand next to the table where Erica was sitting. He pushed a button. "If I may now play the video I've entered as exhibit D."

No, he would not let all the rage igniting inside him explode at Brett

Robinson. And he would control the overwhelming need to set his own record straight in the eyes of the beautiful woman looking down on him right now.

Sonny's own face appeared. His recorded voice announced:

"I have never been monogamous." He grinned, sitting on a director's chair on the Parisian set of Heartbreaker, *in which he played an American ex-patriate who made a career of seducing lonely, rich women. "Monogamy is a foreign concept to me. It's something I hope never to learn, or try to understand." He laughed.*

Brett Robinson hit a button. Sonny's image froze—mouth open, eyes half-shut.

"Now, Mr. Whittaker, you established for viewers of *Entertainment Exclusive*—broadcast around the world—just how you feel—"

"Come on," Sonny said. "That was twenty years ago."

Brett's gold cufflink glimmered as he pushed PLAY. The younger Sonny appeared. What he would do to be thirty-five again: *Smooth face, no lines forming like parentheses around his mouth. No silver threads streaking his combed-back black waves. No worry or paternal anxiety glinting in his eyes. Just a where's-the-next-party sparkle.*

"I'll never marry," Sonny said, puffing a cigarette in a black holder, "Show me the most gorgeous woman," he looked into the camera. "Believe me, I'm meeting them right here in gay paree." He turned to the reporter. "I wouldn't take the plunge for all the money in the world."

"Children?"

Sonny laughed. "Not that I know of."

"Objection!" Myles shouted as the reporter kept talking. "Words spoken two decades ago are irrelevant."

"Mr. Myles," the judge said. "Your client's previous thoughts on marriage and children may, indeed, pertain to today's proceedings. Mr. Robinson, rewind, please."

Myles sat down as electronic gibberish filled the courtroom.

The reporter asked, "Would you like to have a child someday?"

"Who can say," Sonny said with a more serious tone. "I don't know if this is the kind of world I'd want to inflict on some tiny human being who didn't ask to come here."

"Now," Mr. Robinson said. "Mr. Whittaker, your interview of decades past still rings true. You marry one of the most gorgeous women in the world—Erica Haynes—but she and the beautiful daughters she gave you are not enough to stop your insatiable sex—"

"No, I'm different now!" Sonny shouted. He shifted, resting his elbows against his ribs. That only made him feel hotter, by pressing his sweat-soaked shirt into his torso. He took shallow breaths of stuffy air.

The judge's eyes were boring into his burning cheeks, but Sonny could not turn and look up at her. He would not meet her questioning gaze with the insult of Brett Robinson's words hanging between them.

"You set women on fire with your passion," Brett Robinson glared down with those blazing blue eyes, "suck them in with red-hot desire, then abandon them in the smoldering ashes."

"Objection!" Myles shouted. "Your honor, is he going to question my client or testify?"

"Mr. Robinson!" Simone said, knitting her brows. "You are flirting with a night in jail. The objection is sustained."

"Mr. Whittaker," Brett said, turning to Sonny. "I have a grown son and daughter—"

The judge coughed. Why was she looking at Brett Robinson as if she couldn't breathe again without hearing what venomous new insult would squirt from his fangs next?

"And men like you," Brett said, narrowing his eyes, "are every father's nightmare—"

The gavel cracked.

"Mr. Robinson!" the judge shouted. "When you complete your questioning, and I mean questioning, not interjecting your own personal feelings into this trial, we will make arrangements for you to enjoy the accommodations of our fine jailhouse this evening."

Brett's nose flared slightly as he glared up at the judge. He squared his shoulders, as if deflecting her punishment with a rooster-like rise of his chest.

"Mr. Whittaker," Brett said with a playful glimmer in his eyes. "Your name connotes romance and passion in the hearts and minds of women around the world. Even in casual conversation, the name Sonny Whittaker is synonymous with 'handsome, romantic hero.'"

"Those are the characters I've played in my movies," Sonny said.

"Now, would you agree, that for most of your adult life, you have taken full advantage of the Sonny Whittaker phenomenon, as the ultimate philanderer, playboy—"

"No!" Sonny shouted. He shot to his feet. "That's wrong!"

"I am who I am," he said softly. "I will not apologize for being Sweet Sonny Whittaker. An actor who has played many roles as a globe-trotting

Casanova. A man whose life, for years, imitated his art all too closely. But I'm different now."

He grasped the wooden edge of the judge's bench, meeting her gaze.

"Yes, I am a man full of passion," he said softly, "I love women. I love making love." Flames of emotion stung his eyes, blurring the only person who needed to hear this. "But the best part of my life is hearing those little girls call me 'Daddy!' or to feel little arms around my neck when they say, 'I love you, Daddy.' Because—"

"Your honor!" Brett shouted. "This is not a one-man play."

Judge Thompson removed her glasses as she stared down at Sonny. Her *moonbeam gray* eyes narrowed as if she would send him to jail, too.

"I have so much love to give," Sonny said. "So much creative vision to share. But if the lies spoken today succeed in stealing those two little human beings who keep my heart beating, I will drop dead right here."

70

The soft light of sunset poured into Norris's hospital room, illuminating the white styrofoam carton that Marie had picked up at their favorite Indian restaurant. She perched on the side of the bed, raising another forkful of tandoori chicken and basmati rice toward Norris's mouth.

"It's delicious, but I'm full," he said. "I know I'm way out in left field. Someone tries to steam me to death, and I wake up craving my mom's favorite ethnic dinner."

Marie smiled. She wanted to keep the contented glaze in his eyes, and convince him to rest, now that he was conscious. He did not need to think about what was happening in court. And until he was better, the stalker was caught and the trial was resolved, she did not want to think or talk about whether marrying him had been a mistake. Even though every day since she'd said "I do," her heart had ached with doubt.

"Marie, my savior," Norris said with a raspy tone. "Snap out of it. You look like you're down for the count—"

"I'm fine," she said, shaking her head. "Just want to keep you on the road to recovery."

"Why?" He let out a strange laugh. "So you can keep plunging the depths of my scarred psyche? Does it give you a rush, peeking into the mind of this producer of whom Hollywood myths are made?"

She stroked his still-pink cheek with the back of her hand. "I just want to bring my new husband home."

Norris grasped her hand. His eyelashes drew together.

Marie gasped. "Norris, why are you looking at me like—"

"If you *ever* tell a soul," he groaned, just over a whisper, "the truth about how my wife died, or that I'm seeing a shrink—"

"Norris," Marie said with a calm voice even though her insides were jittering. "Why are you worried about this right now? I've always assured you of the utmost discretion."

"I'll make you out as a seductress who preys on unsuspecting and troubled men," he said. "I'll have you investigated. No license, no clients—"

Marie stood, running her trembling hands over her pumpkin-hued satin blouse and pleated wool pants. "Where is this coming from?"

"Nightmares, maybe," Norris said, "when I passed out in the sauna. About your friends, Erica's trial. What does Simone Thompson know about me? And what'll she try to use against me? How bad it would look and sound for anyone to know I need help—"

"Relax, Norris. First, Simone is not that type of person. Even if she knew—"

"Does she?" He grabbed her hand.

"No." Marie pulled her hand back. She picked up the food carton and dumped it into a trash can next to the dresser. "No one knows."

"I don't need any negative publicity when I get out and recast *The Colony*," Norris said. "The civil rights groups will already be on my ass for getting rid of their beloved Sonny Whittaker. But after this trial—"

"Norris, you can't just cut him out," Marie said. "He's got a contract—"

"I can do what I want," Norris said, shifting against the pillows.

"Right now," Marie said, pulling his hair over one shoulder of his blue nightgown. She looked into his eyes. "Just think about getting better."

So I can tell you I made a mistake. That I want out of this farce of a marriage . . .

"I need you to be there for me," Norris said softly. "My savior. When I face the critics to get the movie back on track. I need you by my side. The visual impact—"

His words stabbed Marie's heart. She was his doctor, spouse and propaganda tool.

But nothing more. And she would rather be alone.

"Daddy!" Erica shrieked as she dashed into the room. Behind her came the doctor who wore a pale blue lab coat and carried a clipboard.

"Doctor," Marie said as he approached Norris. "Are all the test results in?"

Brett Robinson strode in. He immediately picked up the phone next to Norris's bed and demanded: "Any messages? Sheila? I need Ryan to talk to the judge. She's trying to put me in jail for the night—"

Marie bit down a smile as she fingered her choker. *Simone, girl, this man must've really made you mad . . .*

"I have to say, Mrs. Haynes," the doctor said, flipping Norris's pale palms to examine red knuckles, "your husband here worked some real movie magic on this one."

Suspicion slithered through her mind. Had Norris feigned heat stroke? Had he staged the whole terrifying ordeal in the sauna? The vandalism? Was he Narcissus? If so, had he killed the lead actress in his movie?

Marie stared at the clean-scrubbed contours of the doctor's face. Her voice lodged somewhere in her tight throat, behind her long scar. The idea of living with a killer . . . the kind of person who robbed her of her own parents as a child . . .

Stop! Norris has serious issues, but my husband, my patient, is not a killer.

"Despite the superficial burns," the doctor said, "Mr. Haynes did not suffer heat stroke. Just mild dehydration, shock and temporary loss of consciousness."

"I'll be out of here and home in a New York minute," he said playfully, reaching for Marie's clammy hand.

Erica crossed her arms and tossed her hair over her shoulder.

"So that's it!" She glared at the doctor. "You scare us to death, then oops! He just fainted. Sorry for the scare!"

"Ms. Haynes," the doctor said softly, "your father was initially showing all the signs—"

Erica pressed a palm to Norris's forehead. "Don't you guys know everything gets reported triple wrong in the media? My boyfriend said one station reported Daddy was dead!"

"Erica," Marie said, walking around the bed to put a hand on Erica's shoulder. "Let's keep it calm and quiet for your father. Norris, want to get some sleep?"

"A good idea," the doctor said.

Norris straightened. "Aren't the girls coming to see me?"

Erica exhaled loudly, pulling away from Marie's hand. "Sonny better not have the gall to come up here. Is that allowed, anyway?" She spun with questioning eyes toward Brett, seeing only his back and the top of the phone.

"Get some rest, Mr. Haynes," the doctor said. The curtain around the bed fluttered as he headed to the door. "Flowers," he called back.

Marie followed him. A cluster of private security guards and LAPD officers handed her a tall vase wrapped in pink paper.

"Wait," she said, taking the small white envelope stapled to the top. "Please take those to the nurse's station for them to enjoy." She slid a finger into the envelope and pulled out the card as she re-entered the carpeted room.

"Sonny's not budging," Brett said.

Marie froze.

"Then offer more!" Norris whispered angrily. "I just need this PR nightmare to go away. Quietly."

Marie held her breath. Her heart pounded in her ears.

"If someone offered me that much," Erica tapped fingernails on the metal bed rail, "it's a no-brainer."

"Whatever it takes," Norris said. "Get him away from my movie, my family."

The small card trembled between Marie's fingers. A woman's delicate handwriting said:

Norris—Until you're big and strong again, your casting couch lies cold, so let my Oscar-worthy performance in court be audition number one for Jenn Ryder's empty role.—Cheyenne.

Marie's heart thundered. Casting couch? Were they trying to bribe Sonny? Tamper with the trial? And was Cheyenne implying that she had been dishonest on the stand?

She turned to leave the room. The metal ceiling track screeched; the curtain sliced back.

Erica scowled. "Daddy, she was listening."

"So what." Norris said with a glare that chilled Marie to her bones.

71

Simone hurried out of the bank, into the dinnertime stream of pedestrian traffic on the Third Street Promenade. Now that she was finished with her five o'clock meeting wtih the loan officer to talk about helping the orphanage, Simone shivered with a sudden sense of vulnerability and exposure. Even faces inside the vast window of the corner bookstore looked suspicious.

I should not have slipped away without the police escort. Even though as she strode past chic restaurants, hip clothing stores and neon-lit cineplexes, she was just blocks from the courthouse. She would walk back, then allow the squad car to follow her home. Just to play it safe. Simone hurried along the pedestrian courtyard aglow with tree lights and vendor carts offering funky jewelry.

"Cool collar!" a teenager in bell-bottomed jeans and a sequined apple hat said, as she and two other girls walked by amidst the spicy scents of a Mediterranean café.

Simone grasped the big fox pouf on the long black cape she had borrowed from her secretary. The black felt cowboy hat, the dark glasses—her reflection in the pane glass of an Indian restaurant was unrecognizable. But if someone really wanted to get her—

"Excuse me," Simone said. She took long, quick strides past a woman pushing a baby stroller, then a blue-suited man with a briefcase who was furrowing his brow and fingering a bandaid on his chin.

Her heart pounded. Narcissus could be anyone, anywhere. *I found Jenn all the way in Brazil, with her face melted; she's dead, and the same attacker wants me—*

"All these people," Simone whispered, pressing past a woman in a brown leather dress, two men in sleek black suits, a TV crew. Media trucks, police cars and limousines clogged the street. Officers stood guard on the sidewalk, and two others flanked the glass door. "What—"

"I need shots of Sonny Whittaker with his paintings," a man shouted from the open side doors of a gray Channel 8 van at the curb. "They want it fed back to the station right away—"

To the right, on the other side of an enormous corner window, colorful paintings lined the white walls, stretching up two stories over hundreds of people. A blue light illuminated a saxophone player on a small stage. Beside a staircase leading up to a balcony with two pine doors, blinding light came from a flash on a camera. Long red fingernails grasped it; behind it swayed twisted-up brown tendrils, red ruffles around the collar of a tight black jumpsuit. The woman smiled: silver braces.

"That's Paulette," Simone said. As long as Paulette were going to indulge her paparazzi fantasy without drawing the line at her personal relationships, Simone would stay as far away from her as possible.

She walked faster.

But stopped just as quickly. Because just inside the window, Sonny Whittaker stood with two silver-haired men. He was pointing up at a painting of giant gold bubbles. He wore all black—turtleneck, pleated trousers, leather belt and loafers with silver buckles. And his hair, pulled back in a curlicue ponytail. He turned, his smoky eyes lingering on her, the tiny lines around his eyes softening for a moment as he studied her lips—

No, he couldn't possibly recognize me like this . . .

Simone turned in front of the van. She would cross the street, and get as far away from Sonny's art show as possible. The last thing she needed right now was for him or anyone else to see her near him.

"Hey, miss!" a high-pitched, masculine voice called behind her, punctuated by heavy footsteps. A man in a shiny maroon suit coat, white ski goggles and baggy black jeans towered over her on the right. "I want to talk to *you*!"

Simone pressed into the crowd, but he craned to look in her face. She looked down—

A red dot on the front of her coat. Like a laser dot. The kind a rifle makes on its target—

Simone stepped toward one of the police officers.

"I am Narcissus!" the man screamed, thrusting his arms upward.

With a collective cry of shock, dozens of faces from the gallery crowd spun toward him.

Police officers lunged—

The man ran into the street. "It is me!"

Tires screeched. Cops ran.

The red dot zigzagged on Simone's chest. Was someone aiming a gun?

"Everybody inside!" an officer shouted. He outstretched his arms, pressing Simone's back, ushering the crowd toward the door like a shifting amoeba.

"No," Simone said. "I—" The red dot was on her shoulder. She turned to the officer, but instead faced a woman with black net over her face, extending down from a tiny hat on her slicked-back hair. The woman was frantically speaking German to a man in a white suit.

"What's going on?" a man cried over the man's shouting in the street.

"Is that Narcissus!" a woman shrieked.

"Everyone inside," a police officer said. "Just a precaution."

The crowd swept Simone into the gallery. Heart pounding, she scanned the crowded room for a quiet place to use her cell phone. Perhaps in one of those upstairs rooms, she would call the court, ask for her police escort to pick her up, take her back to her car—

"Champagne, madam," a tuxedoed waiter offered a tray of bubbling flutes. An elbow jabbed her back. A foot stomped hers. And Paulette's flashing camera was aiming her way.

A strong hand gripped her elbow.

"I would recognize those lips anywhere," he said deeply, playfully.

Simone—still in her hat, sunglasses and big fur collar—gazed up at the paintings. "I can't stay here," she said without turning to him. "It's a mistake—"

"All hell is breaking loose out there," Sonny said. "Come upstairs and wait it out—"

She turned to him. "No—" The affection in his smoldering eyes made all the people, the chatter, the music blur to a rosy haze. His spicy musk sent a tingle through her. God, just a few minutes alone with him . . . no . . . yes . . . she could think of nothing. No worries, no fear, no sadness, no questions. Just profound comfort, as if she were swathed in silk from head to toe.

He pulled her arm; she stepped with him. Quickly, she kept her head down, following him through the crowd, up the open spiral staircase and balcony crowded with poseurs, into a ruby-painted lounge softly lit by beaded lamps and oversized, crimson couches and chairs.

"Sonny, it's not how it looks," she said, standing at the center of the cozy room. Pink-orange rays shot down from a skylight.

"May I call you Simone?" his deep voice boomed through her as he approached in his sleek, impeccably fitted black.

"You'll be calling me an ambulance if I don't take off this hot cape," Simone said, tossing the wool and red-brown fur onto the couch, along with the hat and sunglasses.

He stepped close. Lush lashes fringed pupils that glowed with tiny glimmers of gold and olive and topaz.

"Simone." Her name came through his lips like a dollop of steaming caramel sauce, pouring over the edge of a silver ladle, taking a tempting and small eternity to melt onto a voluptuous mound of ice cream.

"Si . . . mo . . . ne," he said, drawing out each syllable. "I love that name. It's mysterious. Sad, almost. Like a sigh, and a moan, put together."

She breathed him in, closing her eyes. She sucked his expelled air deep into her lungs, imagining each molecule floating down her windpipe, clinging like dewdrops to those cluster-of-grapes-looking sacs of alveoli. Then penetrating her bloodstream, his air becoming a literal part of the miraculous chemistry that kept her heart pumping.

"Tell me," he said, glancing up at the pastel rays streaming over them. "Tell me why you came to me. At twilight." His hot breath tickled her cheek.

"I don't have words," she whispered. "I can't—"

"Please," he said, "Whatever brought you here, I need to know you don't believe the lies." He cupped her jaw with his hand. The pad of his thumb stroked her bottom lip. As softly as a feather, as sensuously as a long-awaited kiss.

"Shhh," Simone said, making her lip press into his thumb. She resisted the urge to suck it . . . him . . . into her mouth. Because the answer was a dizzying swirl inside her head, steaming down to a hot gush of lust between her legs. Her response laid in the sensation of her soul twirling with his in a magical mist around them. Even though the rules and restrictions and possible danger outside that door were threatening to rip them apart, robbing them of this undeniable attraction, and their very lives.

"Sonny," she said, shaking her head. "I'm risking too much—"

His fingertips stilled her lips. She wrapped her fingers around his.

"The answers are in your eyes," he whispered. His face blurred through her hot tears. They streamed down her cheeks, over her lips, between the damp tangle of their fingers. His lashes formed a sensuous awning as he watched the wet salt of her wounds roll down the back of his hand. Then the teardrop perched on her knuckle, catching the rosy orange glow from the skylight.

Slowly, he bent closer. Simone savored a fresh waft of his amazing scent. He lowered his parted lips. And pressed them into the back of her trembling hand. The burning tickle of his tongue touched her knuckle. He pulled back, casting up enchanted eyes.

"I was put here to kiss away your tears," he whispered. "Tears that confirm you feel the way I do. That this profound passion comes once in a lifetime. If at all."

Feverish heat radiated through her. She had to taste him. Not Sweet Sonny Whittaker the movie star. But the man whose presence was colorizing the black-and-white grayness inside her heart into a Technicolor fantasy splashed with vibrant swirls of violet, scarlet and orange.

He leaned forward, lips parted. His fingers slid under her chin, tilting her lips up to his. He came toward her in excruciatingly slow motion. Ever so close . . .

Fire.

A red swirl flashed behind her closed eyelids, in her brain, flowing like lava through her body. She did not move, nor did he. Just the gentle touch of their lips, and the heat flowing between them, that was enough for this moment. He tasted sweet like champagne, yet salty, too.

He was raw man. Lighting every inch of her on fire. From her neck, aching to feel his lips. To her nipples, straining against her bra, stiff and yearning for his mouth. A blazing zigzag down through her middle, behind her belly button, shooting down her legs, weakening them, making them tremble, then ricocheting back up from her toes, up, up, between her thighs, exploding in a creamy, throbbing slick between her legs.

Then escaping upward, through her throat and mouth that longed to suckle the essence of his manhood, to taste liquid *him*.

She moaned. He kissed harder. Wrapping strong hands around her waist, pulling her up and into his firm chest. Plying her lips as if he, too, viewed this as a life-or-death taste test.

She kissed him back, harder, sweeping this hot wet welcome with her tongue, needing more. The static of rushing blood filled her ears, along with the savage pounding of her heart. She threw her head back, letting out a cry of longing and lust. His fiery mouth trailed over her jaw, down her neck, where he parted his lips—

"Yes," she moaned with a lusty rasp. The sensation of his tongue on her neck, on the smooth and hypersensitive plane just between the hard tube of her throat and that fleshy muscle on the side, yes, right there . . .

"I can't do this yet," Simone gasped. "Not until—"

He sampled her neck again. His tongue trailed up, over her jaw, lapping up her cheek—

A gust of music shot into the room. The door was open.

"Sonny, there you are!" a woman said.

And a silver flash filled the room.

72

In a downtown high-rise office building, Paulette Barnes's heart pounded as she walked through the sleek lobby of *Famous*. She ran her fingertips along the frosted mint green glass wall, admiring the way it was back-lighted for a futuristic effect. Just like the stainless steel lamps and chairs, and the metallic curve of the countertops.

I am loving this! Working for such a chic place! Now I just have to impress the editor with my pictures of Sonny Whittaker's art show, and get another star-studded assignment . . .

With her camera bag over one shoulder of her leather coat, Paulette took bouncy steps to make the ruffles of her yellow blouse flutter and accentuate her chest. She loved the way her belt cinched her flatter stomach. She was six pounds lighter, though a little dizzy from hunger, in just a few days!

"Your ID?" said a woman behind the receptionist's desk. With gothic-black hair and a tight pink crocheted sweater, she raised glittery brown fingernails to cover the mouthpiece of a phone headset.

Paulette flashed the lacquered ID card dangling on a cord around her neck. The woman nodded, and Paulette strode past a wall of framed *Famous* covers, into the newsroom.

How cool that Roxanne Jones had hooked this up! Maybe, somehow, Paulette could even do some work for Roxanne's upcoming TV show. More money, more status, more fun! Paulette tingled. Her braces tickled the insides of her lips as she smiled; this afternoon she had written a slew of checks—that would not bounce—to the orthodontist, the boys' school, the Mercedes Benz dealer and car insurance company, and the kitchen contractors. For heaven's sake, if she did this long enough, she and Ted might even buy a bigger house, or build a new one altogether!

Soon I'll be able to pay off the kids' tuition for the year! Ted will be so proud of me. Marie and Simone will be, too, after they see that I've finally found my passion in life . . .

"Paulette!" a tall man in a white turtleneck and dark denim baggies rounded the corner with a gust of the hippest new designer men's cologne. His eyes lit up behind glasses whose lenses were tinted the same redwine hue as his hair. "Luck is on your side tonight. One of my photogs is stuck in London—" He shook his head. "Anyway, we need you."

"Count me in," Paulette said, following the editor into his small office. A mint green glass lamp hung from the ceiling, illuminating boxes and papers and pictures cramming the metal desk and credenza.

"Cool." He clicked on the computer. "We're talkin' big money, but big stress, too."

"Just give me the who, what and where," Paulette said.

"Here," the guy said as a blue grid appeared on his monitor. "Okay," he said, facing Paulette and fanning his ink-smudged fingers. "Picture this: gorgeous woman meets rich, famous man on a tropical island. We get an anonymous tip that sparks fly. They come back to reality. And she's the judge for his divorce, the wife being none other than Norris—"

A cold gush filled Paulette's head, as if all the blood had suddenly drained. She closed her eyes, but her brain swirled even faster.

"Paulette?" the editor asked. "This works well for you, since you just covered the Whittaker art show—"

"Okay." Her voice came out in a squeak.

"Now," he said. "What we need, is for someone to keep constant tabs on this judge. We haven't confirmed anything yet. But hang out around the courthouse, her home, and I hear she jogs everyday—" The guy crossed his arms. "Listen, this'll be a hot scandal, when we prove it. But if it bores you—"

"No," Paulette sighed, shaking her head. "Not at all. Tell me exactly what you need."

73

As the pink light of morning shimmered on the ocean, Simone pulled into the small parking lot at The Tree House. The loan officer had agreed to meet her here before court, to further assess whether the bank could help resolve the orphanage's financial problems.

"Whose cars are these?" she asked, closing her own door next to a silver Lexus, a BMW and a Lincoln.

Perhaps the loan officer would say yes out of sympathy that the house was dark and quiet this morning. The children were at a hotel—thanks to an anonymous donor—until the heat and electricity were turned back on. As she dashed around the house, Simone glimpsed her watch. Just forty-five minutes until she had to be on the bench; Joseph Myles was next in line to question Sonny Whittaker.

"What the——"

Simone's heart pounded. In the sprawling backyard, a cluster of well dressed people stood by the ocean, looking at big white scrolls. Floor plans. The nun was raising her arms, her face twisted with fear and anger.

"You are trespassing," Simone announced as she ran toward the people who were no doubt from Lindo Designs. Sister Margaret squeezed her hand as she said, "Leave now, or I'll call the police."

"Who are you?" asked a man in a hard hat.

"Simone, Simone. Look at you now." The sleek towering woman with flowing brunette hair, a tailored blue suit dress, and a striking face that beamed superiority . . .

"Rosa," Simone said, numb with shock.

"The face of Lindo Designs," Rosa said. "When my husband died, I inherited the company. Now I'm keeping his vision alive. You can afford to buy one of my condos——" Rosa still had a cutting tone that had reduced Simone to tears so many times as a child. Rosa raised an arm toward the ocean. "Now you can invite all the children to live with you——"

"Leave," Simone said. "We still have time——"

Rosa smiled, looking around. "Beautiful grounds. But that old house," she nodded at the man in the hard hat. "Tomorrow, midnight, I want the wrecking ball."

"You are so heartless, Rosa," Simone said.

"I'm not like my mother," Rosa said, "taking in abandoned animals, letting them live for free. Oh, I have a message from the loan officer. He won't be here. He knows where his bank's bread and butter comes from."

"Why are you doing this?" Simone demanded.

"Why did you make bad things happen to my family?" Rosa asked. "My grandfather, my brother——"

"That is so ridiculous," Simone said.

The nun's clammy fingers clenched Simone's hand. "Young lady, charity is a virtue. And God rewards and protects those who have it."

"Money is enough reward for me," Rosa said. She stepped close to Simone. "Has Sonny Whittaker tried to fuck you, like he fucked my mother? That's why my dad hates him."

Simone stepped back, out of Rosa's expensive perfume, away from her aura of arrogance and hatred.

"But dad can't show it. Since his movies——"

Something cold sliced through Simone, but her face remained stiff.

"—are so good for Brazil," Rosa said. "But if he's with you now, he's as condemned as this old house. What a miserable life—"

Simone reached into her purse. She pulled out her cell phone. "Yolanda, put me through to the sheriff's office, please."

"Come on, gentlemen," Rosa smiled at Simone. "Our business is done for now. This place is mine."

"Come inside," Sister Margaret said as Rosa led the men away.

In the office, Simone dialed her mother in Washington.

"Tell me!" She gripped the phone so hard, her fingers ached. "You knew Rosa was trying to buy the orphanage, didn't you? Are you the one who told her about it?"

"She does not talk to me. I don't—"

"I don't care. But if you want to redeem yourself for all the pain you've caused me—"

"Oh, Simone," her mother sighed. "What have I—"

"Go tell Mr. Anderson to write a check right now, to stop Rosa from kicking little children out of their home!" A poster-sized portrait of the kids hung over the desk. It blurred through Simone's tears. "Now!"

"He is not a generous—"

"Now!" Simone shrieked.

"Your own father," she quavered. "He could afford it, easily."

Simone stomped. "Who?! How can I ask him if I don't know his name?"

"Simone, I'm getting on the next plane to LA. I need to tell you in person."

74

Hours later, Simone ached with fatigue after grueling hours of Mr. Myles's questioning of Sonny on the stand. And damn Brett Robinson for getting his own lawyer to keep him out of jail. She stopped at Yolanda's desk to pick up a stack of pink message slips.

"This just came." Yolanda handed over a large brown envelope. "Paternity test results for the Whittaker case."

"I'll need a few minutes to review them before—"

"Simone, what the hell is this?" Charlie asked angrily as he stormed toward her. He held up a snapshot, its image obscured by the glare of over-head fluorescent light. His eyes were wide and bloodshot.

"Charlie, I'm not in the mood for a guessing game," Simone said, extending a key past him to unlock the door.

Her heart was exploding. If he were holding the picture of Sonny Whittaker licking her face last night, her credibility would be lost. "Don't tell me you're jumping on the paparazzi bandwagon, too—"

"I demand an explanation," he said.

She grasped the edge of the picture: orange and pink sky. Lush greenery framing boats bobbing in turquoise water.

"I warned you," Simone said. "And there's proof—"

"Simone, you and Sonny Whittaker look like you're starring in the remake of *Promise Me Paradise*," Charlie fumed, "just before the torrid love scene."

"We're not even touching," Simone said, turning the key in the lock. "I was trying to find a boat to get the hell out of there."

"This picture is worth ten thousand words," Charlie said, "Most of which are X-rated and highly offensive to the Judicial Tenure Commission—"

"I'll be making a ruling as early as tomorrow," Simone said as she stepped into the office. "You told me to stay on this case. So don't tell me we've wasted all this time—"

"If the media gets hold of this," he said, following her into the office, "they'll skewer us like a shish-kebab."

"Where'd you get that picture?"

"Today's mail," Charlie said. "Addressed to me. No return address."

The blood rushed from Simone's face; she felt cold.

Where else had this picture been mailed? And what other images might have been captured? Tumbling on the beach, browsing the merchant stands in a thong, joining the samba dancers . . .

And who had taken the pictures? *Paulette?*

75

In the courtroom, Sonny Whittaker fumed as he sat next to Myles for the third morning of the trial. Exhaustion tugged at his eyelids, his shoulders, his mind, even as he watched the judge settle into her chair.

"I have reviewed the results of the emergency paternity test," Judge Thompson said with a steady, solemn tone.

"Keep your cool, man," Myles whispered, "no matter what happens. I'll deal with it. I covered all our bases on the record this morning."

"Those two Cassandras behind us," Sonny whispered without turning toward Cheyenne and the young woman whom he knew was not his daughter. "They have nothing to do with why we're here."

Sonny stared forward and up. He ached to see that the woman who was holding his fate in her delicate hands, the woman whom he had tasted last night, did not believe he was some louse who would drop his seed, spawn a human being, then take off for twenty-five years. But the fluorescent lights cast a silver sheen over the lenses of her glasses; he could not see her eyes.

"The technician assures me," Judge Thompson said, "the blood analyses for Sonny Whittaker, Cheyenne Moore and Katie Moore are more than ninety-nine percent accurate." The judge glanced down at a white sheet. "The test results show"—she cleared her throat—"that Sonny Whittaker is the father of Katie Moore."

"No," he groaned, just loud enough for Myles to hear.

Myles stood. "Your honor, I request a second test. At another lab."

Brett Robinson, who was leaning toward Erica as she whispered with a loud, disgusted tone rose to his feet. "Your honor, I pray the court will waste no more precious time on this."

"Counselors, after a fifteen-minute recess, be prepared to deliver your closing arguments."

Sonny watched her with unblinking eyes. *Please look at me . . .*

In the ear-splitting second that she cracked the gavel, her gaze raked over him. Fury festered and bubbled behind gray pools. They cast a potent, paralyzing spell over him.

No . . .

Sonny felt horribly alone. Persecuted. And sure that the angst searing his insides would boil right through his sweat-soaked skin.

76

Simone's eyes stung with sleeplessness as she looked out on the hushed court, just grazing sight of Sonny's pleading, tender gaze. The curious faces in the audience. The riveting stares of Joseph Myles and Brett Robinson. She just had to get through these next ten minutes, and trust that things would not blow up in her face and destroy her.

"Mr. Robinson, Mr. Myles, now that you've delivered your closing arguments, I have one announcement before my decision," she said. "For purposes of this trial, I have stricken from the records the paternity test involving Sonny Whittaker, Cheyenne Moore and the woman she claims is their child.

"That aspect of this trial has raised too many questions for me," she said. "Whether Mr. Whittaker fathered a child out of wedlock a quarter century ago is irrelevant to today's proceedings of whether he is, right now, a fit and preferable parent for his daughters."

Brett Robinson shot up. "Your honor, a great deal of time and energy—"

"I've made my decision, Mr. Robinson. Sit down." Simone rested her elbows on the bench, stroking her left knuckle of her balled fist with the fingertips of her right hand. She kept her shoulders squared, chin up.

Damn her mother . . . If one of these men were indeed her father, and it became public knowledge, whatever decision she made in this case could have career-ending consequences. And somehow expose her inappropriate, unethical, despicable-in-the-eyes-of-justice liaison with the man pleading with his eyes before her.

"Mr. Robinson," she said. "Please sit down."

Brett Robinson took his seat next to Erica.

"The court has decided in the case of Erica Haynes Whittaker versus Sonny Whittaker—"

Brett Robinson balled his left hand on the table, ran the fingertips of his right hand back and forth over his knuckles . . .

"—that full custody of Asia Whittaker and India Whittaker will be entrusted with their—"

Simone's hands, hidden from the court, formed another mirror image . . .

That's him. Brett Robinson is my father . . .

77

Sonny Whittaker wanted to shout out to the judge to stop watching Brett Robinson. Yes, that gesture—tickling his fist with his fingertips—was unique. He'd only seen one other person do that . . .

Sonny's heart pounded. They were so similar . . . *butterscotch cream . . . sandy hair . . .* bright blue-gray eyes . . .

My God . . . that's her fa—

"Father," Simone said. "The children will remain in the full custody of Sonny Whittaker."

A rumble, a low whisper, rippled through the audience.

"No!" Erica shrieked. "I want them!"

Simone glared. "Ms. Haynes, sit down or you will be expelled. As their mother, Ms. Haynes, you will have the right to visitation for two weekends per month. Details of those visits are to be worked out between Mr. Whittaker and Ms. Haynes, or the legal representation thereof."

The judge continued. "As for alimony, I have considered the fact that Mrs. Whittaker has been supported by the Haynes family for the past four years, since verbal separation from Mr. Whittaker. And because Mr. Whittaker's income greatly diminished immediately following the marriage, I am ordering Mr. Whittaker to pay a nominal amount of alimony, to be determined after the court has reviewed Mr. Whittaker's financial records."

"Jackpot," Myles gushed. "Congratulations, man. The better man always wins. You placed your bets, and boom! Victory is ours!"

Myles glanced at Brett, who said something about "emergency appeal."

"But be prepared when Brett Robinson fights this," Myles said. "It's not over yet."

Simone slammed the gavel without looking up.

"This case is now adjourned." In a flash, she was a flutter of black down the steps, vanishing through that big door. Without a backward glance.

But Sonny would find Simone. He would thank her. On his knee.

78

"Just a few moments of peace," Simone whispered as she slipped into the scalding bath. Early evening sunshine poured through the small, white wood-shuttered window over the peach tiles, casting a steamy glow over the fizzing bubbles, the looped oval rug, her rose bathrobe hanging behind the door.

If Brett Robinson is my father, do I really want to know? She yanked out the clips holding up her smooth French roll. The steam and water droplets on her fingers transformed her hair into corkscrews that tickled her cheeks.

"What if I'm black?" she whispered, immersing her mouth, her ears.

The doorbell rang. Simone stiffened. "If my mother is just now showing up—"

No, she just wanted to concentrate on where to go from here. Testify in Sacramento next week. Get back to work. Discreetly finish what she had started with Sonny Whittaker. And her father—

She imagined a wedding—Brett Robinson walking her down the aisle toward Sonny Whittaker at the altar.

"Absolutely never." The doorbell rang again.

A gnawing urge to confess radiated up from her gut. Where, exactly, she had crossed the line between her personal feelings for Sonny Whittaker and the facts of the case, she did not know. But she had passed over it, and that was wrong. And that grave error could only come back to haunt her.

Pounding echoed from the front door. If she didn't answer, the cops out front might think something was wrong. In her thick terrycloth robe, the belt tied at the waist, Simone's warm, wet feet trailed over the tiled floor, up the front hallway.

Through the gold glass on the front door: cops standing on each side of Sonny Whittaker. Flowers, a silver box and a dark green champagne bottle jutted from under his arm.

"No way," she sighed. He was talking, and the officers were smiling, as the cop with a five o'clock shadow on his sunburned face reached to knock again.

Sonny's smoky eyes focused on the window—

Simone gasped. Now, could she finally let go and succumb to their soul-deep attraction? No. It was too soon after the trial. And she did not need two witnesses to whatever may unfold. She would tell him to leave, that it was not appropriate for a defendant to make a house call.

She opened the door. "May I help you, Mr. Whittaker?"

The western-style fringe across the chest and arms of his brown suede coat fluttered as he raised the gifts. "Offerings to the goddess of family law and justice," he said. "A thank you."

"I don't accept gifts for doing my job," Simone said. Wet hair dripped on her cheek, which burned with self-consciousness under the officers' stares. "But I appreciate the gesture."

"May I come in for a moment?" Sonny asked. "I braved a media battalion in front of my house to get here." He waved toward a black Jaguar parked at the foot of her walk, between two squad cars. Thank goodness no media trucks were here—

"Just a few minutes," Sonny said.

His deep voice calmed her, making her forget all the questions.

"Officers," Simone said, meeting their stares. "Thank you in advance for your discretion."

"Of course, Judge."

Sonny stepped inside. She closed the door.

"You shouldn't be here," she said. A water droplet rolled down the back of her leg. "This isn't right—"

"I like your hair like that." He stepped close, staring down with smoldering eyes and a hungry wolf look that made her nipples poke against the terrycloth.

"Sonny, it's more complicated than—"

"Champagne?" He raised the bottle. "My girls said to thank you. We just had dinner to celebrate—"

"Sonny, you don't understand. What I've done is so, so wrong—"

He plunked the presents on the table. "Yes, Simone. I understand perfectly well."

Why did his eyes make her feel like that? Light and dizzy, as if her body were turning to mist and floating up to heaven? Why did the sight of him make her forget everything?

"Sonny," she said, savoring his scent. "We should wait—"

His hands grasped her waist. He pulled her up into him, where she wanted to burrow forever, hiding, feeling nothing but the intoxicating euphoria of his spirit spinning around her.

"Simone." His voice boomed through her. "Simone." Deeper still.

A searing hotness seeped through her, as if his presence were melting her flesh and bones into a sweet pool of butter right here on the cool hallway tiles.

"Simone."

Her lips parted, she moaned.

His hot mouth pressed into her damp forehead. Then his open lips and hot breath trailed, barely touching, her eyebrow, her eyelid, lashes, her cheek, the tip of her nose, sliding like wet satin onto her lips . . .

Static rang in her ears. A drunken languidness weakened her knees. Another moan escaped her chest, pressing into him.

We are one. But no . . .

She pried from his embrace, pressing palms against the wall behind her, staring at the man who terrified her and electrified her all at once. "Sonny, we can't—"

He stepped toward her, his mouth saying yes, yes we can. Now, forever.

She placed his hands on the belt of her robe, their fingers lacing as he untied it. It fell open; his gaze fell to her breasts. The hunger in his eyes—

She gasped, arched her back, raising her tingling nipples toward him. And he, almost in slow motion, reached out to trace them, transfixed.

He raised an open hand next to her cheek, without touching. She felt its heat, its power, its strength. He ran that hand, trembling fingers dropping feather-soft touches on her jaw, down into the hollow of her neck, her collarbone. His hand, as if he were feeling her energy force and absorbing it, fueling his own soul with hers, he traced his hand down her chest, his palm brushing the swollen curve of her breast, the nipple.

She quivered as the heel of his hand continued down between her breasts, the center of her stomach. His fingertips touched the super sensitive space around her belly button; she shivered. The robe slid off her shoulders, catching on her bent elbows.

She had to sit down, lay down, or she would faint. She grasped his wrist, but his open palm continued downward. Covering her like Adam's fig leaf. His palm petting the soft hair, a finger slipping into the steamy slick . . .

Simone cried out.

His hand moving outward, curving around but barely touching her trembling thigh, circling to her buttocks. He pulled down the robe, letting it slip to the floor. He turned her, falling to his knees, biting the round mounds of sensitive flesh that had cushioned her today as she announced his fate . . .

She turned to face him; he pressed his face into her soft, smooth belly, arms wrapping around her, clutching her back, her waist, hugging her on his knees. She gripped his head, pulling him into her, through her. And he sobbed.

79

As he walked into Simone's bedroom, Sonny cradled her in his arms with the same tenderness and trepidation as the first time he held his newborn babies. Now, finally, making love to her would be as divine and momentous as if God had ordered him to paint a flawless masterpiece to earn entry to heaven.

"Simone," he whispered, as he sunk into the plush comforter on the cherrywood sleigh bed. "Always look at me like that."

She turned away. "No, what I did, it's so wrong." She pulled the blanket over herself. "The guilt, it feels like acid in my veins. In the morning, I'm going to talk to the chief judge—"

He placed a fingertip on her lips. "Shh." He sat down, pulling her and the blanket in his lap. "God or fate brought us together—"

"Sonny, you don't understand what I've done."

"No, you don't understand. The universe put me and my family in these hands." He raised her cupped palms. "And you are taking care of us. You're keeping us together. Don't you see, this is on another level—"

She closed her eyes, hard.

He pressed her palms to his bare chest, over his pounding heart. "We have this beautiful gift. We have to protect it—"

"Sonny," she whispered, looking up through silvery swells of tears. "There's so much at stake for me. I could be disbarred. All I've worked for, my reputation, the children who need me—"

"I need you, Simone Thompson. Our magic together, it made the sunset flash for us, in Brazil. Just admit to me, that we are the missing links in each others' lives—"

She stared back, her *moonbeam gray* eyes flashing questions.

"Simone, admit that every moment we've been apart for the past week, you have ached for me the way every inch of me has ached for you."

She closed her eyes.

A firebomb of panic exploded inside him. He would make her admit that she wanted him until her dying breath. And he would persuade her to forget about undoing the miracle of her ruling today. And the one sure way he could do that, was to consummate their spiritual attraction.

The task that lie ahead was the marathon he'd been training for all his life, practicing on countless women, breasts, vaginas. Hours of study, learning, exploring, understanding, perfecting his stroke, his thrust, his touch. All had prepared him for this.

"Simone," he said softly. With his eyes he projected his goal:

I am going to make love to you with such exquisite passion and precision, you will completely submit to me. Mind, body, soul.

I will make you shudder and scream until the word "confession" no longer forms in your mind. Until the questions in your eyes are quiet, and you are absolutely certain that I am the one and only man for you.

I will plant my seed in you, creating the miracle of a human being—half me, half you—from our primordial bond. You will purr with carnal delirium as the sun rises. And you will be mine. Now. Forever.

The tiny hairs on the back of his neck rose. His nipples stiffened. And flames of determination sent an infinite supply of adrenaline and blood and virility to the place where he needed it most.

"Simone," he said deeply, laying her on her back, peeling away the blanket like the outer petals of a rose, exposing the pristine and velvet bud that would bloom to perfection under his touch.

"Yes, Sonny," she whispered, arching her back, offering her breasts. "I hear you. I feel you." But uncertainty burned in her eyes.

"Let me taste you again," he whispered, balancing over her. "Your beautiful mouth."

She stared up, parting her lips. He pressed his mouth to hers, plying gently, savoring her pillowy pucker sliding like hot satin under his bite. His open lips brushed her long, elegant neck. She grasped the back of his head, moaning, writhing.

He combed his fingers into her hair, ran his cheeks over the smooth skin of her ribs, her abdomen, her thighs. Every inch was more luscious than the one before. Creamy, quivering.

"My God, Simone," he groaned as her fingers wrapped around his throbbing length. Gentle and firm, she massaged just right.

"I want all of this," she whispered. "All of you. Now." Her lashes fluttered; her lips poked out slightly. And she looked like that man who had tried to destroy him in court.

"Simone."

She stared up, something flashing in her eyes, transforming her face. A mysterious power zigzagged through her, around her, like an energy force, engulfing him in its crackle and hum. His skin felt hotter, a low buzz filled his ears. He shivered, probing her eyes for answers, feeling suddenly stunned by her mystique. He was languid, terrifyingly vulnerable as he balanced over her—

In a flash, she raised her legs up around his waist, wrapping her thighs around him like pliers twisting a cap off a bottle. She grasped his arms with her hands. In one dizzying moment, his shoulder, his hip, his leg sunk into the bed. She rolled him onto his back . . .

"Simone, what in the world are you—"

She knelt over him, a knee on each side of his waist, eyes beaming down.

"You want to dominate me, don't you, Sonny Whittaker?" She glanced at the TV. "Like in your movies—"

He laughed softly. "Am I that predictable?"

"You want to rock my world, so I don't know up from down?" The intensity of her sparkling eyes stole his voice. "Don't you?"

Slowly, her knees slid outward; she lowered herself toward his bare stomach. He imagined his huge erection pointing up at her behind, as luscious as the round tops of two buttered muffins.

"But is a man like you . . ." she said with a soft, sultry tone. Her bare folds of womanhood glistened inches above his stomach. "Sonny Whittaker—are you really ready to submit yourself, all the way, to one woman?"

She pressed her hot pussy into his bare belly. "To me?" she purred.

He groaned.

"As an equal, a partner," she moaned, slowly grinding. He imagined the dewy folds—those hairless lips, the swollen bulb, the sweet cream—branding him as hers. "Mmmmm." She tossed her head back, then looked down at him hard.

"But I have no evidence, Sonny Whittaker, that you," she gasped, "can, or will, submit to me." She licked his ear. "If I risk everything for you, I have no guarantee that next week, next year . . . you won't go back to your old ways—"

"No!" he gasped.

He envisioned himself a molten flow of blood and breath, bubbling beneath her. The pressure and throb of his arousal was excruciating.

But not as painful as the burn of defiance and rage rumbling through him. Never had he felt so vulnerable or weak. Or powerless. No one drove his boat, or controlled his body. Especially in bed.

"Simone, kiss me. Now."

Her eyes glowed with playful refusal. The metaphysical power radiating from her created an otherworldly energy force humming around them. He viewed this moment as if God were endowing them with their own private twilight, bathing them in a pastel kaleidoscope of spiritual, cosmic energy that would forever change their senses of touch, taste, smell, and sight.

Yes, each beam of red, orange, magenta, gold and lavender dancing around them, charging the air, was melding their blood and bones and breath into one, searing their spirits into a swirl of light and golden sparks so bright, it blinded him, made him cover his eyes with his hands. He wanted to submit to its power, but he cringed ever so slightly back into the blankets with terror over its consequences. It brought to mind the Brazilian word that meant both love and death.

It was nothing short of magic. And they hadn't even consummated the act yet.

"Simone," he whispered deeply, pulling her hands toward him, needing to kiss her and plunge his electric wand inside her to carry out this celestial fusion of flesh. "Kiss me."

She leaned forward, lacing her fingers with his, squeezing his hands, pressing so that his elbows balanced her.

"Yeah, Sonny, I'll kiss you." She slid with shocking speed, not her face and mouth, but her hips. She thrust forward, branding his chin with the hot, wet slick of femininity between her legs.

"Oh, Si—"

Her luscious, bald pussy silenced him.

With an open mouth he met the slippery lips, kissing, his tongue dancing with her swollen velvety clit as if it were her tongue, savoring the salty-sweet liquid essence of her. As she balanced on her knees, the insides of her thighs brushed his cheeks the same way her palms once grasped his face as they kissed. And she gently circled her hips, the same way her head had moved slightly as they French kissed before.

He slid his tongue up through the dewy doors to this most prized temple, making his oral offering with expert licks, wanting to swim and slide up into the safety and warmth and nurturance of her womb. The place where all life begins, where this immaculate bond would, in the heat of this most carnal ecstasy, conceive a new body of their love.

"Sonny," she moaned, anointing his face—

"This is how I want to die," he whispered. "Drowning . . . suffocating in this canal . . ."

But terror boiled inside him. The rawness of the moment, the surprise, the stunning potency of her lust, her intellectual clarity in the heat of the moment, made him tremble to his toes.

80

With a new surge of determination, Sonny reached for her thighs. He would gently place her on the bed and tame her with more exquisite love-making than any woman could fathom.

But she slid back, downward, slipping her clit into his belly button.

"How—" The searing sensation sucked away his breath.

The sweet-soft flesh fit into him like a perfect puzzle piece. The ornament around her birth canal melding with the spot that had connected him as a clump of cells to his mother's blood, giving him oxygen and nourishment to grow into a human being, a man, now completing the circle, the cycle.

"Simone, lay with me." He gently grasped her thighs to pull her down, next to him.

Under him.

But she slid over the length of his throbbing erection. Sitting on it, moving up its length and back, she radiated heat like a blowtorch. As if she were trying to solder a lead pipe to the steely plane of his groin.

"Oh, girl."

She slid back and forth, tossing back her head. Satiny moans escaped her pouting lips—*sex on a soundwave.* Circling her hips, knees bent at his sides, her elbows raised as if she were going to run fingers through her hair . . .

She was a gilded butterfly, fluttering over his towering stamen, making him bloom beneath her, enticing his hot pollen sac to spray life-giving golden dust—

No! He was the great bee. He had chosen this single, exquisite rose from a sprawling garden of every variety. Now he had to land on top of her plush velvet petals, penetrate, dominate, fertilize—with his mighty stinger.

He grasped her knees, trying to sit up.

She thrust back . . .

Slammed him inside her.

All of him. With shocking speed. And frightening force.

It paralyzed him. He lay, staring up at her, savoring the mind-numbing sensation radiating from the center of his being.

For a moment, she was still, squeezing her hot tube of flesh around him. Then she fell forward, grasping the inner parts of his upper arms, pinning him down. The tip of her tongue trailed his parted lips.

And she slid upward. Down. Up, down. Clawing his arms, pressing down for balance, pumping faster. Harder. Panting, moaning, swirling her hips, skin slapping skin—

An opalescent sheen glistened on her shoulders, stomach, thighs. Her bouncing breasts hypnotized him. The pressure and tingle and friction turned his mind to a psychedelic swirl.

"Dominate me *now*, Sonny Whittaker."

Words jammed in his throat. A groan burst through his throbbing lips.

She kept fucking him hard, not bouncing, but sliding at just the right angle. Like a jockey. Yes, she was riding him like a jockey. Treating him as the stallion he'd wanted to be all his life. Especially now. But he did not want to be driven, controlled, dominated, steered.

I want the power. But my God, she'll make me come like this . . .

"Simone," he groaned, bucking.

But his very bones were an orange-red flow of lava oozing through his muscles, melting them, sucking them into a steaming, unstoppable river of molten rock. For a small eternity, he lay quivering, staring up in awe at her energy. How long had she maintained this bionic pace? How could she take the violent ramming of his hugeness, so deep and fast?

She was trembling, her legs, her hands, her lips.

And he—

A mighty tremor began to take hold.

"I dare you," she gasped, "to dominate me, Sonny Whittaker." She licked his mouth, his chin, his cheeks. "I'll be your equal. Your partner—"

He bucked again. She pounded harder. A salty bead of sweat dripped from her nipple into his mouth. "But I still dare you—"

A deep, almost sinister groan rose from his quivering gut.

"Oh, sweet girl," he panted. "You don't . . . don't challenge . . . Sweet Sonny Whittaker—"

"You challenged me," she shouted, thrusting.

He raised his trembling arms. She lost her balance, but pushed him back down, resuming her upper-arm grasp. Her ferocious pace. She was about to suck his very blood, his breath, his blast of seed . . .

Another stroke, she shrieked and shivered . . . her beautiful face glistening and twisting . . . a long, deep cry floating from her open panting mouth.

And he . . . the tremors, he couldn't stop them.

A terrifying convulsion sparked.

Hot-cold sweat prickled from his head to his toes.

And the air around them ignited.

A blast of light.

Unbearable heat, sucking away his breath, boiling his blood.

Fusing their skin, their hearts and their souls into one quivering moaning gasping tangle of energy. The explosion in his mind was so awesome, so potent, it felt as if they could float like mist into a more celestial dimension, where there would be no need to confess or dominate or fear or cry or feel anything except this absolute ecstasy.

"Simone," he cried as his soul liquefied and soaked her core. "My Simone."

She collapsed, resting her ear over his thundering heart. Hot droplets fell to his chest.

"I'm yours, Sonny Whittaker," she purred. "All yours."

81

Simone nestled a cheek into Sonny's bare chest, savoring an inner peace and serenity she had never known. She did not feel attached to her languid body which lay tingly-numb next to his long length under the blankets. She wanted to let his heartbeat, his breathing, his warm energy lull her like this forever, undisturbed by all the sinister forces outside the door.

"Simone," he whispered. "I want us to make a life together. A new life. Away from the Pandaemonium of LA."

"My work—"

"You can make a difference for children," he said. "My children. Our children. Perhaps the children of Brazil."

She turned on her side, her elbow, to look into his eyes. Was he asking her to have a baby? Or adopt his daughters? Move away with him to a place she despised?

"I'll never go back to Brazil," she said.

"Then the islands," he said.

"The volcano could stay active for years," Simone said.

"Simone, work with me. The threats on your life should be enough to—"

"They strengthen my resolve."

"What are you trying to prove? Why are you always pushing yourself so hard, doing so many things for so many people all at once? Do something for yourself. Slow down, enjoy—"

"My father—"

He gave her a strange, knowing look. "Simone, sometimes there are questions in life that, it's better if we never get a straight answer."

"You sound like my mother."

"I heard a rumor as a kid. This boy on my street said he saw my father, on the corner at night, kissing the cigarette girl from the nightclub around the block." Sonny chuckled. "But I worshiped my mom. And my dad, he was like God to me. I didn't want to know the truth. So I punched the guy. Knocked out his front tooth. And he never mentioned it again."

Simone sat up. "But Sonny, all my life—"

"Think about the rest of your life. What it would mean."

"I need to know—"

The phone rang. "I'm not answering," she said. If her mother were just now bothering to call, twenty four hours after she was to arrive here, then Ruth Thompson would have to wait until morning. And the media, anyone else, forget it. The answering machine clicked on. After her recorded voice and a beep, a deep, familiar voice boomed:

"Simone! What the hell is going on?!"

She sat up. It was Charlie, sounding furious: "Turn on *Entertainment Exclusive*. Are you out of your mind?" She pushed a button on the remote. Brett Robinson's face appeared on her TV.

Sonny clasped his large hand over hers. "Simone, don't ruin this magical moment. That man is the anti-Christ. If I never see him again—"

How could she have not fully admitted the resemblance before? The way his lashes came together, his lips, his complexion . . .

". . . woman from my past," Brett said, standing in front of the huge gray blocks and panes of glass forming his ultra contemporary mansion.

Next to him, holding a microphone was Roxanne Jones as he said, "has just come to town to inform me that a relationship we had before I came to LA, resulted in pregnancy. A secret pregnancy of which I was never informed—"

Sonny sat up. "A case of life imitating your own lies. Blowing up in your face, motherfucker!"

"Yet, that child grew up knowing I was her father," Brett said. "And now, she is launching an all-out campaign of vengeance, in one of our nation's most sacred forums. The courtroom."

Simone's stomach burned. *God, don't let him say it . . .*

"No!" Sonny groaned. "That loathsome—"

Brett turned to the camera. "I have just learned," he said with a cracking voice, "that Judge Simone Thompson is my daughter. And that she is avenging my innocent absenteeism for the past thirty-five years by ruling against me and my clients."

Acid rose in her throat.

"Judge Thompson," he said, "is poisoning my client's right to a fair trial with her own personal agenda. Keeping two little girls away from the mother who loves—"

Sonny's glare was burning into her cheek. A heave rippled up from her gut. But she could not look away from her father—*yes, my father*—on television.

"And as if Judge Thompson were not creating sufficient scandal by knowingly and purposely ruling against her own father," Brett said into a cluster of microphones, "I have evidence that she may be romantically involved with the defendant." Brett held up the snapshot taken in the gallery, just a few nights ago.

"Oh my God." Simone clenched her gut.

The cameras zoomed into the picture: Sonny licking her face.

"Those who know Judge Thompson might recognize her gold scales of justice ring," Brett said. "And the similarity of her skin tone with mine, and her hair color. And her eyes—"

"Mr. Robinson," a reporter said. "What does this mean, that just today Judge Thompson awarded custody to Sonny Whittaker?"

"I am filing an emergency appeal with the Court of Appeals," Brett said, "for an emergency stay of enforcement of her ruling today. Hopefully the higher court will send the case back, so another judge can decide that my client should have custody of the Whittaker children, while Judge Thompson is investigated for misconduct."

"Hell no!" Sonny bellowed.

"It is a mockery of justice," Brett Robinson said. "Simone Thompson will be punished for this brazen abuse of power. Not only will I demand she be removed from the bench and disbarred, but I will rock that courthouse until my own client gets justice in the form of having her two little girls back home in her arms. Permanently."

Vomit shot up Simone's throat. But she could not move. No, not with Sonny withdrawing from her like that, cringing from her.

"Simone," he demanded. "What does this mean?"

She turned to him. The horror and knowing twisting his face . . .

Simone darted to the bathroom. Her bare skin chilled and took on an eerie grayness in the light of the television.

A burning gush of shock, pain, fear . . . it was a mighty fist gripping her middle, squeezing out her breath, flinging her over the toilet, heaving up the horror of this moment.

"Simone!" Sonny shouted from the bathroom doorway. "What does this mean?"

The pressure behind her eyes, the raw burn in her throat, her trembling fingers, pounding heart . . . She turned toward him. Nude, he was shaking, his nipples stiff, his manhood tightly withdrawn into his body. His name came through her sour lips in a cough.

"I tried to tell you," she shouted. "And Charlie. I didn't know he was my father until—"

His glare sparked another heave.

"My worst nightmare!" Sonny shouted.

Simone crumpled on the cold tile. A chilling stinging hailstorm pummeled her conscience with regret and fear and the dizzying realization that she would be stripped of everything.

82

Paulette Barnes stood facing Simone's house, camera in hand. All around her, satellite masts rose over media trucks, journalists spoke loudly into their microphones for live reports, and camera operators strung tangles of cables across the curb near two LAPD squad cars.

I can't believe I actually raised my camera and clicked away . . . as Simone stood dripping wet in her bathrobe, letting him inside . . . And I'm the only one who saw . . .

Yes, she had been watching the courthouse, and her friend's home, all the while telling the *Famous* magazine editor that she had witnessed nothing out of the ordinary. Now the scandal was out—she'd watched Brett

Robinson on the monitor in Roxanne's satellite truck just a few feet away. In fact Roxanne was sitting in the passenger seat, talking on a cell phone, raising her beautifully waxed brows and nodding. But Paulette did not want to be the one to help crush Simone's career.

"Paulette!" Roxanne called, leaning out the window. "Tell us what you got, earlier tonight. My producer," she said, raising the phone, "is orgasmic over here—"

Paulette gripped her camera. Her head spun with the image of Sonny Whittaker striding up to the door in his sexy western-style jacket, chatting with the cops who were watching the house. Then, with wine and flowers, going inside for hours!

"Paulette!" Roxanne called impatiently.

But, was it in her heart—even for all the money in the world—to hand over the most incriminating image yet of Simone's alleged romance with Sonny Whittaker?

83

Inside her bathroom, Simone bristled as the doorbell rang. A media mob was no doubt gathering on her front lawn. Simone stood; her robe was on the floor in the foyer. Sonny was getting dressed in her bedroom as she strode to the hallway. She would peek out, then not answer.

Pounding on the door grew louder as she approached.

"Simone!"

She snatched up her robe, threw it on, and flung open the door. The bustle of media trucks, camera lights going on, cops trying to keep the street clear and reporters off the lawn . . . it was a blur around Ruth Thompson.

"Simone—" Her mother stepped inside with red-rimmed eyes, a trembling chin, mussed hair.

"Don't!" Simone pointed. "Don't speak my name."

Simone wanted to knock her down for what she'd done. Sonny came up the dim hallway, buttoning his shirt. He stepped into the soft light of the entryway.

He cast his beautiful smoky brown eyes on her. But the terror, the pain, the disappointment in them—it made her gasp.

84

Sonny strode past Simone and an older woman, toward the door. He had to get away from Simone until he figured out what was going on. Whether irreparable damage had been done to his family.

"Sonny Whittaker?!"

He turned to an older woman with Simone's nose, her delicate jaw, the same slim neck and shoulders. He kept striding toward the door, looking down at her, and said, "You are a despicable human being."

Simone's mother huffed. "Well isn't that this the pot calling the kettle black."

Simone stepped between them. "What's your problem?"

Ruth glared up. "You don't remember me, do you?"

Sonny grabbed the doorknob. Through the small window, he saw the media mob at the foot of the walk, around his car. "Dammit!"

"They could be here until morning," Simone said.

"What are you doing here!" her mother shrieked. "With my daughter!"

Sonny scowled at her. "Don't say one more word to me. You are the antithesis of motherhood. You and Brett Robinson belong toge—"

"Well a womanizing bum like you doesn't belong with Simone!"

Sonny looked at Simone. "I want your car," he said. "I can back down the driveway and get away. I'll have someone bring it back."

Simone nodded. She was pale, her eyes flashing pain.

"Rio, 1975," her mother said. "After the reception with the ambassador to Brazil—"

Sonny squinted down, then back to Simone. "Where are your keys?"

She skimmed the table, which held the unopened champagne bottle, the red roses, the silver box. "Right there." She raised the keys. "This one."

"Some things don't change," her mother said.

"Shut up!" Simone started to lead him back down the hall.

Her mother grabbed his arm. "I'm the one who kept the ambassador occupied while you fucked Bianca Anderson!"

Sonny snatched his arm back and took the keys from Simone, their fingers brushing. He followed Simone to the back door to the garage.

"I need answers," Sonny said, turning up his collar, "from my lawyer."

Sonny dashed into the garage. He shot the SUV down the driveway, turning away from the sudden glare of TV camera lights. Then he screeched away.

85

In the dim entrance hall, Simone's mouth was bitter and gritty with the taste of vomit as she turned toward her mother.

"Is Brett Robinson really my father?"

Her mother's eyes were glassy. She nodded.

"Why did you go to him first?"

Tears spilled from Ruth's eyes. "I don't . . . I don't know."

Simone tightened her lips. "Tell me!"

"To ruin Sonny Whittaker's trial."

"What do you care about him? That garbage about Bianca! What was that?"

"The truth."

Simone didn't want to think about whether it was true. The idea of Sonny touching Bianca . . . even decades ago . . . no, her mind would not go there.

"I hate how you've lived your whole life through her!" Simone said. "Bianca is everything that you couldn't be—beautiful, rich, sexy—you thought, because you had me! And deep down, admit it, you're just plain jealous!"

Her mother shook her head. A few strands of her straight, dark hair fell from the antique silver clip over the shoulders of her slim navy blue wool coat.

"Bianca saved me when I was alone and pregnant," her mother said over the deep chop of a helicopter above the house.

"Let's go in the living room," Simone said, turning her back on Ruth Thompson.

"Bianca and Greg," her mother said, sitting on the couch. "They were clients at the law firm. I was a clerk, but when I got pregnant, there was no job protection—"

"How'd you meet Brett Robinson?" Simone asked.

"Delivering papers to his courtroom," her mother said, smiling slightly. "It was lunchtime. No one was around. I told him I wanted to become a lawyer. My goodness, was he handsome. Those eyes, they hypnotized me." Ruth stared hard at Simone. "Your eyes. I remember, I was shaking when he invited me to the little Chinese place next to the courthouse."

Simone crossed her arms. "Don't tell me I was conceived in a court-house."

Her mother shook her head. "No, he was a gentleman. A married gentleman. We would go to an apartment. I thought it was his, but I was nineteen! I think in the back of my mind I thought he'd help me pay for school."

"Anyway, it wasn't until after Brett moved to California to start his own firm," Ruth said, "I didn't know how to reach him. Then the firm fired me. And Bianca, her assistant had just quit in the middle of getting ready for a big event with President Eisenhower. She hired me, for a few days, but I did such a good job—"

"She turned you into a slave," Simone said, "and you let her. Just like that soap opera in Brazil, about a white slave." Simone glared at her mother. "Why were you trying to protect him by not telling me? You said a judge told you we had to be apart! That was a lie!"

Ruth cried, "He was a judge! And by leaving me, he was saying we would be apart."

"You are so selfish."

"Bianca—"

Simone shot to her feet. "Of course! Forget what your own daughter thinks or wants or needs—"

"I promised Bianca. She said she would take care of us, as long as I never tried to contact him. That he was scum for getting me pregnant and leaving—"

"He didn't know! How can you blame him?"

"Bianca said Greg could be a father to you—"

Simone scowled. "That's—"

"And that you'd have brothers and sisters."

"You are sick."

"Admit you got a good education!"

Simone spun, glaring. "Yes, in how *not* to be when I become a mother."

86

In the soft glow of nightlights in the twins' bedroom, Kindred lowered the volume on the TV, so they would not awaken. Or see their father fleeing the judge's house.

Our father.

On the screen, TV lights illuminated just enough of his cheek, his ear, his profile, to show that it was Sonny fleeing the scene of his crime of passion in *her* dark blue BMW SUV.

"*Entertainment Exclusive* is hearing from sources," Roxanne Jones said into a microphone, standing in front of a black Jaguar in front of Simone Thompson's house, "that this car is registered to Sonny Whittaker. We will stay on this breaking story that raises serious questions about the state of our legal system—" Kindred turned off the TV, staring at the dark screen.

This is not the plan. Yes, he was supposed to keep custody, so they could stay here in the house together. But he was not supposed to fall in love with someone else. Especially not her.

"You're the smartest nine-year-old I've ever met," Miss Simone said, *wrapping her arms around Katie in the big playroom at The Tree House.*

"Always looking at me with those big eyes," Kindred whispered with a digusted tone. "I thought she was so nice. That she *cared* about me."

But Simone Thompson had just been studying Katie, like a lab rat, while her parents fought over her in court. And first chance Simone got, the bitch seized the opportunity to grab the first rung on her career ladder—

"By stepping all over my face!" Kindred seethed.

Telling on Mommy, making me go with Dad . . . my birth father, Peter Moore who couldn't take it when Mommy told him her version of the truth. What a pathetic wimp, taking his own life, not caring what would happen to me.

Kindred had done the math so many times. On a rational level she knew that Sonny Whittaker could not be her father—Kindred was conceived months after filming wrapped for *Come Back,* when Sonny was working on another project in Italy, without Mommy . . .

But her mother had told her so many times, and made her believe it.

"I wanted a perfect life, like theirs," Kindred said, peeking into the spaceship bed at India's curl-framed face, then Asia, sleeping under frilly covers. "She told me it would happen."

Kindred perched on the edge of Asia's bed, stroking her velvety warm forehead. She and India would be eight on Monday. A time for a new beginning, or the final act in their little lives.

Mom was always saying one day he would realize he's always been in love with her, that he would finally ask her to marry him, and he would live with his three daughters and his wife, happily ever after.

She said things would fall into place. Change your name, forge records from the prestigious school, get hired as his nanny, and things will fall into place. Make him love you as the true daughter that you are, be perfect, and things will fall into place. Scare him, have someone break into his house, write the poems, so Sonny Whittaker would realize the emptiness of his narcissistic ways, that there's only one woman for him.

"You'll see," her mother would say, spinning in that old lace dress in the candlelight of her shrine. "Our secret drama will soon bring us all together as the happy family we were meant to be."

But remember, make Asia sick enough to go to the doctor so she'll have to give blood for the surprise paternity test, and everything will fall into place.

"Wrong again, Mom," Kindred whispered. "It's all falling *out* of place. I'm not his daughter. You're not his wife. We're all screwed."

And that bitch judge was to blame.

"Simone Thompson will not get a second chance to ruin my life," Kindred said.

87

On the porch of a glass and white wood condominium overlooking the ocean in Marina del Rey, Sonny banged on Myles's door, not caring that it was nearly one in the morning. He had to find out what was going on, and what it meant to the decision already made today about his family being together.

Myles answered, eyes sharp and angry. He wore jeans and a brown sweater. "How long have you been fucking the judge, man?"

Sonny shook his head. "Myles, what happens now?"

Myles narrowed his eyes. "Sonny, for once, you should've asked that question before you let your dick get between you and what you want. I saw you leaving her house on TV—"

"The trial is over—"

Myles looked disgusted. "*Was* over. Brett Robinson is gonna turn that courthouse upside-down."

"Then stop him."

"I did. We won today," Myles said, leading Sonny through a hall, toward a TV in the dark sun room. "But maybe the judge was ruling in your favor for another reason—"

Sonny shook his head, trying to block out the sound of his own name, and a reporter's ominous tone.

Myles pointed to the TV. "You just gambled away the jackpot, man. Brett came over tonight, still trying to push Norris's little buy-out plan."

"That motherfucker." Sonny studied his friend. "What if we throw that back on him in court? Say he's trying to put undue influence on us?"

Myles shook his head. "Lawyers make out-of-court settlements all the time."

"Just tell me," Sonny seethed, "what we have to do now, so that my children stay with me!"

"Brett is asking the Court of Appeals to review Judge Thompson's decision, while she's investigated for misconduct. The case could get sent back to the chief judge, who'll give it to another judge to decide temporary custody." Myles's voice softened. "Sonny, man, the odds are against us right now. Big time."

Sonny's insides glowed red hot. He thought his skin would burst with the pressure of his rage. How could he have let lust blind him once again and suck him into a temptress trap? The choking fear of losing Asia and India snaked around his throat with even more brutality. As if the publicity over Brett's defaming theatrics during the trial hadn't smeared his reputation enough, the blaring TV and his face on the screen and the car whizzing away from Simone's house . . . it made him want to run, escape from this surreal nightmare.

I can't. I'll do whatever it takes to keep my family together. If another judge were to reverse Simone's ruling tomorrow, he would take the girls away.

"Bright and early," Myles said. "I'll pick you up."

"I'll see myself out." Sonny spun, dashing into the kitchen, where he called home; Kindred answered.

"Pack the girls' things right now. With their passports. Yours, too, Kindred."

"I couldn't sleep, anyway," she said. "We'll be ready."

Sonny ran to his car. This drama with Simone, with his life, his family, had just nullified the power of the courts in his mind.

88

Friday morning, the half dozen reporters doing live broadcasts in front of the courthouse did not stop Simone Thompson from walking with her head high in sunglasses and a long black trench coat. She would go inside, find out from Charlie exactly what was happening, and stay composed. No matter what.

"It's like a plot from one of his romantic films," Roxanne Jones announced toward a cameraman, a few yards away. "Sonny Whittaker's magnetism is so strong, it seems even the judge overseeing his divorce and custody trial is powerless to her passion—"

Simone walked more quickly.

"Judge Thompson." Roxanne ran toward her, aiming a black microphone. "Will the sex scandal force you to resign?"

A media swell consumed her, shouting questions, shoving microphones in her face, red lights aglow on TV cameras, photographers clicking.

"What was Sonny Whittaker doing at your house last night?"

A man shouted, "How does it feel now, knowing you're black?"

"Another case of courthouse corruption," a reporter on the lawn said into a microphone, "and here is the judge involved. This time, it's not money and the mob influencing justice. It's sex and a Hollywood star."

Every word was like a razor shredding her reputation, turning her peaceful white sail to rags, stopping her, sinking her. As were thoughts of Sonny's horrified face . . . her mother's pathetic act . . . Brett's gloat on TV . . .

Simone raised her chin, pushing through the doors. Security guards forced the reporters back, so she could hurry to the elevator, up to her office. She picked up a stack of messages and mail from Yolanda's desk.

"Simone," Charlie said, his face taut as he paced in front of the door to her chambers. She unlocked the door without looking at him; he followed her inside, where she flipped through the messages from reporters, Marie and Sister Margaret.

God help me, if I don't work a miracle today, all those kids will be homeless . . .

"I am so disappointed in you, Simone." Charlie slammed the door. "Have you forgotten that your individual actions as a judge, on and off the bench, affect the reputation and integrity of the judiciary as a whole?"

Simone met his glare. "Charlie." Her tone was flat and hoarse after a sleepless night. "I tried to tell you. Repeatedly. Tell me what happens now."

"You didn't say you'd be bedding the defendant or sneaking off to see him during the trial!" he shouted. His oar-like hand made a bristly sound as it brushed over his cheeks. "You'll not be assigned any cases until this is resolved."

"Charlie, I always wondered just how tenuous my status on your A-plus list was," she said, noticing a flier for the black judges association on her desk. Where had that come from?

"Thanks to a complaint filed by Mr. Robinson," Charlie said, "the Judicial Tenure Commission is investigating exactly what happened and when, and how that influenced your decision. After they decide whether you've committed misconduct—"

"That could take weeks or months," Simone said. "Am I supposed to just sit here and paint my nails—"

"You should've thought of that—"

"I did!"

"As for the Whittaker case," Charlie said, "I'm following the order of the Court of Appeals and reassigning this case to Judge Johnston for a temporary custody determination—"

"Charlie! He won't do what's right for those little girls! He'll do whatever he can to flaunt his grudge against me—"

"You've compromised your judgment to the point that I cannot listen to anything else you say." Charlie bolted from her chambers. The door rattling in the wood frame shattered Simone's already fragile nerves. She raised a trembling hand to meet the sob twisting her face.

89

Just down the hall from Judge Thompson's courtroom, Sonny sat next to Myles, with Erica and Brett at the other end of the table. But this time, rather than Simone, a slight, gray-haired man whose eyes radiated malice shuffled papers up on the bench, whispering orders to a woman who kept sitting down and getting up to hand things up to him.

The judge's eyes raked over the courtroom, lingering on Sonny's probing stare with blood-boiling potency.

"I don't like this guy," Sonny whispered to Myles, who was writing on a yellow pad in the still silence. He had the same look in his eyes as Erica had shown this morning. Just a short while ago, in the hallway, Erica had said: *You literally just fucked yourself, Sonny. Thank you!*

"This whole process is wrong," Sonny said. "This guy knows nothing about me, my family, or Erica for that matter."

"This process is what we're working with, man," Myles said with a flat tone. "The Court of Appeals sent the case back to the chief judge, who put us right here. Just remember, whatever happens, it'll only be a *temporary* decision about custody—"

"She already made the right decision," Sonny said. He looked up at the judge.

Sonny's chest squeezed. He had the same dizzying sensation of that day, during a hike through the Amazon years ago, he stared down a wild boar. It grunted, with sharp tusks poised to puncture his flesh. But Sonny obeyed the guide's whispers to stay still, even as the animal urinated on his boots. Right now, Sonny's heart thundered. Because he knew, even standing still, staring down that man up there, he was about to get gored.

90

On the vast porch of The Tree House, disappointment and terror widened Sister Margaret's eyes as she stood next to a towering stack of boxes.

"The children will be split up," the nun said. "Little Mick tied his ankle to his bed this morning. Saying he will not leave the only family he knows—"

Family. Her own family, her life, was now being boiled down to sixty-second radio and TV reports headlined by the words "sex scandal."

"Sister, don't pack another thing until you hear from me."

Back in her chambers, Simone dialed Brett Robinson's office. "I need you to send an urgent page to Mr. Robinson," she said.

"This is highly unusual, Judge Thompson," the receptionist said.

"Do you relay messages for Sheila, his other daughter?"

"Why, yes, of course. Especially now that the Cesarean is scheduled—"

"Then please ask him to come to my chambers immediately following his hearing with Judge Johnston."

A short time later, after asking Yolanda to keep Charlie away, Simone adjusted the blinds to let in a soft glow for this moment she had dreamed of all her life. A knock, a fluttering heart, a jolt of rage, and she opened the doors to her to let her father inside.

91

A hot sheen of sweat broke out under Brett Robinson's dress shirt as he looked into his daughter's face. He wanted to reach out and touch her, to pull her into his arms and rock away the pain and anger in those eyes.

Eyes just like mine. Eyes that melted away the tough persona he showed the world to win in court. Now, looking at his firstborn daughter made him lightheaded with paternal longing and regret. Anger at her mother. And fear of how this woman might try to avenge all those years of longing. He would have to protect himself, just in case she would try to twist the knives of guilt already slicing his conscience.

"Simone," he said softly. "Beautiful girl, I didn't know. No idea."

She stood, staring with wide eyes and trembling lips. Like a wave of emotion, a slight pink hue rose up her neck, flushing her face, filling her eyes with silver tears. He wiped one from her cheek with his thumb. Then he pulled her—this delicate and intelligent and floral-scented woman whose longing was so raw it made him twitch—into his chest.

She banged her fist on his shoulder, sobbing, trembling.

"I hate her for not telling you!" she cried. "I hate her!"

"I'm here now," he said softly. "I am so sorry this happened to you—"

"Part of me hates you, too, for having an affair and never checking to see if you'd left a baby along with it! Me!"

Simone pulled back. Through wet, red eyes she asked, "Tell me one thing. If you had known, would you—"

Brett bit his bottom lip. "Oh, baby." He laid his head on her shoulder, incredulous to the idea that just yesterday he had entertained such insulting thoughts about her behavior in the Whittaker case.

She banged his shoulder again. "You wouldn't," she accused. "If you had known my mother was pregnant, I bet you would've given her some money and said, 'take care of it.'"

Brett bristled. He squinted down at her. "Do *not*," he said with a hard tone, "assume that my sometimes ruthless quest for victory in the courtroom would have any bearing whatsoever on the decisions that I would make as your father."

"Does that include reporting me to the Judicial Tenure Commission?" Simone demanded. "They're investigating me for misconduct."

"That's work," he said. "And I did it before I knew—"

His every muscle ached under her sad gaze; Simone was just months older than Sheila. "If you had any idea how much I cherished the experience of holding and rocking my babies—"

She turned away. "I never had that," she cried softly. "I wanted it more than anything—"

"Maybe I can start to make up for it," Brett said, taking her shoulders, turning her.

Her wet, red-rimmed eyes sharpened as she asked, "Why are you such a bastard in the courtroom?"

"No, baby, that's work. Theatrics. The courtroom is my stage. And I act my ass off to win. But this—" Her face blurred through his tears. "This is real. This is blood, a new beginning."

She tightened her lips. *My lips.*

"If you mean that," she asked, blinking hard, "why did you go to the media first?"

"Norris Haynes is my richest client," he said flatly.

Simone pulled back, crossing her arms. "Money. Money is more important than me."

He glanced around the office. "I'm here. These tears are real. I'm here for you now, Simone Thompson. Any interaction you and I have had in the past—in these chambers, in that courtroom—it's all null and void."

"Couldn't you feel me aching for you for the past thirty-five years? Couldn't you feel me wishing and waiting and wanting so badly—"

He pulled her close. "Shhh. I'm here now." The idea of Sheila enduring such emptiness as a child, it made him shudder. "Simone, I want to make up for us both being innocent victims in your mother's cruel secret."

He pressed a piece of paper into her palm. "My home number. Call me anytime. For any reason. Or no reason at all. You don't have to say who you are, just ask for me. Clients call at all hours—"

"So you're going to keep our"—she drew her brows together—"what is this? A relationship, an acquaintance? I'll tell you what, it's not a secret, the way you announced it all over TV!" Her eyes flashed anger.

"I just don't think it's a good idea to welcome my love child with open arms to our family gatherings. The triplets are coming and, I don't think Sheila can take it—"

Simone blanched. She handed back the paper with his phone number.

"All or nothing. This *love child* needs more than just an occasional clandestine phone conversation with you. I need my father to tell me how I'm supposed to react, whether I should feel differently, now that I know I'm half black! And tell me how proud you are of what I've accomplished without you!"

"Simone, listen." He grasped her hands, holding them up like a bouquet. "I may not show it, but I have the utmost respect for you as a person, and as a jurist. You are one hell of a judge. Your compassion is so strong, I've sometimes sat in awe that you never let the importance of your position or the theatrics, interfere—"

"Until now."

"You are human. And Sonny Whittaker, he's a pretty fine cat, I have to say."

She wrinkled her brow. "But you ripped him to shreds out there. You hurt him. And you're hurting me." She closed her eyes, squeezing them shut, shaking her head. She pursed her lips, opening her eyes. "You know, I became this because of you."

"Because of the Katie Moore trial?" Brett asked softly. "When you testified?'

"No, even before that," Simone said, exhaling. "The only thing my mother would say about you is that the judge decided we couldn't be together. So I decided to become a judge to prevent other little girls from not knowing their daddies."

"Oh, baby," he said over a burning lump in his throat. He stared into her glassy eyes. "Baby girl. I am so sorry."

She pulled back. "Then put your money where your mouth is. Redeem yourself for my suffering by helping a hundred other fatherless children keep their home."

Brett stiffened. "I'm not sure that money is the solution. But tell me what you need, and I'll give it some thought."

92

Sonny Whittaker hurried through the side door of his home, into the cobalt blue and yellow-star-painted hallway. Early evening sunshine glowed on the jade tiles around six suitcases, lined up at the foot of the back wooden staircase, under the new alarm pad.

"Kindred! Asia! India! Time to go!" Sonny grabbed the banister, calling upstairs.

"Josh," Sonny said. "Load these into the Land Rover. Jared, get Kindred and the girls. You're both coming with us."

All of them would be long gone, by the time Erica and the sheriff's deputies arrived to steal his children. Myles could keep his plan to file an emergency appeal—come Monday morning—that could take a week or more to get the courts to return custody.

Now, they had just enough time to get to the airport for the flight to Brazil. Sonny had purchased the E-tickets over Myles's cell phone, and alerted Rico Miranda, in the men's room of the courthouse, just moments after that male judge dealt his blow.

"Daddy!" India flew from the landing, arms and legs outstretched like a bat, into his arms. Asia stepped down, wrapping thin arms around his waist. "Daddy!"

He squeezed them, smelling their coconut shampoo.

"I just heard," Kindred said. He pulled her close for a hug.

"Ready girls?" he asked. "Paradise awaits."

"Yeah!" they chimed.

The doorbell rang at the same time.

"I'll get it, Mr. Whittaker," Guadeloupe called from the kitchen.

As the girls slipped on their jackets, Guadeloupe returned. "It's Simone Thompson."

"No," Sonny helped India with her jammed zipper. "Tell her to go away."

"But she—"

"Sonny." That soft, loving voice made him turn. "I have to talk to you."

"You've said more than enough," he said, hating the raw pain in her eyes.

"Please." She looked at the suitcases, the girls, Kindred, who glared at her.

"Kindred," he said, glancing at his watch. "Be ready in five minutes."

He led Simone into the foyer. "What?"

She took his hands. "Sonny," she said. "I want to help you."

"Are you going to pursue a relationship with that"—he envisioned Brett in court an hour ago, gloating as the judge ripped out his heart—"*man*. Your father?"

She nodded slightly. Sonny pushed past her. A new jolt of urgency—to get away from her, to get his children out of town, out of the country, away from the wrong arm of the law—propelled him through the back hall.

The alarm beeped as it did when any door or window opened.

Good, the guys were loading up the car. He strode faster.

"How 'bout we go shopping tonight?"

Erica. In the house. With deep voices. Sheriff's deputies.

Sonny bolted into the back hall.

"Daddy why are the police here?" India cried. She ran to him, a blur of black curls and banana yellow denim. "Daddy!" She clawed up his shirt, clamping her legs as if she were climbing a rope. He lifted her with one arm, pulling her quaking body close.

Asia looked between him and Erica, then Kindred.

"They're not going with you, Erica," Kindred said. "None of us is." Jared and Josh stood in front of the girls.

"Oh isn't this special," Erica said, glaring over his shoulder. "I don't want that bitch, or these guys, around my children. C'mon, India, Asia. Time to go with Mommy."

"No!" India shrieked. "Don't let them take me, Daddy! I won't go!" She buried her face in his neck.

"Get her," Erica said to the deputy.

Sonny glared at the kid half his age with a gun. He held India tighter. Her tears drenched his neck.

The man's footsteps thumped as he approached.

Asia flitted behind him. "Daddy! I'm not going with the police again."

"Come with Mommy," Erica snapped.

The deputy came closer, holding out his hands. "Let's make this easy, Mr. Whittaker." The other deputy followed. "We don't want you to get into any more trouble tonight."

Simone let out a soft sob behind him.

The deputy raised two hands behind India's back. "Mr. Whittaker, seriously, let's make this easy on everybody."

"Touch her and I'll kill you."

Jared and Josh formed a wall of shoulders between Sonny and the girls, and the officers.

"Sonny," Simone pleaded.

"Mr. Whittaker," the officer said, "we don't want to arrest you for threatening an officer tonight. That would only hurt your chances—"

Erica stomped toward them.

"Move!" she shouted up at Jared and Josh.

"Gentlemen," the officers said with warning looks.

In a blur of hair, Erica grabbed Asia's arm, then India's.

Sonny would not play tug of war with his daughters' bodies, his own flesh and blood, hurting them even more.

"Sonny, just do as they say," Simone said softly. "You'd be powerless in jail. Just trust the appeal—"

"Get out," he said so deeply it hurt his throat. He could not look at her.

The deputy pried India's shoulders back.

"Get your hands off my daughter."

"She has to go now."

"Get her!" Erica shrieked from the door.

Kindred stepped toward him. "India, sweetheart, let's go with Mommy. I'll be with you. Then pretty soon we'll be back with Daddy and your cousins."

"Kindred you're not coming," Erica said.

"Yes I am. Girls, you want me to come, don't you?"

Asia ran to Kindred, grabbing her hand. Kindred glared at Erica.

The deputy stepped closer, wrapping his hands around India's arms. He pulled. She tossed her head back, banging his forehead, screaming. "Daddy, no!"

Sonny closed his eyes, giving her one more squeeze, kissing her hair, her soft cheeks, looking into her sad amber eyes. He bent to lower her onto her feet. She held on, as Asia joined the hug. He squeezed them both, savoring this sacred moment that his heart was being ripped from his chest.

"We'll be back together soon," he whispered. "I love you more than life." Sonny was sure his heart stopped beating as a deputy picked up each girl.

"No!" They screamed. Over the deputies' shoulders, looking back at him, their little arms and fingers reached for him, eyes wide, mouths open, shrieking "Daddy!"

Kindred kissed his cheek, and slunk behind them. With them outside, Erica peeked back through the door: "You and your new girlfriend have all the time in the world now." She slammed the door.

93

Sonny dashed down the hallway, into the family room. A staticky sound, a grainy image of the terrace in Montserrat. Yes, Kindred had programmed the television to videoconference.

"Are you there, Grandmama?"

Her silver hair, her billowing black dress, her warm eyes filled the screen. "Sonny," she said. "They tried to get me to leave." The cowrie shells on her braids tumbled over her shoulders as she looked back at the house. Rocks and dust rolled down the lush slope, down the roof. "The government folk—"

"The volcano?" Sonny gasped.

"We had some rumbles," Grandmama said. The screen went blue—
"No!"

"—patio at the restaurant. Conch next door, he's gone. But this is my home—"

The picture zigzagged black and white. The sound faded.

"—roots are here," Grandmama raised an arm toward the trees and plants ringing the lagoon. "I won't leave your grandfather, either. And the sunset tonight"—serenity glowed in her eyes—"those rings of fire again, Sonny, I told you. But you'll make it. Might get singed, but you'll get through just fine."

"What about the girls?" Sonny asked.

A thunderous roar. The picture shook. Static blared. "All of you, those rings of fire," she said. "Bright green tonight, too. Evil is comin' at you—"

Big rocks crashed onto the roof behind her. Another roar and a hissing noise. "Grandmama, get out of there!" he shouted.

"I'll be watching over you," she said.

The screen when blank.

"No!" Sonny fell to his knees. "No!"

94

As Simone sped northbound on the San Diego Freeway, the red taillights ahead reminded her of the bloodshot eyes of Asia and India and Sonny. The sirens and horns and blasts of trucks were their cries. And the squad car tailing her was a constant reminder that she was still in danger. Anger eroded the relief she finally felt at connecting with her father. "Marie," Simone said into her cell phone.

"I've been trying to reach you," Marie said. "I think I know who Narcissus is. Can you meet me at Cheyenne Moore's house?"

"Is she—" Simone wished the gridlocked lanes of vehicles would speed up.

"Just meet me," Marie said. "It's—"

"I know where it is," Simone said. "On Beverly Glen in Bel Air."

A short time later, she pulled up to an English-style country manor, its two stories of fieldstone covered with ivy. Yellow light glowed from square-paned windows upstairs.

"I think Katie Moore is alive," Marie said. "Not the girl who was in court. One of my clients. And I think she's also the stalker—"

"What?"

"It's a classic case of multiple personality disorder." Marie held out an eight-by-ten picture. "Look, a computer composite of what Katie would look like today."

Simone gasped. "Sonny's nanny. She left his house with Erica. Call Norris—"

"I moved out tonight," Marie said. "I called, but couldn't get through—"

"We have to warn him!" Simone grasped the door latch. "I'll go tell the police, they can find—"

"I already called my sources," Marie said. "They're watching Erica and the house, but they need more evidence before they can get a warrant—"

Knocking on the window. Paulette appeared through the glass on the passenger side. Simone shot out of the car, stomped around.

"How could you!" she shouted.

"I didn't!" Paulette said. Her hair shook over her leather jacket. She wore jeans and high-heeled boots.

"Then how did Brett Robinson get that picture you took of us at the gallery?" Simone demanded.

Paulette's braces glinted in the light of the squad car's headlights. "Ted," she said softly. "He found the picture. He told someone at the agency about it. They made some calls, got a bidding war going—"

Simone's heart pounded with rage. "A bidding war over that picture of me?"

Paulette nodded. "A couple TV stations, and Norris Haynes. I guess he won, and gave it to Brett—"

A string of expletives danced on the tip of Simone's tongue.

Until screaming silenced them all.

It sounded like two women, inside the house.

Marie got out, stepped onto the grass.

The screaming was getting louder. More vicious.

The police officers radioed for backup. Then they walked through the open gate, up the driveway, to the stone porch and double doors.

A piercing scream.

A flash of white, like a falling dove.

A horrible thud.

Simone, Marie and Paulette ran toward the body on the grass.

It was Cheyenne Moore.

95

Marie watched Sergeant Len Earnest take quick steps on his short legs as he dashed from the squad car at the curb toward a crew from the coroner's office. They zipped a black body bag around Cheyenne Moore.

"Thanks for the tip, Dr. Cartwright," he said, taking off his hat to stroke bushy gray-brown brows. "We think we got her."

Marie nodded. She had to see Kindred Germaine with her own eyes, to know that Narcissus was off the streets. "Sergeant," she said, "These are my friends, Paulette Barnes, and Simone Thompson."

"Upstairs," the sergeant said, "they found all kinds of stuff that Narcissus would have. A computer, lots of books on poetry and Greek mythology, daffodil plants everywhere."

"Excuse me," Paulette said, glancing toward Cheyenne's body, "do you have a photographer here?"

"No ma'am—"

"I didn't do it!" a woman shrieked. "It's my sister!"

At the open double doors, two police officers held the arms of a woman. She had long dark hair and a flowy yellow print dress. Her narrow face was pale, her feet bare. "You can't do this!" she screamed.

"Turns out," the officer said, "Cheyenne has a crazy sister. "Does the name Myra Michaels ring a bell?"

"I remember," Simone said somberly. "She was attacked, on campus. After her play—"

The sergeant nodded. "Bingo. She was beautiful, wanted to be an actress. But after they messed up her face, she got real reclusive, real weird after that."

Marie studied the woman as police led her to a squad car in the driveway.

"That's not Narcissus," Marie said, shaking off a chill. "She's still out there, plotting to kill."

96

Inside Cheyenne Moore's shrine to Sonny Whittaker, Simone swallowed a heave amidst the candles, the pictures, the movie playing on the television, the book.

I have to help him, comfort him. But how?

"I thought I had seen some stuff," said a Los Angeles police officer, using tweezers to hold a clump of dark hair. Marie had convinced the officer to let Simone come up to this rooftop greenhouse while officers photographed the ledge outside where she'd fallen or been pushed.

"I know the man is fine, but damn," the cop said. "The woman lost her mind." The officer pulled a stack of pictures from a drawer. "Look, she even got him with that judge he's havin' an affair with."

Simone gasped. That was her and Sonny in Brazil, talking on the dock. How would Cheyenne have gotten that? She hadn't even been aware of anyone taking that same snapshot that Charlie had. Then today's paper, with a photograph of her next to a picture of Brett Robinson, under a headline: EVE'S POISON APPLE FALLS RIGHT UNDER THE TREE.

"You okay?" the officer's eyes widened. "That's you!"

"Simone." Marie rushed in. "You're so pale—"

She steadied herself with a hand on Marie's shoulder. "I'm going to him," Simone whispered. "I can't live with this—"

"Wait." Marie said. "Simone, be careful."

Simone sped to Sonny's house, but the housekeeper said through a crack in the door, "He is gone tonight. To Brazil."

"Please tell me," Simone said. "Is he at Sanctuary in Bahia?"

"Yes."

Simone imagined flying there, finding him, comforting him.

Facing her demons. She shivered.

But his little girls' screams echoed in her head. And it was her own father's lawyering that had wrenched them from his arms.

Sonny needs me. I'm going.

97

Kindred stepped inside the Haynes home, using the all-purpose credit-card style passkey that she'd lifted from one of the AlarmTech technicians when he removed his toolbelt. Just like she'd done when she went spray-painting in the screening room. Just like the morning she'd sent Norris on an extra-long sauna.

She couldn't believe that bitch Erica had kicked her out of the car and dropped her off at that corner! Even though the girls were screaming for her!

In her purse, Kindred still had the twins' passports with all the credit cards and cash she would need for the three of them, when the time was right. When they could all be together again with Daddy, in a faraway place. Jared and Josh, too. They'd looked pretty pissed off, having to stay at the Whittaker house tonight.

She dashed through the kitchen, up the front stairs, where a private security guard was coming down.

"Hey, Kindred." His narrow, freckled face lit up with a smile, under bangs parted like missing teeth on a brown comb. "Erica said you wouldn't be coming back."

"Yeah, my mom got sick. I had to go check on her. But she's okay now."

"Cool," the guy said. "The girls are asleep. And Mr. Haynes, the doctors put him on so many drugs, he'll be sleeping for a week. Hey, how 'bout we get some coffee together, in the kitchen?"

"Sure," Kindred said, smiling, "in a few minutes."

She dashed up to the twins' room.

"Wake up, little angel girls," she whispered. "It's time to go see Daddy."

98

At the gate at Los Angeles International Airport, as Simone sat waiting for her flight to Brazil, she pulled out her cell phone. Inhaling the scent of gourmet pizza at the nearby Wolfgang Puck restaurant, she dialed the number written on the slip of paper that Brett Robinson had given her today. After three rings, he answered.

"Brett," she said softly. Red electronic letters flashed her departure time on the monitor behind the counter, just above a flight attendant as she checked in two young women chatting about the wild abandon they intended to have at Carnival. "This is Simone. You said to call—"

"It's late," he said with a grating tone.

"I need to talk—" She fingered the paper that he had discreetly placed on her desk before leaving her chambers.

The line was silent.

"So you kept my number after all," he said without emotion. "I've been thinking about what it all means, being a parent. About you, and what I said." He exhaled loudly. "What I do, it's not a game. Your mother could have easily done to me what just happened to Sonny Whittaker today. And it would have killed me, losing Sheila and Scott—"

Simone rode the hot wave of resentment that surged through her limbs and washed her mind in red. Sheila and Scott Robinson, who grew up with their father and their mother, not knowing they had a half-sister on the other side of the country, wishing she could be there with them.

"Brett—"

"If you don't want to call me Dad yet, let's think of something else, a nickname." He laughed. "Just not 'Half!'"

"I'll think on it. But right now, I need to know if you can help me."

"You're really asking a lot," Brett said. "This is very sudden."

"Exactly."

99

In Brazil, Sonny Whittaker stood at the long, dark wood bar dividing the kitchen and cavernous living room of his bungalow at Sanctuary. He balanced a phone on his shoulder while attempting to pour sugarcane liquor into a crystal tumbler.

"Myles, how much longer?" He stared through the wide open rectangle of dark wood framing the turquoise slice of paradise. The cool liquid splashed his left hand; he tossed it back, letting it burn down his throat.

Rico Miranda offered a white towel, dabbing the spilled booze on Sonny's hand.

"Sonny," Myles said over the crackling line. "Just be patient. The judge is reviewing my emergency motion to return custody to you. But the investigation"—loud static blared—"could take weeks or—" More static.

"Myles?"

"—a chance to get them back," Myles said over the hiss. "But not if you do something rash—"

Silence.

Sonny glared at the phone in his hand, ready to throw it into the surf. Rico took it. "Sorry, my friend. Phone service to the States is a hit or miss endeavor down here."

Rage shot like flaming arrows through his head, his fingers; he had to relax. His chest squeezed. "What was I thinking?"

Rico laughed. "A beautiful woman? We know what you were thinking."

Sonny hurried onto the back porch.

Outside, Rico held out a hand. "Lay in the hammock, my friend. Indulge in the pleasures of Carnival tonight. You will forget everything."

"I can't forget," Sonny said deeply, joining Rico on the step, letting the hot sand burn his bare feet. Sonny guzzled his drink. Worrying about legal decorum and consequences had gotten him nowhere but trouble over the past week. So why should he let rules keep him apart from his own flesh and blood? Why couldn't he act on his paternal instinct to shelter and love his own children? Who was that man, that judge, to make such a life-altering decision?

Then again, trusting that the base, primordial instinct and attraction for Simone would work out for the best had backfired. So how much stock should he place in instinct? The instinct to protect his children. The instinct to bond with a woman, physically and spiritually.

It's so strong. With every heartbeat he saw her face . . . crumpled in the agony of passion as they made love . . . a light sheen of sweat on her skin . . . her grave composure as she read her decision . . . her puffy-eyed plea last night at the house that he let her help . . . the sparkle in her eyes as he whispered, "Simone."

"Sonny, she has cast her spell. You will die ten times before your passion fades," Rico said, tossing a shell into the white foam. He smiled. "You are lovesick, my friend."

Sonny stared up at the blazing sun. "Why!" His shout echoed over crashing waves, screeching birds, rustling palms overhead. "Why!" He ached for Grandmama's comfort and counsel.

Rico patted his back. "I have the perfect cure for a broken heart. Her name is—"

Sonny glared at him. "I couldn't touch another woman now. Simone has stolen my soul. And my family." Sonny gripped the glass so hard, he imagined it cracking, slicing his fingers, dripping red blood into the white sand.

"Simone is my elixir. For eternity. But if I don't get Asia and India back, I swear, man, I'll be like that myth of Miguel—"

"Throwing himself into the sea after his lover died," Rico said. "Visit the *pai de santo*, my friend. He will ask the spirits to bring her and your girls, back to you."

Sonny shook his head. "No, I did that once. The guy took my twenty bucks and mumbled nonsense. It was ridiculous."

"Believe, my friend," Rico said, pointing toward a tiny island in the distance. "Noah, he can see. He knows. He has the power."

An eery flash in Rico's eyes made Sonny stare for long moments. Until footsteps echoed inside the bungalow.

"I had the chef make up a special meal for you, my friend. All your favorites—" Rico turned. His eyes grew wide.

Sonny spun.

Simone.

100

She stood in the open doorway, framed by the white sheers draping the bed. The bamboo ceiling fan, and the ocean breeze, billowed her loose hair over her shoulders. She was knee-buckling sexy in light blue jeans and a white cotton blouse. Beside her, the vines of purple bougainvillea hung next to the spiral staircase. And the sunshine lit up her *moonbeam gray* eyes.

Sonny's heart thundered as he stared, letting her aura wash over him with the soothing warmth of those gentle waves lapping the sand nearby.

But he stiffened with rage. Because her face transformed under the crimson cloud of rage in his mind, into the man who had stolen his children. The man who had assassinated his character in the courtroom, for all the world to hear. The man whose selfish, vengeful act of taking his story to television before speaking with his own daughter, who devastated her . . .

"Go away." His lips hurled the words like rocks.

She flinched, but did not look away. The twenty feet between them was so charged, he expected to see white and blue veins of electricity crackling from him to her and back.

"Leave, Simone."

"Go easy, my friend," Rico said, standing up. He slipped away via the beach.

Sonny raised to his feet on the burning sand. She walked toward him, staring hard, telling him with her eyes that she was going to help him no matter what. If he refused, would he be missing out on some link that could, still, help? Or would she only botch things further for his family?

His core melted as he watched her liquid walk, hips forward, squared shoulders and raised chin broadcasting control and power.

"No, Simone."

"Sonny." Her deep *silk on a soundwave* tone reverberated in his head. "Sonny, I'm going to help you get Asia and India back. Safe and sound. Then and only then, you can decide whether you'll ever speak my name again."

She stepped close. He inhaled her: a hint of perfume and the lingering scent that clings after a long airplane ride, blended with the sweet-salty musk of fear and hope.

"I don't want you here, Simone." But just saying her name, and looking at her, she was the dose of pure opium that he craved. How profound and disturbing that she was possibly the reason—and the remedy—for his problems.

And I love her. I love . . . no . . . I worship this woman.

The image came to mind of falling to his knees like a samurai, sliding his razor-sharp sword into his gut, then working its beautiful, ornate handle back and forth. It would be suicide to try to live without her. Yet the intensity of their passion, when they made love the other night, had been deadly as well.

"Sonny," she whispered, placing warm fingertips on his cheek. The blinding sunshine made her eyes glow with eery brightness. And her touch set off an explosion inside him.

He wrapped his arms around her, pulling her shoulders into him. He smashed his mouth into hers, meeting no resistance. Wild, deep kisses. He had to taste that she felt the same for him. That she could help him.

"Simone," he groaned into her neck, biting, licking, sucking.

She threw back her head, moaning. Then, clawing his shoulders, she jumped up onto him. Long legs wrapped around his waist, lips locked onto his.

He lost his balance. They crashed onto the hot sand. He dug his fingertips into her ass, making her moan.

He thought of nothing. Nothing but the base, animal urge to satisfy his lust by ramming himself between her soft, wet walls of flesh.

She clamped her hands around his head, squeezing her legs so tight he groaned. She took his upper lip between her teeth, gently biting, licking.

He had to have her now. He ripped open her blouse, rubbing his face over the creamy mounds of her breasts. She clawed his head, his hair, pulling him closer. He pulled off her blouse, her jeans, her panties, sandals. Sand burned and scratched and cradled him, covering their clothes, their bare skin.

She sat on her knees, unbuttoning his shirt, unbuckling his belt, unzipping his pants. Clawing down his white briefs. Her eyes radiated girlish awe yet womanly understanding and appreciation of what this rod of hot flesh could do for her. He savored the moment of his hugeness throbbing under her raw, needy gaze. Her eyes moved from its tip, a ripe plum swaying before her, along a vein zigzagging down its long length, to a nest of blackness. She stroked its sides with her fingertips, forming an A as if praying. Leaning forward, she opened her mouth.

She glanced up, as if to ask permission.

He closed his eyes.

Slowly, she took him into a chamber of liquid heat. Sucking softly, stroking back and forth with her lips. She grasped the backs of his thighs, pulling him closer. And she pressed the searing slick of soft flesh between her legs into his thigh.

Her mouth was wet fire. He melted into the velvety coarseness of her tongue, rimming round and round his outer tip, her wet lips sliding back and forth with just enough pressure, her fingers pulling and twisting just right. His hands clamped into her hair, guiding himself in, further, deeper. Hot, soft flesh of her mouth, the back of her throat, the insides of her cheeks, her slippery lips . . .

"Simone," he said more deeply than ever.

She sucked and licked and stroked his length with those beautiful fingers, slipping one back to cup and massage the mighty storehouse of his seed, then, stroking the sensitive stretch of skin just beyond.

"Oh, Simone," he groaned.

She laid back on the sand. "Make love to me, Sonny Whittaker. Fuck me till I can't even crawl to the water's edge."

He reached down, grasped the outer sides of her thighs, raising her up. He yanked her down onto his huge erection, loving her fingernails in his back, her agonized cry echoing up to the deep blue sky. He fucked her, balancing on his sword, up and down, spinning.

They rolled, kissing ravenously, moaning, panting. Then he carried her to the bed. Clumps of sand fell from their damp bodies, sprinkling the cool white sheets as he laid her down.

He pumped into her, harder and harder. Making her eyes roll back into her head. Causing her mouth to drop open in a gasp, a scream, a desperate gulp for oxygen. Covering her lips with his mouth, making her breathe his breath.

Then, onto the dark wood circular staircase leading up to the beachside balcony, providing the perfect balancing point for his knees, just below her spread legs. He was inhaling her female scents with the fiendish need of a cocaine user snorting their drug. Injecting her essence into the red blood boiling in his veins. Licking her skin, lapping up every bead of sweat, every milky drop of lust, with the thirst of an alcoholic. Nibbling, licking, sucking her as a food addict savors every morsel. Pounding, fucking, sweating, panting. Staring into those *moonbeam gray* eyes, lost in complete rapture.

101

Hours later, Simone sat up in bed, clutching her stomach. She was nude, and the soft swirl of white sheets brought to mind a cozy nest that was about to get walloped by a violent storm.

"Come on," Sonny said, offering a silver forkful of Brazilian beef. "It melts in your mouth."

Her gut cramped. She pushed away the lavish tray of food angled over the sheets. "My stomach is doing flips," she said.

Sitting naked before her, Sonny put the meat in his own mouth, then dabbed his lips with a linen napkin. "We need strength."

She stared up at the whirring ceiling fan. "All these questions."

"I guess it would be shocking to find out you're black," Sonny said, spooning up beans and rice. "And the child of that—"

"I don't feel any different," Simone said. "But would my life be the same, if I'd known all along that I'm biracial?"

"You are you," he said.

"Would I still want to help kids? Would I still be a judge?"

"Would you still be this delicious?" Sonny asked, diving toward her ankle with an open mouth. "Worrying about it won't help. If I think about the fact that my daughters were taken away"—he shook his head— "I have to have faith that things will work out. Quickly."

Simone laughed to keep from crying at the sight of her buttery leg contrasting with his deep bronze cheeks. And the golden strip of trimmed hair between her legs versus the black waves on his head. He reached to the dinner tray, then danced a cool cluster of purple grapes over her breasts, causing the nipples to stiffen. He traced the fruit along her neck, her jaw, over her lips.

"My question to you is," Sonny said, "would Brett Robinson have marveled at you the way I do Asia and India, if he'd known when you were born?"

Simone's stomach burned.

"It seems impossible that someone as destructive as him," Sonny said, disdain hardening his gaze, "created you."

Simone bolted to the bathroom.

A stranger—framed by a sandy cloud of corkscrew curls set by the steam of sex—looked back from the mirror. A stranger with eyes that inspired tragedy and terror. A stranger who did not know what she was supposed to think or feel or say. Now that she embodied all the socio-political weight of being part of another race.

"Who am I?" she whispered as her lips twisted into a sob.

Sonny wrapped his arms around her, cradling her in the warm firmness of his body. He rested his chin on top of her head, looking at their reflection.

Hot tears stung her eyes as he kissed her hair. His arms formed a W over her chest; he cupped her shoulders in his palms. Simone closed her eyes, forgetting everything except this amazing security . . .

"All these spectacular curls. Wear your hair natural for me." Sonny turned her around. "Simone, let's go out tonight. To see the Brazilian lust for life, even among the poorest of the poor—"

"I've seen it," she said.

"But it's time to face your fears," he said. "Let's get rid of that once and for all. And your race, we can appreciate the beauty here and help you—"

Simone shook her head. "No, Sonny, I can't. It took everything out of me to get on a plane to come here. Then the taxi ride, all I could see, all I could hear, was that old woman—"

"I want you to face the fear and get over it!" His voice deepened with anger. "Just like I'm trying to do right by waiting. For justice. Myles says—"

"Sonny, I came down here to help you—"

"Judge Simone Thompson," he bellowed. "Do you fuck every vulnerable father who comes before you? Trying in some sick way to fill the void for your own daddy?" The blaze in his eyes stole her ability to speak. This was pure, unbridled Aries fire. Charring her Cancer crab's shell, scalding her inside and out.

"And your own pathetic family drama!" he shouted. "Why did you let that soap opera have a public premiere during my trial?"

"Sonny, you're as much to blame! You know the effect you have on women. Using it to make a soap opera of your own life—"

"Are you gonna go back to your important job and play more games with people's lives? Just for the *fuck* of it?" His eyes threatened to burn a hole right through her. "You know, Simone Robinson, maybe there's more of your bloodsucking father in you than you want to admit!"

"Maybe you're more like the man he described during the trial," she shot back, "than you want to believe. Maybe you knew from the second you saw me, that I was the judge, and by seducing me, you could influence my decision—"

She tilted her chin upward under his glare.

"Maybe," he accused, "you're on daddy's bank roll, and this was rigged from the start. Dazzle the defendant out of his senses with those eyes, that sultry voice, and voilà." He pounded the wall. "The court hereby declares: you lose, Sonny Whittaker. No more kids, no more movie, no more dignity, no more life! Now go wallow in misery!"

"I will!" Simone screamed.

102

Sonny's insides boiled with guilt as he approached her, sitting at the bar in the bungalow. She was frantically dialing the phone, speaking flawless Portuguese.

"Leave me alone!" She slammed down the receiver, turning her back to him.

"Simone, will you ever accept an apology?"

She spun off the stool, standing. "We need to get one thing straight, Sonny Whittaker. Even if you never see me after I leave in the morning—"

He stepped toward her. "No, please stay—"

"Let me tell you—I have never even *hinted* at violating the strict code of ethics governing my commitment to justice."

He shook his head. "Simone, I will regret what I said until my dying breath. I don't really think—"

"Then why'd you say those horrible things?"

"I was venting."

"Venting? Those were the most vicious words ever spoken to—"

He took her hand.

"Some of what you said, I can turn back around on you," she said. "About seducing every woman you meet. Or using your charm to get whatever you want from anybody."

She scowled up at him. "Maybe you even thought it was working on me. Because you willingly played this game, knowing your heart and soul were on the line. Asia. India. Me."

For a second, he saw a glimmer of himself in her. A woman not afraid to shoot back. Erica's response to arguments was to storm away, slam doors and cuss in the most unladylike manner.

The feisty sparkles in her eyes made him laugh softly. "Guilty on all counts, your honor." He took her hands. "Now there's something that might help us both tonight," he said softly. "Simone, I will not breathe again until you accept my apology, with the woefully inadequate excuse that I am absolutely raw inside."

Sonny's entire being ached with the need to protect and soothe her. And he was sure, Noah could help them both. Now he just had to convince her to go.

"Simone," he said softly, staring into her glassy eyes. "There's a man, a *pai de santo*—"

"No!"

"I haven't talked with him in awhile, but I've gone to him before."

"A lot of good that's done you." She shot to her feet, snatching up the phone again.

"Simone, you can't go the rest of your life carrying all these things that are haunting you. It's ridiculous—"

She threw down the phone. "I'd do better with a soup can and a string!"

He took her hands. "Please, go with me—"

"You call me ridiculous! You're the one who wants to visit a witch doctor in a grass hut."

"You of all people should understand the power—" He held his palms up. "I can feel it all around us."

"I can still feel the power of all the mean things you said to me tonight," she said. "Tell me you don't really think—"

He stared down at her.

Something flashed in her eyes. And she ran out of the bungalow, onto the beach. Sonny followed. "Simone!"

"Leave me alone!" she cried, running toward the ocean. He sprinted after her.

"Simone!" She stopped at the moonlit fringe of vegetation at the water's edge, panting. Hair blowing in the breeze, the spaghetti strap of her tank top falling down her arm.

My God, what a flawless vision. He would paint it later: "moonlight angel." But now, the raw emotion and energy coursing through him ignited in another way.

103

Simone could feel him coming toward her, trapped here by the ocean and the jungle flora. Her mind throbbed with the brutality of all he had said in the bathroom a short while ago. Yet, deep down, she wanted to understand and forgive, as she hoped he would do for her.

His large hands slid from behind, circling her waist. She slid away. "No, Sonny, I—"

"I apologize," he said with tender eyes that melted her soul, "for crossing the hairline between love and hate."

Her lips parted. The idea of him touching her again, of their bodies pressing together . . . she closed her eyes, savoring the swirling sensation behind the blackness of her eyelids. Everything seemed symphonic—the water crashing on the sand, the breeze rippling through the trees, the cries of birds overhead.

"Simone," Sonny whispered deeply. His hot lips pressed into her mouth. She let out a tiny moan. That third energy of their togetherness made her want to go inside him, through him. It deluged her senses, arousing a hot swell between her legs. She clawed his cheeks, sucking, biting, melding their tongues. She crushed her breasts up into his chest, ground her hips into his. She was dizzy with hunger for him; her every cell ached.

In an instant, she was nude, and so was he, and her backside was pressing into warm, wet sand, waves tickling her toes, her calves, her thighs. Staring up at the full moon, as she ran damp palms down the length of Sonny's back, over the firm rise, down to rock-hard thighs.

"I can't live without you," he groaned as his huge hardness slipped between her legs. Parting the glistening gateway to the deepest chamber of her heart, turning her mind to a golden swirl.

"Aaahh," she cried. How exquisite he was, stroking so slowly, taking her upper lip, then her lower lip, into his mouth, gently sucking. Panting into her neck, pressing his searing mouth there, making her quiver and cry out and say his name over and over.

Wave after wave of euphoria and serenity and goosebumps danced through her every cell, stirring her soul to a magical spray of sparks heating the air around them.

"Nirvana," he groaned.

If only her mind could be this numb and blank all the time. If only her heart could pound with this heavenly love and lust, without the cold fist of conscience smashing it to bits.

The violent fusion of two minds and two bodies blinded her, wracked her with violent tremors, and sucked her into a level of love consciousness so deep, she closed her eyes and fell asleep, blanketed by the ocean foam and this man she had to have until her dying breath.

Simone awoke in his arms, between the soft sheets of his bed. Through the open wood-slatted doors, an orange haze hung over the ocean. She sat up, not knowing the time or even the day.

"Good afternoon," a woman said in English.

Simone gasped, turning toward the voice. It was a maid, wearing the traditional Bahian white lace skirt, an off-the-shoulder white blouse and matching head wrap. As the woman adjusted the sheet, several strands of tiny pink, green and blue beads rolled along the smooth skin of her neck. "I was just closing the doors. It is so bright."

"What time is it?"

The woman laughed. "Sleepytime, we say at Sanctuary. Rest, now. And when you're ready, I bring lunch."

Simone's mind spun over where she needed to be, what she needed to do, what she needed to say. All her problems back home were lined up in her mind like sprinters at the starting line at a track meet, waiting for the gun of wakefulness to shoot off, so they could run circles through her head all day.

No! Somehow, knowing she was powerless at this moment to resolve the problems, she chose to think of nothing. And that was no resistance for the heavy tug of fatigue on her mind and body. So she closed her eyes, snuggled back into Sonny Whittaker, and indulged in the oblivion of sleep.

104

That night, Simone tensed as Sonny stopped his boat about ten yards from an island that would fit inside her courtroom. Waves rolling onto the beach glowed lavender under the full moon; the whispering dark palm and poinciana and almond trees swayed in the salty breeze.

And there, on the sand, a small campfire illuminated a hammock, four oversized chairs made of rough-hewn sticks and a small table. Just beyond stood a hut of vertical bamboo logs under an umbrella of leaves; yellow light filled its open, arched door. There was no dock, no dinghy.

"What, is this a swim-in appointment?" Simone asked. The water was so clear, an occasional fish or garland of seaweed or a shell shimmered under the aqua-lunar glow.

She had never been to a *pai de santo*, but she'd seen several at official gatherings for the ambassador. The idea of whether they really could communicate with spirits was terrifying, so she never spoke with them, or looked in their eyes. But now, in case Sonny was right about it helping, she just wanted to go through the motions and get this over with.

She turned to Sonny, who was pushing buttons near the steering wheel. A rattling chain, a low hum, the anchor plunked into the water. He killed the engine. "Sonny—"

"The water is knee-high. I'd ruin my propellers if—"

"What about our feet, when sharks decide it's time for a late dinner?"

"I've done this before," he said, taking off his leather sandals. He opened the white gate at the back of the boat, then splashed feet first. The water swirled around his bare knees. He held out his hands. "Come on."

"You're serious."

"Come on, Simone."

"Does he know we're coming?"

"I'm sure he heard the boat. But I haven't talked with him."

Simone perched on the side of the boat, then slipped into the warm water. Thank goodness she had changed into shorts and a tank top, not bothering to put on the white sneakers still on deck.

She took Sonny's hand; a smile lifted her cheeks as they splashed toward shore. She tingled with the wild adventure of the moment, and even a faint glimmer of hope that somehow this would calm her fears about her career, her father, her racial identity, the consequences of Sonny's case.

"*Senhor* Whittaker." A low, deep voice rumbled out of the darkness. A red dot glowed in the shadows near the chairs; a moonlit waft of whatever he was smoking rippled upward.

Great, he's stoned. Real sage advice we're about to get.

"Do not be cynical, girl," he said in English.

Simone gasped.

He stepped from the shadows, swathed in white from a thick turban to the fluttering hem of his gown. In Portuguese, he told them to sit at the table, where joss sticks filled the air with woody incense and tiny flames danced on small black candles dripping onto a batik cloth.

Simone glanced at Sonny, who nodded slightly and stood behind a chair for her to sit down. She did, across from the *candomblé* priest; Sonny sat between them, facing the ocean, holding her hand.

"Let go," the man's eyes—milky whites around onyx pupils—projected such potency, the tiny hairs on Simone's arms stood up straight. But she could not look away from his long, thin face. His skin was ink-black, smooth and taut and soft-looking as a child's, despite wiry white hairs sprouting from his ears.

The man held a straight arm toward the space between Simone and Sonny. Then he closed his eyes. Simone imagined, had she been in another frame of mind, this would seem outrageous, laughable. She would think this guy was a pretender, putting on a show to take an American movie star's cash. But she could feel, deep down, an inexplicable and otherworldly force emanating from him.

And it made her quiver. With his hand still outstretched, he began to mumble, and his hand started making tiny circles in the air, like the pendulum over a ouija board.

Slam! The man's open palm hit the table so hard, one of the incense sticks rolled off, into the sand. A tiny droplet of wax stung Simone's hand. He threw his head back, inhaling.

"Fight it," he whispered. "Around you, together, terrible danger. She is coming tonight." The man cupped his ears. "Confusion—"

The man sat forward, clawing a handful of cowrie shells from a coconut bowl in the sand. He held the shells to his sharp, protruding cheekbones. As he shook them between cupped hands, his thin, wide mouth split; corn-cob yellow teeth glistened. He rolled the shells on the table like dice. When they tumbled into no particular pattern, the man's gaze darted from them to Simone and back. He held his palms upward, staring at her hard.

"Two things you must do," he said. "First, visit the *pelourinho*, tonight. Go to the place where your ancestors' blood poured into the streets, where the mulatta felt your pain. Go there, lay down. Look up at the moon—"

Simone went numb.

"—as she died. Ask her—"

The man leaned forward, raking up the shells with his long thin hand with the speed and precision of a craps dealer. But this time, as he shook them, he murmured African-sounding words, then let them clatter amongst the candles and incense. A "Sssss" sound came from between his gritted teeth. "The old woman, the snake lady at Carnival—"

Simone's blood turned ice cold.

"—she is dead. Her daughter, with your eyes. Stoned by a mob, for the curse. She . . . wanted to punish you—"

Simone glared at Sonny. With a quavering voice, she said, "How much did you pay him to trick me?"

Sonny, with wide, haunted eyes, shook his head. "No—"

The yellow ovals of flame on the candles disappeared. But there was no wind, no sound of a deep breath being blown. Not even the rustle of leaves. The water was still as glass.

"You must," the man said deeply, only the whites of his eyes, his turban and his gown visible, as he was shaded from the moonlight, "you must go to a *candomblé* ceremony tonight. Both of you. If you do not, you risk death."

105

Sonny could feel Simone's terror and torment, and suspicion, as the *pai de santo* whispered into the handful of shells, shaking them, letting them rain through his fingers onto the tablecloth. Sonny needed answers and guidance. He wanted assurance that everything in every aspect of his life would be fine.

"You, Sonny Whittaker," the man ran a flat hand a few inches over the shells. "There is a spirit from the islands—"

Goosebumps prickled Sonny's skin.

The man lit the candles with a match. "She is trying to warn you—"

Sonny leaned forward, gripping the edge of the table.

"A beautiful woman, silver hair, she is watching over you," the priest said, shaking his head. He pressed his hands to his ears. "So much noise! The energy in one place. Action."

Sonny grasped the man's waxy hand. "What is Grandmama's warning?"

The man's eyes widened. He clamped long, bony fingers around Sonny's grip. "Someone you thought—" The man slammed his back into the chair. His eyes grew huge. He took in a sharp breath.

"What is it?" Sonny cried. His every cell exploded with panic.

How stupid and selfish of him to leave the States to brood here. He should go back, tonight, to make sure the twins were safe. They were at Norris's house—where Narcissus had already broken in—twice. And indulging in carnal pleasures here with the woman who caused it all— Sonny could feel disdain shooting from his eyes as he looked at Simone, sitting there trembling and looking at the priest with eyes wide with terror.

What was I thinking to leave my flesh and blood in jeopardy back in LA? Why should I help Simone when she is to blame for this Hellish period of my life? I have to get home . . . now . . .

The man shot up in a great flutter of white fabric.

"Come," he said, striding toward the water on leather thongs adorned with cowrie shells. "There is no time."

106

Simone shivered with déja-vu as she and Sonny and the priest climbed out of the boat in the marina at the mainland. The man had sat at the back of the boat, entranced, for the whole ride, while Sonny drove in silence. He had not even looked at her, and when she called his name, his knuckles whitened on the steering wheel. Her hand on his shoulder made him cringe. So Simone had sat in the passenger seat, shivering with dread.

But she could feel his desperate need to call Los Angeles, or find out the time. Now, on the edge of the city of Salvador pulsing and exploding with the lusty energy of Carnival, Simone's every muscle convulsed. She did not exactly know what the *pai de santo* was going to make her do—or why she was going along with this bizarre charade.

God help me . . . Simone followed the *pai de santo* and Sonny into the jammed street, past a three-story-high glittering pink float, holding a samba band and rows of women dancing in their silver-sequined high heels at twelve beats per second, shaking bodies covered with pink feathers over nipples and crotches, and huge, plumed headdresses.

The smell of aphrodisiac cow's hoof soup wafting from a steaming pot on the corner . . . fireworks booming in the sky . . . deafening shouts and screams of costumed, masked revelers jostling her body . . . homeless little boys hawking lace and cigarettes . . . old men peddling coffee as they sat on chairs made of rags.

Simone focused on a twist of white fabric on the back of the priest's turban. Pressing through the crowd, she held her breath, trying in vain not to feel the awesome energy rattling her very bones. The warmth and comfort she had felt from Sonny a few hours ago was now an icy wall between them as the trio made it up to the giant elevator at the two hundred foot bluff connecting the lower city to the upper city. Minutes later, they strode onto the jam-packed pelourinho. Her white sneakers crossed the cobblestone square lined with huge colonial mansions.

Even though the actual pelourinho, or whipping post, had been removed two decades ago as a humanitarian gesture, Simone could still feel the centuries of evil. She could, amongst the ear-splitting percussion of samba drums and the screams of revelers, hear cries for mercy as bloodstained strips of leather sliced and stung black skin . . .

Simone's head whirled. She sucked in a mix of sweat, salt and spices. The priest put his waxy hand on the back of her neck, pressing scratchy hair against her sweaty skin. "There," he said, pushing her toward the center. The kaleidoscopic swirl of skirts and antique lampposts and grilled balconies over chic boutiques and cafés . . . it all blurred.

Simone shook her head. "I don't want to—"

"Lay down," the *pai de santo* said, his stare as sharp as knives. "It was here."

Simone tightened her mouth. "No. This is crazy." She cast a pleading gaze at Sonny. "I'm not doing this."

She gasped. Sonny's eyes were bloodshot, puffy, and saying, *You deserve this, for what you did to me and my family.*

The priest's hands pressed down on her shoulders.

"Sonny!" She pushed up on the man's wrists. But he was so strong.

All around, people were laughing, dancing, kissing. Oblivious.

Simone's behind slammed the hard cobblestones. It was dark, with samba feet and calves slicing inches from her head and body. She gagged on a gust of alcohol and urine and sweat.

I'll suffocate down here . . . get stomped to death . . . She tried to stand. But the priest's white gown fluttered over her. He raised his hands toward the giant almond and poinciana leaves arcing over the square. He straightened his arms over her, raised them toward the celestial void above, then lowered them. Simone stared straight up. Right into Sonny's eyes. He was glaring down at her . . .

"No!" she screamed. Her every cell convulsed with terror. She found the strength to bolt up. On wobbly feet, she would run away—

The priest pushed her back; Sonny caught her under her arms. His hands gripped each other under her breasts, over her heart. A waxy black palm pressed over her eyes.

Simone envisioned the young woman—buttery skin, silver-blue eyes and sandy curls—trembling on the smoking pyre, facing the blood-hungry plantation owners . . . the unfathomable pain of fire . . . staring up at the mocking moon . . . and dying, right here in a city where every corner has a baroque church offering salvation from gold-encrusted altars, where the ever-present spirits of her ancestors should have saved her.

The priest yanked back his hand.

And a spectrum of humanity danced around her. Faces and eyes of every shade, hair of every texture, laughing and loving and celebrating with Dionysian abandon . . . There were no titles here of judge or lawyer or doctor or actor. It was just a mass of humanity, going with the flow of life and loving every second. Embracing each other as kin, celebrating as if tomorrow might never come.

And suddenly, Simone's mind gushed with the realization that she could release the death-grip on her job, and the way it somehow gave her purpose and identity. The same for her race. A label, new or old, meant nothing. The people smiling and laughing and tossing their heads back in celebration all around her, their *joie de vivre* sprang from deep within.

I can love myself no matter who I am. Or what I am. Or who I'm with. I already know I'm a good person. A kind, helpful person who deserves love and respect, who can share it tenfold with everyone. Anywhere.

Simone had the sense that what was happening to her life and career back in Los Angeles was the universe's way of bringing her this moment of epiphany, and had she not endured the past few days, she might never have tapped this awesome geyser of inner peace.

It was so strong, her leg muscles slackened. But Sonny held her up.

107

In Brazil, Kindred tugged Asia and India by the hands, up the wooden steps on the side of the bluff above Sanctuary. Fireworks boomed overhead, lighting up the sky and illuminating the otherwise dark rocks and staircase.

"Come on!" Kindred said. About ten more steps loomed before they would reach the shadowy patio behind the pale yellow house where the set of *The Colony* sat empty. "This is where we're supposed to meet Daddy."

"It's too late!" Asia shouted, pulling her hand back. "Daddy would never want us up here in the middle of the night." She crossed her arms, staring down at the beach crowded with dancing people, blaring bands and glittery costumes.

Kindred squeezed her hand around Asia's little wrist.

"Ow!" Asia said, twisting her face. "You're pinching me!"

"I said come on," Kindred said.

India's eyes widened; she paled. "Kindred, why are you mad?"

Kindred tossed her head back and laughed at the black sky. "For a lot of reasons. And if Daddy doesn't hurry up—"

"I want to go to bed!" Asia cried. "Call Uncle Rico, so we can go to our bungalow—"

"We're staying right here for now," Kindred said.

"You weren't supposed to take us away from Mommy," Asia accused.

"How long do we have to wait?" India asked.

Kindred grasped both their wrists harder, pulling them up. Their ponytails bounced; fireworks cast a red, then a blue glow over their denim jeans and white T-shirts. "I said come on, little angel girls," Kindred said, turning toward the water glimmering under the full moon. "Watch the bay, for Daddy's boat."

"Where's *Dharma's Dream*?" India asked. "Daddy's slip is empty."

"We'll go up," Kindred said. "I'll light a fire, and we'll wait."

Asia and India stomped up to the top of the staircase.

"Here," Kindred said, handing them a handful of wish ribbons she'd brought in the pocket of her oversized jeans. "Sit at the table and make wishes for Daddy to come back really fast."

"I'm scared," Asia whined. "We shouldn't be here alone, in the dark, without Jared and Josh!"

"We don't need them anymore," Kindred said. "Here, I'll make you a necklace." She knotted a blue ribbon around Asia's neck. "And if you keep complaining—"

"I don't want this!" Asia cried, hooking her fingers inside the shoelace-style string.

Kindred raised her hands and shrugged. "Sorry, no scissors. Now sit down!"

She gripped their ponytails and guided them to the table. India's eyes widened, reflecting the crimson and gold and green sparks lighting up the sky.

"Things are different now, girls," Kindred said, stepping toward the barbecue grill. She pulled a newspaper from the makeup table, bunched up the pages, and shoved them under the grill with kindling wood. "It's time for a big change."

The orange-red flames illuminated terror in the girls' eyes as they watched her from the table. The shock and frozen-stiff confusion on their faces stabbed her heart. But not as harshly as the raw pain now surging up from the places deep inside, where Kindred had been hiding it for so long. Still, her insides tingled with relief, now that she'd finally helped her mother end her misery—

"Yes, jump!" Kindred screamed on the roof as her mother stood at the edge, the wind blasting her lacy gown and black hair. "He doesn't love you! He loves the judge who ruined it for all of us!"

Kindred dusted off her hands, then took long, quick steps toward the twins. She stroked their trembling backs.

"Don't look so scared, little angel girls," Kindred said with lullaby softness. "This story will have a happy ending, when Daddy gets here. You'll see."

108

Sonny glimpsed All Saints Bay as the priest led him through the crush of bodies. The man moved through the crowd like a vapor cloud.

"Come," he called, turning back with a scowl.

Sonny could feel Simone behind him, but right now, through this filter of panic and worry—her very existence repulsed him. Deep down he knew his feelings were quite contrary; he had even felt a glow of relief when serenity washed over her face as the *pai de santo* pulled away his hand.

But Sonny just wanted to follow the priest to the *candomblé* house. If Grandmama had a message for him, he needed to hear it before anything else. He needed to call the States, to check on the girls, but he had no cell phone. International calls here—he'd been put on hold for thirty minutes or more trying to call LA—often felt like an exercise in futility. And getting anything done amidst the chaos of Carnival seemed impossible.

The priest snatched Sonny's and Simone's hands; he pulled them up a steep, narrow street lined with houses dyed like Easter eggs in mint green, pale pink, faded yellow. Then, with a glance up at the moon, the man led them into the doorway of a house the color of washed-out aquamarine.

A gust of garlic and farm animal and chanting and frantic drumming shot from the dim, crowded room . . . A sea of tan, raisin and cream faces parted for the *pai de santo*. The man directed Sonny past blue and brown and black eyes glowing with recognition, his name pouring out in whispers over lips thick and thin, pink and brown.

"Come, there is no time!" the priest whispered. He pulled Sonny to the center of the sweltering room, and began chanting.

Sonny's insides flamed with fear and anxiety and urgency. Everything swirled—from the young woman on the floor, entranced with the initiation of a priestess, droplets of fresh chicken blood on her shaven head, as her lips mumbled with the spirit; the glistening bare-chested men pounding drums with painful-looking speed and force; the two older women in traditional white lace turbans and dresses staring with hard eyes at Simone, just an arm's length from him, pleading with tear-filled eyes, tightening trembling lips.

He turned to the *pai de santo*; a circle of chanting men just like him surrounded Sonny. Suddenly the priest cupped his hands to his ears.

"The noise!" he shouted over the drums. "They are all screaming now!" He clawed Sonny's arms, stared into his eyes with spine-tingling focus. "Your grandmother. She says go! She says let your angel help you. She sent the angel with the eyes—"

The priest turned slowly toward Simone. His chest rose and fell slowly; his lips parted as if he were sighing. Then his eyes opened wide. He spun toward Sonny.

"Go! Your babies are coming. But you may be too late!"

"Where are they?" Sonny's limbs burned with panic.

"Go now! They are coming . . . where they will find you."

But who would bring Asia and India here? Erica, Norris—was he going back to work on the film without him?

"Who are they with?"

The man's eyes glazed. "Someone you love. She is sad—"

Sonny pried his gaze away; he looked at Simone as she bit her bottom lip. Wet streaks glistened on her cheeks in the candlelit haze. Was the priest talking about Simone? The girls were not with her . . .

"—someone you love and trust," the priest said. "The daughter of Gertrude—"

My God, Kindred.

Cheyenne's daughter . . . living in my house . . . tricking us!

Sonny's blood caught fire. He spun toward the door, taking Simone's hand. Was Kindred also Narcissus? Did she kill Jenn and Cheyenne? Try to kill Norris? And how could she get the girls away from Erica, out of the country? Sonny's chest rose and fell in violent heaves. *Are my little girls in the hands of a murderer right now?* He closed his eyes.

Grandmama, protect us, please. Let me find them alive.

The priest pushed his back. "Go to them, now!"

Sonny stumbled onto the street between a jester and a woman wearing a bikini of tiny mirrored circles with matching shoes. His trembling legs threatened to collapse. Simone gripped his upper arm.

"Sonny," she said firmly. "First we need to find out if what he said is right. We need a phone."

"No, we should go to Sanctuary," he shot back. "That's where she would bring them. I was going to bring—"

"Let's make some calls first," Simone said, glancing around. "Come on."

She led him down the steep cobbled street, turned around a few corners, and there . . . the familiar and comforting blue and white logo of American Express above an office in a pale-yellow storefront. The fluorescent lights were on, and a woman was inside, on the phone. Simone knocked. But the woman shook her head, tapping her watch. Simone pulled her wallet out of her purse, flapped it open and clanked her metal judge's badge to the glass. The woman inside studied it, then cracked the door.

"I need to make an urgent call to the U.S. ambassador," Simone said firmly. "I am a judge, from Los Angeles. Two little girls may be jeopardy—"

The woman opened the door.

"Can you get him some water, please?" Simone asked as Sonny paced amidst the noisy revelry penetrating the front window.

Simone snatched up the phone, dialing with lightening speed. She stared down with taut lips, but after a moment, they relaxed.

"I need help. From Mr. Anderson."

Sonny seethed. That woman was not ever going to help him. He gripped the brass doorknob, but there were so many locks and bars on the door . . . Simone was telling him with her eyes to wait while she explained what was going on. "They're the innocent victims here. Do it for them, to make up for"—her voice cracked—"everything."

Then she dialed again. "Marie."

Sonny exhaled loudly. How could they trust Norris's wife?

"Marie, it's Simone. Can you hear me?"

She nodded for long moments. "When?"

Simone turned gray.

Sonny stepped close. "What?"

Simone hung up, then looked at him. "The girls disappeared from Norris and Marie's house. Erica was out. But Marie says she thinks she saw Kindred driving away with Asia and India—"

"My God," Sonny groaned over a sandpaper throat.

"They haven't been seen since."

109

Inside the Haynes mansion, Marie's heart pounded as she kissed Norris's forehead.

"Get well soon," she whispered toward his sleeping face, framed by a fan of hair on the taupe silk pillowcase.

After returning to the house to look for the twins, she had to help the police search for the Whittaker girls. If Tabitha and Kindred and Katie and Narcissus were all one person . . .

Marie shivered.

No, those little girls will be found tonight, safe and healthy.

Then Marie would check into a hotel and get on with the business of whatever was necessary to get away from Norris. As her husband, as her patient. With all the medication he had taken tonight, he would probably sleep for days. That would give her time to start the process of ending their marriage.

Marie turned away from the bed.

A strong hand gripped her thigh. Norris groaned.

In the soft light, he opened his eyes. They glowed with a plea for her to stay and comfort him. Her parents, Jesus, the usual barrage of images and emotions began to play . . .

Norris's eyes glinted in that way that chilled her. But no, she would not stay here under threat that he might ruin her reputation and career, or worse. She had dealt with fear all her life, and won.

And right now, her worry over the well being of Sonny Whittaker's two little girls was far more pressing than her own.

So she turned, strode toward the door, and—after putting her seven-carat canary diamond on the dresser—Marie Cartwright left.

110

Kindred tossed another log into the brick barbecue pit on the patio; giant flames and red embers shot up toward the leaves.

"How long are you gonna make us wait here?" India demanded, yanking on the wish ribbon tied around her neck. "You're scaring us—"

"Your daddy is scaring me," Kindred said, "by taking so long—"

Asia's long lashes fell heavily to half mast; she jolted awake. She pulled at the wish ribbon choker. "This is too tight."

Kindred yanked a pair of scissors from a chest of props and supplies by the doors to the house. "What do 'ya know? I found some scissors." Kindred dug a finger between the ribbon and Asia's neck. "Hold still, honey. Just one snip and it'll all be over."

"No!" Asia cried as the shears came toward her.

"Stop!" India said, shooting up so fast, the chair fell over. She grabbed Kindred's arm. "Stop it!"

Kindred spun. The force made India fall to the tiled ground.

India stood back up, then pounded little fists into Kindred's hip.

"Don't hurt my sister!" India shouted.

Kindred grasped the base of India's ponytail. She pulled her, shoved her into a chair next to Asia. "One more bratty outburst like that, I'll tie you down until Daddy gets here."

"He's not *your* daddy," India snapped.

"Yes," Kindred said, smiling. "Yes, he is."

111

"Sonny, slow down!" Simone screamed over the roaring motor and splashing water. "We can't help them if we're dead!"

He faced forward, driving his boat, without slowing down. His knuckles turned even whiter on the steering wheel. Simone stood next to him, her arms folded. She could taste his fear. And she kept hearing the *pai de santo* say, "You may be too late."

She stared toward land. They were only a few minutes from the marina, which even from this distance looked like a watery beehive of festivities. To the right, on the public beach, people dotted the jagged rocks. To the left, the bungalows at Sanctuary glowed behind dancers on the beach.

Was Katie there with Sonny's daughters?

Simone looked up to the luxury homes shrouded by dark patches of greenery on the bluff. People filled the lighted patios and—

She gasped. "Sonny," she shouted over the roar. "Is anyone using the set house tonight?"

Sonny glanced up. His brows drew together. The house was dark, but a red glow reflected off the trees above. He sped even faster.

Simone watched, praying that the little girls were safe. This time, for Katie Moore. For the tragedy that was her life, even before the whole courtroom debacle with Judge Johnston and Simone and Cheyenne Moore and the girl's father's suicide. Had she heard the *pai de santo* mumbling in Portuguese the words "old spirit"? As if Katie were a tormented soul coming back to life for more suffering on earth?

She remembered hearing Bianca say so many times that Hell is here in the human life, and that spirits are reincarnated as punishment for past sins, or reward for charity and generosity and love. Simone had often wondered, what had her spirit done way long ago to deserve a mean mother and the cold empty void of no father?

Deep down, beneath this horrific fear, Simone felt at peace with herself for the first time ever. But she did not want to acknowledge and savor it until she knew Asia and India were safe.

"Fuck!" Sonny shouted as they approached the marina. "Someone's in my slip!"

He turned toward the beach at Sanctuary. Slowed a bit, quit the engine. Soft sand scraped the hull, metal clanked on rocks. And Sonny splashed over the side, running up the beach, into the huge flailing octopus of flesh and deafening percussion.

Simone ran behind him, glancing up and around to see if her mother had in fact asked Greg Anderson to flex his muscles and come to the rescue. *God help us . . .*

112

Sonny's legs ached, his lungs burned, his mind exploded, as he ran up the stairs scaling the bluff. He had to find his daughters safe and alive. He would do whatever necessary to wrench them from the grip of crazy Cheyenne's deceitful offspring. Whatever necessary. Then he would decide how to handle everything else, including the beautiful, intelligent woman sprinting past him.

"Wait," he huffed. "We don't know what—" He gasped. "She may have been watching for us, she could ambush—"

"Sonny, I knew Katie when she was a little girl," Simone whispered. "She used to like me."

He panted, "You're on her hit list, too."

Simone slowed, creeping silently up the final steps.

The scent of burning firewood wafted down. With crying.

That was Asia.

Another adrenaline rush propelled Sonny upward, next to Simone.

They stopped just below the top step, listening but not seeing.

"And this is for all the times," Kindred said angrily, "I took a paycheck from my own father!"

"Kindred, stop!" Asia whimpered.

"This is for all the lies that bitch told me," Kindred shouted, "making me think your daddy was my daddy, too! Making me hate *you*, Asia, and *you*, India Whittaker. For having the life I always wanted, but that judge stole from me!"

Panic and rage—as potent as the fireworks blasting in the sky— exploded inside Sonny's gut. He ran onto the patio. The girls were sitting on one side of the long rattan table, one on each side of Kindred, facing him. Behind them, red-orange flames and sparks rose from the barbecue grill, casting an eerie shadow on their faces.

"Daddy!" they cried in unison.

He would grab the twins—

Asia and India tried to push away from the table.

Kindred grabbed each of their ponytails, holding them down. One wrong move, and she could shove them onto the fire.

"Kindred, honey," Sonny said with a fake tone of affection. "Whatever is upsetting you—"

Her eyes glowed with hatred toward him, then Simone.

"You still have no idea!" Kindred shouted.

Sonny stepped closer. "Kindred, let go of the girls."

"Mom said we'd all be together," Kindred said. "But now you commit the ultimate insult, by bringing *her*—" Kindred's eyes shot venomous arrows at Simone, who was stepping close.

"I should punish you both now," Kindred seethed. She pulled the girls' hair, making their heads jerk toward her. "Let's let being seven years old, like I was, be the turning point for happy lives gone bad."

113

Simone held out her hands as she stepped closer to Kindred and the twins. She had to calm her down, so Sonny could grab the girls, and pull them to safety.

"Katie," Simone said softly. The fire heated her cheeks; the smoky burning-wood smell made her squint. "I want to help you—"

"Your way of helping kills people," Kindred said. "My dad died because of you!"

"No," Simone said, stepping closer. "I had to tell the court what I saw. Your mother was not supposed to treat you like that—"

"You should've left us alone!" Kindred screamed. She shot to her feet, yanking the girls up. Chairs tipped and crashed. She pulled the twins toward the roaring fire in the barbecue grill. "Now leave *him* alone! Or all three of us will die!"

She pulled the twins even closer to the flames.

114

In Beverly Hills, Brett Robinson jogged past a thick green hedge on Sunset, holding large manila envelopes under his arm. At the corner of Doheny, he jogged in place during the red light. A week ago, he never would have considered this.

He shot across the street in the headlights of Benzes and BMWs and Jaguars. Then, at the corner, he stopped and pulled up the hood of his nylon jogging suit. He scanned the addresses: the *Los Angeles Times*, the Judicial Tenure Commission, Channel 8. Then he dropped the envelopes in the mailbox.

The papery thud brought to mind the single white sheet inside: a copy of the million-dollar check to Judge Johnston, signed by Norris Haynes. A check dated the same day Judge Johnston awarded custody of the movie producer's grandchildren to his daughter.

The same day all hell broke loose in my daughter's life . . . because of me . . .

Oh, and just for good measure, the envelopes included a few snapshots of the judge frolicking in his birthday suit—unbeknownst to Mrs. Johnston—with those busty centerfolds in his chambers, the night his three colleagues were sent to prison for taking bribes from the mob.

Brett tapped the top of the mailbox, then sprinted down Sunset.

115

On the patio set, Sonny dove toward Kindred, Asia and India. The heat of the fire stung his cheeks. But he would die before he would allow one hair on his babies' heads to get singed.

"Triple jump, Daddy!" Kindred screamed. She shot toward him, pulling the girls by the ponytails. They each had about a dozen wish ribbons tied around their necks.

The twins shrieked.

All three of them slammed into him; he tottered backward, onto the stone patio. A few inches to the left and all four of them would have crashed through the waist-high glass wall, over the cliff, onto jagged rocks.

Kindred was on top of him.

The girls cried out.

Heart racing, Sonny tried to analyze the various thuds of their fall: had their heads hit the stones? His back ached, his skull had made a terrible crack sound, his backside throbbed.

"Run, girls!" Simone shouted.

They started to scramble. But Kindred clawed their necks, yanking them up by all those damn ribbons. They let out horrid screeches.

Simone dove toward them.

"Bitch!" Kindred screamed. She shot to her feet. "I hate you!"

Sonny gripped the trembling girls. He tried to stand.

Kindred shoved Simone's chest.

Simone fell backward, toward the staircase. Kindred kicked her. Simone thudded down the steps. Disappeared. Silence except for the partying below.

In a flash, Kindred charged them. She grabbed the girls' neck ribbons; their heads jerked. Little gagging sounds escaped their mouths. Tears dripped down their cheeks. They stared at him, then Kindred, then him, with terrified eyes.

"Kindred," Sonny said. He wanted to grab her, hit her, knock her out of the way. But one wrong move, she could snap the twins' necks. "Let the girls go. I'll help you, if you let them go."

"I wanted us to be a family, like she promised me," Kindred said with blazing eyes. "I found him dead because of you! When she told my father that you're really my dad, he couldn't take it."

"I'm not your father," Sonny said. "It's impossible—"

"Say you're my dad!" Kindred shouted. "I wanted to believe it all this time. I told myself it was true—"

"Kindred," Sonny said, his mind spinning, his heart pounding. "Let go of the girls. We can talk about it—"

Over Kindred's shoulder, out of her line of sight, Simone appeared at the top of the steps. She crept behind Kindred. Then with speed and stealth, she locked an arm around Kindred's neck.

Kindred gagged. She kicked; her white tennis shoe shot forward like lightning. She smashed it between Sonny's legs.

A horrible groan escaped his lips.

Blinding pain shot up through him. He could not breathe.

116

In the San Fernando Valley, Paulette Barnes held the phone away from her ear as Roxanne Jones's angry voice shot into the cool nighttime air. She kept pacing in the eerie glow around the swimming pool in her back yard.

"You just need to know," Roxanne said, "the next time somebody sticks their neck out to help you, don't punk out, like you did me—"

"It didn't feel right," Paulette said, stepping toward the diving board.

"I wouldn't be wasting my time calling you right now," Roxanne said. "But a whole lot of folks spent time and energy on me, to get me here. Now I like to help out people who remind me of myself. With that same look in their eye, like you had—"

"I'm so sorry," Paulette said softly. "I really am—"

"You *are* sorry," Roxanne said. "I thought about having you as the roving photographer for my new show. Which debuts, by the way, in a couple months."

Tears streamed down Paulette's hot face. She glanced at the white-paned windows of the ivy-covered ranch-style house, where Ted and the boys were sleeping.

"Wastin' my time," Roxanne said with a slight Southern drawl. "Makin' me look like a fool in front of *Famous*. You know what a good gig that was?"

Paulette slumped onto the diving board, letting the cold, sandpapery surface scratch the bottoms of her bare thighs. She had told the editor that no, she had not seen Sonny Whittaker entering Simone's house.

"Sorry doesn't begin to describe you," Roxanne snapped.

Paulette sobbed as she pushed the OFF button on the phone. "Maybe on other stories," she whispered, "but I couldn't sell out Simone."

Paulette's stomach rumbled. Right now, she would go inside, make some buttered toast and milk, and figure out how she and Ted could start digging out of this conscience-bruising abyss of debt. Without paying for it with friendships and self-respect.

117

Kindred's eyes were wide and wild as she glared at him. She was still holding the girls by those strings around their necks.

"Let go or I'll kill them now!" Kindred screamed back to Simone.

Simone released the chokehold.

Kindred yanked the girls to the hammock, shoved them down. They clung to each other, trembling and crying as the brown crochet cradled them like peas in a pod. They looked at him with huge, pleading eyes, even more desperate than the night they were taken away.

Sonny found the strength, despite the throbbing pain, to shoot up to his feet. He dove toward the twins.

But Kindred pulled a machete from under the hammock. The long silver blade glistened in the light of the moon and the fire. She cackled at Simone: "Does this look familiar, Esmerelda?"

She sliced it through the air toward Simone, who raised her hands and stepped back. "Katie, we can help you."

"I made a fire for you." Kindred pointed the blade closer to Simone, pushing her toward the barbecue grill.

Sonny straightened as the pain faded. He wanted to jump on Kindred's back. But she was within striking range of the girls' heads and Simone's chest. And one more step back, Simone would catch fire.

Kindred turned to Sonny. "Eenie, meenie, miney, moe," she said with a quavering voice. "Pick one, Daddy Whittaker." Kindred pointed the giant knife at Asia and India, who sobbed and cringed.

"Them," she said softly. She pulled the blade up to her forehead.

"Me, or her!" She sliced it toward Simone, whose eyes grew enormous. A quick glimmer, like a warning, as she shot her gaze toward the thick, dark greenery behind him. Were the police coming? Did Kindred have an accomplice?

"Kindred, honey, we already are a family," Sonny stepped forward, close enough that she could deliver one deadly whack.

Her gaze softened. She lowered the machete a few inches.

"Think about it," he said, stepping even closer. A quick glance at the twins; they watched through finger masks. "You are a daughter to me. You live with us. You travel with us. Holidays—"

"But," she said, her chin quivering, "you pay me. Just like Guadeloupe and the gardeners. If I were your daughter—"

"Kindred," he said softly, holding out his hands, "if you'd feel better about it, I can deposit the money into a fund. You can even change your name to Whittaker—"

"You're pretending! You pretended to love my mom. You promised her things. Lies! You made her crazy. And she took it out on me!"

Sonny could feel Simone trying to tell him something. A warning?

Kindred swung the blade toward the hammock. She sliced a few thin ropes just above their heads. The girls shrieked, covering their eyes.

"Kindred, listen to me!"

"No!" she screamed, raising the machete above her head. Her eyes grew huge with rage and malice. He was looking into all the years of pain and terror that losing a parent could inflict on a child's heart and mind. "You listen to—"

Pop!

A tiny crimson dot appeared on her forehead.

Kindred's eyes widened further.

A dark circle, the size of a blueberry, replaced the red dot. The machete clanged to the stone tiles.

And Kindred slumped forward. She crumpled at Sonny's feet. A grapefruit-sized hole at the back of her head glistened.

The girls . . . their eyes were covered with their hands.

Sonny spun; a man in black from head to toe, holding a long black rifle, stepped out of the bushes, near the stone statue of the goddess of love and death. Several other men, dressed the same, stepped out of the darkness.

And Sonny, barely able to inhale, or stand, or speak, lost himself in the quivering embrace of his three angels.

Epilogue

As she stood at the balcony overlooking the ocean, Simone Thompson closed her eyes to savor this newfound sense of serenity and peace. She focused on the gentle sound of the warm breeze rustling the leafy arch over the patio set. And she tilted her face toward the warm streaks of Brazilian sunshine dancing around her.

"Everyone in their places," the director said through a megaphone, across the patio by the cascade of bougainvillea and two black cameras.

"You ready for your acting debut, Mrs. Whittaker?" Sonny's deep voice made her open her eyes. "With a kiss for good luck?"

Simone smiled up at Sonny as he pulled her into his chest, toward the same style of silky olive tunic that she now wore. They turned toward the horizon, which shimmered blue and green as fluffy white clouds tumbled across the endless sky.

"Never in a million years," Simone said, "did I think I would actually leave the bench and join *you* on a movie set." Even though the Judicial Tenure Commission had decided that she had not committed misconduct during the Whittaker trial, Simone was enjoying her extended sabbatical from the bench. And savoring the delights of a new adventure as a wife, stepmother and thespian.

"The Oscar buzz is louder than ever," Sonny said. "I hope Norris can hear it while he's being indicted. Tell me your new daddy didn't have something to do with uncovering that fat check Norris wrote to Judge Johnston—"

"I'll never tell," Simone said, peering toward the waves and white sand below. "All I know is, Marie is down on that beach right now, recovering from that wrong turn down the aisle."

"Myles is down there somewhere," Sonny smiled. "I've never seen him so relaxed. It was sensational this morning—Josh and Jared had him out on a jetski."

"That must've been when I was writing a letter to Paulette," Simone said. Her friend had penned a touching apology, and Simone had responded with an invitation for Paulette to bring Ted and the boys down for a visit—as long as she left her cameras at home. Meanwhile, Paulette said she was still struggling to pay her bills, hoping that her new job at a portrait studio would tide her over until cash flow picked up at Ted's sports agency.

The patter of little feet made Simone turn back toward the set.

"Double jump!" India and Asia chimed. One girl leaped into Sonny's arms; the gold band on his left hand glimmered. The other girl sprung into Simone's embrace. The twins gave each other a high five.

Thank goodness a higher court had upheld Simone's custody ruling, after throwing out Judge Johnston's decision. He was suspended and charged with bribery.

"You're cool for a new mom," India said as the scent of coconut wafted from her dark curls.

"Now we have two moms," Asia said. "Daddy, can we call Mommy in Milan tonight?"

"Of course," Sonny beamed. "I only wish we could call Grandmama, too. Now, little angel girls, take your seats."